Praise for T. I. Lowe

T. I. Lowe has created an impeccably researched, emotionally compelling new novel. You will root for Avalee as you immerse yourself in the restoration of not just a forgotten town, but of a heart that could never be forgotten.

> **MARYBETH MAYHEW WHALEN,** author of *Every Moment Since* and cofounder of The Book Tide, on *Lowcountry Lost*

With a full cast of quirky characters, T. I. Lowe has offered a beautiful reminder that there is hope for those who feel forgotten. *Lowcountry Lost* is a love story for abandoned buildings, lonely hearts, and empty arms, overflowing with southern sass and folksy charm.

> **CHRISTINA CORYELL,** author of the Backroads series

This is my kind of story! Yes, the DIY girl in me was hooked by the makeover of the town . . . but oh, there's so much more. Second chances, secrets, healing (and a hot Irishman on a motorcycle). Most of all, an ending I didn't see coming. This compelling tale of restoration on every level will stay with me a very long time. Highly, highly recommended!

> **SUSAN MAY WARREN,** award-winning, USA Today–bestselling author, on *Lowcountry Lost*

I loved Avalee from the start. Maybe it was her voice or the broken heart she is trying to mend. I could feel the humidity of the Lowcountry and see her tuck that pencil behind her ear. I felt the ache inside for her hidden losses. A good story will take you deep into these places of the heart. This story does that and more.

> **CHRIS FABRY,** author and host of *Chris Fabry Live,* on *Lowcountry Lost*

T0191296

T. I. Lowe had me at "ghost town" but got me right in the feels! This book is guaranteed to make you rethink the dead places inside of you—the ones caused by heartache and tragedy. These are the ghost towns that can be renewed, and *Lowcountry Lost* doesn't disappoint. A poignant, relatable story, this one hit close to home for me, personally—three times over. You'll know what I mean when you read the book. It's a Top Read of 2024!

JAIME JO WRIGHT, bestselling author of *The Lost Boys of Barlowe Theater* and Christy Award–winning *The House on Foster Hill*

Immersive, transportive, and divinely transformational, *Lowcountry Lost* lays the blueprint for hope after loss. An up-close-and-personal renovation of the heart, with a generous smattering of Lowe's signature southern charm and cheeky wit. Please don't miss this one.

NICOLE DEESE, Christy Award–winning author

T. I. Lowe mixes serious issues with her own unique sense of humor and style, and her Sonny Bates is a force to reckon with. . . . A terrific read!

FRANCINE RIVERS, *New York Times* bestselling author of *Redeeming Love* and *The Lady's Mine*, on *Indigo Isle*

Lowe delivers a powerful coming-of-age story set on a Magnolia, S.C., tobacco farm in the 1980s. . . . The many colorful Magnolia characters, particularly the eccentrics of First Riffraff, rise to support Austin and nicely round out the slow-burning romance. Lowe's fans will be thrilled.

PUBLISHERS WEEKLY on *Under the Magnolias*

Under the Magnolias is a beautifully told tale about loss, mental illness, connection, and finding both yourself and your capacity to heal.

GRAND STRAND magazine

A family's collapse under the weight of dysfunction and mental illness becomes a luminous testimony to the power of neighbors and the ability of a community's love and faith to shelter its most vulnerable residents. Readers will close the cover with a smile and a long, satisfied sigh.

LISA WINGATE, #1 *New York Times* bestselling author of *Before We Were Yours* and *The Book of Lost Friends*, on *Under the Magnolias*

With lyrical prose and vivid description, T. I. Lowe masterfully weaves the story of a teenage girl's quest to protect the ones she loves most in the wake of unthinkable tragedy. *Under the Magnolias* is a moving portrayal of the power of family—the one we're born into and the one we create—and the resilience of the human spirit. In this memorable and moving story, T. I. Lowe has hit her stride.

KRISTY WOODSON HARVEY, *USA Today* bestselling author of *Feels Like Falling*

T. I. Lowe has done it again! I loved *Lulu's Café*, but I love *Under the Magnolias* even more. There is so much to admire about this book. T. I. writes with amazing grace and beautifully depicts the cost of keeping secrets when help might be available. This story is filled with rich, lovable characters, each rendered with profound compassion. Austin is an admirable young woman—flawed, but faithful to her family—and Vance Cumberland is another Michael Hosea, offering unconditional, lifelong love. *Under the Magnolias* is sure to delight and inspire.

FRANCINE RIVERS, *New York Times* bestselling author

On a tobacco farm in 1980s South Carolina, we meet smart and spunky Austin as she struggles to keep the family farm together and raise her six siblings and mentally ill father. With a wide cast of fun, offbeat characters, a mix of heartbreak and humor, and a heaping handful of grit, *Under the Magnolias* will delight Lowe's legion of fans!

LAUREN K. DENTON, *USA Today* bestselling author of *The Summer House*

What a voice! If you're looking for your next Southern fiction fix, T. I. Lowe delivers. Readers of all ages will adore the spunky survivor Austin Foster, whose journey delivers both laughter and tears. Set smack-dab in the middle of South Carolina, this story will break your heart and put it back together again. A must-read.

JULIE CANTRELL, *New York Times* and *USA Today* bestselling author of *Perennials*, on *Under the Magnolias*

Plain-speaking and gut-wrenching, T. I. Lowe leaves no detail unturned to deliver a powerful story about a family's need for healing and their lifelong efforts to run from it. This is no "will they or won't they" romance. Rather, it's a thorough exploration of the hidden depths of the heart.

ROBIN W. PEARSON, Christy Award–winning author of *A Long Time Comin'* and *'Til I Want No More*, on *Under the Magnolias*

I loved *Under the Magnolias*! . . . Austin Foster is one of the most memorable characters I have ever read.

SESSALEE HENSLEY, Barnes & Noble fiction buyer, retired

LOWCOUNTRY LOST

LOWCOUNTRY LOST

a novel

T. I. LOWE

Tyndale House Publishers
Carol Stream, Illinois

To all the parents who had to say goodbye before saying hello

In memory of
Max Duval
Kimberly Payton Clark
Barrett Cooper Clark
Virginia Krooswyk

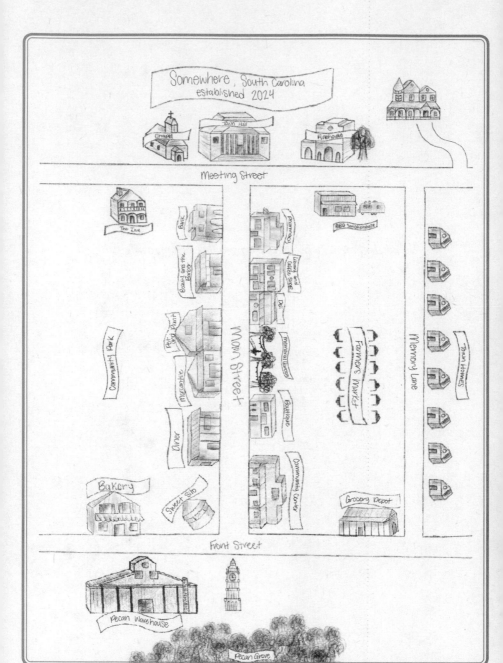

PROLOGUE

A GHOST TOWN IS A ONCE-FLOURISHING TOWN wholly or nearly deserted, usually as a result of the exhaustion of some natural resource. The landscape of North America is riddled with such places of abandonment. Buildings, streets, furniture, sentiments, hopes, dreams . . . all left behind without so much as a backwards glance.

Can a person be a ghost town? I believe I am. Once-flourishing, yet now just so dang exhausted. Similar to an abandoned town, everyone and everything abandoned me but the trauma, the grief it produced, and the silence that followed. I could do nothing but accept the forsakenness while the passing years began to weather my soul. Rusting the hinges of my heart until the corrosion made it nearabout impossible to open to anything or anyone.

I wonder if the folks who deserted those towns ever grew homesick. Did they ever have the feeling they'd left something of value behind?

CHAPTER 1

JANUARY

"Cell phones carry ten times more bacteria than most toilet seats."

Grunting, I focused on the gleaming white porcelain just past my nose. "Hello, Mr. Random."

A smooth, masculine chuckle echoed around the restroom from behind me. "Your face is in a toilet. Not so random, my darlin'."

"Good thing this one is brand new, so . . ." I grunted again, wrestling the hundred-pound thing into place. "No bacteria to worry about. Hand me the wrench." I held out my hand and wiggled my fingers. Cool metal touched my palm, but it felt wrong. I looked at the screwdriver and then narrowed my eyes at the handsome scoundrel screwing with me. "Seriously, Des? We don't have time for you to be actin' cute." I settled onto my haunches and rummaged around in the toolbox. Holding up the adjustable wrench, I gave him a pointed look before turning back to the toilet.

Desmond preferred to leave the dirty work to me, instead sticking close to the design aspects of a project. But I didn't mind.

3

Demolition and restoration were my regularly scheduled therapy sessions. For the sake of my sanity, I tried my darnedest to never skip an appointment.

"Thirteen minutes," he warned. "That ribbon cutting is waiting for no one."

"I can't believe the entire grand opening is hinging on a back-ordered commode. Seriously, why was a commode, of all things, on back order? In all my years working construction I've never . . ." I shook my head and placed a small level on the seat. When the bubble settled precisely in the middle, I turned on the water valve and waited impatiently for the tank to fill.

"It's the world we live in nowadays. The only thing that makes sense is that nothing makes sense."

Trying to wrap my mind around that hogwash, I tossed the tools in the toolbox and closed the lid. "That made no sense."

"Exactly." Desmond offered his hand and helped me to my feet. His brown eyes, nearly the same shade as his skin, swept over me and landed near my feet as a groan worked up his throat. "Darlin', please tell me you have another pair of shoes to change into."

I glanced at my scuffed work boots covered with paint splatters and huffed. "No way was I going to chance dropping a toilet on my foot without these."

He planted his hands on his lean hips. "But they don't go with your dress."

"No one's going to care about my footwear. Besides, the dress is long enough they barely show." I did have a pair of sandals in my truck, but the chance to mess with Desmond was too fun to pass up.

He made a *tsk*ing sound. "You're just shy of six-foot. Hate to break it to you, but your dress isn't that long."

"No worries." I placed the lid on the tank and wiped my hands on the floral maxi dress. The vibrant pink flowers matched my fresh manicure. The name of the polish seemed perfect for this conversation: *Short Story*. "Go get the inspector, so he can see this baby flush and pass us."

"Sure thing, but for the record *I* care about your footwear." Desmond reached behind me and unraveled the band holding my hair out of the way. He tousled it until the long brown waves looked intentionally messy. "Better. Besides those hideous boots, you look like a proper lady." He winked.

Stifling a laugh, I watched his lithe body saunter out of the public restroom. Dressed to the nines, as always, in a navy three-piece suit and shiny leather shoes, Desmond Grant could have been a world-renowned fashion model, jet-setting around Europe, instead of my fixer-upper partner in South Carolina. I'm glad he chose the latter. Certainly, the man had made life more tolerable these last five years. I had hoped maybe with time we could have become more than platonic, but it never happened. Toeing the threshold of turning forty, the idea of me finding anything past platonic with anyone seemed to be an idea fading faster than cheap wallpaper.

Ten minutes later, I quickly shook the inspector's hand and sprinted out of the building just in time to clap as the new owner of the Library Café cut the ribbon.

Twenty minutes after that, I sat at a table with my other business partner Nita as she bounced her ten-month-old daughter on her lap. The baby giggled, but I paid her no mind. Instead, my gaze swept over the impressively long line of customers waiting to order from the selection of sandwiches, salads, pastries, and specialty drinks of their choosing.

"It still amazes me how perfectly good buildings like this old library are just abandoned." I motioned around, admiring the original dark wood flooring, wall paneling freshly painted in a creamy caramel hue, and iron chandeliers. The space mingled perfectly with the rich aroma of coffee and cinnamon.

"Good thing we found this one before it sat for too long," Nita said and then cooed at her daughter. Such a sweet moment. So sweet, in fact, that I had to look away.

"Yeah." I took a sip of my honey latte, but it suddenly tasted bitter. I placed the paper cup on the shiny surface of the table and studied one of the library catalog cards underneath the thick layer of clear resin.

Organized Crime—Fiction
Grisham, John
The Firm 1st ed. 1991

I'd hand-selected this one and other mystery suspense cards, but Desmond came behind me and sprinkled in romance titles. Each table in the café held a scattering of them and book checkout slips, some dating way back to the 1920s. Those slips of paper held too much history and nostalgia to toss, so we'd turned them into art instead.

Desmond helped me figure out how to incorporate many of the old treasures left behind in the library. It never ceased to amaze me what people cast off without thought. Okay, so maybe I could be classified as a low-key hoarder, but still.

"The long librarian's desk made a perfect order counter and those bookshelves lining the back of the café, holding mugs and supplies instead of books, great use of our resources." Nita smiled, looking and sounding every bit the salesperson she was. I'm glad we stumbled upon her a few years back at an estate sale where she actually talked me into buying a few things I had no use for. The woman could sell sawdust to a lumber mill.

I returned her smile. "This one turned out great. Unique enough to draw people in without being over-the-top kitschy."

Nita shifted Joyia to her other leg. The tiny human refused to sit in the high chair. "It's packed out, so clearly we nailed it. Once again."

I was the self-appointed ghost hunter, tracking down abandoned buildings to flip. Desmond did all the design plans and purchases. And Nita had an uncanny knack for finding the right person who would be a perfect fit for the newly revived place. We were a dang good team and Lowcountry Lost had already made a name for itself within five years of being in business. We began by flipping homes, but quickly moved on to businesses, helping withering towns have a fighting chance with new revenue. But none of that compared to our next project.

"Where'd Des run off to?" Nita asked, no longer cooing. "I need to get this little lady home for a nap soon."

I craned my neck, scanning the group, but no towering, sharply dressed man stood among them. "I have no idea. He's probably in the media room, showing off his bougie couches." We both laughed. Desmond had turned the old media and archives room into another seating area and dressed the room with two burgundy velvet settees, a wrought iron chandelier dripping with teardrop-shaped crystals, and a chunky coffee table he'd found at another estate sale. Cozy with a relaxed ambience, customers would definitely want to stay awhile.

"Well, I need a refill. I'll see if I can round him up while I'm at it. Hold Joyia for me, will ya?" Nita began to rise while holding the baby toward me.

I held my palms up. "I can't . . . I'm allergic."

"Good grief, Avalee. Just hold her for a few minutes." Nita tried again but I shook my head.

"I might break her."

She laughed, rolling her eyes. "You're ridiculous. Kids aren't that fragile."

Maybe not in Nita's care, but in mine . . . Well, that was a different story and no way would I chance being responsible for another child's well-being ever again.

Never. Ever. Again.

"I'll get you a refill. My treat." I shot to my feet and darted away before she could argue. While waiting in line, I sent Desmond a text, telling him to get his behind to our table so we could discuss our next project. Soon I returned with the coffee and Nita returned to the subject I wanted no part of.

"One of these days Mr. Right is going to sweep you off your feet, and you'll change your mind about children." Nita planted a kiss on the side of Joyia's forehead as the baby made an absolute mess with a sugar cookie. Was she even getting any of it in her mouth?

I shifted in my chair, preparing to get on my soapbox. "Mr. Right is a myth the romance industry invented just to sell naive women movies, books, products . . . It's the same reason Santa Claus and the Easter Bunny exist."

Nita stared at me blankly. "Wow . . . Bitter much?"

More than I care to admit. I shook my head. "Just being realistic."

Truth be told, a man resembling Mr. Right had already put on the act of sweeping me off my feet, and boy did it leave a lasting mark when we both stumbled and fell. But Nita didn't need to know any of that. When I left Beaufort to start over, I left the delusions of romance behind too.

Thankfully, Desmond sidled up to the table, his leather portfolio tucked underneath his arm. Grimacing at the cookie chaos across from us, he chose the seat beside me and started shuffling through some papers. "Let's talk business."

I motioned for him to get on with it, but Nita spoke up. "The saloon passed inspection and the power was turned on yesterday, so it's all clear for you to move in." She wrinkled her nose. "Are you ready to go live among ghosts, Avalee? I still can't believe you're not creeped out about it."

I lived with ghosts on the daily, so a ghost town seemed like the perfect place for me to reside. And how cool would it be to live in a saloon? We'd been working on remodeling it since last fall in our spare time, converting it into our home base. With a little over three thousand square feet, we would be able to hold large group meetings downstairs and I could live upstairs comfortably.

I shrugged. "Work crews will be in and out, so I won't have much alone time with the ghosts."

"Even after what our research found out about this place?" Nita shivered and made the sign of the cross. "They say you can hear children's laughter, and the broken clock tower sometimes chimes even though the bell clapper is sitting on the ground."

"A ghost town can't go by that title without some urban legends seasoning its history. South Carolina is known for such. We've all heard of the Lizard Man."

Nita sat up a little straighter, her dark eyes widening. "I haven't heard about a Lizard Man."

Desmond chuckled quietly. "Over in Lee County. People say there's a swamp thing damaging vehicles and generally terrorizing folks."

Nita gasped, holding Joyia closer. The baby, thinking it a game, squeezed her mama in return.

I snorted. "It's just a legend. We need to focus on the facts, not hearsay."

Nita shook her head. "No way would I be able to stay out there until the town's complete."

Although the facts were sparse, it had been enough to capture my attention and hold it for the better part of my life. Norm, South Carolina, was founded way back in the 1800s, but after they built that new road in 1938 it pulled the plug right out of the poor town, slowly draining all the life from it. Now it sat in the middle of nowhere, but we had a solid plan on making it a somewhere. We'd even been given permission to rename the town Somewhere. Clever, right?

"Avalee won't be on her own much. I'll be staying with her off and on throughout the duration." Desmond clasped my arm, his touch soothing as always. "But, honey, just so we are clear. The first time I hear any creepy kid's laughing or that broke clock chimes in the middle of the night, I'm out."

I nodded. "As long as you take me with you."

Desmond released my arm and tapped the top sheet of paper. "We meet with the investors and some heads from the county on Monday. That'll give Avalee the weekend to move in. We'll do a walk-through of the town and present the plan of action."

"How do you feel about the investors bringing in their own engineers and such?" Nita asked while going through what looked to be about an entire package of baby wipes to clean the cookie goo off Joyia's chubby cheeks.

I moved my phone to my lap just as Joyia swiped a grubby hand toward it. "We've worked with subcontractors before. This will be no different. They've already approved my proposal, so I'm fine with having the extra help to get it accomplished."

"Are y'all sure we haven't bitten off more than we can chew? It has to be done by the end of September. Since we don't officially start until the first of February, that only gives us *eight months*." Nita was always the optimist of our team until we talked deadlines.

"We thought the Palms was too much to take on, but we managed it just fine and look how spectacular that turned out," Desmond said, offering Nita a confident wink.

This one would be Lowcountry Lost's largest project by far, with the abandoned vacation-resort-turned-retirement-community coming in second. The Palms gave me hope we could pull this off too. Sort of . . .

"Funny enough, the town's footprint isn't much bigger than the Palms," I said, proud of myself for sounding like the optimist of the group for a change. "We got this."

Six years ago, when my life collapsed, I picked up and moved away from Beaufort to get away from the ghosts. After I settled in Lexington, I purchased my first flip house, intending for it to be my starting-over home. Before the restoration was even completed, I received an offer for the house I couldn't refuse. My Grandma Maudie didn't raise no fool, so I sold it and hunted down another house to flip, and then another, thus spurring me to obtain my general contractor's license and to form Lowcountry Lost. After my failed date with Desmond, I didn't waste much time convincing him to partner with me.

It was hard to believe how my life had flipped during those years too. Sure, parts of me were still broken, unfixable repairs, but at least it was livable again. And that was saying something, because I sure as heck didn't think that was possible. I could only hope the patch-ups held.

CHAPTER 2

FEBRUARY

Exiting the saloon, Desmond and I walked along Main Street of soon-to-be Somewhere, South Carolina, our heads craning and angling around to survey our new challenge lining the dirt road. I could already envision our plans for the old buildings situated along both sides of the street. Just beyond the saloon, which would eventually become the town's community center, would stretch a clothing boutique, a deli, a combination coffee shop and library, and at the end of the block, a pharmacy. On the other side of the street would be a candy store, an old-fashioned diner, a mercantile, a pet store, barbershop, and bank.

The wind swept through the vacant area, kicking up dust, and I half expected a tumbleweed to roll on by at any moment.

"Are there tumbleweeds in South Carolina?" I asked Desmond while I tested the sturdiness of a handrailing leading up to the old fabric store, destined to become a deli. The darn thing broke off in my hand, freeing a shower of mortar from the brick wall. Sighing,

I leaned the rail against the building, adding that to the extensive fix-it list.

"Dunno," Desmond mumbled while cupping his hands to the grimy window and peering inside. "I want that armoire in there for the new mercantile store. We need to make sure the subcontractors and work crews know to save all the furniture, even if it's questionable." He leaned away and used a monogrammed handkerchief to wipe off his hands.

"Those vegetable bins from the feedstore will be good to use too. It's bizarre how much stuff was just left behind here." I motioned for us to continue walking. We'd done this very thing more times than I could count in the last year while waiting to win the bid for the town. Thankfully, some bigwigs with deep pockets thought restoring the town would be more beneficial than leveling it for yet another housing development. With big cities such as Charleston and Hilton Head experiencing a great urban sprawl, it was a wonder they didn't go that route.

Even though the decaying relics were barely holding on to their rotting clapboard siding or crumbling brick facades, they never gave up their Southern charm of yesteryear. My attention battled between which rundown building to settle on. Thick vegetation seemed determined to choke what life was left out of the deserted town. Or maybe my perspective was wrong. Was it holding tight to those last vestiges? Only time would tell.

Desmond began whistling a tune. It sounded vaguely familiar.

I glanced at him out the corner of my eye. "What song are you going for there?"

"The one from that western where the cowboys mosey into town." He puckered his lips and tried again.

Cocking my head, I listened closely. "I think your whistle is broken."

"Probably because I'm still half asleep." Desmond yawned. "Why didn't we remodel the coffee shop or diner first for the home base?"

"Because the saloon is on the corner of Front and Main. It made better sense. Plus it's always been Maudie's favorite building in town, too, so how could I not."

"Ah, the lovely Maudie. When will she be paying us a visit?" Desmond asked, breaking out into another yawn. I'd brought in carafes of coffee for the meeting but he'd have to wait until everyone arrived to get into it.

I checked the time on my phone before shoving it back into my pocket. "I'm sure she'll be gracing us with her appearance regularly. Especially since it's her fault I've been obsessed with this place nearly all my life."

My mother died before I turned two and my father never seemed to know quite what to do with me, so I'd become my grandmother's sidekick by default. Always by her side. Either in the workshop behind her house creating, or in her consignment store selling the creations, or in her old pickup truck on junking trips to pilfer any useful materials—cabinets, windows, doors, flooring, etc.

On one junking trip, Maudie had brought me out here to see this ghost town. We'd spent the better part of that day wandering building to building, and an eeriness had clung to me as heavily as the dust had clung to every surface. Dishes on a lunch counter, unopened whiskey bottles on a shelf behind the bar in the saloon, a pair of glasses folded on top of a newspaper beside the register at the diner. It looked like the residents had just up and left, leaving their belongings behind.

There had been so much there for the picking, but Maudie didn't take one thing, saying it felt too much like grave robbing. Ever since that trip, the little ghost town never completely left my thoughts, and now the time had finally arrived that I could do something about running off the ghosts and breathing new life into the town.

The alarm on my phone went off just as the sound of vehicles drawing closer broke through the surrounding trees.

I shut off the alarm. "One thing about being out in the middle of nowhere is no one can creep up on you. You'll hear them well before they reach the town." I started to make my way toward the saloon where we were to meet.

"Wait." Desmond grabbed my hand, pulling me to a stop. "We've come a long way, darlin'. From flipping little ole homes to entire towns. I want you to know how proud I am of you."

I squeezed his hand. "Aww, thank you."

He gave me a once-over. "But would it have killed you to dress up for the first meeting with the 'illionaires'?"

I scoffed. "I plan on getting some work in after the meeting. Surely the illionaires will appreciate that more than fancy clothes." The investors were a mixture of millionaires and billionaires. Talk about intimidating times a billion. We'd nicknamed the group *illion-aires* to make ourselves feel a little better about that. "It wouldn't kill you to wear something besides three-piece suits. Soon the temperatures are going to get cranked up and your purty self is going to wilt. I can pick you up some T-shirts and jeans from Walmart."

Nose upturned, Desmond shuddered. "No thanks. By the time my talent is needed, the buildings will have brand-new central air systems."

Desmond didn't believe in denim. The man wore a suit most days. Shoot, he probably even had one made out of silk to sleep in. And don't get me started on his outrageous collection of pocket squares and fedoras. Today's square was a hand-dyed blue number that really popped with the light tan suit.

"Let's go meet the illionaires." Overwhelmed and giddy, I waved him on ahead of me as car doors began opening and closing around the corner. As soon as I spotted the group of investors, I realized Desmond and his suit would fit right in with the other suits. And I would not. "Gentlemen, Mrs. Waxman, welcome to Somewhere, South Carolina."

"I really like the sound of that. A much better ring to it than *Norm*." Jonas Brumfield, the designated spokesperson of the group, shook my hand and then Desmond's.

"If you'll follow me." I led the men and the lone female of the group inside the saloon. "Coffee and breakfast is set up on the bar. Help yourself and feel free to take a few minutes to explore." I stood off to the side and watched their reaction to the restored space. The freshly sanded and stained bar gleamed, stretching the entire length of the left wall.

"Nice touch with the piano." Jonas pointed to the upright, freshly polished and looking ready to turn a tune.

"Thanks. We pushed all the tables to the back to accommodate our conference table. Typically, everything will be spread out and the piano will be more of a focal point."

Murmurings of approval and praise followed the group around as they pointed out the restored corbels along the edge of the bar, the repaired crown molding, the stained-glass window behind the bar . . .

The idea of adding my mark to this town's history sent a wave of excitement zipping along my shoulders and back. Tamping it down, I grabbed a cup of coffee and settled in a seat beside Jonas, who sat at the head of the table. I'm sure a man like Jonas never sat anywhere else.

Once everyone had taken a seat, I began my spiel. "As you know, we've renamed the town Somewhere, South Carolina, to make it stand out. How many times have you heard the phrase 'Let's go some-where?' Well, let's give folks Somewhere to go." I grinned and the investors nodded in agreement.

"We have a few new investors here today. Would you mind giving us a brief summary of the plan of action?" Jonas waved a hand for me to continue.

"The folder before you has all the details but I'll give you a brief summary." I paused a minute to allow them to flip through the paper-work. "Our plan outlines how we'll transform each of the two-story buildings on Main Street into various businesses. Including: a few restaurants, specialty stores, pharmacy, small bank, a barbershop . . ."

"What about the outdated businesses?" Jonas prompted.

"The fabric store is set to become a deli and beside it, the little theater is going to be turned into a coffee shop with the town's library on the second floor. The county found room in their budget to add a small public library here, so all costs for supplies and employment will be their responsibility." I flipped the page even though I had the revisions practically memorized. "On the other side of the street, we're turning the post office into a bakery and moving an old grain silo over and transforming it into an ice cream parlor. It'll be on the corner where a service station used to be before it burned down. And the hardware store will become a mercantile. Think country-style Walmart."

"And you're lining up who will run the businesses?" an older gentleman named Kendrick Adams asked. He owned just about half of Georgia, last I heard.

I looked him in the eye and nodded, something Maudie taught me always to do. "Yes, sir. Several are already under contract. Our business partner Juanita Aguilar is handling that. She works remotely but will be stopping in throughout the project."

Desmond nudged my arm. "Tell them about Diesel."

I rummaged around my folder until finding the paperwork. "Juanita struck gold with this interesting man. His name is Diesel Miller and he already owns three other retro barbershops around Charleston. He looks like he should be running tattoo parlors, full sleeves on both arms, rides a Harley. He has an MBA and is also the president of a motorcycle club that focuses on ministry work."

Jonas guffawed. "That's impressive."

"His daughter Jillian just completed cosmetology school, so he wants to open this up with her. Half beauty salon, half barbershop called Beauty and the Barber." I passed the renderings for the salon around the table. "The black-and-white tile flooring is original and we also discovered an antique barber chair and a box of scissors and such in the back room. All of it will be used somehow."

"It will be one of my favorite projects," Desmond spoke up as they continued to study the renderings. "The coffee shop and library will be too."

"I agree. We've just completed a similar project in Lexington." I passed around pictures of the Library Café. "But this one will have a theater theme. There are lots of memorabilia we can use. Old film reels, costumes, ticket stubs . . ."

"Why not keep it as a theater?" Jonas asked, drumming his fingers on the table.

"It's too small, only seating twenty or so people. Plus we have other spaces set aside for entertainment." Desmond pointed to the folders in front of each man. "It's all detailed in there. Juanita has already found a young couple to lease the coffee shop. The wife will run that, and her husband has already been hired by the county to be the librarian. Nice twist, right?"

Agreeing remarks trickled around the table as we went over each building's concept. They all looked like a bunch of excited little boys when I explained how the large Greek Revival bank building on Meeting Street, the former Calhoun Brothers Bank, would become the new firehouse.

"We're covering the cost of the renovation, but who's fronting the money for the fire truck and equipment?" Tony Rossi asked. He looked like he'd walked off the set of *The Sopranos* with his gold pinky ring and flashy watch, black hair slicked back.

I briefly met Lore Waxman's eyes before returning my attention to Tony. "An investor, who wishes to remain anonymous, has set up a trust to handle the firehouse expenses."

In a group of high-powered men, Lore knew it would become a one-upping competition if they found out she had invested a great deal more than them, so she contacted me directly when she found out we didn't have enough funding for the firehouse. She lost her high school sweetheart in a fire almost fifty years ago, so, of course, she was adamant that we make the town as safe as possible.

"That's great," Jonas spoke up and several murmured similar sentiments.

"Each building will have a collection of memorabilia to showcase the history of what it once was." Desmond passed around idea boards.

"Makes me want to live here," Kendrick commented, leaning back in his chair and steepling his fingertips over his paunchy midsection.

"Well, you're in luck, sir." I gave him my best salesman smile. "Most buildings will have apartments on the second floor, to attract new residents. With new housing developments creeping closer to the town by the day, the reasonably priced apartments won't be a hard sell, but I'd hurry if I were you. There's been a lot of interest in them."

The illionaires chuckled, knowing good and well they had enough means to secure something they wanted even after the fact.

"The smokehouse over on Meeting Street will be remodeled into a catering venue with an industrial-grade kitchen, and we're having a thirty-foot Airstream remodeled into a food truck that'll sit permanently next to it. Nita has a barbeque pitmaster under contract to run both of them."

"That'll be fun," Jonas commented, looking at the renderings for the Airstream.

As we went over the plans, a low rumble began to build. Only one person I knew rode a motorcycle, but Diesel wasn't supposed to be coming out today. *Or was he?*

Moments later, after the noise of a beastly bike shut off, a man in a gray suit—minus a tie—pushed through the door while taking off a matte gunmetal-gray helmet. That face . . . too familiar . . . too devastating. All the oxygen was sucked out of the room as the door shut behind him, suffocating me. Taking a shallow breath, I blinked slowly to try to clear my vision—because I couldn't possibly be seeing what I was seeing—but it didn't work.

"Sorry I'm late. I had to pick up the blueprints." He held up a long plastic tube as confirmation. Blueprints? Why would this man need blueprints or be in this room disrupting my carefully constructed peace?

Confused and on the verge of freaking out, I searched the other faces at the table, but none looked remotely concerned by the revelation that just strode into my saloon like he had every right to be there. *What the heck is going on here?*

"This is Rowan Murray, our top structural engineer from Greenville. He'll be overseeing the renovations as well as the town house builds." Jonas met him by the door and shook his hand before leading him over to the group of investors. More introductions were made and the chatter around me was probably others welcoming him, but the deafening roar in my ears blocked it all out. The only thing I could do was gape in shock, as if rigor mortis had set in, specifically in my mouth and throat.

Rowan's eyes swept over the table until landing on me and I held my breath again while inwardly chanting, *Please don't say it, please don't say it . . .* Thankfully, he didn't say anything to me, but he settled in the chair directly across from me and continued making eye contact like this was no big deal. *Ha!* Nothing could have been further from the truth.

"Avalee Elvis is our lead on this project and she was going over the game plan." Jonas motioned for me to continue, but I couldn't move. Or speak. Or hardly breathe. Was my heart even working? *Oh yes*, the roaring in my ears answered, *still beating, albeit feverishly.*

The silent pause grew well past awkward. Finally, I managed to regain some motion in my left arm and slid my portfolio in front of Desmond. I tapped the top paper, and God bless him, he took the hint.

"I'm Desmond Grant, Avalee's partner, as most of you know. We've set this week aside for structural inspections and demolition. We plan to move any and all salvageable furniture and materials into the shipping containers we set out by the clock tower. Our goal is to preserve as much of the old charm as possible while updating the town with new-world function. We'll determine what and where to use . . ."

The loud roar in my ears hit a new volume, drowning out most of the meeting as I tried processing what had just happened. Did Rowan know I would be a part of this project? He didn't seem too surprised when our eyes met, but he'd always been one to mask his expressions. Not me. From the intense flush of my face and glassy unfocused eyes, surely everyone in the room was witnessing my sudden duress.

And, hello, how could I not? Just mere inches away sat my first and last *everything*.

First crush.

First kiss.

First love.

First heartbreak.

Last kiss.

Last love.

The six years apart—and a few leading up to that—had aged both of us, but on Rowan the age only improved his appearance. Not even the sparse sprinkling of gray through his coppery brown hair or the fine lines at the corners of his golden-brown eyes could lessen his appeal. Dang it, he looked vibrant and healthy, as if getting rid of me had done him good.

That hadn't been the case for me. The mirror reflected a depth of despondency in the lines around my lips, and the dark circles under my eyes bore witness to the insomnia that had become a normal part of my nightly regimen. I had a feeling my irregular sleep patterns were about to get even worse.

Desmond touched my forearm to get my attention. Being hyperaware of the man sitting in front of me, I noticed when he zeroed in on Desmond's hand on my arm.

I looked to Desmond and then Rowan, finding his gaze on the hand still caressing my arm. *Good. Let him make assumptions.*

"Is there anything else you'd like to add before we conclude?" Desmond gently squeezed my arm before letting go.

I couldn't summon my voice, so I shook my head.

Desmond's brow pinched but smoothed just as quickly. "Okay then. I believe we're ready to get this show started. Please help yourselves to more coffee and such. Then we can do a quick tour of the town."

While the investors were distracted with refreshments, I went out the back exit undetected. My phone began vibrating in my pocket almost immediately. I turned off my location finder app that I shared with Desmond and Nita so I could disappear for a while. Ignoring the texts and calls, I crossed Front Street, and after making sure the coast was clear, I slipped inside the old clock tower. Dark and dusty, no bigger than ten by ten, it was the perfect hiding spot for someone in need of a good ole meltdown. I hunkered down in a corner, pressed my back against the rough bricks, and hung my head between my knees. There I remained until the world slowed its spinning enough that I could call for help.

CHAPTER 3

THERE'S SOMETHING STRANGE IN THE NEIGHBORHOOD . . . That darn *Ghostbusters* song played in my mind as I put the phone to my ear and listened to it ring. *Who ya gonna call?*

"Whatcha know new?"

"Maudie!" I nearly yelled.

"What's wrong?" All the playfulness from my grandmother's tone had disappeared.

"I can't do this," I whispered on a hiss. From my hiding spot, I heard deep voices and then the sound of vehicles driving off.

"I don't know what it is you think you can't do, honey, but you've got moxie like no one else. Sure you can."

"No. You don't understand." I leaned my head against the brick wall and stared up at the spiderweb-draped rafters and mechanical parts of the clock that no longer worked. "Rowan. He's here."

It grew quiet on Maudie's end of the phone and then a whispered, "Oh . . ."

"Yeah. *Oh.*" I rubbed my forehead and took several deep breaths. "I can't do this."

"Oh, honey . . ." Her pitying tone confirmed she understood. "You gotta grow up and put on ya big-girl pants."

I sat up straighter and grimaced. "Say what?"

"You heard me. You're an adult. Act like one and do your job."

I switched the phone to my left ear, thinking I couldn't be hearing her right. "But it's *Rowan*!"

"He's just a man."

"*Just a man?* How can you even say that? He was my *life* until . . ." I shuffled to my feet and dusted off the seat of my pants. "Until we destroyed each other."

"That's a bit dramatic. You're both still breathing." She sighed heavily into the phone. "Take this as an opportunity to show him you're not that broken shell of a woman he walked away from."

My eyes began to water. Sniffing, I whispered, "But there are parts still broken." I blinked away the next wave of tears. "Shoot, not just broken spots but complete sections missing. Ripped out. You know those parts are never gonna mend right again."

"I do know that. You know that. Heck, even Rowan knows that. Just . . ." Maudie sighed again. "Just see this through. For your own sake. Prove to yourself how much stronger you are now."

Overhead, a flock of birds flew in and found perches among the rusted clock gears that hadn't moved in years, scaring the tater out of me. Flinching, I clamped my lips shut just in time to catch a screech. Rubbing my chest, I scanned the space overhead. This structure stood three stories tall. The first floor was an entry space but worked pretty well as my hiding place. The second floor housed the clock, and the third held the bell. Nita was searching for a clocksmith to see about fixing it. I made a mental note to check on her progress.

"Are you still there, Avalee?"

"Yes, ma'am." I swiped my hand over a rung in the ladder mounted to the wall. A cloud of dust rose up, stinging my nose and setting off a fit of sneezes.

"Bless you."

"Thanks." Sniffing, I wiped my nose with the collar of my shirt.

After a few beats of listening closely to make sure my sneezing hadn't drawn any attention, I whispered, "I thought I was stronger . . . But now . . . seeing him again after all this time, it just proved how delusional I've been. I'm really freaking out." I lifted my foot to kick a dented metal bucket but thought better of it and paced in a tight circle instead. I knew I couldn't hide out here forever, but I certainly didn't want to be found just yet.

"You know what's the best remedy for freaking out, don't you?"

I doubted I wanted to hear her answer but asked anyway, "What's that?"

"Good ole hard work. Don't you have some demolition that needs to be done?"

I rolled my neck and then my shoulders. "Tons."

"Sounds like therapy time then. Go tear something up."

But that meant I'd have to leave my hiding spot. Even though Desmond had been blowing up my phone for the past hour, I still didn't feel capable of facing anyone or anything beyond these crumbling confines. The irony wasn't lost on me that I was ghosting in a ghost town.

"Go get to it, sugar," Maudie spoke again.

"Yes, ma'am. Love you. Bye." I ended the call abruptly. My grandmother hadn't told me a dang thing I wanted to hear, but I guess that was for the better. The phone vibrated in my hand. I tapped the text message icon and read the newest text from Desmond.

Just tell me you're ok.

I skimmed back over the other ones he'd sent that I'd ignored while hiding.

What just happened?

Where are you?

This new guy keeps asking about you. You have some explaining to do, young lady.

Not ready to sift through all the baggage those questions carried, I answered his last. **I'll be OK. In need of a bathroom and something for a headache.** I added, **Is the new guy gone?**

Desmond replied after a few seconds. **Inspecting the big bank. Where are you?**

Heading up to the apartment for a bit, but if anyone asks, I'm not here. PLEASE.

Desmond didn't reply, but at least I knew all that I needed to know for the time being. With the confirmation that Rowan would be on the other end of town, I pocketed my phone, cracked open the door, and peered outside. Again, the coast was clear, so I dashed across the road and snuck up to my apartment. I opened the door and nearly peed my pants.

"Avalee Elvis." Desmond sat casually on the couch, but his clipped tone spoke of his seriousness.

"Give me a minute before you start in on me." I held up a finger and darted into the bathroom.

After doing my business, I moved to the sink and slowly washed my hands. I turned off the faucet and dried my hands. If I stayed in here long enough, would he grow bored and leave? Deciding to give it a try, I rummaged through the drawer of hair ties and bandanas. I selected a gray bandana since the color matched my mood and tied my hair back with it. Then I opened the medicine cabinet, took the bottle of Excedrin off the middle shelf, and shook out two tablets. Popping them in my mouth, I turned the water back on and sipped from it like a drinking fountain. I glanced in the mirror and noticed an eyebrow hair in need of plucking, so I got out the tweezers and went to work.

"I'm not leaving, so you might as well come on out of there," Desmond called.

Staring at my frowning face in the mirror, I grumbled a few things under my breath before saying out loud, "Why me?" When my reflection didn't answer, I put away the tweezers and opened the door.

Desmond angled his head and looked at me expectantly as I walked out of the bathroom. "What happened in that meeting?"

I swiped my tool belt off the counter, fastened it around my waist, and checked for my safety goggles while avoiding his scrutiny. "Nothing."

"Bull." He slowly rose from the couch and collected his leather portfolio and iPad, beating me to the door within seconds. "That was anything but *nothing*. Who's Rowan Murray to you?"

I grasped the doorknob, but Desmond reached over my head and pressed his palm against the door to keep it shut. Huffing, I gave him the simplest reply I could think of without lying. "Just a guy I grew up with."

Desmond shook his head. "Nuh-uh. Try again please." Seconds ticked by until he got the hint that my lips were remaining shut. "If this is going to be a conflict of interest we need to figure out how to handle it."

I rubbed my temples where my pulse hammered against my skull. "I don't feel like it."

He clucked his tongue. "Wow. Way to handle whatever this is maturely."

Eyes and nose burning, I studied my boots. "Please. Let's just put a pin in it for now."

Desmond pushed out a long exhale, sounding as frustrated as I felt. "Answer me this, are you safe?"

Was I? Nothing felt safe, that's for sure. Especially my sanity and my carefully constructed walls. I mumbled a "yes," anyways. I was safe in the way Desmond meant.

Desmond dropped his hand from the door and checked his watch. "I have to head out to another meeting. I'm already late because of your little disappearing stunt." He wrapped an arm around my sagging shoulders and pressed a kiss to the top of my head. "Call me if you need me."

Nodding, I followed Desmond downstairs. He gave me a hard look when I peeped outside before exiting the building. I knew I was acting like a lunatic, but there were no cares to give in that moment. My survival instinct was stuck in flight mode.

Desmond paused by his car. "You sure you're okay, Avalee?"

"Yep." I kept my head down and pulled on my work gloves.

Desmond mumbled something that sounded a lot like "liar," as he slammed the car door and drove off.

Checking for any signs of Rowan and finding none, I crossed the street, not stopping until I stood inside the old post office. I took a deep inhale of musty air and looked forward to the day I could do that and smell only the yeasty goodness of freshly baked bread and pastries once we transformed this place into a bakery.

Gloves and safety glasses on, I picked up the sledgehammer and swung toward the orange X spray-painted on the mail room wall. The impact sent a burst of plaster crumbling to the floor and a vibration along my arms. It almost stung. Good. I needed that jolt to release the tension. As tears dripped down my cheeks, I raised the hammer and slammed it against the wall again.

Soon, the jarring rhythm of beating down the wall and the ever-growing pile of debris captured my total attention. Well, almost. It would take a heckuva lot more demolition than one wall to make me forget about the ghost who just returned to haunt me along with the bevy of regrets that would surely be conjured due to his presence. Good thing the entire week's schedule was filled with just that.

As I took out the last piece of the wall, a deafening roar had the loose windowpanes and my heart rattling. I stood still and listened as the motorcycle rumbled in place for several agonizing moments before finally peeling down the street and away from Somewhere. Once the sound of it completely faded away, I finally took my first easy breath since Rowan had shown up. It would be short-lived, that I knew, considering he'd be here off and on until this project was complete. With that as the perfect motivation to get to work, I scanned the room for my next victim.

I turned my sights on a busted cabinet. Past the point of repair, I decided to put it out of its misery while I was at it. My boots crunched against the debris on the floor as I widened my stance in front of the cabinet and swung at it like a major league baseball player. Three swift swings in, a letter fell out the back of it. I squatted down and retrieved the yellowed envelope, postmarked 1896 and addressed to a Louis Jefferson. One of my favorite parts about demo days were the secrets so often discovered. Secrets hidden within walls, underneath floorboards, wedged behind plumbing or furniture.

Intrigued by the possibility of perhaps a love letter or something on those lines, I moved over to the window for better light and took off my work gloves. The flap opened easily, as if time had robbed it of the adhesive. I pulled out the single sheet of paper and read the note in cursive writing.

Dear Mr. Jefferson,

I'm writing you in regards to the three heifers you refuse to return. They were not our son's cows to give and I expect you to respectfully give them back by the fifteenth. We need to bring them to sale or we'll need to mortgage the farm again. My boy says your daughter has already moved on to a new suitor anyway. She ain't even got all her teeth, so I still don't understand for the life of me why he'd give three perfectly good heifers for her in the first place. My boy, he has all his teeth and the doctor done fixed that lazy eye, so it really is her loss.

You have until the fifteenth or I'm taking my complaint to the sheriff.

Regards,
Jasper B. Reaves

Snorting, I pulled my phone out and took a picture of the letter, sending it to Nita and Desmond with a quick text. **Found the first demo treasure.** I figured it would reassure Des I was okay.

Nita replied first with a laughing emoji, followed by a cow emoji.

Desmond's reply popped up before I put the phone away. **Who knew folks were that petty before the days of social media.** He attached a GIF of a snaggletooth woman grinning.

LOL. Still refreshing to read something handwritten in this text and email times we're living, even though it's hate mail. I sent an envelope emoji and a mean face emoji.

Nita: **Not sure I could manage anything handwritten. They stopped teaching that stuff.**

Her comment made me feel my age. A flash of a memory popped in my head of me showing a certain boy in our fourth-grade class how to write a cursive *R*. Blinking the memory away, I focused on the phone screen as it lit up with new text messages.

Des: **You can't, Nita. Your writing is chicken scratch.**

Nita: **For that I'm mailing you a hate letter.**

Des: **While you do that, I'll be shopping for the perfect frame for Avalee's letter. That has to be put on display once the bakery remodel is complete.**

Nita: **That'll surely bring in customers!**

Chuckling at their banter, I closed out the text app and placed my phone in my back pocket.

Feeling a little more on level ground now, albeit temporarily, I put the letter to the side and got back to work. I couldn't quit laughing over the unexpected letter. Better than crying over things I had no control over, I guessed. It figured I'd find hate mail instead of something sweet or sentimental. It wasn't even endearing. No love, not even someone else's, for me.

Loveless. Story of my life.

CHAPTER 4

THE SOUND OF PROGRESS MET MY EARS as I hurried outside at daybreak a few days later. Work trucks filled with subcontractors and crew members were pulling in and parking along Front Street. I buttoned my gray work jacket to ward off the February chill and waited by the corner while everyone unloaded their equipment.

Desmond walked over, looking debonair as always. "You ready to get this show on the road, darlin'?"

"I've been ready to do this for at least two years now." I picked up my thermos and took a sip of coffee as we started up Main Street.

"You should have worn that pretty pink Carhartt jacket I bought you. And the beanie that matches."

"There's nothing wrong with what I'm wearing for a day of demolition."

Desmond flicked his wrist and checked his gold watch. "It's not just a day of demolition. Remember the TV crew will be here in about twenty minutes to interview us."

"Shoot. I forgot about that." I looked him over. Of course he was dressed to the nines in a navy suit and a camel trench that matched his fedora. "But this will have to do."

Froid Bellamy shuffled up, wearing navy coveralls. His furry hat made him look like he had a raccoon curled up on top of his head, tail and all. "This town reminds me of a lost city you see in the jungle where all the vines start overtakin' it." He pointed a gloved hand at no building in particular. Nature had been having its way with the abandoned area for quite some time, but today that would be coming to an end. The potential was there. It was up to us how to bring it forth.

"Good morning, sir. I thought you and Fred weren't due until after the demo was complete." I gave him a quick side hug and continued walking. "Nice outfit, by the way."

The sixty-seven-year-old gentleman straightened his furry hat, pretending to primp. "Me and Fred figured you'd need some interestin' folks to be on the TV."

"*Interesting* is about right," Desmond mumbled, eyeing the strange hat.

Froid and his twin brother could wear whatever interesting outfit of their choosing as long as they helped me see this project to the end. They were the best wood craftsmen this side of the Mississippi. Plus the brothers knew how to keep life fun, handing out smiles wherever they went. I, for one, could use all of that I could get.

I patted him on the shoulder. "I'll let you know about the interview, Froid. First I need to do this meeting."

Desmond and I climbed the steps of the courthouse, which had been designated as the morning meetup. While the crew, mostly burly men and a few tough-looking women, sipped from thermoses or soda bottles, I filled them in on the game plan.

"We already did the testing for lead paint, asbestos, and mold. Results were expected but still grim, so we had all that addressed before y'all arrived. The production calendar will have frequent updates, so be sure to check it often. We want everyone to be on the same page at all times. It'll look worse rather than better for a while, as most of you know. Just trust the process. Remember, even though we all have our own tasks, we're a team with the same goal." I motioned around us. "Bringing this ghost back to life."

Keeping my eyes peeled for a certain team member, I answered a few questions. Thankfully, Rowan hadn't shown up, so maybe he'd jetted off on his shiny new bike and would stay out of my way. I'd been able to dodge him successfully for three days straight, so maybe my luck would hold for a change.

"A lot of the buildings will become different businesses than they were originally. Like this courthouse. It will become the town hall. And Fanny's Fabrics is going to be turned into a deli." I hitched a thumb to my left. "The Calhoun Brothers Bank will be the firehouse. There are signs on the doors and I've made a map to help keep us from getting confused." I handed over a stack of maps to Froid, who stood at the front of the group. He took one and then passed the stack to the guy beside him.

"A reasonable dent has already been made in the demolition, but there's still plenty for us to get knocked out. The sooner we finish tearing the town apart, the sooner we can get to rebuilding it. With the time constraints, it's necessary to juggle the electrical and plumbing crews at the same time. Every building must be rewired to pass code, so it's a big order. The saloon is complete. As well as the pecan warehouse." I pointed down the street where the top of the warehouse could be seen just over the line of buildings to the right. "That's going to become an events venue, but for now you're welcome to have lunch and bathroom breaks in there. Make a mess, clean it up. I ain't your mama, so this is the only time I'm sayin' it." I gave them all a pointed look. Work crews and tidiness had never been synonymous, but a girl could hope.

Desmond cleared his throat. "Also, for now the firehouse, the feedstore, and the flower shop are off-limits. Signs have also been posted on the doors as reminders. We have to get further inspections made before touching those buildings."

I glanced at my clipboard while Desmond scanned his iPad. I still liked the old method of printouts. Something he'd relentlessly teased me about. "If something has an orange *X* painted on it, then it's to be trashed. Put everything else in the shipping containers down by the old clock tower. I'll be around if you need anything."

The group divided and I followed Desmond to the old clock tower.

"Let's start the interview here. That way they can pan down Main Street and capture the entire ghost town and the crews getting to work." He reached over and fussed with my hair.

Laughing, I batted his hand away. "Knock it off."

A brightly colored news van pulled up and a bubbly redhead hopped out the passenger seat. Haley introduced herself and went over some details while the cameraman set up. They were busy, we were busy, so she assured us it wouldn't take too long. Of course, Froid and Fred crashed the interview, wearing identical outfits to highlight the fact that they were twins. If it weren't for Froid having a good thirty pounds on Fred and Fred being about an inch or so taller, they could have pulled off being identical.

Haley brought the microphone closer to her lips. "I studied the map you sent and it made me wonder why such a tiny town would have two banks."

"There's a pretty interesting story behind that," I commented. "So back in the day there used to be a wealthy family. They owned the Calhoun Brothers Bank. The big one on Meeting Street that we're turning into the firehouse. The Calhoun brothers, Don and Von—"

"Twins like us?" Fred interrupted, poking a thumb in Froid's direction.

"Yep. And well . . . they ended up having a falling out."

"Money does that, ya know," Froid supplied.

Fred clucked his tongue. "Ain't that the truth."

I returned my attention to Haley and the microphone she held in my direction. "So they went their own ways. Don kept the big bank and Von opened the smaller one on the corner. About a year after that, there was a bank robbery at the big bank. Whoever pulled it off knew a lot about the vault, making rumors fly that the brother who owned the smaller bank was involved."

"Von wouldn't do that to Don," Fred declared, his raccoon hat flopping around as he shook his head, as if he knew the bank brothers personally.

"How much money did they get away with?" Haley asked, unbothered by Fred's interruption.

"This part is kind of funny. They ended up stealing groceries instead of money."

"Humph." Froid crossed his arms. "You're making this up."

"No. For real. I have copies of the newspaper articles to prove it. The bank teller had spent her lunch break grocery shopping, but she didn't have enough time to bring the groceries home. She placed her groceries in bank bags and tucked them in the vault, so her boss wouldn't know. The robbers grabbed the grocery bags, thinking it was money, which meant the poor woman was the only victim of the crime."

Haley laughed softly. "That was quite an interesting tale. I'm sure we'll be hearing more of them as the revitalization project gets underway." She moved the interview along, asking questions about our timeline and such.

Thirty minutes later, Desmond and I waved goodbye to the news van as it drove off.

"I wonder where your friend is at today. He would have been a good one to interview." Desmond hummed, going for nonchalance, but that simple statement held a whole heckuva lot of weight.

Avoiding his scrutiny, I stared down at the clipboard in my hands. "Who?"

He clucked his tongue. "You know who. Or is he more than just a friend?"

"Don't start with me." I started to walk off but Desmond gripped my arm.

"Remember that pin you put in the Rowan conversation? It's starting to slip out."

My eyes narrowed as I said through gritted teeth, "Then shove it back in."

Desmond mirrored my stern expression. "Maybe I'll just have this conversation with the man himself."

I gasped. "You better not."

Desmond opened his mouth just as his phone began to ring. He checked the screen and sighed. "I need to answer this."

Relieved, I breathed a little easier. "No problem. I need to get to work."

Rolling his eyes, Desmond walked away. But I knew my friend well enough to know he would be back for another round about Rowan sooner rather than later.

I made my way up the street to the old theater. The small stage and five rows of seating needed to be ripped out and cleared away before we could begin converting it into the coffee shop. After donning my work gloves, I gripped the armrests of the first chair I reached, giving it a firm wiggle to test how secure it was to the floor. A solid yank, then another, and the rusted nails came loose. Soon, I got into the rhythm of destruction, going through each row like a tornado.

Good ole hard work, I'm talking about the kind of backbreaking all-consuming variety that allowed me to disengage from the world outside of the task at hand. Exerting myself also reminded me that my body could be used for a good purpose. That even though it had betrayed me in the worst way, it did know how to function purposefully.

Hours passed, the coat ended up on the floor and my shirt sleeves were rolled up. I paused to dab my forehead with the back of my arm, wiping away the combination of dust and sweat. That grit felt like progress.

Like Pavlov's dog, I was triggered by the sound of a motorcycle to instantly search for a dark corner to hide in. In a panic, I scanned the room and decided to scramble out the back and creep over to the rear entrance of the saloon. A solid plan, or so I thought until my getaway went sideways.

My childhood and teen years could be summed up as one giant dare. And all the small dares that added up to create the big one could be blamed on one person, or hellion as Maudie often referred to him. One of those dares went down at the state fair in the livestock tent.

Twelve years old and invincible, I took the dare to climb into the piglet enclosure. A candy apple waited for me as a reward if I pulled it off without getting caught. I made it inside with no hiccups and was about to hop back out when this fat sow came out of nowhere and bulldozed into me, knocking my feet right from under me. Just above the squealing and oinks I heard cackling. The hellion's honey-hued eyes and his devilish grin were the first thing I saw on the other side of the fence just before one of the livestock workers came over and helped me out. Then the worker escorted me to the exit, banning me from coming back. I hated getting caught, because the hellion never reneged on a dare so I didn't get the candy apple.

Now, as I stood in the narrow hallway leading to my apartment, I had another standoff with the hellion in question, and that dare flickered through my thoughts. Just like the mama pig and the livestock worker caught me, I'd been caught once again. No way around it, doggone it.

"Your hair . . ." He held a hand up toward his forehead and waved his fingers. "It's different."

"They're called bangs." I blew the long fringe from my eyes, thinking how bizarre our first words were after everything we'd been through and then the long separation. Did he seriously want to talk about my hairstyle?

"You've never had those before." Rowan took a step forward, giving me a thorough once-over. "And your nails are painted."

I glanced at my freshly manicured nails, shined up in a bright orange color the nail tech called *Toucan Do It If You Try*. I needed that encouragement as much as the cheery color.

After losing all I'd lost, I came pretty close to losing myself altogether. My dad, of all people, took me to get my first manicure. He had the mindset that tossing money at something, even a broken daughter, could fix it, so I received a spa gift certificate the day after Rowan walked out of my life. The manicurist talked about self-care during my visit, something about shifting focus onto the little things to take a break from the big things. That stuck with me and so my manicured nails gave me something to focus on during the heavy days. It reminded me I was still here and needed to keep breathing.

A curious look creased Rowan's face as he leaned into my space and took a deeper breath. "And you smell different."

"Because I *am* different." I retreated but didn't get far before bumping into my door.

The dang man had been waiting for me and now we were just holed up here, practically circling each other as if we were preparing to go a round or two.

I crossed my arms to shield myself. "After ten years apart, the first thing you want to discuss is my appearance?"

"Six years," Rowan corrected.

"We might as well count those last years before you made it official." I expected him to become chagrined and argue, but no. He left that subject just as easily as he'd left me all those years ago.

"The changes look good"—he tipped his nose closer to my neck and inhaled—"and smell good on you, even though I prefer your other perfume."

"People change. That's life." Shrugging off the shiver he provoked, I shoved him away. "You're different too. I can't get over you driving a motorcycle." I sized him up. "Are you also hiding tattoos underneath that designer suit?"

His eyes flashed, reminding me of warm honey, and then he smirked. "Maybe." He flicked the top button of his shirt without actually unfastening it. "You're welcome to find out."

Oh, no. He used that flirty tone! The one with the lilt wrapping around his pronunciation. What was the matter with me? One minute I'm trying to cut him down with a glare and the next we're easily falling right back into a familiar flirty banter. Chemistry had never been our issue, but attraction alone couldn't carry a relationship. Something we found out in the hardest of ways.

I held my palms up, ready to shove him if need be. "Knock it off.

Just . . . explain to me why you're suddenly here, after all this time, disrupting my town?"

Rowan dropped the playfulness and grew stoic. "Your town? Nah, I'd say this town belongs to those investors who hired me to assist in this revitalization project. I'm here to do my job. Plain and simple."

Nothing with this man had ever been plain and simple. Difficult from day one. He may have changed in some ways, but clearly that part hadn't.

Now we were back to the tense stare down. I placed my hands on my hips and squared my shoulders. "I have work to do, so hurry up and say what you need to say."

Rowan finally gave me some breathing room, retreating a step, and ran a hand through his wavy brown hair, the hall light catching on the natural copper undertones. "We're going to be working together the better part of the next year. We need to get over ourselves and make this work."

I sputtered a laugh. "We couldn't make our *personal* relationship work. You're delusional if you actually think we can make a *business* relationship work." My phone pinged just as I heard a large truck pull up on the street below. "That's my lumber delivery. Need to go. How about you stay out of my way and I'll stay out of yours." I shoved past him and hurried down the stairs, practically running.

"Avalee!" Rowan called out, but I hightailed it.

In an effort to self-protect, I fell back on my typical way of handling things, avoidance. I stuck to emails while dodging Rowan's calls and text messages. Always picking another part of the small town to work on after checking his schedule. It worked for a solid two weeks until it didn't.

In the middle of taking down a busted door in the pharmacy, I heard the front door open and slam against the wall. "Hey! I don't need another broke door!" I glared over my shoulder and found Rowan storming my way, chest bowed out like a bull on a rampage.

"I've had my fill, Avalee. This ain't working for me. You will not reduce me to email exchanges."

"It's for the best."

"For who? You? Like I said, it ain't working for me." He ran his fingers through his hair and gave me a stern frown. "When I need to speak with you about a matter pertaining to this project, I expect you to answer your dang phone like a professional."

I gave up on the door hinge and jabbed the air between us with the screwdriver. "I ain't got time for this."

"You don't get it, Avalee. I'm not here to cause you any trouble."

"No. *You* don't get it." I harrumphed, the ache of exhaustion getting heavier by the minute. "Just looking at you hurts me."

Lips drawn tight, Rowan grew still and looked off to his left.

Before I could spew off anything else, Rowan caught my wrist and pulled the tool out of my grip. In a blink, he had the door free from the rusted hardware and leaned it against the wall.

Returning the screwdriver to me, he took a deep breath and lowered his voice. "I know how important this town is to you. I'm here to help make it happen. Same goal as you. I'll do my best to leave you alone as much as possible, but please . . . just answer when I call." He pivoted and walked out a lot slower than he'd entered, chest no longer bowed.

Watching him go, I wished I could hate him, but that had proved to be as difficult as anything relating to Rowan Murray. And the man had no idea how, even when he wasn't in my presence, it was impossible for him to leave me alone. In last night's rendezvous with insomnia, he'd starred in every sleepless thought.

CHAPTER 5

MOVING TO SOMEWHERE, SOUTH CAROLINA, had been a permanent decision. One that I couldn't go back on now that I'd closed on the sale
of my house in Lexington just a few days ago. Sure, I could pick up
and start over again, but I'd grown weary of that task. As old Southern
ladies liked to say, I wanted to grow a sit, put down some roots, and
let them settle deep right here in the sandy soil of this part of the
lowcountry. Somewhere was supposed to be my new solace, but with
Rowan hovering nearby with all our ghosts, solace had abandoned
me and a heftier burden of anxiety took its place.

Rubbing my tired eyes, I slumped against the pillows haphazardly
tossed on the bed and surveyed my new bedroom. I'd spent the better
part of the night unpacking all of my belongings. Belongings that
held pieces of Rowan no matter how many times I tried purging him.
My gaze landed on a trinket box on the dresser across from my bed.
It held more than one piece that included Rowan, but one specific
piece came to mind and several memories it evoked.

The day I fell in love with Rowan Murray should have been a sign
that things would never work out. We'd been such fools.

Maudie gave Rowan the nickname Rowdy not long after we became friends in the third grade. He'd just moved to South Carolina with his family from a small village in Northern Ireland, but after only a few weeks it seemed he'd been a part of my life all along. The guy entertained bad ideas like a professional host. And he always figured out how to rope me in as his assistant. Divvying out dares was his forte and I was always the sucker going along with it.

Summer before junior year of high school, Maudie sent me on a picking day trip with Rowan just south of here at an abandoned train depot. The two of us were already inseparable by that point, so we were quick to agree to the adventure that would surely hold a dare or two. After we loaded up a few benches and an old desk, Rowan quickly settled on the day's dare. *I dare you to climb inside that caboose through the roof.*

Sounded simple enough. All I had to do was climb up the metal ladder attached to the side of the caboose and shimmy through the roof hatch. I recall gazing up at the caboose and asking what my prize would be. He promised me a giant chocolate milkshake from my favorite ice cream shop on the way home. We'd worked in the stifling heat for hours by that point, filling the back of the truck and a trailer full of treasures, so the idea of a cold treat had me accepting the dare without much thought. I gripped the hot rungs on the side of the faded red caboose, worrying my hands would blister, and made quick work to the top. It took a few yanks to get the corroded latch undone and without thinking the plan through, I dropped inside. A few seconds of standing in the middle of the dimly lit space, I realized the error of my ways. Everything inside the musty cabin was bolted to the floor, so I had nothing to stand on to get back out the top. And the windows and exits were welded shut, something we should have checked beforehand.

Ten minutes in I began to panic. Fifteen minutes, I started screaming bloody murder, swearing I was close to having a heatstroke. Yelling for me to calm down, Rowan tied several tarps end to end and fished me out through the hatch like he was a master angler. Never a scrawny guy, but that day he found some superhuman strength to get me the heck out of there.

Once our feet were safely on the ground, my best friend gathered me in his arms, apologizing profusely. *I'm so sorry, a stór. So sorry.*

It was the first time he'd ever called me that. *A stór*, my treasure. His words had been coated heavily with his accent, each syllable curled with a lilt. I'd heard it before when it was just us and he'd be excited or angered by something or someone. But that day at the train depot was the first time I had a physical reaction to it. A static sensation ran along my shoulders, and my heart fluttered like a lightning bolt had zapped it. And I never felt the same after that.

Rowan calling me *a stór* and sounding like a full-on Irishman— the combination formed into a magnet and the next thing I knew, I'd smashed my lips against his. Not very graceful, mind you, but when I began to withdraw, Rowan followed as if he were under the power of a magnet as well. We kissed until the panic-riddled adrenaline rush transformed into something else entirely.

Maudie said we'd been joined at the hip before that junking trip and joined at the lips after. There was a lot of truth in that, no need in denying it.

Now, unraveling myself from the bedding, I stood up and crossed over to the dresser. Flipping open the lid to the trinket box, I stared inside, easily finding the smashed penny, no longer a circle but an oval. I ran a fingertip over the smooth copper before pushing it to the side and plundering around until catching a glimpse of tarnished silver. Without picking it up, I stared at the antique claddagh ring. No fancy gemstones, just a crowned heart held by two silver hands.

At homecoming during our senior year, while most kids in our class attended a bonfire after-party on one of the nearby farms, Rowan took me out to Sands Beach and got down on one knee right there on the little sandy shore. He proposed, sliding his great-grandmother's claddagh ring on my finger, placing it on my left hand with the heart facing away from me, signifying my heart belonged to him. And it truly did belong to him. Until it didn't.

Snapping the lid shut on those thoughts, I shoved the trinket box into the top drawer and slammed it shut. Out of sight, out of mind, and all that. With the punch list for the bakery waiting to be knocked out, I'd lollygagged long enough. Needing to feel a little more confident, I chose my pink Carhartt pants with only one small tear at the knee and a dark gray T-shirt with our Lowcountry Lost logo on it. Two *Ls* flanking a palmetto tree inside a circle. I thought it looked pretty classy for a construction company logo. I tucked in just the front of my shirt, going for a trendy carpenter look, and pulled my hair into a high ponytail. After shoving my feet into my gray steel-toe work boots and preparing a thermos of coffee, I set out to make some headway on that punch list.

As I made my way down the street, I caught sight of Rowan over by the mercantile shooting the breeze with Fred and Froid Bellamy, two of the most talented albeit slowest woodworkers in these parts. Even though Rowan looked up before I could turn tail and run, he didn't acknowledge me. Just one glimpse my way before turning his back. Apparently, the man was holding true to the promise he made me yesterday to leave me alone unless necessary.

Fine by me. I had plenty to do without having to deal with him. I cracked open the front door and the scent of drywall dust and spackle assailed me. Ah, the smell of progress!

First on my list was tiling the wall dividing the service area from the kitchen, the area that used to be the post office's large storage room. The boxes of tile and the tools needed were waiting by the wall, so I got straight to work. First, inspecting each cement tile, taking them out of the box and laying them in stacks. With a creamy white background, the grayish-blue baroque stamp really stood out. Only four pieces had chips, which was minimal damage. One time, while working on a flip, I ended up with five cases of smashed tile. Maudie always said if life served up smashed tile, make a mosaic. So that's what I did. Thankfully, I wouldn't have to do that today.

Hours later and with tile halfway up the wall, I heard someone's heavy shoes enter the front. I glanced over my shoulder and cringed.

"Cute outfit," Rowan said as soon as he made it to my side.

I iced the back of another tile with mortar and contemplated ignoring him altogether, but darned if it didn't feel nice that someone noticed. Typically, as a construction worker, I didn't receive compliments on my attire unless it was about my Gatorback tool belt with ergonomic memory foam for added back support. "What do you need, Rowan?"

"We need to discuss this wall before you tile it." Rowan pointed toward the wall, half of which was already dressed in the gorgeously rustic tile.

"Umm . . . It's a little too late for that now, dontcha think?" I waved the trowel at the tiled section, giving him my best *duh* expression.

Rowan settled his hands on his lean hips. Dressed in a white button-down with sleeves rolled to the elbows and a pair of slate blue trousers, he looked like an annoyed schoolteacher. "It won't support the weight of those heavy tiles."

I almost lost my grip on the trowel. "What? Why not?"

Pulling a small stud finder out of his back pocket, he moved to the wall and ran it along the untiled top half. It didn't beep nearly as often as it should. "Wall studs are supposed to be a minimum of sixteen inches apart. As you can see, the closest ones are thirty inches. Some more than that."

"How on earth did someone get away with that?" I picked some mortar off my thumbnail and glared at the offending wall, trying to disregard him standing so close that I could smell the crisp notes of apple and sandalwood in his cologne.

"Building inspectors probably weren't even a thing back when this was built."

Pinching my eyes closed, I groaned. "This is a lot of wasted tile and time."

"The tile's a bit *garish*, so maybe it's a good thing. Now you can rethink your choice."

I tried not to let it show but I was quite impressed that he used such a word to describe tile of all things. I also tried my darnedest to ignore the effect that his accent had on me as it slipped through the word, blaming anger for the heat creeping up my neck. I focused on the insult instead.

"Clearly, you have no taste in tilework. These are handmade encaustic tile."

Rowan shrugged one shoulder, still unimpressed.

Growling a huff, I jabbed the trowel at him and a few globs of mortar flew in his direction but didn't hit the mark. "You could have told me before now."

"Yeah? You already know how remarkable we are at communicating." Rowan scrubbed his face and mumbled something behind his hand. Dropping it, he leveled his gaze on me, a hint of remorse in his honey-brown eyes. "I'm sorry, but let's face the facts here. This wall won't hold the weight of this type of tile."

I walked away and came back with the sledgehammer. "How's this for communication?" I reared back and swung, producing a good-sized hole. "There. Problem solved. And here's another fact for you. My team and I are in charge of this project. Next time something like this comes up, we are to be told about it immediately."

"I'm part of the team!" His scowling face colored.

"You're only here as a favor to the investors!" My voice rose with each word.

Rowan threw his hands in the air and growled. "You went from ignoring me to now yelling at me."

"Because you don't listen . . . This seems oddly familiar." I shook my head.

Rowan turned on his heel and stormed away, tossing a sentiment or two over his shoulder. "I'm not doing this."

"Yeah? You walking away seems oddly familiar too!" I whirled around and swung the sledgehammer with all my might. "And this tile is not garish!" I yelled, as chunks of tile rained onto the floor. Guess life was handing me shattered tiles once again.

Rowan muttered something but I was too busy pummeling the

wall to catch any of it. I kept on until nothing but the rickety wall studs remained.

I marched behind the building, where a stack of newly delivered lumber sat. Fishing out some two-by-fours, I began the process of starting over. Story of my life.

CHAPTER 6

MARCH

Working to avoid Rowan and then bickering with him when we had no other choice but to talk had become part of my workday routine. I'm not proud of that. And the good Lord knows I never thought in a million years I'd find myself in this predicament. How had this become my life? Today began a brand-new month, making me more aware of the clock ticking rapidly toward our deadline, so I knew I needed to just put on my big-girl pants like Maudie suggested over a month ago and figure out how to work with Rowan as peacefully as possible. Darned if every time I had tried, though, he would do something to undermine my efforts.

As I tackled removing rotted and damaged sections of the flooring in the mercantile, I couldn't get the man out of my head. Just yesterday, he weaseled his way in on the smokehouse project. With new windows in place, the squat cinder block building only needed to be dressed up on the outside, so I was framing it out so a crew could wrap it in charcoal gray tin siding. One minute Rowan just wanted to help and then the next he had to tell me a better way of doing it by using jacks to keep the furring strips level. Sure, he may have been right, but still. It caused me actual pain to be that close to him. How could he not see that?

My pocket vibrated. I freed a hand from a glove, fished the phone out, and glanced at the screen. "Speak of the devil . . ." I muttered before answering with a casualness I didn't feel. "What's up?"

"Can you meet me in front of the flower shop in a few minutes?"

I looked around at the work needing to be done, wishing I could get away with saying heck no. "Give me a half hour." I hung up and pocketed my phone before he could reply. An hour later, I put away my tools and met Rowan at the flower shop.

Out front an excavator sat idling.

While Rowan wrapped up a phone call, I examined the clapboard building with a grimace. Ironically, Mother Nature had woven it with thick stitches of vines and foliage. She was doing her darnedest to reclaim it, but I wasn't ready to let go.

"We need to clear it out."

"The only thing holding this building together is the kudzu." Rowan signed something on a small clipboard and handed it to the guy with the machinery. "Sorry, Avalee, but we have to count this one as a casualty."

"No way. We can—"

"It won't pass code."

I had almost forgotten about the distinct finality his voice held when he meant business.

My heart began pounding as the operator put the excavator into gear and it rumbled louder. My throat tightened but I managed to speak around it. "We're supposed to be saving the town. Not tearing it down."

Placing his hand on my elbow, Rowan moved us out the way and motioned for the guy to get started. "Some things can't be saved. You of all people should know that."

The severe honesty of his words struck me to the core and my knees nearly buckled. Unsteady, I blinked against the sting in my eyes and yanked my arm free of his grip.

Rowan sighed heavily. "Look—"

I held a palm up and shook my head, not wanting him to try soothing the pain he'd just caused. It would only add more salt to the wound. "Tear it down then." I turned and stomped away.

"Avalee! I'm—"

"No!" My steps gained momentum, even though my legs felt weighted, not from my work boots but the debilitating grief he'd nearly unleashed from inside me. I needed to get away from him and fix the lid back into place.

That's the thing with grief, long expanses of time can go by with it lying dormant, but one tiny phrase or suggestion can trigger it. It happened to me about a year back. Out junking with Maudie, I found a family tree made out of a slice of a tree trunk at an estate sale so similar to the one I'd made a long time ago. The names were etched along the tree rings instead of in a traditional tree branch style. I thought I was so original with my idea. Clearly, that hadn't been the case. Eyes blurred, I stared at the tree slice, thinking that family did the same thing with their family that I did with mine. Just carelessly discarded it. Surrounded by people milling around the dusty house, an invisible monster attacked me. Crushing my heart in its fist while slamming the air out of my lungs.

As the splintering sound of wood being snapped at the jaws of the excavator reached me from behind, I dodged through an alley so I couldn't turn and see the destruction. Mad at Rowan and mad at myself, even though the exact reason for the anger eluded me, I hid out for the remainder of the workday in the chapel.

Avoidance had become a dance quite familiar to me. Avoid a subject or situation altogether. That had been my first approach with grief. Just avoid facing any part of it. At some point, after hitting rock bottom, I started counseling. Then I attended one session of group grief counseling at my counselor's insistence, but I figured out real quick that was not my cup of tea. One guy was there to discuss losing his pet, I think it was a cat, and how he hated that animal with a passion. Yeah, *hated*. Another woman spoke extensively about her grief over losing her grandmother, a woman she'd only met two times, but how horrific it had been on her anyway. No judgment here about either, but it made me realize sharing my heartache of losing my children with complete strangers who had different losses didn't work for me. I found no appeal in airing laundry, dirty or otherwise, so that had been the first and last group session I attended.

Sure, grief never looks the same from person to person. I get that, I just had no desire to express mine so vocally. Some like to critique others' expressions of grief. *She didn't cry enough. She cried too much. He shouldn't have been smiling at such a tragic time.* I could go on and on, but the point is everyone mourns differently. Just as there are many ways to grieve, so are there many different forms of therapy. My therapy came in the form of demolition and restoration.

While hiding, I swept out the chapel, dusted away the cobwebs from underneath the pews and along the rafters, and took down two broken chandeliers. Even managed to order the parts needed to fix them with my handy-dandy smartphone. With nothing else I could do without my tools, I made a punch list of everything that still needed to be done. Wood floors refinished. One of the side windows had a cracked windowpane that needed replacing. Central heating and air. A small side room behind the altar would be transformed into a restroom.

By the time the last work truck pulled out and left the town silent, the sun had set. With an excess of frustration to work out of my system, I hauled a portable battery-operated light over to the feedstore.

As I finished setting up the high-powered light and focused it on the floor, my phone vibrated in my pocket. I pulled it out and read the text from Desmond.

You're not in the feedstore, are you??

I huffed a slight laugh. Since we tended to work all over the place, Nita decided we needed to follow each other on the Life360 app. It cut down on the repetition of asking each other where we were. I liked the idea of someone knowing my whereabouts since I'd started staying in the ghost town alone.

I typed a reply. **You're not stalking me on that app, are you??**

Just making sure you haven't disappeared. FYI—the feedstore is still off-limits.

IK. I won't be long. I glanced around the dusty space. The floor planks matched the ones in the mercantile. Between the water damage and some staining, there was only enough salvageable flooring for one building. Since we didn't know what to do with the feedstore just yet, I decided to swipe some to patch the mercantile floors. Definitely, a robbing-Peter-to-pay-Paul flooring situation.

With my face mask lowered to block out some of the funky stench and potential mold spores, I walked along the creaking floor, noticing that it gave in some spots. It felt like being on a rickety boat on the verge of going under. I feared this building would end up sinking, so to speak. Rot had gradually encroached around windowsills and doorways. Plus there was a good bit of water damage due to a hole in the roof. Every surface appeared swollen from moisture and coated in mildew. And where the water hadn't gone, termites had. Feeling uneasy, I gave the run-down building a sweeping glance. Too many shadows and cobwebs. Shaking off my apprehension, I placed my portable speaker on an upturned bucket and pulled up my Imagine Dragons playlist with the tempo full of attitude. "Enemy" filled the small room as I picked up my tools and scoped out the perfect spot to begin destroying something.

"Sorry about this," I whispered to the building before stabbing between two loose boards with my crowbar and wiggling it until the nails began popping free. I gave the loose board a good yank, losing my balance and stumbling into the vegetable bin. Rubbing the sore spot on my hip, I looked down and noticed something behind the bin.

"Someone lost their shoe?" I mumbled, picking up the little blue canvas sneaker and glancing around for the other one. Not finding it, I tossed the shoe aside and refocused on tearing out the flooring.

Soon I got into the rhythm of the music and floor demolition, losing myself in both. As I turned to stack another board, movement in my periphery jolted me out of my headspace. I looked to the right. A low-hanging cobweb swayed in the breeze coming through the broken window. I huffed a laugh and got back to work, but it happened again only minutes later. This time the fine hairs on the back of my neck rose. I remembered Desmond talking about the Lizard Man and darned if I didn't picture him lurking outside. With the crowbar clutched firmly in my fist, I paused the music and eased over to the back window, fully expecting to find a green scaly monster with yellow eyes there. Nothing but darkness showed past the stoop.

"Get a grip, Avalee," I muttered, taking a step away from the window. As I turned away, something rustled nearby. Holding my breath, I strained to hear, but minutes passed with nothing. Sound or no sound, I'd had enough. I was sure it was just my overactive imagination, but I decided to call it a night anyway. Pulling the mask off, I took out my pocketknife just in case and made a mad dash to the saloon.

I fumbled to get the door open and once I got inside, I slammed it shut and leaned against it. After a few moments, my heart rate settled down and I felt foolish. I started to head upstairs but paused. Before turning in for the night, maybe I should take a look at the mess next door. I could wait until morning, when there would be better light. But maybe not having better light would help lessen the sting of losing the flower shop.

I opened the door again and checked the street. Seeing no sign of any type of boogeyman, I rounded the building and came to a halt in front of the pile of rubble that no longer resembled potential. Nope. It stung anyway. It astonished me that something that had stood for decades could be so easily taken down. Gone within a few hours.

I aimed my phone's flashlight over the pile of splintered wood, where it caught on something shiny. Climbing over a few boards, I squatted down and could now see that it was actually a metal box about double the size of a cigar box. I reached in and wiggled it out, almost losing my balance in the process.

"Des would kill me if he knew . . ." I stumbled back to solid ground without breaking my neck and popped the lid open, finding inside a dozen or so metal crosses. I picked one up and shined the phone light on it. *In loving memory* was engraved on the front. "Figures I'd find funeral keepsakes."

Shaking my head, I straightened and stretched my aching back. With the box wedged under my arm, I stood there as a sad thought surfaced from the debris. This building was my relationship with Rowan. It started off with so much potential, but we weren't as structurally sound as I thought. One devastation after another chipped away at our stability until our marriage collapsed. Damaged hopes and dreams left scattered and discarded in disrepair.

I checked the time on my phone. Only a little after ten. An entire night lay before me, which would be fine if sleep would be gracious. But that wouldn't be happening with all the memories stacked in my head, waiting their turn to pester me. I pulled off my work gloves and inspected my nails. Several had chips in the *Welcome to the Jungle* green. My eyes lifted to the withering vines among the pile of rubble. How fitting.

After a quick Google search, I found a nail salon located inside a tattoo parlor with late-night hours. It was only a thirty-minute drive from town. The ratings and reviews were great, and a quick phone call secured me an appointment for eleven, so I changed out of my dirty work clothes and took off. Fun thing about manicures, my world could fall apart in both the literal and physical sense, but shiny, pretty nails was something I could control. If I felt like pink nails, done. Purple, absolutely. Never a *no* in the nail world. I was so sick of *no*s.

I followed the GPS to Ink & Polish. Shades of red and black decor with metal and glass accents, it was everything I pictured for a tattoo parlor. Buzzing from tattoo guns could be heard over the alternative rock music. Those guns and the clients receiving the ink were hidden behind privacy partitions, but several people were scattered around a waiting area.

A few college-aged girls, dressed in hip-hugging jeans and crop tops, were sitting on a leather couch, giggling over photos in a portfolio. The lone brunette looked up and smiled.

"You can sit with us." She scooted over. "They said to wait here."

I glanced around, wondering who *they* were, but finding no one behind the counter. "Uh, sure. Thanks."

"Are you here for the half-off special?" Her hazel eyes glittered with enthusiasm as I settled down beside her.

"Half off?" I shrugged. "I didn't know anything about it but I'm down for a discount."

Moments later, a door opened from the far left and a tiny woman appeared. She had a stark-white mohawk and was wearing a red skater dress. Her arms were covered in exquisite watercolor designs. "I'm Dayley. Y'all can come on back." She turned on her biker bootheels and vanished again.

The brunette sprite stood and turned to me. "Let's go."

I tried to wave her off. "Oh, I can just wait here for my turn."

"Don't be silly. You should totally join us. It'll be more fun in a group." She smiled with lifted eyebrows. I would have been willing to bet she was captain of a cheerleading squad.

Giving in, I shuffled behind the lively group, thinking it wouldn't hurt to see what sort of nail art they went with. It might give me some inspiration.

We stepped into a fairly large room. A long metal counter housed displays of earrings and more unusual jewelry.

Dayley pulled on a pair of black latex gloves. The little snap echoed around the brightly lit space. "Who's first?"

I gave the area another scan and found no nail polish or manicure tables. Only a few leather chairs, similar to the ones at the dentist, and a rolling stool. Suddenly, that same feeling I got every time I walked into the feedstore came over me. The one that said something was off.

"She is!" The brunette gave me a little shove, making me step forward. This girl was starting to annoy me. Refraining from giving her a withering side-eye, I moved to join Dayley.

"Pick your hardware." Dayley pointed at the jewelry as I caught one of the girls sizing up her belly button in the mirror beside the counter.

Realization finally hitting me, I sputtered a nervous laugh. "No, no, no. That's . . . I don't want my belly button pierced."

"Aww. You poor thing. No need to be scared." The brunette, who seemed to have designated herself as my guide for this evening's bad decisions, latched on to my arm. "I'll hold your hand. How about that?"

I shook her off and put some distance between us. Seriously, someone needed to school this chick on personal space. "Piercings aren't my thing. Not that there's anything wrong with them. It's just that I saw a video one time of a girl getting her piercing stuck in her zipper. They ended up ripping that sucker completely out!" I shuddered, pressing my hand over my hidden belly button. "And you know how the video rabbit hole goes. The next video I watched showed an infected belly button piercing. Seriously *gross*. It was super swollen and—" I buttoned my lips when I noticed everyone looking up at me with slack jaws. One glance at Dayley told me not to unbutton them. I wanted to hunch down to make myself smaller, but that was impossible when surrounded by a group of petite women that I towered over.

All at once, an intense chatter broke out. Some started chickening out while the others tried guilt-tripping them into going through with it. The room grew hotter.

Dabbing the sweat from my upper lip, I added in a higher-pitched voice, "Not that you girls would have any of those issues. I'm sure Dayley here keeps everything sanitized and your pants are so low on your hips, no way will the zipper-ripper happen to you!"

Two of the girls moved toward the door but before they could make a run for it, a heavily tattooed man walked in, making them jump. "Day, what's going on in here?"

Dayley shot me a severe glare while pointing at me. "This woman is freaking everybody out."

I whirled around to the big guy. "I didn't mean to! I just wanted a manicure!" I held up my hands and wiggled my fingers.

The big guy's lips twitched. "What about a tattoo instead?"

My back stiffened. "Nothing against them, but I read this article about allergic reactions to the ink and . . ." I stopped myself when he barked a deep laugh.

"I'm just messin' with you."

Dayley nearly growled. "Good grief. Kline, get this woman out of here before she runs off all your business!"

Still chuckling, Kline motioned for me to follow him. "Come on. Starla is in the back room."

I trailed behind him, ready to make a detour to the exit if need be. "Does Starla have nail polish?"

"That she does." He led me to another door, this one to the far right. Sure enough, the back housed a nail studio. This rambling building reminded me of *Alice's Adventures in Wonderland*, one room leading to another one and then another.

The tension began to slowly drain away from my shoulders as I moved inside.

"Yo, Starla!" Kline shouted. "You got a client."

A woman with purple hair and a killer winged eyeliner emerged from a storage closet, carrying an industrial-size bottle of acetone. "Hi." She had to be at least a half a foot shorter than me but gave off a boss babe vibe large enough to make a grown man feel small.

"You might have a troublemaker on your hands, hon," Kline said from behind me.

Shoulders stiffening right back up, I shook my head. "I promise I'm not. That was just a misunderstanding." I hitched a thumb over my shoulder like that explained it all.

Kline let out another deep chuckle as he exited the room.

Starla disregarded the big guy's comment and my rebuttal, as if trouble was nothing new. "What color are you in the mood for?" She showed me to her manicure table with a giant rack displaying every shade of polish imaginable.

"Something dark," I insisted, settling into the black velvet high-back chair. The tufted back felt luxurious. Dimly lit with wrought iron chandeliers and perfumed with a spicy scent that hung subtly in the air, the salon was goth glam with a spa-like ambience. "This place is gorgeous."

"Thanks." Starla ran a long pointy nail in matte gold over the bottles of polish, clinking against each one until stopping on a bluish black with flecks of silver. "Dark like this?"

"What's the name of it?"

She plucked it from the rack and read the bottom, *"Insomnia."* She raised a pierced eyebrow.

"That's perfect." Seriously, that choice was a no-brainer. At least I'd have something pretty to look at while I lay awake in bed.

As Starla began removing my old polish, I replayed the ridiculous scene that just went down in Dayley's room of terror. Rowan would have gotten such a kick out of that. Knowing him, he would have picked out the jewelry and gone along with it until the last minute just to mess with them. He'd always been a quicker thinker than me.

The smile creeping onto my lips vanished. I'd ventured out to this place in the middle of the night to get my mind off that man, not sit here and muse over him. Unable to stop my train of thought, our argument about the flower shop from earlier highjacked my mind.

Some things can't be saved. You of all people should know that. I rubbed a free hand over my heart, feeling like a zipper-ripper had gotten ahold of it.

CHAPTER 7

BEING A GENERAL CONTRACTOR MEANT I WORE VARIOUS HATS—or gloves. Today's were yellow rubber gloves, perfect for cleaning a blackened fireplace. The hope was that after washing away decades of soot, salvageable stonework would be revealed. It would lend ambience to the coffee shop and help make it a perfect place to gather. I admired my sparkly dark blue nails before slipping on the rubber gloves. I'd made it back to my apartment a little after midnight, but by my estimate, I'd only managed to get about two good hours of sleep.

Sighing, I dipped my sponge into the bucket of soapy water, and sharp fumes of vinegar wafted from it. It smelled like progress to me. Only an hour in, I'd made just that. A fourth of the fireplace now showed off beautiful gray and creamy red bricks.

"Little Avalee," Fred announced as soon as he shuffled inside the coffee shop.

I dropped the sponge into the bucket of water and sat back on my haunches, amused that he continued to call me "little" after all these years, when I was at least a foot taller than him and his brother. All through school I was the tallest in my class, until senior year when Rowan and a few other guys finally caught up and passed me by a few inches. "What's up?"

"This here kid is lookin' for work." Fred hitched a thumb toward a tall, lanky guy with blond hair. "You needing some under-the-table kinda help?"

I scrutinized Fred and then the young guy towering over him with slumped shoulders. "What's your name?"

"Bash," he answered in a clear, deep voice, sounding older than he appeared.

"How old are you?"

Bash looked off to the left. "Nineteen."

I smashed my lips together in a thin line, knowing what I was about to suggest was a bad idea, but darned if it wouldn't be nice to get someone else to work on cleaning the soot away while I got some construction done. "You got a last name?"

He studied his worn sneakers. "Yes, ma'am."

Bash reminded me of the summer help Maudie used to take on, saying sometimes kids just needed a break without question. I gave Bash the same inspection my grandmother used to give. No track marks on his inner elbows. Complexion pale but not sallow. Skin clear of any pockmarks. No dark circles under his steady blue eyes. Even though his sandy-blond hair was long and shaggy, it looked clean, like he had some respect for himself.

When Bash didn't supply a last name, I asked, "How about teeth. You got all yours?"

Behind his closed lips, Bash ran his tongue over his teeth. "Got 'em all, yes."

I watched closely as he talked and all I saw were two rows of white, slightly crooked teeth. Deciding he passed the inspection, I went over my terms. "Ten an hour under the table. Show up on time and work until we call it a day. No drugs, no alcohol, and no attitudes allowed on site. You reckon you can handle that?"

"Yes, ma'am."

"Good. Start by cleaning the rest of this fireplace." I pointed to the stonework and waited for him to gripe about the work being beneath him, but Bash surprised me by getting to it without any lip. I took off the rubber gloves and handed them to him. "I'll be in the pharmacy next door. Come find me when you finish."

"M'kay."

"We got ourselves a talker on our hands," Fred joked while following me out the door.

"I think he's all right." I rotated my shoulders a few times and rolled my neck. Why did fatigue make the entire body pay for it? "But would you mind helping me keep an eye on him?"

"Not at all." Fred patted my shoulder. "Me and Froid will be setting up right here in this alley." The brothers' work van began backing in as if on cue. "We gonna be workin' on makin' the custom bookshelves for the library today."

"Sounds good. Thanks, Fred," I tossed his way before entering the pharmacy. An electrician was pulling new wiring on the back wall. "I need to work on framing the two new walls for the urgent care clinic," I told him. "Will I be in your way?"

"Nah. Should be good. The sooner you get that wall up the sooner I can pull wires for it too."

I checked my watch. "Give me a few hours and I'll have it done."

Halfway through the framing, I guess my lack of sleep from the night before caught up with me. I aimed the nail gun and misfired, missing the board completely. A ping rang out as the nail glanced off the floor. Hoping no one had seen my blunder, I blinked the bleariness away and surveyed the new divot in the cement floor. "Shoot."

"Yeah, you did." Desmond appeared from out of nowhere and took the nail gun out of my hand. He switched it off while giving me a careful once-over. "I believe it's time for a break." He knew me well enough to see the signs of exhaustion that I was able to hide from everyone else.

"Anybody seen my jacket?" Froid interrupted before I could

protest. He ambled inside and looked around. "I left it by my work-bench but it's gone."

Various mumbled *no*s answered him. It had been a long, busy morning and there were no cares to give about a misplaced jacket.

"But it's my favorite," Froid huffed.

"It's blue, right?" I asked him.

"Yeah."

"I'll keep an eye out for it. Someone probably picked it up by mistake."

Froid meandered away, still grumbling about his coat.

Bash walked in and scanned the room until finding me. "I'm finished with the fireplace."

"Who's this?" Rowan asked from behind me, making me jump.

I gestured toward the young guy, noticing Fred scooting inside. "This is Bash. He'll be giving me a hand around here. Bash, this is everyone." I was too tired to make introductions past that.

"Bash . . ." Fred spoke up. "That yo' real name?"

"It's short for Sebastian." Bash fidgeted, not making eye contact with anyone.

"Oh, that's fancy." Fred smiled.

"Not really. I'm named after that crab from *The Little Mermaid*." Bash finally met my gaze. "What do you need me to do next?"

Before I could answer him, Rowan cleared his throat. "You out of school for the day? It's not quite noon yet." He checked his watch dubiously.

"I'm finished with school." Bash studied the floor.

Rowan's eyes narrowed. "How old are you?"

Bash looked up and met Rowan's stare. "Nineteen." His tone held a challenging quality, but it didn't strike me as disrespectful.

Glancing around, I read the room and the room appeared not to be buying it. I bought it, but I weren't paying full price for it just yet, as my grandmother would say. Speaking of, I summoned my inner Maudie and said, "Bash, I need you to head over to the pecan ware-house. It's to the right of the clock tower. You'll see the sign. Clean the restrooms and the kitchen area and anything else that needs to be done. The cleaning supplies are under the kitchen sink." Once again, I expected him to grumble about the unpleasant task, but he was out the door before I could comment any further.

"You sure he's nineteen?" Rowan muttered before Bash was completely out of earshot.

Ignoring him, I turned back to the framing and held my hand out for the nail gun still clutched in my friend's grasp.

"Avalee," Desmond warned, placing the gun on the floor instead of giving it to me.

"Don't start with me, Des. I really need to get this finished. I'm fine."

An eyebrow arched dramatically underneath his navy fedora. "The last time you said that to me, you picked up this beauty mark." Desmond lifted my hand and traced the two-inch scar on the back of it. A broken windowpane had gotten the best of me back in the fall. I may have fallen asleep standing and leaned against it . . .

Rowan leaned in to get a look. "What happened?"

I tugged my hand from Desmond's grip. "Nothing."

"Just take a break, darlin'." Desmond lowered his voice. "I'm not taking no for an answer."

I shut my eyes for a moment to get away from the pity in his but quickly reopened them when my body swayed. "Fine." I shuffled down the hallway and grabbed my thermos and clipboard from the room we were using for storage. If Des was forcing me home, hopefully I could at least get some paperwork done.

Hushed voices came from the hallway. I stilled a moment to listen.

"What's going on with her?" Rowan whispered.

"Can't you look at her and tell?" Desmond answered and then grew quiet for a moment. "She's exhausted."

"Why?"

"I'm not sure that's any of your business." Desmond sounded a little hostile.

I hurried out into the hallway, catching them off guard. "Both of you need to mind your own business," I snapped. "I'm heading to my apartment for a while to catch up on some paperwork." I pushed past them and made my way to my apartment.

I kicked my work boots off by the door and slogged toward the bathroom. Insomnia was a beast that required all sorts of tricks to combat it. Hot showers were one of them. Although I was dead on my feet, I climbed underneath the scalding hot water to help relax. Barely drying off, I skipped getting dressed. With my bedroom door closed and the blackout curtains blocking any light, I set my alarm and collapsed into bed.

I could have sworn I had just closed my eyes, but the alarm going off indicated that had happened two hours ago. Still too tired, I hit the snooze for the next half hour until finally waking fully. I shoved the covers off and swung my feet off the bed, taking a moment to get my bearings. Parched and stomach growling, I shrugged on the oversize T-shirt I'd worn to bed last night and went to find something to eat.

I opened the bedroom door. Coming up short, I let out a blood-curdling scream.

Rowan jumped off the couch and searched the room. "What's wrong?"

Clutching my chest with one hand, I motioned toward him with the other. "How'd you get in here?"

Rowan relaxed. "Des let me in." He called him Des, not Desmond. Great. They must have become friends while I'd slept.

"Why'd he let you in here?" Since Des had permanent use of my guest room, that kind of made the apartment his home, too, so I couldn't complain about him inviting Rowan in. No matter how much I wanted to.

"He had somewhere to be but didn't want you left alone." Rowan resettled on the couch and picked up his laptop.

"I'm a grown woman. I don't need a babysitter." I crossed my arms and stayed put by the bedroom door. "You can leave."

"I will soon. First, I thought you'd like to see the plans for the firehouse." He nodded toward his laptop screen.

Grumbling under my breath, I pushed off the bedroom door, crossed to the fridge, and grabbed a bottle of iced coffee. I joined Rowan on the couch and let him go over the plans for converting the large Greek Revival bank building into a firehouse, while I chugged down some caffeine. I had too much to do to let this lack of sleep get the best of me.

Truth be told, the restless nights had gotten a heckuva lot worse since Rowan had showed up so unexpectedly. I'd just have to figure out how to get through the next six months and hide my fatigue better. I made a mental note to search for a magic undereye concealer.

"Hey." Rowan tapped my knee with his. "You fall back asleep?"

"Nah." I yawned and stretched, then refocused on the 3D image on his screen. "I like the idea of keeping those light fixtures above the bay." I pointed at the rendering with my empty bottle.

Rowan exited out of the file and closed the laptop. "Des told me you suffer from insomnia."

"Des has a big mouth."

"Have you tried medication to help you sleep?"

"Yes, but they make me have weird dreams. I'd rather forgo sleep than have nightmares." Flashes of me pushing a dead baby in a stroller sent a shiver down my spine. That one had plagued me for years now. Why was it that a good dream faded but nightmares stuck around to haunt?

"How long has this been going on?" The concern in his voice made my eyes sting.

Blinking several times, I focused on the empty bottle in my hands. "Since you left."

He grunted as if he'd been punched.

My head snapped up and I met his glassy eyes. "It's not your fault."

The muscle in his jaw flexed. "Then whose is it?"

I shrugged. "It's life, Rowan . . . Can we just drop it?"

He opened his mouth but then closed it, deciding to keep whatever comment to himself. Fine by me. This encounter had already been awkward enough.

At first, I believed the insomnia was God's way of not letting me give up after my life imploded and Rowan left. Had it been up to me, I would have crawled into bed and never gotten up again. After two weeks of staring into the dark each night, I got up. I figured if I kept myself busy to the point of exhaustion, sleep would return. I figured wrong.

I listened to the droning sounds of power tools down the street for a while, wishing Rowan would just go ahead and leave already. It hurt to be around him again. I doubted the time would ever arrive where it didn't.

"They were green yesterday."

Blinking out of my reverie, I glanced at him. "What was green?"

He tapped the top of my hand, resting in my lap. "Your nails. They look nice."

I moved my fingers until the flecks of silver caught the overhead light. "Thanks. It was either this or getting my belly button pierced."

"Say what?"

"Just kidding." *Sorta.* "I got a manicure after work." I pulled my hand away when I noticed him reaching for it. "I need to go finish framing that new room in the pharmacy."

"It's already finished."

I frowned. "How?"

"I finished it before coming up here to relieve Des."

Des. Rowan using the shortened name irked me. It also irked me that the two of them thought I needed a sitter. I had a sneaky suspicion Desmond did this on purpose to force me to face Rowan. That was just inviting trouble and I'd had enough of that to last a lifetime.

"You didn't have to do that and you sure don't need to be baby-sitting me."

Rowan gave me a wry smile and shook his head. "You're welcome."

Swallowing my pride, I mumbled, "Thank you." I expected him to tease me now, but he dropped it.

"So I see you've brought the twins on board." Rowan nudged my leg. "I haven't seen those two in a long time."

"I send work their way any chance I get. You can't find that type of high-quality craftsmanship nowadays."

"Or slower work."

I shrugged. "I don't care how slow they are. Fred and Froid served our country for nearly thirty years apiece. They've earned the right to be as slow as they want."

I thought it was quite endearing how the twin brothers did everything together. And I do mean everything. They'd joined the navy together right out of high school, married sisters on the same day, and took over their father's custom cabinetry business after they retired from the military. They'd worked with Maudie over the years and then began teaming up with me on projects once I started Lowcountry Lost.

"Yeah, but they spend more time on breaks than on work. Yesterday I straight-up watched Froid measure a board, break for something to drink, cut the board, break for a snack, then repeat that for each board." Rowan chuckled.

Smiling, I shook my head. "They're paid by the project, not hour. As long as it's done by September, I don't care." I hitched a shoulder. "Besides, those two silly men are a twofold of exceptional craftmanship and entertainment. I spent an entire afternoon listening to them debating the merits of barbecue sauces. Froid has convinced me mustard-based sauce is supreme."

"Well, I have to agree with him on that. Maurice's BBQ Piggie Park in Columbia will convince any vinegar-based fan to change their ways."

My mouth watered. "You're making me hungry. Change the subject."

Rowan checked something on his phone. "Permits came through for the firehouse reno. We have a lot of work ahead of us."

"That's what Des keeps saying, but I'm confident we can get it done on time. I've even factored in delays and such."

Rowan shifted beside me. "Des said you two were just friends."

"Yep."

"You sure?"

I snorted a laugh and looked at his frowning face. "Yes. Why's that so hard to believe?"

"He lives with you."

"No, he doesn't. I let him stay in my spare bedroom when he stays over for work."

"So he's fine with you walking around half naked?" Rowan perused my bare legs, blatantly so.

I tugged the hem of my shirt down a little further. "Had I known there'd be an intruder in my living room when I woke up, I would have gotten dressed."

"I don't mind it." He kept his attention focused on my legs, making me feel completely naked.

"Stop flirting." Still holding the hem as far down as possible, I stood, which put my bare legs right in his face. So close I could feel his warm breath on my thigh.

"Just stating facts." A deep groan rumbled up from his chest. "I've missed these mile-long legs."

My heart thudded hard, hearing the inflection of his hidden accent coming through. That accent only made a showing when he was worked up, angry, or . . .

Cheeks warming, I pointed toward the door and backed away. "Put the Irishman away and get out."

"Or I could stay . . . I remember something we used to do that helped you relax pretty dang well." He winked, the devil.

I gasped. "Rowan Connor Murray! Get! Out!"

Grinning, he collected his laptop and stood, but paused at the door and spoke over his shoulder. "Let me know if you change your mind."

I grabbed a throw pillow from the couch and hurled it toward his head but it bounced off the door as he closed it behind him.

"That man . . ." I stomped to the bathroom and glanced in the mirror. Shocked, I leaned over the sink to examine the rosy hue of my cheeks and the smile on my lips. "Clearly I need more sleep." That was the only thing that made sense. Surely if I'd been in my right mind, I would not have gotten all swoony over my ex. Shaking my head, I turned on the shower and hopped under the spray before it could heat up. The icy water did very little to ease this newfound libido of mine. Good gracious, I thought that thing exited years ago never to return, just like Rowan.

The next six months stretched out before me, looking a lot like torture if I didn't get my head screwed on right.

CHAPTER 8

I GOT CAUGHT SHOPLIFTING ONCE. I stole a candy bar after my father refused to buy it for me. When the store owner tried taking it from my pocket, my father claims I pitched a fit, refusing to give the candy back. There was a problem in the getaway though, considering I hadn't even reached the age of four yet. Maudie had laughed, brushing off my crime, when my father ranted about it later that day. *She's just a baby and doesn't know any better*, she'd defended. But Dad didn't let it go so easily. *First it's candy, then it's bigger items, like cash or cars.*

I never moved past food thieving, thank you very much, but someone on this worksite sure had. I scanned the smaller crew assembled around the steps of the town hall. Most of the demo had been completed, so just mostly the subcontractors were on-site this week. "Blake's hard hat has been missing since Friday, my goggles vanished yesterday, and now an entire bucket of fried chicken just walked off from the tailgate of my truck?" I shook my head, aggravated that my nice gesture had been stolen, literally. "Stealing that

73

chicken is taking this too far. We're all hungry, so someone needs to fess up."

"A chicken bandit," Rowan quipped. "This is ridiculous."

Glancing over my shoulder, I found him standing right behind me in the same plaid button-down shirt he'd been wearing last week when he let that darn accent out while flirting with me in my apartment. "I've got this," I said low enough for only him to hear. He looked like he wanted to say something. Instead, he gave me some space, leaning against one of the white columns and crossing his arms.

"Don't forget that whole bag of cookies I brought," Fred mentioned. "They were homemade."

I gave it my best shot to ignore Rowan's shadow bearing down on me and waited for someone to come clean, but no one did. "Fine, if one more thing is stolen, then all y'all are fired." I stormed down the steps. "Now get back to work!"

Hungry and fuming, I stomped down the steps with cookies on my mind. I'd tucked my own bag of cookies from Fred's wife behind the counter at the coffee shop earlier. Maybe eating a few would be a good enough lunch for now.

Bash met up with me. "I finished cleaning the light fixtures." Since joining our work crew a week ago, he had continued to be a guy of few words. Only stating the finished task and waiting for me to give him instructions for the next.

"I could really go for some fried chicken. You know how to cook?"

Lips firmly pressed together, he shook his head. Bash had also been consistent with not reacting to my lame attempts at humor.

"Well, shoot." I stopped walking and looked around, trying to think of something for him to do. There were over a hundred light fixtures he'd had to clean, no small task, so I wanted his next task to be a little more pleasant. "Fred and Froid could use a hand with the bookshelves for the library. Go find them. Say I sent you to stain the ones they have finished." He was already on the move. "You good with that?" I called after him.

"M'kay," Bash said over his shoulder as he walked with purpose toward the twins' work van.

I stepped inside the coffee shop and paused for a moment to take in the changes. A counter stretched across the back of the room and would eventually have barstools placed in front of half of it while the other half would be for ordering and pickup. The rustic fireplace took up most of the right side of the room, soot-free thanks to Bash. With his help, I had attached a broken wood beam for the mantel after cutting it down to size. Satisfied with how it had turned out, I crossed the room toward the counter, but a rustling sound gave me pause. It sounded a lot like that cookie bag.

"Doggone it, those are my cookies!" I yelled, rounding the counter.

The thief yelped like the guilty and I squealed like a pig, but then he had enough nerve to try making a run for it with the bag of cookies. I took off after him, both of us darting past Rowan as we made it out the back door.

"What the heck?" Rowan hollered from behind me.

"Thief!" Arms pumping, I charged through the woods, but I quickly lost sight of the scoundrel in the overgrown brush. I veered to the right, getting slapped in the face by a low-hanging branch. Wiping something off my cheek, not taking the time to see what it was because frankly I didn't want to know, I moved away from the tree and its snares and gave up the chase.

"Where'd he go?" Rowan asked as he came to a stop beside me.

I braced my hands on my knees and tried working some oxygen into my lungs. "I don't know, but . . ." I inhaled and exhaled. "He stole my cookies."

Rowan breathed normally, as if we hadn't just sprinted a half mile. "You think he's our thief?"

"What do you think?"

He lifted a shoulder. "Makes sense. He's probably just hungry."

I turned around in a circle, hoping to spot the mangy thing. "Okay, but what would a dog need with my work goggles and a hard hat?"

"Maybe he's trying to open his own construction business." Rowan said this with a straight face but cracked into a grin when I laughed at the absurdity of that. "We could go left. See what we can see." He pointed toward a thicket of heavily moss-draped trees.

That familiar statement pushed me from the woods and straight into my past. *See what we can see.* Rowan had said something similar to that quite often during our childhood—and getting into trouble normally followed it.

"Avalee?"

Ignoring the peculiar mix of nostalgia and sadness, I shook my head. "Nuh-uh. I'm not chancing a case of red bugs over a mangy mutt." I moved around him and retraced my steps through the woods.

I swung by the saloon to leave my lightweight jacket and chug a bottle of water. That's the thing about March in these parts. Mornings are typically chilly, but once the sun is settled high in the sky, the day heats up considerably.

"What are you working on next?" Rowan asked, startling me out of my thoughts. I didn't realize he was following me down Main Street.

"I'll be at the town hall. I need to cast a resin mold of a section of plaster crown molding so I can repair the damaged areas." I came to a halt just before the tall steps and angled my head back to get a good look. The stone exterior had aged well, unlike the rest of the town.

Rowan stopped beside me. "I like how this building and the old bank are both Greek Revival. Nothing like the rest of the town, but it somehow works, don't ya think?"

We stood shoulder to shoulder, a little too close in my opinion, and surveyed the white stone and ornate pillared exteriors. "Yeah. I like all the plasterwork and marble floors inside too. These two buildings are going to be beautiful landmarks once again. I can't wait."

"You need any help?"

I felt his gaze on me but kept looking forward. Hadn't we already agreed to give each other space? Clearly he'd forgotten, but I didn't feel like being rude and reminding him. I worked a small smile on my face to soften my answer. "Nah. Thanks though."

Rowan still hesitated, looking between the building and then me. "Let me know if you change your mind. I'm free for the next little bit."

"Sure."

We parted ways and I went inside, veering to the left and entering a meeting room where earlier I had set up a makeshift table—two sawhorses and a sheet of plywood—with all my supplies on top. I pried open a window to let in some fresh air. Glancing outside, I noticed the side door to the chapel was slightly ajar. I made a mental note to locate a doorknob to replace the missing one and got to work on making my mold.

An hour of steady work flew by as I cast the mold and then waited for it to set up. While I cleaned up my mess a noise rang out from next door. Wiping my palms on the side of my jeans, I decided to walk over and check on things, maybe figure out a way to secure that door. As I reached the open door another noise drew my attention. Behind the pulpit, lounging on Froid's blue jacket and gnawing a chicken wing, was that thieving dog. He had made himself right at home in a church, of all places.

Rolling my lips inward to keep myself from laughing, I propped a shoulder against the doorframe and watched him tear into my crew's lunch. The lunch I purchased as a thank-you for their hard work. Not sure this one had done anything to deserve it besides being rather slick.

When the dog fished out his third piece of chicken, I decided to speak up. "You're going to have a stomachache if you eat all that."

The chicken leg fell from his mouth, and I kid you not, the dog pawed it under the coat.

"Too late to hide the evidence now, buster."

His eyes swung from me to the doorway I was blocking.

I eased to the floor, thinking I'd appear less intimidating, criss-crossing my legs. After several minutes passed and I'd done nothing but sit, the dog must have decided I didn't pose a threat. He finished off the chicken leg, walked over, and dropped the bone at my foot like an olive branch.

I laughed. Even though he was filthy, I gave his swollen belly a rub when he rolled over. "You're too friendly to be abandoned . . . Yet you have been, haven't you? You poor sweet thing."

"Who are you baby-talking to?" Rowan said as he came in from the front entrance.

I rubbed behind the dog's ear when he tensed, instantly putting him at ease. His tail went back to thumping happily against the worn wooden floor. "The chicken bandit is my new buddy."

Rowan stopped by the end of the front pew and just stared at me and the dog. He pulled his phone from his pocket and aimed it at me.

"What are you doing?"

"Capturing this moment with you and your buddy."

Blushing, I stood and dusted off my pants. "Come on, dog, you need some exercise after all that food." I patted my leg and he actually followed me.

"He needs to be checked out if you plan on keeping him around."

"You really think that's necessary?" I eyed the dog as he pranced down Main Street like a proper pooch.

"Yeah. He might have rabies or something. Better to err on the side of caution." Rowan pulled his phone out and began typing. "There's a vet's office a town over. Let's load him up in your truck." He started to walk off but I grabbed his arm.

"Wait. I think we need to ease into it, maybe take him for a ride on the side-by-side first to see if joyrides are even his thing. If that goes well, we'll get him in my truck."

Rowan gave me a sidelong glance full of *you gotta be kiddin' me.* Shaking his head, he crossed the street to my truck, opened the door, and let out one of those earsplitting whistles. Next thing I knew, the dog loaded himself up and seemed rather excited for an adventure.

"Show-off," I muttered, doing a quick trash sweep so I could find the passenger seat.

Sure, Rowan whistling like that and having the dog instantly obey was impressive and kinda hot, but darned if I'd tell him such.

➤

Luckily the vet allowed walk-ins, but that meant our entire afternoon was spent sitting in a waiting room that smelled like wet fur and flea powder. Not the most comfortable of situations to be in with your ex, mind you.

Our turn finally came, but then another hour lugged by with them running a gamut of tests on the mangy mutt. Yes, he had fleas and a few ticks, but no rabies. Yes to hookworms, no to heartworms. Once all that had been figured out, they started loading him up on the vaccine shots while I kept apologizing to the poor thing. I was a frazzled mess even before we met the doctor.

A jolly-looking man in scrubs walked in and introduced himself as Dr. Lagotto. "And what's this fellow's name?" He glanced over the chart. "Elvis?"

I shook my head. "No. That's just my last name. We don't know his name."

"Ah. You found him?"

Rowan chuckled. "More like he found us."

"Well, I'm sure you'll figure it out." Dr. Lagotto examined the dog, just as the vet tech had done, which made no sense to me, then went over the blood work. "I believe he's roughly four years old. With the long snout and black patches in his brown coat, he's possibly a mix of German shepherd and Labrador. He's malnourished and has a few patches of mange. I'll give you a list of everything we administered today and we'll send you home with everything else you'll need."

After Dr. Lagotto answered our questions, one of the assistants gave the dog a bath to treat the fleas and mites. Then we went to the front desk to retrieve the prescriptions and the bill.

"Five hundred dollars? That can't be right!" I scrutinized the paper, thinking a hundred seemed more on the right lines, and handed it back to the receptionist. "Can you check this?"

She shifted in her rolling chair and coughed. "It's correct. We accept all major credit cards."

"I bet you do," I muttered, fishing for my card, but Rowan beat me to it. "No," I protested. "He's my . . . my dog. I'll handle this." If he heard me, Rowan didn't let on. And the young woman happily accepted his card.

"Here's a goody bag." It was nothing more than a sample bag containing two Milk-Bone treats and a coupon.

"Gee thanks," I mumbled, eyeing the dog as he perked up from beside me. "Don't even think about it." I wasn't sure I wanted a living being to, well, keep alive, but seemed this one wasn't taking no for an answer.

Once we were all piled in, Rowan cranked the truck. "I guess we need to head over to Target or something for supplies. You wanna see if there's a PetSmart nearby?"

"Oh heck no. We ain't having a bougie dog. We're going to Walmart." I cringed, realizing I'd slipped and said *we*. I guess I couldn't claim sole ownership, considering he'd paid that hefty bill.

Chuckling, Rowan backed out and drove over to Walmart. But this dog might as well be bougie, because Walmart stuck it to us too.

"Three hundred dollars! For a dog bed and junk! Seventy bucks for just the bag of dog food."

"But that Milk-Bone coupon saved us a buck fifty," Rowan said with enough sarcasm to make me snort.

I pored over the receipt on our way back to Somewhere. "Clearly I'm in the wrong business."

The pitiful dog laid his head in my lap and gave me puppy dog eyes, as if apologizing. I couldn't help but smile at him and scratch behind his ear.

"He's rather soft since they washed him." The coarse hair now had a silky texture.

Rowan released one hand from the steering wheel and ran his

palm along the dog's back. "We need to figure out a way to wash him with that medicated shampoo."

I thought about it for a minute before coming up with a solution. "There's one of those galvanized water troughs in the shed behind the feedstore. We can use that as a tub."

He tapped the steering wheel with his thumb to the beat of the song on the radio. "That'll work."

We made it back to Somewhere, but the dog decided he liked hanging out in my truck. Leaving him to that, we started unloading all the canine couture. That's what I was calling it anyway.

"Let's set him up in the saloon." I twisted the doorknob, using my hip to open the door, and dumped the bedding in the front corner.

Rowan came in with the giant bag of dog food draped over his shoulder and I tried not to appreciate how nice that looked. "I'm pretty sure he's an outdoor dog."

"Then why'd he set up camp in the chapel?"

Rowan scratched his cheek, the five-o'clock shadow darkening it. "I suppose you're right."

We headed back out for another armload only to find the dog still sprawled across the front seats.

"You reckon he's okay?" As soon as I asked, the dog lifted his head and popped off a friendly bark, apparently letting me know he was just chilling.

"Guess joyrides are his thing." Rowan winked at me while managing to scoop up all the bags from behind the seats in one fell swoop and turning to go inside.

Flustered and needing some space, I told him, "Just set everything by the door and I'll get it all squared away."

He spoke over his shoulder, "I don't mind sticking around to get him settled."

How could I tell him I'd reached my limit of spending time with him without sounding like a jerk? "I got this. Thanks, though." I took the bags from him and stood in the doorway, clearly saying goodbye.

Fortunately, Rowan had always been good at leaving without

much prompting. Saying nothing more to me, he veered to the open door of the truck and spoke quietly to the dog. Guiltily, I watched for a hot minute before turning away and going inside to turn the front corner into a doggy condo. Just as I finished placing the food and water bowls by the fluffy bed, I heard Rowan's motorcycle fire up and then speed away.

Breathing a little easier, I fished a giant piece of rawhide from one of the bags and went to see about coercing the dog out of my truck. That worked fairly well, him being a good sport and following me inside to check out his new digs. He sniffed the food bowls and then the bed before picking up the rawhide treat and trotting out the door.

"Hey! Get back here."

Did he listen? No. *Just like a man . . .*

I trailed the mutt all the way down the block and right into the chapel. He climbed onto the front pew and seemed perfectly content with just holding the treat in his mouth.

"Don't you want to try out your new bed? That thing cost a hundred bucks." I waved a hand at the open door. "It's a pillow top orthopedic. Way fancier than my own bed."

The dog gave me his final answer by tucking the rawhide under his paw and closing his eyes.

"Fine. Stay here. You know where your food is. I'm not bringing it down here to you. That's where I'm drawing the line." I eyed the shiplap, whitewashed walls and the dark wood floors and pews. The place held a soothing quality to it, so I didn't blame the dog for wanting to stay, and I also saw no harm in it for now.

I petted his head and the scruffy animal sighed, softening my heart toward him even more.

CHAPTER 9

DAYLIGHT SAVINGS IS A TRICKY GIFT. Sure, days are longer and you can get more done. But days are longer and you have no excuse for not getting more done. That covers the evening part of the tricky gift, but have you ever forgotten to reset your clocks the night before, only to wake up to a morning of confusion? One time Rowan and I forgot and the next morning we arrived at church to find an empty parking lot. Dumbstruck, we thought Jesus had come back and left our sorry behinds. Talk about a way of making you check yourself real quick. We never made that mistake again. Too bad we made so many other mistakes, though.

Adjusting to the time change combined with a restless night had me starting slow today, but we had a big task ahead of us, so I was already on my second thermos refill and another pot of coffee was on the ready in the saloon.

With heavy machinery beeping and revving in the background I addressed the work crew. "This is pretty straightforward, boys. Like stacking Legos." Standing in the middle of a circular foundation, I pointed to the giant galvanized steel rings laid out in a line down Front Street, five in total plus the dome-shaped roof. Yesterday's task had been to disassemble the old grain silo, so we could relocate it here on the left corner of Front and Main. "The crane and forklift will move the pieces into place and we are to secure them."

"Where'd this come from?"

I glanced at Lester, the reporter from the local news station. So caught up in the excitement of raising this building, I'd already forgotten they were here to film today. I pulled the bill of my cap down lower, hoping to conceal the dark circles under my eyes. "The silo was originally on the land where the town houses are being built. It stored grain back in its heyday and now it's being given a new purpose. Sweet Silo will be an artisanal ice cream and candy shop."

I answered a few more questions from the reporter before sending him and his filming crew next door to the bakery, where Desmond was supervising the light fixtures installation. Then I got to work helping to bolt the silo sections together once they were properly in place.

Midday, a catering truck rolled up from Maurice's BBQ Piggie Park. The driver and two servers said the bill was taken care of for the lunch treat for the entire crew. I'm talking at least thirty people. It sure blew my bucket of stolen chicken out of the water and I knew Rowan, who had been a no-show in the last few days, was responsible for it. The workers loved it, nonetheless, and I'd be lying if I said I didn't enjoy it too. We chowed down on pulled pork smothered in mustard-based barbecue sauce, sweet coleslaw, and hush puppies.

Nearing dusk, Sweet Silo stood tall and proud. I sat on the front steps of the town hall, petting the lazy dog sprawled out beside me while gazing down the street at the new addition. I liked how it stood out, definitely making a statement.

Desmond exited the coffee shop and walked over. "Who is this?"

"Des, this is the dog. He's really into belly rubs and can make entire buckets of chicken disappear." I told him about the thieving debacle.

Desmond, not much of an animal lover, patted the dog's head featherlight with just the tips of his fingers. "What's his name?"

"I have no clue."

Desmond *tsk*ed. "He needs a name."

"Let's try out some until he answers to one." I climbed to my feet and jogged down the steps. Several paces away from the dog, I called, "Hey, Rover." No response. "Here, Spot, here!" Nothing.

Desmond gave it a try. "Harold!"

I wrinkled my nose. "Really?"

Desmond shrugged and tried again. "Chief!" Still nothing. "Oscar!"

Several rounds in, we gave up.

"Just come up with one and start calling him by it. Eventually he'll get that you're talking to him."

I studied the scraggly dog, trying to figure out something that suited him. "He won't stay out of the chapel so I think I'm gonna call him Preacher whether he responds to it or not."

"So you're just going to let him stay in the chapel?"

"I tried to bribe him into moving to the saloon, but he weren't having it. But the sly dog manages to sneak over there long enough to empty the food and water bowls each day while I work. No matter how appealing I make his space in the saloon, the dog keeps wandering back to the chapel. He's been wandering around this town like the unofficial mayor for months. No use in changing the order of things now."

Desmond checked his phone and thumbed out a text. "Are you sure having a dog on a construction site is a good idea?"

"He's not bothered anything . . ." I began but amended that when Des gave me a hitched eyebrow. "Well, except for the little bit of stealing, but he's been on the up-and-up since I had a talk with him a few days ago." I rubbed the dog's back as his tail wagged. "Ain't that right, Preacher?"

"Good grief," Desmond grumbled. "I didn't peg you for one of those crazy pet ladies who baby talks to the animal. Please don't start collecting them."

I rolled my eyes and sat back down on a step. "One is enough."

A shiny black truck with giant tires and dark tinted windows pulled up at the curb and Rowan climbed out of it. Of course he'd have the latest king cab as well. Bachelorhood really suited him.

Preacher darted to him, nearly plowing him over. Rowan's throaty chuckle echoed down the street. The man looked so darn happy it made me sigh.

Desmond hummed.

I cut him a glance. "What's that hum for?"

Grinning, he straightened his silver cuff links. "Oh, nothing."

We watched Rowan roughhouse with the dog for a while, not even bothering to speak to us first before horsing around. On his knees, playing tug-of-war with a rope toy, the man finally looked up and acknowledged us. "Des. Avalee. The silo looks good."

"Thanks." I waved toward our metal jewel that instantly ramped up the town's charm. "Can you believe the illionaires wanted to just trash it? I've been trying to give them lessons on spotting treasure, but I think they're a lost cause."

Rowan sat beside me. "What other treasures have you unearthed around here?"

"So far, a hate letter, a dog, a teenage boy." I laughed. "We've even found a house."

"A house?"

"Yep. There's an old Victorian hidden in the woods behind Meeting Street. Complete with a turret and gingerbread trim. Built in 1876, but it's held up considerably well."

"Huh. How have I not seen that?"

"It's down a narrow lane that's overgrown, so it's pretty easy to miss. Fine by me, I want it to stay overlooked until I can talk the owner into selling it to me."

"You want that house for yourself or for a flip?" Desmond asked.

"For myself. It's my dream home. It reminds me of a dollhouse my father gave me one Christmas." I remembered playing with my dolls alone, pretending they were real and that they were my family and that we were all happy and not lonely.

Rowan gave me a measured look, knowing all about that doll-house. We shared a small smile, probably recalling the times I made him play dolls with me. He said if I ever ratted him out, he'd deny, deny, deny.

"Well, good luck with getting it. I'd love to restore a Victorian." Desmond's phone began ringing. Rising to his feet, he fished the phone from his pocket and silenced it. "I need to return this call and then I'm going to head out."

I said, "Okay," but I wasn't too okay with being left alone with Rowan.

Desmond must have picked up on my tone. Eyeing Rowan, he bent and placed a kiss on the side of my head. "Y'all have a good evening."

"You too," Rowan said, his tone not quite friendly.

Silence settled around us once Desmond's car disappeared.

Rowan shifted beside me and sighed. Even with all the time that had passed since we were together, I could still read him like an open book.

Knowing he had something to say, I braced myself and said, "Just spit it out, already."

He scratched the side of his neck and sighed again. "I thought you said you and Des are just friends."

I held back a laugh, finding his poutiness beyond amusing. "That's correct."

Rowan met my eyes. "You let your friends kiss you?"

Giving in, I laughed. "He kissed my head."

"So. It's still a kiss."

Since Rowan wanted to pry, I decided to play along. "We did go on one date." I yanked the elastic band out of my drooping ponytail, finger-combed my hair, and then gathered it into a messy bun.

He grumbled something under his breath, accepting the ball the dog offered and then throwing it. Preacher took off after it.

"It's none of your business, but by the time dinner was over we'd decided to be friends." I held my hand out as Preacher trotted back with the ball. He dropped it in my palm and I threw it. "I guarantee *you've* had plenty of dates in the last six years." I expected him to be blushing or looking smug when I glanced at him, but he was shaking his head.

"None."

I scoffed. "None? That's a little hard to believe." Rowan had never been one for lying, but this seemed a bit far-fetched.

"My friends would invite me out and try setting me up with another friend, but . . ." Rowan made a somber face. "None of them were you."

Glancing around for a way out of this, I spotted the new addition to the chapel. "I installed a doggy door." I sprang to my feet. "Come check it out." I jogged down the steps and looked over my shoulder.

Lips pressed into a frown, he remained sitting on the step.

I placed my hands on my hips and gazed up at the orange and purple sky for a few beats before returning my attention to the sulking man. "We can talk about this town or the dog." I slashed a hand through the air. "Nothing else."

"Why not?"

"Because I don't want to." I winced, realizing that sounded a lot like what I'd told Desmond a while back, when he tried pushing me to talk about my ties to Rowan. I just didn't think any amount of talking would make a difference. It certainly couldn't change the past. "But I would really like to show you the doggy door."

"Guess I'll take what I can get," Rowan said so quietly I almost missed it. He finally stood and walked with me to the chapel. "I've never seen a doggy door on a church before." He bent his knees and inspected it as Preacher darted inside. A moment later, the dog poked his head out and barked, seemingly quite happy with his newer, easier access to his favorite place. Rowan petted him. "I'm not sure whatever religious organization that comes in will be fine with a dog coming and going as he pleases."

"I had a talk with Jonas. Thank the good Lord, he's a dog lover. He's putting the stipulation about it in the contract, so they have to agree to it."

"That's good . . . Weird, but good." He straightened as the dog darted outside and started trailing a butterfly.

"His name is Preacher."

"Yeah? How'd you figure that?"

I shrugged. "It suits him, since he's always pacing the altar in the chapel."

Rowan chuckled. "I suppose you're right. We better give him his bath before it gets dark." He whistled and Preacher followed as we started toward the saloon where we had the tub set up outside by the back door.

The nightly ritual of tending to Preacher had become a team challenge, whether it was to apply ointment or give him his meds. It was awkward—yet so familiar—to work with my ex-husband, but I sucked it up for the dog's sake.

I turned the water hose on and dropped it inside the metal tub. "Oh, I almost forgot to thank you for the lunch today. The crew devoured it. Nothing's left."

He smiled but didn't comment further. That was Rowan though. He had never been one to show his left hand what the right one was doing. He gave to simply give, not for recognition.

We made quick work of filling the tub and getting the supplies situated while the dog trotted loops around our activity.

"I've finally decided what to do with the old home goods store next to the mercantile."

Rowan glanced up from removing Preacher's collar. "Yeah? Let's hear it."

"A pet store with maybe a small plant and garden section. The new park the county is putting in backs up to the store. I think it would be neat if we installed a pet-washing station just outside the building."

Rowan chuckled. "Sounds self-serving." He tipped his head at the dog.

I smiled. "Maybe a little, but you saw how packed out that vet's office was. People are crazy about their pets nowadays. Nita is already reaching out to some people who may be interested in running the store."

Rowan gestured for Preacher to get in the tub and the dog immediately obeyed. I seriously thought we'd found the smartest stray dog in the history of stray dogs. If we could just get him to quit stealing. Just the day before, I caught him with someone's insulated lunch bag.

For him to have been so filthy the day we discovered him, Preacher sure loved a bath. He also loved making a game out of seeing which one of us he could soak first.

Laughing, I reared back to try escaping the spray of water. "Stop, you menace."

"We would have been great parents, don't ya think?"

A few years back, I ran smack-dab into a sliding glass door. I didn't see it coming. Wind knocked out of me, I bounced off the glass and landed hard on my backside. Rowan's question slammed into me just as hard, leaving me unable to breathe for a few stunned moments.

Rowan held his palms up to block another water attack from Preacher, totally oblivious to the invisible line he'd just crossed.

My eyes began to sting, blurring my vision. "You maybe. Not me."

He finally looked at me but had enough nerve to act affronted by my answer. "How can you think that?"

"Seriously, Rowan?" If I could have unfrozen my body, I probably would have punched him. I pushed to my feet and threw the bottle of dog shampoo against the brick wall. The lid popped off and left a long streak of white shampoo on the red bricks, but I wished it would have exploded to match how my insides felt. "You forget about the children I already failed?"

Rowan bowed his head and groaned. "Avalee—"

Storming inside and slamming the door, I didn't hear anything else he said. I locked the back door and then locked myself in my apartment. I fired off a text, telling Rowan to finish up with the dog and then leave. He replied before I could close the text app. **I'm sorry.**

"Not as sorry as I am," I muttered to the phone before dropping it on the bed.

The only coping mechanism to get me through the last decade had been focusing all my energy on work. Maudie was constantly on my case, saying work alone wasn't much of a life, but I found it to be the only way I could breathe.

Mentally going over the day's progress, I climbed into the shower with intentions of staying there for a good long while. As I bent my head forward so the shower jets could pound against the back of my neck, I reviewed each step in reassembling the silo today. It had gone off without a hitch, made possible by all the planning and preliminary prep work. I made sure the foundation was properly set by allowing it to cure for an entire week.

Maybe that had been the root of Rowan's and my problem. From the get-go, we seemed to rush everything. Shoot, he proposed while we were still in high school, and like an idiot, I said yes. Then we rushed right into marriage the summer after we graduated.

"Err!!" Unable to avoid the deluge of memories pouring down faster than the shower water, I turned it off and grabbed a towel. I wrapped it around my midsection and made it to the bedroom before falling to my knees by the bed. I didn't know whether to pray or scream as the faint scent of ginger and molasses wafted from another dark memory.

The first time we found out we were pregnant was near the Christmas of Rowan's sophomore year of college—no, I didn't further my education right away. I was too busy making dumb choices. So anyway, that Christmas, I made gingerbread cookies. Some were women with rounded bellies and some were gingerbread babies. We brought the cookies to the family gathering. When our family figured it out, the look on their faces was priceless.

How horrific it had been to turn around just a month later and tell them I'd lost the baby. Everyone said that it just wasn't meant to be and that we could try again. Shell-shocked and devastated, I could only nod.

The doctor had said in a clinical voice, "Your baby is no longer viable."

I remember sitting on the paper-lined exam table, confused and swaying in a cloud of disbelief. My mind snagged on the word *viable*, and while the doctor continued his clinical talk, I began thinking of words that sounded like *viable. Reliable. Sustainable. Unable.* Then I put the words together. *My body wasn't reliable and was unable to be a sustainable carrier of a viable baby.* I'm pretty sure I suffered a small breakdown that day, or perhaps those thoughts took up space in my brain for no other reason but to distract me from the horror of the situation. Even after I left the doctor's office, my brain kept getting hung up on certain words. Like *miscarriage*.

The definition of *carriage* is the act of carrying. The prefix *mis-* means wrong or bad. I hate the word *miscarriage*. It implies I did a bad job carrying my babies.

Marriage sounds pretty darn close to *carriage*. Instead of divorce, it should be called mismarriage.

CHAPTER 10

APRIL

My father and I have never been what you'd call close, but it wasn't either of our faults. We liked each other well enough, but we could never figure out how to get over this awkward divide between us. I'm fairly certain that chasm had been created by my mother's death. She was the missing piece to our relationship.

Every now and then, Dad would get the wild idea to work on filling in that divide. One of those wild ideas led us to the Land of Oz. Tucked in the mountains of North Carolina, the theme park was on my bucket list of abandoned places to visit, which proved my father did pay attention to me to an extent. It'd opened back in 1970 but closed only five years later. The weirdly cool park had endured a turbulent history of fires, vandalism, various owners, and years of abandonment.

At the time of our trip, the park was closed to the public, but Dad knew someone who knew someone that set up a private tour for us. We had the entire park to ourselves. Meandering down the worn yellow-brick roads and touring the weathered attractions, I fully expected the scarecrow to shuffle by or for Toto to come scurrying up to yap at us. I kept looking up at the sky for any signs of those creepy flying monkeys, worried they would dive-bomb us.

It's an odd sensation to be fully in awe and a bit freaked out at the same time. That's how I felt that day exploring the Land of Oz. And it's exactly how I felt every Sunday I spent alone in this ghost town. With no work crews beatin' and a bangin' on our one day of rest, that odd sensation followed me around like a pressing breeze. But just like visiting that theme park, I planned to take full advantage of my day alone with this place.

With Preacher on my flip-flopped heels, I lugged my cooler out to the middle of Main Street and placed it between my neon-green lounge chair and a blue plastic kiddie pool. Sunshine glanced off the water, sending sparkles along the blue edge. It was only mid-April, but the heat had already shown up.

"Well, boy, we have sand and water." I readjusted the beach umbrella to cast some shade over the pool. I stepped back and admired my oasis mirage. I closed one eye and squinted with the other while angling my head to the right. "It's almost convincing we're on a deserted island instead of in the middle of a deserted dirt road."

Preacher barked in agreement before leaping into the pool, splashing me in the process.

Squealing, I hopped out of the way and wiped the drips off my leg. "Silly dog."

Tongue lolling out the side of his mouth, Preacher looked up, and I declare he was grinning just before belly flopping, sending waves of water over the sides of the pool.

"You keep that up, you'll be out of water soon." Laughing at his silliness, I slathered on some coconut-scented sunscreen and took a deep inhale. It smelled like beach trip memories, too many of which included Rowan. Growing up, we worked hard for Maudie during summer breaks but played just as hard. We would set out to the beach with a cooler of sodas and ham sandwiches and whatever else we could swipe from our families' kitchens and stay until the sun dipped out for the day. Flashes of frolicking in the ocean, building elaborate sandcastles while daydreaming about our dream home, and laying out on beach towels while the sun tanned us to a crisp. Back then, life only held great possibilities. Too bad we had to grow up and learn otherwise.

My palm skimmed over the old scar on the back of my leg, another memory attached to Rowan. Shoot, thinking about it, he was attached to almost every scar I carried. I cocked my leg out to the side and angled my head to get a look at the faded silvery lines crisscrossing just above my knee. One of those beach trips, I got tangled up in the venomous tentacles of a Portuguese man-of-war. You would have thought, given how Rowan freaked out, that he'd been the one in excruciating pain, but that was Rowan. He always took on my pain, as if it would relieve me from it. The only thing that did was make for two miserable people instead of one. By the end of our marriage, we'd perfected that.

Wiping my hands on the beach towel spread over my chair, I turned on the portable speaker and cued my Island Playlist to add to the spring break setting. The whimsical chords from the ukulele bounced off the buildings on each side of us and gently persuaded my mind to take a siesta from work and worries.

While Preacher had himself a large time splashing around in his new pool, I stretched out on the lounge chair and basked in the sunshine. Sighing in bliss, I closed my eyes and tapped my toes to the beat of the song. I remained in my relaxed beach bum state of mind until the sound of a motorcycle approached town and ruined it.

"Please, not today." I held out hope that Rowan was headed over to the town houses site until I heard footsteps approaching. I wondered if I could get away with pretending to be asleep.

Preacher barked and then commenced to going into doggy rinse cycle, shaking cool water all over my sun-warmed skin, blowing my cover by making me jolt into a seated position.

"Dang dog." I sent him a scathing glare from behind my sunglasses as I lay back down.

Chuckling in that deep throaty way of his, Rowan asked, "What are y'all up to?"

"I'll give you one guess." I swear I was going for sassy but it sounded a lot more flirty.

"Sunbathing in the middle of Main Street."

"Exactly. Not many can say they've done such."

Rowan huffed. "I doubt anyone else has ever pulled off something like this."

I closed my eyes, not wanting to focus on his casual outfit of T-shirt and shorts. Seriously, how could the man make that look as good as his tailored suits? "That's the point of it. Taking advantage of this free pass to do whatever strikes my fancy."

"Humph."

I listened to him walk away, thankful he'd taken the hint. Or not. I peeped an eye open as he set up a fold out chair beside me and settled into it, having enough nerve to prop his feet on the side of my lounge chair right next to my hip. "What are you doing?"

"Taking a page from the Avalee Elvis handbook, doing whatever strikes my fancy." He clasped his hands behind his head and grinned. "I like your orange suit. It matches your nails." Rowan slowly perused my body before settling his gaze on my lower abdomen. I looked down and realized my scar peeped from the top of my bikini bottom. I quickly flipped over.

"It's coral," I muttered, checking my new manicure. I had a standing appointment with Starla at the tattoo parlor. The woman had some kind of magical topcoat that kept my nails looking spiffier much longer than most. *Aloha* was the name of this one, perfect for tropical daydreaming.

A few blissful beats of silence passed before Rowan said, "I'm surprised your grandmother doesn't make you go to church with her on Sundays since you're this close to home."

"Beaufort's still a forty-minute drive from here, but I'll have you know I went to the early service with her." I lifted my head and glanced at him. "What about you?"

"I have a home church in Greenville. I've been watching online since starting this project."

At the mention of Greenville, I couldn't help but wonder what all he'd been up to in the last six years. He'd mentioned his friends trying to set him up, but that was the extent of it. That line he said about none of them being me seemed like one of those ways of answering without actually answering.

My curiosity got the better of me. "You like living in Greenville?"

Rowan lifted both shoulders. "Greenville is great." *Another nonanswer.*

I continued looking at him, willing him to share more, but he didn't. Giving up, I lowered my head and pretended to sleep, hoping he'd do the same. It worked for about an hour and then he started sighing heavily.

I rolled my head in his direction and squinted at him. His nose was already getting sunburned. I thought about offering him my tube of sunblock, but he wasn't mine to tend to anymore. "What's your problem?"

He sighed again. "I'm hungry."

"You're a grown man. Go eat something."

Rowan stood and walked off. Good riddance.

Turning up the volume a bit, I focused on the steel drum beats. Between the tranquil rhythm and the sun warming my shoulders, I slipped into a heavenly lull. Sighing, I began to drift . . .

The chair next to me creaked, snapping me out of my happy place. I stifled a huff, keeping my eyes pinched shut, but then the breeze shifted and suddenly the sweet aroma of chocolate wafted by me.

My eyes popped open and caught Rowan taking a giant bite of chocolate mousse cake. "Where'd you get that?"

"From your fridge." He shoveled another forkful into his trap.

Gasping, I sat up and tried snatching the container. "That's my supper!"

Rowan held it just out of reach. With chocolate smeared on his lips and his nose wrinkled, he resembled the boy I grew up with. "Since when do you have cake for supper?"

I thought about not answering him or coming up with something snarky, but on a heavy sigh, I decided to go with the truth. "Since I can't have any of the big happies of life I've settled for the small ones. Like cake for supper." I held up my hand and wiggled my coral-tipped fingers. "Manicures. And sunbathing in the middle of this deserted street. I figured if I collect enough small happies maybe they'll add up enough that I won't miss the big ones so much."

A heaviness settled over Rowan's handsome features as he stared at the nearly gone piece of cake. Without a word, he rose from the chair and walked off. Several minutes later, the roar of his motorcycle echoed down the street. As the engine faded with his retreat, thick tears fell down my cheeks. I flipped over and clutched the edges of my towel as a sob tore through me.

I hadn't allowed myself a good wallow on losing out on the big happies in quite a while. For one thing, it hurt too darn bad. But also, the last time I wallowed, it sent me into a dark place that I found difficult to come back from. Nowadays I focused on moving forward, appreciating the small happies along the way. It had worked perfectly well until my path led me here to this abandoned town. Being forced to face one of my biggest fails each time I caught a glimpse of Rowan had been agonizing.

Preacher sidled up beside my chair and licked my damp cheek.

Sniffling, I scratched behind his ear. "Such a good boy. You've had enough fun in the sun too?" He'd been snoozing in the shade so he was mostly dry, but I sat up and grabbed the extra towel and dried him off just for something to do to distract me from myself.

The crackling roar of the motorcycle reappeared. I froze, looking over my shoulder, but Rowan didn't emerge from the other side of the building where he typically parked. "What is he doing?" I whispered, but Preacher didn't answer. I certainly didn't want to see him again today while I sported red, swollen eyes, so I stayed put.

Less than ten minutes later, he left again.

Feeling drained from the sun and my mini breakdown, I put away the beach stuff and called it a day. After feeding Preacher, I headed upstairs and took a long shower to wash away the sunscreen and the dried tears. I toweled off and applied some aloe to my slightly red shoulders before dressing in a ratty T-shirt and joggers. The encounter with Rowan had robbed me of my appetite, so I decided to skip supper but knew I needed to hydrate to combat the headache trying to settle in. I opened the fridge to grab a bottle of water but was taken aback by a white box taking up the entire top shelf. The Publix label gave it away but I pulled it out to confirm my suspicions. Yep, an entire chocolate mousse cake. A note was scribbled on top of the box.

Sorry I couldn't give you all the big happies, a stór. —Rowan

And just like that, the waterworks started all over again. I shoved the cake back in the fridge and slammed the door. "Dang you, Rowan Murray!" With my back pressed against the fridge, I slid to the floor, wishing I could melt right into it.

CHAPTER 11

SORRY I COULDN'T GIVE YOU ALL THE BIG HAPPIES, A STÓR. —Rowan

His note played on a loop in my thoughts as I worked alongside the crew the next morning at the coffee shop. Was it ever Rowan's job to give me all the happies, big or small? Most certainly not.

While constructing a framed arch to go above a hallway passage, I tried to recall the traditional vows we didn't recite at our wedding.

To have and to hold from this day forward, for better, for worse, for richer, for poorer, in sickness and in health, to love and to cherish.

Nothing in those vows said anything about happiness, and I knew the vows we shared didn't either. Never one for flowery eloquence, my vows had been simple, promising to love him, be his partner in life, to share the TV remote, and to try to keep him fed. I was almost embarrassed to state them after Rowan busted out legit vows that had every guest sniffling. He'd shared Ruth 1:16-17. *Don't ask me to leave you and turn back. Wherever you go, I will go; wherever you live, I will live. Your people will be my people, and your God will be my God. Wherever you die, I will die, and there I will be buried. May the* LORD *punish me severely if I allow anything but death to separate us!*

Still, no matter how beautiful and heart-tugging, his vows hadn't said a thing about giving me happiness. I hated that he ever thought that cross was his to bear on my behalf. So much so, I couldn't even stomach eating the cake for supper last night. By this morning, I managed downing a piece of that decadent treat with my coffee, though. That didn't mean I accepted the apology attached to it that he had no right giving. If that were the case, I had a heckuva lot more to apologize for than he did. If our marital sins were stacked side by side, mine would surely tower over his.

Banishing those thoughts, I focused on finishing the last section of the arch. Wiping the sweat off my brow with the back of my hand, I let out a long breath. I motioned for Bash to follow as I grabbed us each a Gatorade from my personal cooler. "I'm spittin' cotton. Let's take a break."

We sat on overturned buckets and surveyed our work. "Not bad for it only being ten in the morning."

"Yeah." Bash sipped his blue sports drink.

"You did good with measuring and cutting the boards. Would you be interested in learning more stuff like that?"

"Sure." Another sip.

Laughing, I shook my head. "Boy, you sure are a talker." I shoved my shoulder against his and he finally laughed, looking much younger than nineteen.

"I need to check in with Desmond over at the inn. How about you square this away and I'll meet you back here in a bit."

"M'kay," Bash said quietly as he started stacking the small wood remnants into a wheelbarrow. He never hesitated with whatever task I assigned him. He beat most of us to work each morning and stayed later than anyone else. He took care of tasks before I even had to ask for them to be completed. The boy seemed bound, bent, and determined to prove his worth.

I walked down Meeting Street to the inn that sat directly across from the chapel. The two clapboard buildings were quite similar, with tall wooden doors and ornate metalwork on the windows. *Welcoming* came to mind as I looked back and forth between them. I could hear Desmond inside, his dress shoes click-clacking along the brick floors just before the front door opened.

"Oh, hey. I was about to go looking for you." He joined me out front and we surveyed the building.

Everything, whether a place or event, needed a main attraction. Sounded a little like a circus, but true in so many ways. Sure, we could flip a dozen or so buildings, make this little piece of God's green oasis into something less rusty and overgrown, but it would take more finesse to transform this unknown into something folks would desire to know. We needed to make that happen through key businesses. The Sweet Silo and the saloon were definitely main attractions, but this little inn would be one also from what I glimpsed of Desmond's plans for it.

"It's on the small side but has lots of potential." Desmond's eyes roamed over the outer facade of the old inn as he took off his fedora, scratching at his neat twists before settling the hat back into place. "We're keeping the original floor plan with the upstairs for guests, and downstairs will be social spaces with the reception and dining areas. And in the back will be the living quarters for the innkeepers."

I made a note on my clipboard. "I need to check with Nita and see if she's found any takers yet."

"There's a taker." Desmond rocked back on his heels, smiling. "It's a done deal."

"Oh yeah? Who?"

"You're looking at him." He spread his arms wide.

"Des!" I jumped up and down and clapped my hands enthusiastically, going for silly but meaning it just the same.

"I couldn't let you be the only one of us to own a slice of Somewhere." He tugged on the end of my ponytail.

I swatted his hand away. "Are you going to run it too?"

"My parents want to, actually. They've decided retirement is too boring." Des rolled his eyes, but he didn't fool me. My friend was over the moon.

"That's great. A family affair." I grinned. "I've read over your plan ideas. You wanna do a walk-through and lay it all out for me?"

"Absolutely." Desmond opened his iPad and led me inside.

We made it upstairs after a quick discussion about the first floor, mainly about repairing the brick floors and reconfiguring the kitchen layout.

"You mentioned themed rooms in your notes." I peeped inside a hall closet that would be used for linen storage.

"We only have five rooms, so I want each one to have a distinct South Carolinian vibe." Desmond stopped in front of the first door to the left and knocked on it. "This one will be the Pecan Grove, beside it the Magnolia Room, and on the far end the Carolina Coast." He pointed to the room directly across from us. "That room will be the Indigo Room, and beside it the Train Depot. I'm having wood-carved name plaques made for each door."

"Those are perfect room names and it'll be a good mix of feminine and masculine."

"I'm avoiding bougie for this one." Desmond winked at me before heading downstairs.

"Nothing wrong with bougie. It worked fine for that sitting room at the Library Café, but I agree this place needs to be more on the rustic side. I'm pretty sure I have some pieces in storage from an abandoned railroad station, and you're welcome to pick through the stuff we saved from the pecan warehouse."

"Let me know when you go rummaging and I'll tag along." He made a few notes on his iPad. "You know JP Thornton, right?"

"Yeah. He's that famous photographer from Charleston."

"I've hired him to capture black and whites to correlate with each room."

"That's what's going to set this little inn apart. All the details." I flipped a few pages on my clipboard until finding the town map. It had notations scribbled all over it. I pulled my pencil from behind my ear, ready to make another. "You thought of a name yet?"

"What do you think about the Lowcountry Inn?"

"I think it's a fabulous name. This place is going to be fabulous too." I jotted the name down on the map. "Let me know if there's anything you need me to do."

As we exited the inn, a commotion at the other end of the street caught my attention. A group of men, including the Bellamy twins and Bash, stood around the oak tree beside the firehouse, heads tipped back and pointing up.

"What in the world are they looking at?" I squinted, but we were too far away for me to make out anything.

"We better go find out." Desmond led me down Meeting Street, and once we passed the town hall, the problem came into view.

I ran the rest of the way and elbowed my way through the group until reaching the base of the tree. "Rowdy, what the heck are you doing, dangling up there like a monkey?"

"Rowdy?" Desmond mumbled beside me but I ignored him.

Gripping the thick limb, Rowan glanced over his shoulder, now reminding me more of an upside-down sloth than a monkey. "My shirt and pants are snagged."

"But why are you—?" Deciding it wasn't worth asking at the moment, I patted my pocket for my knife, then backed up a few steps. Giving myself a running start, I jumped and was just able to grab hold of the lowest hanging limb.

"Who's the monkey now?" Rowan hollered from above me.

"Ook-ook! Eek-eek!" Monkey noises erupted from the peanut gallery below us.

"Hush!" I yelled. The tree bark bit into the palms of my hands, but I continued scaling the trunk for another twenty feet or so until reaching Rowan. I straddled the limb and tried catching my breath. The breeze rustling through the leaves and Spanish moss helped. "You mind explaining how you got yourself in this situation?"

Rowan grunted, readjusting his arms that were hugging the limb. He sort of did a pull-up as he kicked a leg out and hooked it around the top. "Later. You got your pocketknife?"

"Of course." I scooted closer and tried to figure out how to free him. "Where exactly are you snagged?"

"The branch poked through my shirt and then got hung up in my belt when I fell." He grunted again, his knuckles turning white.

My heart skipped a beat at the mention of him falling. "Only you would get into such a predicament." I was about to ask one of the many questions I had about this fine mess, but it would have to wait. His arms, as nicely toned as they were, had to be getting tired. I fished the knife out of my pocket and unfolded it. "I'm going to have to cut your belt and maybe your shirt too."

"'Kay." Rowan blinked several times as a bead of sweat dripped into his right eye.

I needed to get on the move before he finished falling, but the realization that I would have to squeeze my hand between Rowan's nether regions and the tree in order to reach the belt had me stalling. I contemplated cutting the back of his belt but it was out of reach.

"Y'all okay?" Fred yelled.

I glanced down and growled. Desmond and Froid had their phones angled up at us. "Really, guys?"

Rowan cleared his throat, bringing my attention back to him.

"Sorry." Leaning over, I caught a whiff of his cologne, making this feel much more intimate than it really was. "Hold very still or I might accidentally cut the wrong limb."

Rowan turned into a statue.

I slid the knife down his torso, keeping the blade pointed toward the tree until I felt leather brush the back of my hand. "Here we go . . ." Carefully, I slipped the blade behind the belt and sliced through it in one go, hearing fabric rip as the branch sprung free with a piece breaking off. "Watch out below!" The guys scattered, dodging the falling debris. I put the knife away and scooted backwards to give Rowan room to right himself.

"Thanks for coming to the rescue." Straddling the limb with his knees touching mine, he gave me a faint smile and a hint of his Irish accent. "My hero."

Heat flooded my cheeks, but I brushed off his comment with a scoff. "Just trying to prevent a lawsuit."

*Tsk*ing, Rowan shook his head. "Say what you want, but you just showed me you still care."

"I care about not getting sue—" My attention caught on the giant hole in his shirt, the exposed skin rendering me speechless. My perusal stopped on an angry red scratch beside his belly button.

"What?"

My gaze rose to meet his. "You have a scratch on your stomach."

Rowan tucked his chin to check, his abs flexing with the move. His faint smile curled into something more impish as he glanced up. "You wanna kiss it and make it better?"

Rolling my eyes, I swung around and began making my way down the tree.

"You used to be all about kissing me better," he said louder than necessary.

"Yeah. And used to be, we were married." I slid until my boot reached the next limb below. "That's no longer the case, so knock it off."

Rowan chuckled but it sounded off, similar to how I felt. We shouldn't have brought up the past and we both knew it.

Needing to get away from him, I jumped when I got about four feet from the ground. I didn't stick the landing, but luckily Desmond was right there and helped to steady me.

"You do realize we could hear everything the two of you were saying?"

I straightened my shirt and noticed a sticky smudge of sap on my palm. "Well, then. I guess now you know."

Desmond frowned, reminding me of a disappointed parent. "Still not enough."

Rowan landed on his feet beside us, nimble as an elite athlete, and brushed away a few twigs stuck in his tousled hair.

Hands on my hips, I glared at him. "Tell me why you were up that tree without a safety harness."

Rowan pulled off his ruined belt and coiled it around his hand. "We were trying to figure out if the tree has to go or if a good trimming is all it needs." He rubbed the back of his neck and scanned the tree above. "So I climbed up to see. Good news is, I think only a few limbs need to be removed. I'm going to see about getting a tree service out here ASAP."

"You should have done that in the first place." I gave the hole in his shirt a pointed look.

"I can take it off, if you'd like." Golden-brown eyes glinting with mischief, Rowan grabbed a fistful of his shirt, but I batted his hand away.

"You're not funny." I glanced at Bash and hitched a thumb toward Rowan. "Bash, just say no to foolery such as this."

"M'kay." Apparently bored by it all, Bash shoved his hands into his pockets and walked off.

I gave it a go myself, shoving my hands into my back pockets and starting down the road, but Desmond caught me before I made it very far. "You didn't actually think you were going to get away after dropping that bomb back there."

"A girl can hope." I wrinkled my nose and smiled.

"*Just some guy I grew up with*," Desmond mimicked my voice, failing to sound anywhere close. "At least your skittish behavior around him makes sense now." Shaking his head and muttering something about a husband, he veered away from me and took off toward the inn.

I hated nothing worse than talking about my failed marriage, but disappointing my friend came in a close second. "Des!"

Without slowing or acknowledging me, he slipped inside the inn and closed the door firmly.

Tilting my face toward the sky, I blew out a long exhale and continued down Main Street.

"Hey!" Rowan called out.

I stopped in my tracks. "Good grief. It's like some weird version of freeze tag." I resumed walking once Rowan fell in step beside me.

"I have something for you in my truck."

I looked at him out the corner of my eye. "What is it?"

He didn't answer, just kept moving us toward his truck parked in front of the saloon. When we reached it, he opened the back door, tossed in the belt, and pulled out a cardboard box. "Remember when Pastor Alvin assigned us to the church sign?"

Huffing a laugh, I propped an arm on the side of the truck bed. "Yeah. He'd tell us what to put on it and we'd figure out a way to mix it up."

Chuckling, Rowan placed the box on his tailgate and took off the lid. *"Anyone who enjoys sinning is invited to join the choir."*

Unable to stop it, I burst out laughing. "Switching the *g* for an *n* seemed like an innocent enough mistake."

"Not to Pastor Alvin. After that one, he put his foot down and took away our sign duties." Rowan pulled out a letter card and handed it to me. "I thought a lot about what you said yesterday about collecting small happies. I picked up this box of letters for you this morning. I thought maybe you could put funny sayings on the chapel's sign. Make it one of your small happies."

My throat tightened. "That's . . . thank you." I flipped the plastic letter *E* end to end. "But, Rowan, my happies aren't your responsibility. Not now and not when we were married."

"I'd like to give this one to you just the same." He stilled my hand and held my gaze until Preacher's playful bark broke the connection. The dog trotted over with his tongue waggling.

"Someone's ready for his lunch." I gave the letter card back to Rowan and scratched behind Preacher's ear. "I better go feed him."

"Okay." He replaced the lid and lifted the box. "I'm going to set these inside the chapel."

Watching him walk off, I couldn't deny the appeal of placing messages on the little chapel marquee any more than I could deny the appeal of the man who gifted me with the idea.

Heaven help me, things were getting stickier than the tree sap on my palm.

CHAPTER 12

DON'T TRY EXPLAINING PUNS TO KLEPTOMANIACS. *They always take things literally.*

I stepped back from the church sign and admired my handiwork. After debating for the last week and a half on how to put to use the letters Rowan had given me, I chose to go with sharing puns. This one seemed appropriate for the first one.

I put away the box of letters and moved to the deli, where Bash was already waiting, wearing the work gloves I gave him yesterday after noticing him working with bare hands.

"Let me give you a little lesson on this type of wall." I motioned for him to join me by the left wall with the orange *X* on it that we'd just added a few days ago, after deciding it needed to go. "Before drywall, folks used these small wood slats." I stripped a section of yellowed wallpaper back to expose the supporting structure behind it.

Bash peeled away a strip and brushed his gloved fingers over the wood slats. "Kinda like that shiplap you used in the bakery?"

Pride had me standing a little taller. This kid paid attention. "Exactly like that. This'll be tedious work, so no rush. Just pry off as many pieces as possible."

He glanced over and eyed the top of my head. "You have a cobweb in your hair."

"Typical work hazard." I pulled a glove off and flicked the cobweb out of my hair, only to have it tangle around my fingers. Wiping it on the side of my pants, I told Bash, "I'd like for us to preserve as many of these wood slats as possible. I plan on using them as a decorative element on the front of the coffee shop's order counter."

After demonstrating a few sections, I left Bash to it and started installing the new sink in the bathroom. I popped in one earbud and cued my music app. A few songs in, I had the sink vanity fitted into place and began connecting the hot water.

"Avalee!" Bash's deep voice rang above the song.

Lowering the wrench from the back of the faucet, I lifted my head and yelled over my shoulder, "Yeah?"

"There's something in the wall."

I rose from the floor and went to the front of the building. "Whatcha got?" I leaned in and peeked through the hole he'd made.

"It looks like some kind of bag." Bash stepped out of the way.

I snaked my arm between the wood slats and fished out a burlap sack. The name stamped on the aged material caught my attention. "No freakin' way . . ."

"What?" Bash drew near, peering over my shoulder.

I opened the drawstring, fully expecting bundles of hundred-dollar bills. Instead, the contents were only a tin can of sardines and a can of peaches. "Figures . . ." Huffing, I handed Bash the bag while hollering for anyone near to come see what he had uncovered.

Several workers meandered in.

"Did you find a treasure?" Froid asked, popping his safety glasses on top of his bald head.

I laughed. "Sort of."

While they passed the disappointing bag around the room, I told the history of it.

Unfazed, Bash stared off at a spot over my head, seemingly less interested in the bank robbery than, say, a fly on the wall, but the rest of the group chatted it up, adding their theories and lots of "what ifs" and "if I were the robbers."

"I would have looked in the bags before taking them," Fred declared as he inspected the bag.

Froid scoffed. "No, you wouldn't. A bank robbery is a swipe-and-go kinda thing. You don't dillydally."

I chuckled. "Sounds like you're talking from experience."

Froid shrugged. "Just common sense."

"Okay." I took the bank bag from Fred. "Time to get back to work."

The guys moved out, leaving me and Bash alone once again in the deli.

"I'm heading out to Beaufort for the rest of the day to work on a few projects with my grandmother." I lifted the burlap bag. "I think I'm going to get her to help me make a display case for this while I'm there."

"M'kay." Bash put his work gloves back on.

"Finish taking that section of the wall down and then you can call it an early day."

Bash shook his head. "I'd rather keep working. The pecan warehouse needs cleaning. I could do that and then do a trash pickup around town."

I checked my pocket for my keys, wondering why a guy in his youthful prime wouldn't want a free afternoon to go hang out somewhere. "If that's what you want. Just wrap up when the other crews do."

With the idea of making a display case for the burlap bag fresh on my mind, I gathered some supplies and loaded them in the back of my truck.

By the time I parked in front of my grandmother's store, I had a solid plan for the display case. Pushing through the door, I found one of Maudie's longtime employees behind the counter. "Hey, Stacie. Maudie around?"

"Hey, girl. Maudie's next door having lunch. She told me to send you over once you got here." She hitched a thumb over her shoulder.

"Thanks." I made a U-turn and walked along the boardwalk. The rich aroma of fried seafood mingled with the briny breeze, making up the scent of my childhood. I'd say the scent of home, but that wasn't the case any longer. The scent of home for me now held notes of sawdust and paint fumes.

I waved off the hostess. "I'm looking for Maudie."

"She's on the back patio."

I thanked the young woman and wove around tables to the patio doors. I came to a sudden halt when I spotted my grandmother's lunch date. But the shock quickly wore off and anger took over.

I marched up to the table. "What's going on here?"

Maudie had enough decency to look slightly guilty. Not Rowan. No, he grinned like it tickled him to be caught red-handed.

"What does it look like?" He lifted his fork containing flaky fish.

I cut my eyes toward Maudie and waited for her to take a long drink from her glass of tea.

She put the glass down and dabbed the corners of her mouth with a napkin. "Rowdy and I catch up when he makes it to town." The familiarity of her using the nickname she'd given him a long time ago sent an ache along my shoulders.

Feeling betrayed by my own grandmother, I crossed my arms. "Oh. So this isn't the first time then?"

"Oh, get over yourself and sit down." Maudie pointed to the empty chair.

Huffing, I yanked a chair out and did as my grandmother said. "I'll sit but I seriously doubt I'll be getting over this."

"Suit yourself, Miss Sourpuss." Maudie waved the waiter over and ordered me a shrimp basket. "And put some extra suga' in her tea. My granddaughter is in need of some sweetenin' up." She winked at the guy and he smiled like he was in on the joke.

The waiter came back in a flash, setting my glass in front of me, along with several packets of sugar. To say this lunch was awkward would be an understatement. My grandmother and ex-husband acted like it was the most natural thing and I sat there poking at my shrimp once it arrived. I had nothing nice to say so I said nothing at all until Maudie kicked my leg.

"Stop glaring at Rowdy like that, Avalee. People at the other tables are starting to get worried you're gonna stab the poor man with your fork."

I tightened my grip on the fork, thinking their assessment sounded on point.

Rowan chuckled. "Our girl is terrifying, Maudie. The first time I met her back in third grade, she punched a boy for making fun of my 'broke' accent." He draped an arm over the back of my chair, ever so nonchalantly. "Remember she got suspended?"

Maudie clucked her tongue. "First of many."

I opened my mouth, ready to defend myself and lay blame on the man beside me, but he plowed on.

"When she returned to school the next week she demanded I be her best friend. Said I owed her as much. I followed right after her, too, no questions asked."

They both laughed. Not me. I sat there stewing over the fact that Maudie had been seeing Rowan behind my back all these years. Peeved that they seemed so chummy and totally disregarding our tumultuous history together. The history that still stung.

"Hello! *She* is sitting right here." I pinned Rowan with a severe glare. "Don't act like you know me. We haven't seen each other in over six years. We're strangers."

Finally, the table fell silent, only the seagulls and ocean waves filling the void for several heated minutes. I stared at the beads of condensation on my glass, too embarrassed to look up.

Clearing his throat, Rowan leaned forward and drew his wallet out of his back pocket. After slipping a hundred-dollar bill onto the table, he pushed out of his chair and braced the back of mine and leaned close to my face, as if daring me to not meet his light-brown eyes. "Six or sixty . . . it doesn't matter how many years go by. You and I, *a stór*, will never be strangers." He straightened and walked away in that familiar loose-hipped swagger, making it hard for me to look away.

"Mercy. He just let the Irishman out. I ain't hot flashed like this in decades."

I turned my glare toward Maudie. "You mind explaining to me why you're having frequent lunches with my ex?"

She swiped the drink menu and used it as a fan. "He's your ex. Not mine."

Something had niggled in the back of my mind since sitting down at this traitorous table and it suddenly clarified. Gasping, I jabbed a finger toward my blushing grandmother. "You knew!"

The fan stilled for a moment in her hand, but instead of owning up, she went right back to fanning herself.

"You knew he'd be on the restoration project." I slumped in my chair and squinted at the waves rolling in just beyond the patio railing. "All this time and you didn't think to clue me in on it."

"You would have backed out like a coward if I had warned you."

Wearing my indignation like a cloak of self-righteousness, I shoved away from the table. "Wow, betrayal *and* name-calling. I feel so special."

Maudie rolled her eyes and stood. "Don't be so dramatic. You are special. And that man hasn't forgotten it."

I halted. "What's that supposed to mean?"

She hooked her arm in mine and gestured for me to move. "It means what it means."

Tension followed us out of the restaurant and kept tailing us all the way back to Maudie's shop. Once we were inside, she asked, "You ready to make those coat hooks?"

Too mad and too confused, I didn't even want to talk to her about the display case but I was already here. Besides that, life had taught me the harsh lesson that another breath was never a guarantee. I didn't too much like my grandmother at the moment for keeping what she'd kept from me, but no way would I squander sharing this experience with her. "Yes, ma'am. I have another project I'd like for us to work on." I told her about the bank bag discovery.

Maudie clucked her tongue. "Well, that beats all. They never found out who the bank robber was, right?"

I shook my head and widened my eyes. "Nope. We found it in the wall of the old fabric store so maybe it was the seamstress."

Tittering, she held the burlap at eye level and inspected it closely. "What's your plan for this?"

"I'd like to make a display case. I have some wood I held onto from the bank demo. Think it'd be neat to use that." Every piece of story we unearthed during the project would be put on display in some sort of manner, no matter how small the discovery. I liked the idea of preserving as much of the original town's history as possible. "I'm going to ask Des to have a placard made for it."

"Where's the material?"

"Back of my truck. I brought a piece of plexiglass too."

"Then let's get to work."

We quickly set up shop and got to work, taking measurements and sketching out the design. I easily fell into the rhythm with Maudie that we'd established years ago.

I handed her a board. "You knew I'd find out about Rowan today."

"Yep." She slid the board into place and secured it with a few nails. "You've been out there in that ghost town for almost four months, and you ain't done a thing to fix things with that boy."

I set the measuring tape down with more force than necessary. "There's nothing to fix. We've both moved on."

"That's a crock of malarkey." Maudie gestured at the board in front of me, so I picked up the tape and measured out fourteen inches. "He doesn't want you to know this, but that first year after the divorce was rough on him."

I snorted, marking a line and then shoving the pencil behind my ear. "Like it wasn't rough on me."

"Of course it was rough on you. I just want you to know he didn't handle it well either." Maudie moved the nail gun aside and reached for my hand. "Talulla and Connor ended up having to place him in a facility for close to a month when he . . ." Her bottom lip quivered.

"When he what?" The words came out just over a husky whisper as I held her watery gaze.

"Rowdy took a bottle of sleeping pills."

I gasped, and the board in my free hand clattered to the cement floor.

"Fortunately, his parents popped in for a surprise visit and he confessed to what he'd done. They rushed him to the ER to get his stomach pumped."

"Why would he do something so . . ." I shook my head, knowing good and well I had thought about doing the same thing more than once.

"I visited him while he was getting treatment, and after he got out, he began visiting me. Don't be mad at me for that." She squeezed my hand and let go.

All at once, fatigue crept over me like a thick shadow. I bent down and picked up the board, moving over to the chop saw to cut it. As the shiny blade sliced the wood in half with ease, I wished there was a tool that could cut away the painful parts of my life's story just as easily. How freeing that would be.

Maudie had always been keen on reading a room, so after she dropped that devastating bomb on me, she gave me some space to process it. We worked mostly in quiet, only talking about the display case and the coat hooks we were making from all of the old doorknobs I had collected throughout the town.

Still numb from what my grandmother had shared about Rowan, I managed to finish the display case just after sunset and head back to my ghost town.

My phone chimed as I parked, but I left it be until placing the display case inside the saloon for safekeeping. I dug the phone out my pocket and read the message from Rowan. **Fed Preacher already.** I stared at the text, wanting to apologize for being sassy at lunch and for everything else I had done to hurt him over the years. Instead, I chickened out and simply replied with **Thanks.**

I checked the saloon but Preacher wasn't there, so I made my way toward the chapel to check on him. I came to a halt in the chapel's front yard when I heard voices coming from inside. I stood by the marquee and listened while rereading my pun. Smirking at the sign, I decided I was just hearing things, but then I heard it again.

I crept up to the door and eased it open, thanking myself for oiling the hinges just this week. Poking my head through the small opening, I peered inside and could hardly believe my eyes.

My grandmother liked to call me *knowsy*, because I liked being in on the know, not left in the dark. Too much in life had to be left up to chance. Why on earth would someone find pleasure in throwing their cards in the wind and just letting them fall wherever? Not me. No sirree!

Perturbed at being left in the dark on this one, I held my breath and leaned past the door opening to get a better look. I knew what I saw, but I still could hardly believe it. Up front, Bash sat on the altar with Preacher by his side. The dog seemed perfectly content while the teenager carried on a lively conversation with him.

"Dude, it was hidden right there in the wall!" With a plastic spoon, Bash smeared peanut butter on a saltine and offered it to the dog. Preacher sniffed the cracker suspiciously before accepting it. "I wonder what all else is hiding in this town?"

A teenage boy, so it seems.

Shaking my head, I watched in amazement. This same kid who had barely spoken since joining my crew almost two months ago was now talking a mile a minute . . . to a dog. Bash hadn't even acted like he cared earlier when we were all checking out the bank bag.

"The only thing inside was a can of gross sardines. One of the guys dared another to eat the sardines, but Avalee threatened to fire anyone who tried opening that can." Bash huffed a chuckle before popping a cracker into his mouth. He fed Preacher another. "I think Avalee is going to display the bag in the firehouse with the newspaper article about the bank robbery. Man, that's something." As he rolled out a sleeping bag, he told Preacher the entire history of the bank robbery, surprising me once again that he'd paid such close attention.

The realization of what was going on here suddenly punched me in the stomach. Was Bash living in the church with Preacher? Surely not . . . Maybe he decided to spend the night since we had an early start in the morning . . . My instinct said otherwise though, so I took a step inside but hesitated. Bash was so skittish. What would happen if I confronted him? He'd probably take off and something told me that wouldn't be a good idea.

Thinking better of it, I slipped back outside. This day had done nothing but deliver secrets I wasn't prepared to face.

CHAPTER 13

MAY

My grandmother liked to quote Proverbs 18:2 to me any time I mouthed off about something I didn't know much about. *Fools have no interest in understanding; they only want to air their own opinions.* Did I have some opinions on Bash and him staying in the chapel? Sure, but I didn't know enough about his situation to act on anything.

Yawning, I flipped the wall calendar beside my fridge to the new month before grabbing a bottle of water. I'd forgotten to flip it this morning, too groggy to do anything but prepare coffee. As if I needed another reason to stay up at night, Bash being homeless now joined the lineup. I'd tried talking to him over the past couple days, fishing for information during the workday, but that kid kept his cards close to his chest.

I glanced at the digital clock on the stove. A quarter till ten, close to being too late for phone calls but I had to talk to someone about Bash. I set the water on the counter and grabbed my phone. I pulled up Rowan's contact, trying not to dwell on why I chose him over Maudie or Desmond.

He answered on the first ring. "To what do I owe the pleasure of this call, ma'am?"

"Hi. I umm . . . I think we might have an issue." I started to bite my thumbnail but stopped before chipping my nail polish.

"What kind of issue?" His playful tone vanished.

Sighing, I plopped down on the sofa and told him about finding Bash in the chapel with Preacher. "He's been there for the last three nights." I had taken up sneaking around like one of the town's ghosts, checking each night and finding Bash stretched out on his sleeping bag.

After a hefty pause, Rowan released his own sigh. "I knew something was up with that kid. What are we going to do?"

"I'm not sure if we should do anything just yet. Clearly, he's going through something. Can't we just keep it to ourselves for now?"

"How old did you say he was?"

"Nineteen, so he's a legal adult."

"A legal adult who's trespassing."

"I know he's here and I'm not opposing it, so it's not trespassing." I stared at the design on the greenish-blue wallpaper, similar to the original floral print but a bit more modern. "I say we let things lie for now."

"But he could be trouble."

I picked at the frayed hem of my oversize T-shirt and noticed a strip of skin beside my knee that I missed shaving. "Preacher approves. Dogs have a sixth sense about a person's character, right?"

"I don't know . . . Preacher might be in on it. Could be a setup to rob you!"

Rolling my eyes, I pulled the hem of my shirt down until it covered my knees. "Good grief, what's he gonna steal? Paint and flooring?"

"I wouldn't put it past him. People are desperate nowadays."

"The only thing this guy is desperate for is to just have a place to be and I see no reason why we can't give that to him for the time being."

Rowan grumbled underneath his breath. "Fine . . . for now."

That sounded a lot like the conclusion to so many of our arguments in the past. Just brush it to the side with no resolution. *Some things never change, apparently.*

Annoyed, I ended the call and headed to bed, knowing good and well no sleep would find me.

I walked into the silo the next morning and found Bash setting up to sand the butcher-block countertop. It was getting harder by the day to not say something to him about camping out in the chapel. He appeared clean enough in a rumpled young dude kinda way, but now his slim frame stood out more. I backtracked to the apartment and popped a breakfast sandwich in the air fryer. Thinking better of it, I popped in another. Once the food finished heating, I grabbed a can of Coke and returned to the silo.

"Good morning."

Bash looked up as he attached the Shop-Vac hose to the sander. "Yo."

I held up the paper plate and decided to give fibbing a whirl. "I thought Des would be here but I got his schedule mixed up. Would you eat this breakfast I made him so it won't go to waste?"

Eyeing the bag, Bash swallowed loudly, poor kid, but played it off with a shrug. "I guess."

"Thanks. I hate wasting food." I placed the food and soda on the counter and decided to give him some space so he could eat without an audience. I hitched a thumb over my shoulder. "I'll be working in the old barbershop first thing but will be back this way to help seal the counter in a bit."

Bash dusted his hands off but didn't make a move for the food. "M'kay."

It felt like I was dealing with the skittish dog all over again, making myself appear nonchalant and walking out the door casually.

Good grief. From the guarded look he gave me, I was undoubtedly a horrible actress, but I couldn't turn a blind eye to someone in need.

I joined the small crew in the barbershop to help frame out the wall partition that would separate Diesel Miller's work area from his daughter's beauty salon. "Here's the plan," I said, showing the guys the drawing and measurements on my clipboard. "Dave, if you start cutting the lumber, I'll help Jonny install." I handed him the clipboard and we got started while another subcontractor worked on roughing the plumbing.

As we worked, the guys discussed their plans for Mother's Day. My insides churned and my lips remained pressed firmly shut. I didn't celebrate the holiday and Maudie understood, but I always sent the famous twelve-layer coconut cake from Charleston's Peninsula Grill to celebrate *her*. With cream cheese icing and freshly toasted coconut, Maudie had been in love with the decadent dessert for as long as I could remember, calling it a slice of heaven. To hear her *ooh* and *aah* over it each time I had one delivered to her made the exorbitant price tag worth it. She was worth it. Used to be, I sent Rowan's mom one, too, but that had ended along with everything else in the divorce.

Having heard all I wanted to hear about Mother's Day, I excused myself halfway through the wall build. "Y'all seem to have this under control. I need to get back to the silo."

The Bellamy twins were supposed to finish up the trim work, but they got into poison ivy while hunting for a spot to fish at during their lunch break yesterday. They'd roped Bash into going with them, but he seemed to have dodged the poisonous plant.

"Hey," I yelled, entering the silo.

The high-pitched whining halted as Bash switched the electric sander off and popped the safety glasses on top of his shaggy head. Instead of saying anything, he just looked at me expectantly.

"I'm going to work on the door and window trim."

"M'kay."

I reached out and smoothed my hand over the curved drywall. The warm white color played nicely with the cedarwood and metal accents. "The drywall team are magicians. There aren't any seams. Did you know the name of the paint color is *Vanilla Ice Cream*? How perfect is that?"

He nodded his head, but I wanted actual words to come out of his locked mouth.

Giving it one last shot, I glanced up at the domed metal ceiling with the industrial-sized fan. "What do you think about this place?"

Bash shrugged, his focus on the retro soda machine still wrapped in plastic, then moving to the ice cream case we dressed with some pieces of weathered corrugated tin. "It's my favorite, besides the chapel."

My chest tightened and it almost slipped out of my mouth to ask him about staying in the chapel, but somehow I managed to keep it in. "This town is starting to feel like home to me." When all I got was another head nod, I gave up and pulled out my measuring tape.

Bash slid the glasses back on and continued sanding the L-shaped counter. I noticed he was meticulous with his work, stopping every so often to run his hand over the grain to check for smoothness. It reminded me of Rowan back in the day when we helped Maudie in her workshop. Refocusing, I marked the piece of trim for the door and stepped outside to cut it.

Lunch rolled around and I stopped Bash before he snuck off to the chapel. "I have a few things I'd like to discuss. How 'bout joining me at the pecan warehouse for lunch?"

His eyes darted in the direction of the chapel, as if contemplating making a run for it, but he nodded his head once and followed me instead.

After warming two containers, I wove around the tables and sat across from Bash. He only had a pack of Nabs and a Sprite in front of him, not nearly enough sustenance for a growing teenage boy. "I made Des lunch too. Now I'm stuck with extras again." I opened the lid to one, the aroma of garlic and herbs escaping. "Spaghetti and homemade meatballs. It's my specialty . . . Well, it's my grandmother's specialty. She makes these huge batches of meatballs once in a while and stocks my freezer with them. The sauce is mine though . . . Well, it's jarred Rao's, which is real fancy marinara, but I added some Italian seasoning."

With a hand wrapped around the can of soda, Bash just stared.

Good grief. I sounded like an Italian cuisine salesperson. When all else fails, Maudie always said to go for guilt-tripping, so I gave that another shot since it worked at breakfast. I slid the container over. "I don't want to waste it, since my grandmother worked so hard to make the meatballs. She'd be so bummed if she found out. You mind helping me out? You're welcome to have it."

Bash finally took it, but gave me a squinty look, making it clear he was on to me. I'd have to figure out how to be more sneaky. And I'd also have to buy more food, because the "extra" container of spaghetti I gave him at lunch was supposed to be my supper.

He tore into it and didn't come up for air until polishing off over half of the meal. He took a sip of soda and I know I heard him sigh, which pinched my heart.

"I'm finished with the sanding. What do you need me to do this afternoon?" He shoveled in another mouthful, slurping up spaghetti noodles with gusto.

I got my protective hen emotions in check and answered. "We don't want to stir up any dust until the sealer is dry. It'll need to dry overnight, so . . ." I flipped through the to-do list in my brain and offered him a napkin. "You ever run a pressure washer?"

Bash wiped his mouth. "No, but I can figure it out."

"I'll show you. We need to get the inn washed up and prepped for the painters." I pulled out my phone and showed him the paint sample for the wood siding. "It's called *Low Tide*. It's a deep coastal blue with hints of green. Des and I both agree it's a perfect pop of color at that end of the street."

Unimpressed, Bash mumbled, "M'kay."

Feeling silly for carrying on about a paint color to a young guy who apparently couldn't care less—or was that just an act?—I put away my phone and shared something I thought he'd appreciate. I dug out a handful of mini candy bars—Reese's Peanut Butter Cups, Snickers, Milky Way, and Three Musketeers—and made a pile between us. I selected my favorite, Three Musketeers, and expected Bash to swipe the Reese's Cups. He chose the Milky Way bars instead. The poor guy was probably burned out on peanut butter.

We cleaned up our lunch mess and I grabbed us both a Gatorade before heading out. We made it just outside before Bash said quietly, "Thanks, Avalee."

His simple thank-you did something to my heart but I didn't want to make it awkward, like hugging him, so I went for nonchalance and said, "No problem."

After we knocked off work for the day, I drove over to Publix to pick up some groceries. Mindfully dodging the Mother's Day gift section, I headed straight for the bakery section and loaded three single-serve containers of chocolate ganache cake into my basket. The hazelnut cake looked pretty good and so I contemplated grabbing one of those too. As I reached for it, a woman walked up to the counter beside me, rubbing a barely-there baby bump.

"I'm picking up an order for Martin," she told the lady behind the counter.

"The gender reveal cake?"

"Yes, ma'am." The pregnant lady grinned, her hand still rubbing her belly.

I wanted to warn her to keep her mouth shut. To yell, *It's too soon!*

The consensus seemed to be on the same page, agreeing to wait until you're past the first trimester to announce a pregnancy. After enduring the first miscarriage, Rowan and I decided to go with that rule of thumb. Nineteen weeks into my second pregnancy, we appeared to be in the clear to let our family in on us having a baby girl we planned on naming Helen, Maudie's middle name. In the midst of ordering a pink cake from the local bakery to share the pregnancy news, I felt an unsettling tug, signaling my body had once again betrayed me.

That time, no one knew. That was supposed to make it easier. Yet, all I felt was a debilitating loneliness. After finally telling my father, he sent Rowan and me on a Caribbean vacation. As if the teal water and fruity drinks could wash away our grief. We pretended it did and I learned a thing or two about pretending during this time too. The truth will sneak up on you eventually and no amount of pretending can fix the damage it causes.

In the middle of the Publix bakery, my truth punched me in the gut, leaving me weak and hardly able to take in a breath. Appetite gone and all signs of gumption disappearing along with it, I placed the entire basket of food into the cake cooler and walked out, a shadow of profound sadness leading the way.

CHAPTER 14

EVERY STATE IN THIS FINE COUNTRY has a little craziness in its history and South Carolina has its fair share. And some of the outdated laws are downright ridiculous. But the craziest part about these laws is that some idiot had to have done the thing for there to even be a law against it. Am I right?

Take for instance, it's against the law to keep a horse in a bathtub. I know it's a horrible thought, but I'd kinda like to see how on earth someone could manage getting a horse in a tub in the first place. Some fool out there managed it at least once for there to be a law forbidding it to happen again.

Another law, nothing can be sold on Sunday except light bulbs. Sure, I get light bulbs, but what about other necessities, such as toilet paper and coffee? For me, those two are much higher on the must-have list than light bulbs.

How about this one—you're not allowed to cuss in public. I don't mind this outdated law. There's enough words in the English language to express yourself without using foul language.

An awful law I'd heard told but one I couldn't find actual proof of being in the books anywhere is that husbands are allowed to beat their wives on the courthouse steps on Sunday and only with a stick. Crazy, right? This one was probably made up by a manipulative husband and other jerks followed suit.

"Isn't it against the law to loiter outside the courthouse?" Des asked as he climbed the steps, making me laugh. "What's so funny?"

I scooted over on the old quilt I'd spread out and motioned for him to join me. "I was just thinking about outdated laws." I told him about the horse law and the one about light bulbs.

Chuckling, he took off his navy fedora and placed it beside him. "You made those up."

"I'm not that creative." I opened the wicker basket and pulled out two wrapped sandwiches, placing one in front of Des and the other in front of me.

"What's on the menu?" He leaned over to rummage around in the basket, his designer watch clinking against the side of it.

"We're celebrating our little town's specialty, pecans." I pointed to his sandwich. "Chicken pecan salad on a croissant, those little jars are spinach salads with candied pecans, and for dessert we have pecan tassies. Nita dropped it all off a little while ago. The sandwiches and salads are from the owner of our new deli, and the pecan tassies are from the bakery owner."

"Ah, you know I love a theme." He unwrapped his food. "But why the courthouse steps?"

"First of all, this is the *town hall* steps, remember?" I handed him a bottle of tea.

"My bad."

"You ever hear about someone getting locked in a department store overnight?"

"Sounds vaguely familiar." He snapped his fingers. "Ooh. That movie *Where the Heart Is*. The pregnant lady got locked in the Walmart."

"I loved that movie. We should see if it's on Netflix and watch it again." I worked the lid off my salad jar. "She had the entire place to herself to do whatever she pleased. We kind of have the same opportunity before the town opens, so I've been coming up with a ghost-town bucket list."

Desmond took a polite bite of his sandwich and chewed thoughtfully while I shoved a loaded forkful of salad into my mouth. "Okay, so picnic on the *town hall* steps. What else?"

I held my fork up, needing a minute to finish chewing. "That's the fun of it. We'll just make it up as we go along."

"So . . . a rock concert in the chapel?" He waggled his eyebrows.

"Nah. Nothing that cheeky, but . . ." I pointed next door at the marquee sign in front of the chapel. Rowan had inspired my bucket list when he gave me the sign letters, but I chose not to share that with Desmond.

"Time flies like a bird. Fruit flies like a banana." He looked confused for a beat and then burst out laughing. "That's so lame, darlin'."

"Expect lame puns on that sign until we pull out of here in September."

"I look forward to it." Desmond toasted my bottle of tea with his.

Working my way through the salad, I gazed down Main Street. "I can't wait to see it all polished up with freshly paved roads, gleaming-white sidewalks, and planter boxes brimming with colorful flowers."

"Me too."

We settled into our meal for a while, enjoying the sunny day and each other's company. Desmond was my friend first and business partner second, so he talked about a date he went on and how it went so well, they'd already lined up another.

"That's great, Des." I pressed my shoulder to his before finishing off my sandwich, which was sweet and savory and fabulous.

"I think you should give dating a go too."

I avoided meeting his eyes. "We already gave that a go. Didn't take, remember?"

"You know what I mean, smart aleck." Desmond pressed my shoulder but with a little more force. "Seems to me your *ex-husband* would like to give it another go with you."

"Des, I'm too busy trying to give this poor town another go to even think about anything else, so please don't keep right on about it." My tone came off a little harsh, shutting the conversation down for an uncomfortable moment before Desmond dismissed it.

"After this is complete, then." He waved a hand and we both looked again down Main Street. A work truck backed into the alley between the diner and the mercantile. "That must be the flooring crew."

"Probably. They're splicing the floorboards in the mercantile with flooring I swiped from the feedstore." I started packing up our picnic. "Speaking of, the floor guy told me they needed more to be able to fix it all, so I need to go grab some."

Desmond gathered our trash. "We still don't have a plan for that building."

I groaned, shooting a look at the brick building with the lopsided sign. *Gibson's Feed and Grain.* "You remember how we felt that one time about that old shoe store over in Clinton?"

"Yeah. It just didn't feel like a good fit for us, so we passed on it." Desmond stood, smoothing his pants legs, and then helped me up.

"That's how I feel about the feedstore."

"I get it, Avalee. I'm at a loss for what to do with it too. And with all the repairs needed, it's going to put a substantial dent in our budget. But we can't remodel an entire town and leave one eyesore."

I blew out a long exhale. "I know. That's why I'm going to make myself spend the rest of the day in there. Gather some more flooring and then start on clearing it out. Maybe whatever it's supposed to be will reveal itself before suppertime."

"Well, good luck. Oh, and don't forget I want the vegetable bins for the mercantile."

"I'll get them moved over there today too."

"I'd join you, but I'm picking up that chaise lounge and wingback chair to have them reupholstered." Desmond put on his hat, adjusting it to just the right angle. "My guy in Charleston can have them done the fastest, so I need to get on the road. Thanks for lunch and"—he flicked his wrist carelessly toward nothing in particular—"for the tantalizing conversation about South Carolina laws."

"You're welcome."

Des strode down the steps and mumbled to himself. "A horse in a tub . . ."

Bash walked out of the chapel as I began down the steps.

"Hey!" I called him over. "My eyes were bigger than my belly. You want the leftovers?" I held the picnic basket a little higher.

Bash shrugged and mumbled, "I guess."

"Thanks." I handed it to him. "I hate wasting food." I didn't want to make it any more awkward than it already was, so I hurried away. "I'll be in the feedstore if you need me."

"M'kay."

Inside the mildewed feedstore, I donned my gloves and surveyed the section of missing floor and the warped cabinets lining the right wall. The air seemed still and too quiet, but that was always the case when I came into this store. Something just never settled right with me about it. Probably because I couldn't figure out for the life of me what we needed to do with it.

First order of business was the flooring, so I hopped over the missing section to reach the good pieces the rain hadn't ruined. Two boards in, something shiny in the dirt below caught on a ray of sunshine coming through the hole in the roof. There was only about two feet from the floor to the ground, so I crouched down and plucked the bracelet easily enough from the dirt.

"Finally, a real treasure." I wiped it on my pants, then held it in the stream of light to get a better look. Rubies set in antique gold. As I looked it over, one of the stones popped out. "Or not . . ." Straightening, I shoved it in my pocket anyway and went back to removing floorboards until I had my little rolling cart stacked with ten more pieces.

After taking the flooring over to the mercantile, I loaded the vegetable bins on the cart and moved them out as well. Even with that complete, it didn't look like I'd made any progress, and no sudden clue had fallen out of a hiding place to tell me what this building needed to become.

Growing agitated, I wiped the sweat from my brow and scanned the ramshackle room. A broken chair overturned, a stack of mildewed grain sacks, dusty jars with *Poison* written on the labels, rat droppings . . . "This place would make a perfect haunted house." I sighed. "Too bad we don't need one."

My phone buzzed with an incoming text. I took off my gloves and read it.

Rowan. **Had to check on another project. Be back in town tonight.**

I replied with a thumbs-up and stared at the screen for a few beats, almost texting him about the fake treasure I'd found. But that would be something I'd send a friend, not an ex-husband. A thought whispered, *But he used to be your best friend*. I whispered back, "Used to! Not anymore!" Between that thought and this gloomy building, loneliness crept over me. Pocketing my phone, I did the only thing that got my mind off such, focusing on work.

Hours passed with me sorting through each drawer and cabinet. The findings were what I expected, damp-then-dried packets of seeds, a few gardening tools, a mildewed Farmers' Almanac dated 1913. Too bad the almanac was in such poor condition or it would have been a collector's item. I tossed the unsalvageable articles in the dumpster out back and made a pile of things that could be saved.

Midway through the second set of cabinets, I reached inside a bottom cabinet and came out with a child's canvas shoe. It matched the one I'd found weeks ago. Shaking my head at the oddity of items we kept finding in this town, I placed it beside its companion on top of the counter. Perhaps I'd find a story to go with the shoes and we could display them somewhere. Crouching down, I stretched my arm into the dark recesses to see what else I could find.

"Please don't be any critters hiding in here," I whispered, while craning my neck out the way and reaching blindly into the dark space. A crinkling sound met my touch as I tapped against some type of plastic. I all but crawled inside the cabinet to get a good grip on it and began tugging. It wasn't heavy but a bit unyielding. I gave it a good yank, finally dislodging what turned out to be a black garbage bag. Whatever was inside the bag clanked around, sounding like sticks.

"Why on earth would someone put a bag of yard debris in here?" I muttered to myself while untying the top of the bag, releasing a musty odor. At first glance, it appeared to be a bunch of sticks like I—

"What the—?"

The bag shifted and revealed something round among the debris.

"No . . ."

The room began to spin as a deafening ring started up in my ears. Dropping the bag with the contents spilling onto the floor, I fell on my backside and crab-crawled away from it until my back met the wall. Stomach churning, I tried to comprehend the sight before me, but it made no sense.

Bones, brown and brittle.

A small skull.

It can't be. Squeezing my eyes shut, I took a stuttered breath and looked again, but the horrific discovery still remained spilled all over the warped floor.

An eruption of sweat broke out over my chilled skin and a spasm shot through my midsection. Clamping my hand over my mouth, I dry-heaved, barely keeping the contents of my stomach down.

Gulping for air, I fumbled for my phone and dialed 911.

CHAPTER 15

IN A CACOPHONY OF SIRENS AND LAW ENFORCEMENT AGENCIES, my quiet little ghost town came to life in absolute chaos. Everything and everyone moved too quickly for me to process, as if each blink of my eye missed minutes instead of seconds. The sensation reminded me of waking up from anesthesia—confused, lethargic, unable to hold steady to my surroundings.

The authorities were quick to shut all work down and evacuate the workers except for me, leaving me alone in this nightmare. Even though I sat on the ground in front of the feedstore while two officers rolled out yellow crime scene tape around the building, my mind was still inside with the skeletal remains of a small human.

Listening to the crackling voices talking in code over radios, I tried to make myself stand up but my weak legs wouldn't cooperate. Shaking my head, I tightened my arms around my knees, still unable to fathom what I just discovered. No wonder that place had felt so strange every time I entered it.

A guy wearing one of those white hazmat suits exited the feedstore, carrying a small black body bag that appeared almost empty. That in and of itself had to be a crime, a life reduced to nearly nothing. Looking away, I bit back a whimper.

The uniformed officers parted for a man in plain clothes. He walked over and flashed a badge, his gun holster visible underneath his jacket. "Detective Wolf. Mind if I ask you a few questions, ma'am?" Ironically, he had a wolfish look about him, but not in a bad way. Jet-black hair, slightly darker than mine, and thick eyebrows furrowed over clear blue eyes, the man appeared intense. Predatorial. Dominant. Good characteristics for a detective, I supposed.

I licked my lips, the texture rough as sandpaper from me chewing on them for the last hour or so. "Okay."

Wolf crouched down in front of me. "I know you've been stuck out here alone for quite a while, so I promise to make this fast and after that you'll be free to go. Okay?"

I nodded, running my hands up and down my arms.

"You're shaking." Wolf stood and disappeared from my view, returning moments later with a jacket. He settled it over my shoulders and helped me to my feet. "I was told you live in the saloon on the corner. Would it be all right if we talk there?"

I nodded again and began stiffly walking that way, with the detective keeping a firm grasp on my elbow. We sat at the conference table on the main level and I gave my statement for what felt like the hundredth time, then answered his questions, while Preacher sat dutifully by my side. With trembling fingers, I petted him while stuttering through the interview. Afterwards, Wolf walked me to my apartment, his hand on my elbow to keep me steady.

"Please let your crew members know they're not allowed back on site until we clear the entire town." The detective handed me a card. "I'll be in touch tomorrow, but feel free to call if you think of anything else before then."

"Okay. Thanks." Unable to produce a smile or farewell, I shut the door and leaned on it for a few measured breaths. I wasn't sure of the time, although the darkening sky was a good indicator. My stomach growled, but I would take the achy emptiness over more nausea. I tried collecting my thoughts enough to figure out what to do next. Calls had to be made, plans for the next few days needed ironing out, material orders would have to be put on hold. But I decided washing off the grime and distress of the day took precedence.

I shuffled to the bathroom, my legs oddly heavy, and turned the shower on. Shucking my clothes, I stepped under the hot spray of water and closed my eyes, but all I could see were those tiny bones and the blue canvas shoes. The crumpled plaid fabric that had once been the child's shirt. Snapping my eyes open, I made quick work of lathering and rinsing.

In zombie mode, I dried off and put on an oversize T-shirt and baggy pajama pants before making my way to the couch and plopping down. Staring at my phone, I truly hated to do what I was about to do over a text message, but there was no way I'd be able to talk, so I sent out a giant group text to all the crew leaders, Jonas, Desmond, and Nita.

Before I could close out the screen, messages began pouring in. I tossed the phone beside me and it slipped between the cushions. Instead of retrieving it, I rested my head on the back of the couch. The shock and adrenaline was starting to wear off, leaving me weighted with fatigue. Even checking my phone would have taken too much energy, energy I didn't have, so I just sat there and listened to the continuous calls and texts coming in.

My mind raced a hundred miles an hour, as if a reel of today's events played in a high-speed loop. The trembling returned and I managed to pull the throw blanket off the armrest and unfold it over me. Sometime in the midst of this out-of-body state, I noticed my cheeks were damp with tears. My physical being seemed to be finally catching up to my emotional distress as I began mourning for that poor child. This wasn't a personal loss, but I felt it all the same. Somewhere, sometime, there had been a family out there, going out of their mind, not knowing what happened to this child.

The high-speed loop transitioned from brittle bones to the black body bag being carried out the feedstore, then to the what-if scenarios that could have landed the child there in the first place. From the pieces of clothing found and the snippets I overheard from the authorities, the remains appeared to be a boy, and I could picture him just like I could picture my own lost children. Carefree, playing and laughing. I wondered if the child's life had been happy until it had been stolen. Or had death been merciful, ending his suffering?

Later in the night, loud stomps echoed in the hallway right before my front door crashed open. Rowan came storming in, reminding me of the Incredible Hulk he liked watching as a kid.

"You forget how to knock?" Irritated at myself for forgetting to lock the door, I slumped further on the couch and pulled the blanket higher to help conceal my face from him.

Suddenly the blanket was yanked from my grasp and Rowan stood before me in a fitted T-shirt and gray sweatpants, looking ready for bed. "I just heard." He knelt and placed his hands on my knees. "Talk to me, Avalee."

A wave of déjà vu rolled over me. We'd already lived this, him kneeling before me, saying those exact words, the day I lost our first child.

I closed my eyes for the sake of my sanity. It would have been so darn easy to fall and let him catch me, but I held the rickety shield of self-preservation in place as best as I could. "It's fine," I said through gritted teeth.

"No it's not. You just found the remains of a *child*. Please talk to me." He touched my chin and tilted my face toward him. I'm sure the sight of my swollen eyes and cheeks damp with tears said much more than any phrase would.

Yanking out of his grip, I glared at him, but my bottom lip trembled, ruining the desired effect. "I said it's fine."

"Fine." Rowan huffed and shook his head. He rose to his feet and then plopped down beside me. "That one word was our downfall."

"Our downfall?"

"Yeah. We tried covering every hurtful thing we went through with that dang word." He held up the back of his left hand and wiggled the ring finger that used to be wrapped in a plain gold band I gave him on our wedding day. "Look what that dumb word cost us."

"A finger? It cost us a finger?"

Rowan dropped his hand and met my glare with one of his own. "Ah, sarcastic humor. Partner to the word *fine*. Just hide our problems within the syllables of jokes. Works every time."

I shoved my hair out of my face. "You can go. Seriously. I'm fine." I cringed, realizing the word had slipped out again.

Sitting in silence, we stared straight ahead for a heated spell. Out the corner of my eye, I saw him toe off his shoes, indicating he had no plans on leaving me anytime soon. Then he reached over and adjusted my blanket, gently tucking it around me, as if I were fragile. How long had it been since someone took care of me in such a way? A stinging started in my nose and bloomed to my eyes and throat. I sniffed and blinked, but it was no use.

Angling toward me, Rowan sighed. "You're not fine, *a stór*." He cupped the back of my neck; his thumb stroked my skin, the touch tender, caring. The heat of his hand and the empathy in his warm brown eyes softened my resolve and released a new batch of tears. "Please. Talk to me."

I finally found words even though they were awfully raspy. "Based on the clothing, they believe the remains are of a boy . . ." My chest caved as a sob hiccuped to freedom. "I found him in a garbage bag . . . How could anyone just throw away a chi—" Voice giving out as the day's devastating events crashed into me again, I fell against Rowan and let him hold me.

Allowing a stranger this close shouldn't have felt so right. But then again, how could this man ever be considered an actual stranger?

What had he said that day in Beaufort? *Six or sixty . . . it doesn't matter how many years go by. You and I, a stór, will never be strangers.*

Too many intimate details connected me to him in a way that

141

made it impossible for Rowan Murray to ever be classified as a stranger. I knew about that birthmark in the shape of a clover on his inner thigh and how he was ridiculously sensitive to the touch in that exact same spot. I knew how he would run his fingertips along my forearm when he was deep in thought. And how, when he was quite tired, he'd always hum this Gaelic song his Scottish grandfather had taught him, a lullaby he gifted to himself. A lullaby I had always counted on him humming to our children one day. I knew about the romantic gesture of his Scottish grandfather leaving his beloved country for his Irish wife, a fact that Rowan was so proud of, always stating that the power of true love could never be held back by any sort of family tradition or rules. I understood the depth of his family roots and how important they were to him. I also knew how I severed the root system the day I demanded he walk away.

No matter how much this all played through my overly emotional mind, I still clung to him like I had a right. I didn't, but I did it anyway. He had offered his shoulder, after all.

My sobs eventually weakened into just whimpers, leaving my throat raw and my eyes uncomfortably swollen.

Rowan brushed the damp hair out of my face. "Have the investigators told you anything?"

"The entire town has to be searched, so they've shut us down for at least the next three days. Longer if need be." I sounded like I had a terrible cold, nasally and hoarse.

"They think that's really necessary?"

"Apparently. I have to keep Preacher here with me while cadaver dogs are brought in. He's downstairs in the saloon." Sometime in the middle of the chaos hours earlier I'd found enough wits about me to bring the dog in.

"Dang . . . That's . . ." Rowan shook his head. "What about Bash?"

"Oh shoot." I sat up, finally making myself retreat a little from Rowan's side. "I forgot about him. When they evacuated the town, he took off too. But he doesn't know we're shut down for the rest of the week." A headache pounded behind my eyes. I rubbed them with the heel of my hands. "I'll be sure to go over to the pecan warehouse first thing in the morning. He's always there around six thirty."

"I'm not all that comfortable with you out here alone right now."

Back stiffening, I dropped my hands. "I'm a grown woman and—"

"I know, but listen . . ." Rowan brushed his fingertips along my forearm just like he used to. I should have made him stop, but I didn't. "We could use that as an angle and ask Bash to camp out in the saloon until all's clear."

"Humph. That's not a bad idea, but there's actually another apartment besides mine." I pointed over my shoulder. "It just needs furniture."

"We can work with that."

I started to point out that this was a *me* problem and not a *we*, but I didn't want to be alone in this. "Okay."

Rowan began combing his fingers through my hair and slowly my head reclined, landing on his shoulder once more. His touch comforted me, and I wished the comfort alone was enough to make everything right. Too bad I knew it wasn't.

CHAPTER 16

MY CHILDHOOD YEARS NEVER HELD ANY NIGHTMARES. My dad, as neglectful as he could be, seemed to be aware of making sure of it. We
had a nighttime ritual when he was in town, and when he wasn't,
Dad made sure Maudie kept the ritual. He always took the time
to read me a book before bed. *The Giving Tree* by Shel Silverstein
will forever be one of my favorites and I've aspired to be that tree
ever since kindergarten, but with a side of feistiness . . . I've thought
many times how perhaps those books and our nightly prayers had
kept the bad dreams away. The sweet dreams disappeared altogether
after I lived through some pretty intense real-life nightmares,
though.

Last night had offered up a tailspin of nightmares, flashes of
skeletons and torment, with very little rest. That's why I couldn't pry
myself out of bed when a new morning slowly began to announce
its arrival, the sky transitioning from dark to gray to pinks just outside my window. Even though I was wide awake, I chose to remain
cocooned under my blanket, as if that would stop the new day from

showing up. It worked for all of ten more minutes until sounds of vehicles pulling in finally forced me out of bed.

Whatever was waiting for me wouldn't wait long, so I made quick work of getting ready for whatever that might be. Trying not to wake Desmond, who was softly snoring in his room, I quietly dressed in worn jeans and a Lowcountry Lost T-shirt. I brushed my teeth and ran a wide-tooth comb through my hair. I didn't have to lean close to the bathroom mirror to see the dark smudges underneath my eyes, but no amount of concealer was going to fix it. This was as good as it was going to get. Shaking my head at my reflection, I decided to leave my coffee fix for later and slip downstairs to check on Preacher.

He stood on his hind legs with his nose pressed against the front window.

"Whatcha see, boy?" I joined him by the window, giving his head a lazy pat while peering out. Three vehicles were backed on the curb. Two patrol cars and one van. Several officers loitered while one uniformed dude unloaded two dogs from the rear of the white van.

Preacher whimpered, his ears perking up.

"Those are working dogs. Not playdates." I patted his head, feeling a bit sorry for the scraggly animal. "Poor baby. I know you're not used to being cooped up. Hopefully, this will be over soon." I moved my attention back to the scene outside and caught sight of a tall, lanky figure emerging from the pecan grove. Bash kept his head down and vanished inside the pecan warehouse in a flash.

"Be a good boy. I'll be back soon." I hurried out the door. Securing it closed behind me so he couldn't get out, I darted over to the warehouse and found Bash in the kitchen plundering through the fridge. "Hey. I have some bad news and I also need a favor."

Bash straightened and closed the fridge door. "What's up?"

"You know what went down yesterday." I paused, hoping I didn't have to go into detail. I shouldn't have bothered worrying with this one; he simply nodded. "Because of that we'll be shut down for a few days while the authorities investigate, so no work today. And no one is allowed in town without permission." I eyed him closely to catch his reaction, but this kid was a pro. He only shrugged like being without a place to squat didn't faze him.

"M'kay."

I wondered if giving Bash a little shake would loosen some words out of him, but refrained. I hoped at some point he'd feel comfortable enough to open up to me. "Not sure what you got going on in the next few days, but I could use some help if you're not too busy?"

Again, he played it off with nonchalance and a bored frown. "Yeah? Like what?"

"I need to keep Preacher out of the investigators' hair. Could you help me with that? We have to keep him inside the saloon since the rest of the town is off-limits."

Bash chewed on his bottom lip, looking uncertain.

"It would really help me out," I interjected quickly. "Detective Wolf said something about needing me to be available to them, so I can't watch the dog and do that. And I can't chance Preacher getting in their way." I pressed my palms together. "Please."

Bash hitched a bony shoulder, seemingly unmoved by my lackluster acting job. "I guess."

"Cool. Great. *Fantastic.* Truly, a weight off my shoulders." I nodded a little too enthusiastically, but the teen, God bless him, didn't call me out on it.

"M'kay."

M'kay. I didn't know much about Bash but at least I knew his favorite phrase, one of indifference, one to shut something down before it picked up speed. Something about that word contraction made me sad, especially for Bash, who seemed to rely on it way too much.

Moving on before I got choked up, I said, "We have a few bed frames in the shipping container beside the clock tower. I'll need you to help me carry one up here to the apartment beside mine. Y'all should be fine in there until—"

"Nah. I'll just stay downstairs with him. I have a sleeping bag."

"But—"

"I'm cool with it." Bash moved past me like it was a done deal, but I wasn't ready to call it.

"Bash, really . . . I don't mind. I already had two sets of mattresses delivered next door. It'll take no time to set up a room." I tried again to reason with him while trailing him outside.

Before I made any leeway about him staying upstairs, the detective walked over, dressed similar to yesterday. White button-down and dark jeans, his shiny badge clipped to his belt with the gun holster strapped around his broad shoulders. The armor of intimidation, I decided to call it. Given the way Bash took a decisive step behind me, he felt the same way.

"Good morning, Miss Elvis." Wolf tipped his head in a way that conveyed Southern gentleman with a side of tough guy, even though there was no twang to his accent. Definitely a transplant, probably from some big Northern city. I was too freaked out yesterday to notice.

"Call me Avalee, please." I hoped I conveyed strong Southern woman with a side of sweet gal.

"Avalee," Wolf amended. "I hate to be the rule police, but we can't have anyone wandering around until the crime scene . . . the entire town, for that matter, is cleared." His stony gaze lasered in Bash's direction.

"No. I get it." I motioned behind me and took a step to the side. "This is Sebastian, by the way, and he's going to help me keep my dog out of your hair. They're going to stay in the saloon."

The detective sized Bash up. "That should be all right."

He escorted us to the saloon, making it clear he meant business. I refrained from rolling my eyes at his John Wayne attitude.

Once Bash was inside with Preacher, Wolf and I stood outside underneath the saloon's black awning, and he explained what the authorities would be doing today. "Each building will be searched and then a sweep of the surrounding woods will be done. The forensic team will be testing for trace evidence, starting in the feedstore, but we may need to search your residence also."

As Wolf talked, it all hit me once again and flashes of that tiny skull rolling to one side in that wrinkled garbage bag popped in my head. Suddenly dizzy, I swayed like a tree being pushed by a gust of wind.

Wolf firmly placed his hand on my shoulder. "Avalee?"

"Sorry," I whispered, sounding like I had gravel in my throat. "It's just a lot to wrap my head around. It still feels like a really bad nightmare."

Wolf squeezed my shoulder. "That's totally understandable."

I took several deep breaths in an attempt to clear the floaters from my vision. The detective's firm grip didn't waver and for that I was thankful, because without that grip I'm fairly certain I would have folded to the ground like a limp noodle.

After several slow inhales and exhales, the ringing in my ears lowered in volume and I could hear a truck approaching. I turned to see a familiar black truck park along the street and suddenly had the urge to run to Rowan and hide in his cloak of comfort. Somehow I controlled those urges and stayed put.

Rowan emerged from the truck with a tray of coffees and a box of donuts. A deep frown darkened his face as he zeroed in on the detective's hand on my shoulder.

I stepped toward Rowan and Wolf's hand fell away. "Those still warm?"

"Yeah." Rowan finally met my gaze. "The *Hot* sign was on . . ." He tilted his head. "You okay?"

"Just a little shaken up from all this." I motioned toward the state vehicles lining most of Main Street. My lips began to wobble.

Rowan stepped closer. "Dang it, I shouldn't have left you alone last night."

"Des showed up after you left. I wasn't alone." I pointed to the second-floor window. "He's still sleeping."

Wolf cleared his throat.

I straightened, trying and failing to put some steel in my backbone. "Detective Wolf, this is Rowan Murray, one of the structural engineers working on the town."

"Sir, no work is allowed until—"

"I know," Rowan said firmly, cutting the detective off. "I just wanted to check on my wife and bring her some breakfast."

"*Ex*-wife," I corrected, but neither seemed to be listening to me. They were too busy giving each other a stare down.

Rowan finally turned his attention to me and held the tray of coffee out. "Bash turn up?"

I helped myself to the one marked caramel latte. "Yeah. He's inside the saloon with Preacher."

Wolf cleared his throat again. "Mr. Murray, I need to speak with *Miss* Elvis about the investigation, if you don't mind. You need to leave the property until further notice."

Rowan gave the detective a pretty intense glare, icy enough to chill the box of warm donuts in his hand. "I can stay if you want me to, Avalee."

I kept an eye roll in check. Rowan had some gall acting like he had any authority over law enforcement. I shook my head instead. "I'm fine."

"Ah, our favorite word . . . *Fine*." Rowan winked at me, then jerked his chin in Wolf's direction, full of attitude, and stepped inside the saloon. Moments later, he came out empty-handed. "I'll be close by. Call me if you need anything." He gave me a hug, catching me off guard, and left without acknowledging the detective.

Good grief. I thought Rowan did away with his alpha-male attitude. Apparently, that stinker had just been carefully tucked away until now.

"Your friend upstairs will need to leave as well," Wolf spoke, drawing my attention to him.

"I'll let him know once he wakes up. What's the plan here?"

"We are going to barricade the main road. As I'm sure you're aware, the news outlets are getting wind of this and are already circling like vultures."

I rotated my neck and shoulders, knowing good and well we had a mess on our hands that extended past the tragedy of a lost life, hard as that might sound.

"I guess that's to be expected." I took a sip of coffee, barely tasting it. "I'll be in the saloon if you need anything."

"Sounds good."

We parted ways and I went inside. Bash was on the floor playing tug-of-war with Preacher. They both had one end of a brightly colored doggy rope, going to town. Face lit with amusement, Bash cackled like a little kid, but as soon as he spotted me, he turned it off and went back to indifferent teenager.

I pointed to the back hall leading to the stairs. "I'm going to get some paperwork done. Y'all have the donuts and there's drinks and snacks in the fridge under the bar, but come upstairs for lunch."

Bash sat on his haunches, holding on to the rope as Preacher continued tugging. "M'kay."

As soon as I made it halfway up the stairs, I heard Bash bellow out in laughter again, the punk.

CHAPTER 17

BEFORE AND AFTER IS THE NAME OF THE GAME when it comes to remodeling. The transformative power of "before" photos of outdated, lackluster spaces, positioned beside freshly updated ones, was Lowcountry Lost's specialty. But a week ago marked a different type of before and after. Before I discovered the remains of that child, our town was a fairly quiet one. After, it exploded into an uproar. Before, we'd only managed to stir minimal interest in the revitalization project. After, people were coming out of the woodwork, wanting to claim a piece of Somewhere, South Carolina. After the authorities gave permission, I naively thought we'd return to work and keep moving forward like we had been before. Instead, the town had become a circus, with the feedstore as the sideshow attraction.

So many news outlets, so many sources wanting the inside scoop. I gave several interviews at Jonas's and the investors' insistence. They brought in a PR team, who spun it into making me look like a hero for finding the child, saying Lowcountry Lost was known for restoring that which had been lost. I didn't want this tragedy to be used to promote the revitalization initiative, but it happened anyway. All of the apartments were now under contract after what felt like overnight. A well-known bank chain in South Carolina purchased the little bank on the corner of Main and Meeting Street. The boutique and deli on each side of the former feedstore were also under contract. The illionaires couldn't have been more tickled. I guess I should have felt the same way, but I didn't.

Offers poured in for the feedstore, too, but I put my foot down on that. No way could I live with myself if anyone came in and made a profit off the loss of a life. Even though the feedstore wasn't for sale, it didn't stop a steady stream of trespassers from sneaking into town to get a peek at it. We'd posted *No Trespassing* signs, but they were all but ignored. Because of this, I had a new problem keeping me up at night. Being the sole resident of Somewhere meant I was also the sole member of the neighborhood watch, running off intruders all hours of the night and having to catch power naps on my lunch break during the day.

A nice breeze swept softly through the truck. With the warmth of the sun as my blanket, I stuck my legs out the open window and propped my boots on the side mirror. Surrounded by the subtle scents of apple and sandalwood, I lay across the front seat, tipped my hat to shield my eyes from the daylight, and dozed off almost instantly.

Later, I slowly emerged from a dead sleep. Noticing the warmth of another person—more specifically, another person's leg that my head had been lying on—I righted myself on the seat and shoved the hat out of my eyes.

Hand flying to my chest, I yelped. "Dang it, Rowdy! You scared the heck out of me."

He lowered his phone and shot me a flirty grin. "I love it when you call me that."

"I should call you a creeper." Grunting, I rubbed my eyes. "Why were you sitting in here while I slept?"

Rowan placed his phone on the dashboard beside an open file folder. "It's my truck." He shot a dubious look out my window to where my dingy blue truck sat beside his shiny black one. "How'd you manage getting them mixed up?"

"I didn't. Yours is cleaner."

His eyebrows rose. "Yours would be, too, if you quit using it for a trash can."

I scoffed, sneaking a peek at the clutter lining my dash. A protein bar wrapper and an empty soda can sat among opened mail and paperwork. "I do not. It's more like my office."

Rowan's narrowed eyes held a measure of skepticism.

I crossed my arms. "Still doesn't answer why you were sitting in here while I was sleeping."

"I had a meeting to get to." Placing an arm along the back of the seat, he leaned close enough I could see the flecks of copper in his light-brown eyes. "Imagine my surprise when I opened the door and found Sleeping Beauty."

"I'm sorry. You should have woken me up and kicked me out." I went to grab the door handle, but his hand wrapped around my wrist.

"It's okay. I rescheduled it for tomorrow."

"Why?"

Rowan's playful expression faded into something more serious. "Because your rest is more important than me playing referee between a spoiled husband and wife arguing over the floor plans for their game room addition for the umpteenth time." His faint Irish accent caught on certain syllables, releasing a flurry of butterflies in my stomach.

Pressing my free hand against my midsection, I settled against the seat and stared out the windshield. On the Front Street side of the saloon we were a little secluded and out of sight of most of the workers, so when Rowan readjusted his hand and curled his fingers with mine I couldn't bring myself to pull away. That night I found the child's remains, Rowan had woken a dormant part of me when he held me while I wept. I hadn't realized I was in dire need for such until I had it once again. I also hadn't taken into consideration the sacrifices Rowan was having to make to work on this town.

"You're juggling a lot by working with us on this project and handling your other clients."

He squeezed my hand. "You're juggling a lot too."

"But I'm in one location doing that. You're having to constantly travel between this and everything else you have to do."

"I'm used to traveling. My firm does projects all over South Carolina and other Southern states. I have one coming up in Alabama mid-July."

My phone rang before I could comment. Freeing my hand, I pulled it out and cringed. "It's Detective Wolf," I shared with Rowan before answering it. "Hello, Detective."

"Hi, Avalee. I wanted to give you an update."

"Okay."

"We're fairly certain the remains are that of a nine-year-old boy who went missing close to sixty years ago."

I gasped. "Sixty years ago?"

"That's what it's looking like. The clothing we found matched what the missing child's report said he was wearing the day he vanished."

"Oh my goodness. Do you know his name . . . No, wait, I'm sorry. I shouldn't have asked."

"It's all right. We contacted his mother yesterday, so the information is being released soon. His name was Douglas Holt."

"Oh . . ."

"Well. Anyway. I promised to keep you updated."

"I appreciate that." I propped my elbow on the door and rubbed my forehead.

"After all this is settled, I wonder if you'd be interested in having dinner with me."

Slack-jawed, I shot a glance at Rowan, worried he had heard, but he only looked curious. No reddening of his face or steam coming out of his ears. "Uhh . . ."

"No pressure. Just think it over. How about I give you a call once we've closed the case?"

"Uhh . . . Okay."

"Take care, Avalee."

"You too." I ended the call and met Rowan's expectant gaze while tucking my phone back into my pocket. "They've identified the little boy. His name is Douglas Holt."

Frowning, Rowan reached for my hand and I let him take it even though it was starting to feel more dangerous than comforting. "You said something about sixty years?"

"Yeah. That's how long he's been missing."

"Great day." He shook his head and rubbed a circle on my skin with his thumb. "I wonder if his parents are even still alive."

"Wolf mentioned they've already contacted his mother, so . . ." I shrugged, blowing out a heavy sigh.

The mood in the cab of the truck grew somber as we sat processing the news. I propped my chin in my hand and watched a green lizard scamper across the hood while wondering how that poor mother had taken the news. Had she been relieved to finally know? Or had it only made things worse? Approaching footsteps pulled me out of my head. I wiggled my hand free from Rowan's and sat up straighter.

The Bellamy twins and Bash appeared beside my door.

"What's up, guys?"

Froid tipped his head at Rowan. "This is an intervention."

I squinted at him. "For what?"

Fred edged closer to the open window and I noticed they were both dressed in matching jean overalls and lime-green T-shirts. "You been driftin' 'round here like a haggard apparition."

"Haggard?" I snorted a laugh and almost pointed out that they looked like green highlighters wrapped in denim. "Wow, Fred. Tell me how you really feel."

Froid waved a hand, as if shooing away the insult. "He ain't meanin' to offend you. We're concerned."

I opened my mouth, but Rowan interrupted.

"Have you even slept since you found that little boy?"

"Did you not just sit here and watch me sleep for"—I grabbed his arm and checked the time on his watch—"almost an hour?"

His eyes narrowed. "At *night*, Avalee. In a bed. For more than an hour. Not in someone's truck or on a pew in the chapel or behind the counter in the silo."

I crossed my arms and huffed. I didn't think anyone had noticed the daily power naps. Cutting a look at the twins and then Bash, who was studying the ground, I realized I had been wrong. "People keep sneaking around town at all hours of the night, trying to break into the feedstore. I nailed boards to block the doors and windows, but it's not stopping the fools."

"We'll take care of it from here on out." Froid motioned to his brother and Bash.

My frown deepened. "Take care of it how?"

"Just leave it to us." Froid waggled a finger in my face. "No more guard duty for you, missy. Stay up in your apartment and focus on gettin' some proper rest."

I craned my neck to get a better view of the teenager. "Bash, you don't have to let these guys rope you into something you don't want to do."

He finally lifted his head and met my eyes. "I'm good."

It didn't look like they were going to take no for an answer. "Fine. Let's get back to work." I opened the door and they backed away to let me out. "Bash, you're working with me the rest of the day in the library."

"M'kay." Hands tucked into his front pockets, he began to follow.

We spent the afternoon laying heavy-duty vinyl plank flooring. Still more groggy than clear-minded, I put Bash on cutting duty while I fit the flooring together to ensure I didn't lose a finger. By the time we called it done, my back was screaming and my knees sore even though I wore kneepads.

"There are premade sandwiches and cups of soup in there." I pointed to the fridge by the saloon bar. "Maudie dropped it all off this morning, like she was feeding an army and not just me, so please help yourself so it won't go to waste." My grandmother had made the trip out here to check on me each morning this week, bringing food and staying as long as she could before having to head back to Beaufort to open her store. I told her it wasn't necessary, that I was *fine*. Of course, she didn't listen.

Even though he looked bored as usual, Bash licked his lips. "M'kay."

I fought the urge to hug him, to declare I'd help him out of whatever mess he'd found himself in. Before I gave in and did it anyway, I grabbed a club sandwich and a cup of tomato soup and dragged my achy body upstairs. After scarfing down the food, I took a long, hot shower and contemplated taking a sleeping pill, going back and forth on whether it was worth the strange dreams. By the time the water began cooling, I decided the pills were probably expired anyway and just settled on ibuprofen for the muscle aches.

Once my nightly routine was complete, I climbed into bed and closed my eyes. I tried praying, asking God for help, but my mind felt like it was full of sludge. Maudie told me once that even though my mind might not know what to say to God, he heard my heart's cry, so I settled on a simple, "Please, God, help."

I forced my eyes to remain shut, but it only lasted until the coolness of the sheets grew warm. Then I stared into the dark for a while, waiting for the weight of sleep to close them again.

When that didn't happen, I gave up and switched on the bedside lamp. I scooted up and reclined against the headboard and took my laptop off the nightstand. Firing up the search engine, I typed *Douglas Holt*. There were several hits, mostly Facebook profiles and one about a semi-famous baseball player. I revised the search to *Douglas Holt missing child cold case*. The first article's headline hit me hard, but I needed to know so I clicked on it anyway.

Justice for the Lost Boys of the Carolinas
Harvey Parker, age 42, was convicted yesterday on three counts of kidnapping and murder. The state is seeking the death penalty.

The article went on to list the three boys' names and details about their deaths. Two were from North Carolina and one from South Carolina. Readjusting the computer on my lap, I skimmed the article until finding my lost boy.

> Nine-year-old Douglas Holt Jr. from Ridgeland, SC, went missing last October. Even though witnesses have come forward and identified Harvey Parker as the man they saw near the Holt home the day Douglas Jr. disappeared from the family's front yard, the serial killer has never confessed. Prosecutors are unable to bring charges against him due to the lack of evidence. Douglas's parents, Douglas Sr. and Loreen, are asking that anyone with information about their son please come forward. The Holts have also tried to arrange a meeting with Parker to plead with him to confess but have been denied access.

"That poor family." My eyes welled with tears, making it impossible to continue reading. I exited out of the article, closed the lid of the laptop, and placed it back on the nightstand.

They say the truth will set you free, but in this case, the truth did nothing but imprison me in a weighty state of despondency. I sat suspended in this funk with my mind reeling. How could anyone hurt a child? I just couldn't fathom how such an evil could exist in a world my Creator made.

My loss hadn't come at the hands of some sick individual, but I felt a keen sense of connection to these parents just the same. Why were we not allowed to keep our precious treasures? I recalled another type of freedom, the freedom of free will. Why on earth had God granted such power to idiotic humans? Clearly, we couldn't handle that significant type of responsibility.

A sob tore through me, taking parts of my trust in humanity with it. I cried until my throat became raw and my nose completely congested.

Changing my mind about the sleeping pill, I tossed my blanket to the side and stood from the bed. I made for the bathroom but a high-pitched scream stopped me. Frozen in my tracks, I cocked my head and listened. Surely, I was hearing things.

Nope. Another scream pierced through the darkness.

"What now!?" I hurried into a pair of jeans and a hoodie. Shoving my feet into my work boots at the door, I grabbed the spotlight I'd been using to flash at intruders, my phone, and a can of Mace.

Loud pops and booms broke out, followed by more screams. Was that gunfire? I hesitated, second-guessing going out there. Froid did say for me not to leave the apartment. I looked over my shoulder at my bedroom, but then more pops and booms erupted, so I darted out the door and barreled down the stairs. The saloon had three exits—one on Front Street, the main entrance on Main Street, and the one that led to the back. I chose the back exit, thinking it would give me more cover. Crouching, I moved around the corner just as a flash of movement zipped by.

"Those crazies are shooting at us!" a man squealed, sounding more like a little girl.

"Try this again and they'll carry you out in a body bag too!" Froid's typical laid-back Southern twang had been overtaken with severe authority.

A spark of something whizzed by me before it exploded just yards away. I peeked from the edge of the boutique building. The moonlight reflected off four figures hustling down Main Street. Two short and stocky, one tall and reedy, and one low to the ground on all fours.

A vehicle cranked in the distance and then tires screeched as it took off like a shot down the road.

Whoops and laughter rang out.

"We stopped 'em, boys!" Fred, I think, bellowed.

"What on earth are y'all doing?" I stepped out and nearly slammed into Bash.

His arms shot out and steadied me.

"Handling things," Froid said.

I clicked on my spotlight and shined it at them, finding the three guys dressed in camouflage with black greasepaint smeared all over their faces. Even Preacher wore a camouflaged vest. "Have y'all lost your minds? You can't shoot at people, Froid."

"We ain't." He dug into his pocket and showed me what was in his palm. "It's just firecrackers and bottle rockets."

I scrubbed a hand down my face. "But they didn't know that. What if they'd had a real gun and unloaded it on y'all?"

Shoulders hunching, the guys clearly hadn't thought about that.

Preacher sidled up to me and nudged my leg with his nose. I petted him, in spite of being right aggravated.

Froid puffed out his chest, showing off the fact that his camouflage jacket was at least a size too small. "That's the second group we ran off tonight, so I call that a win."

I sniffed, unimpressed, and moved my attention to Bash, whose shirt was at least two sizes too big. "You need to take Preacher in for the night. And I'd better not hear of you coming back out here." I expected the normal dismissive *m'kay* but was surprised by his response.

"Yes, ma'am." Bash patted the side of his leg and Preacher followed.

I waited until the saloon door closed behind them before tearing into my favorite troublemaking twins. "What were you two thinking?"

Fred scratched his bald head and looked at his brother. "We . . ."

"Listen, I'm not sure y'all realize this, but Bash isn't in a good place in his life. I don't even know what his circumstances are exactly, but I highly doubt this"—I waved a hand in the air—"would be helpful."

"You gotta know we didn't mean no harm." Froid placed a hand on my shoulder.

"I know, Froid. I know. Just be more mindful, okay?" My heart was already in tatters from that news article and the hurt reemerged, sending a prickle of pain along my nose and eyes. "I don't want anything to happen to Bash."

Arms wrapped around me as I began sniffling. One arm from Froid. The other from Fred.

"We got you, little Avalee." Fred nearly cooed, the comfort a father would give a daughter. The comfort I longed to be given for years, but my father never did.

An engine in the distance suddenly interrupted my breakdown as it drew closer.

"Shoot!" Fred dropped his arms and stepped back. "Here we go again!"

Adrenaline dumped into my veins faster than any IV could ever administer it. "Hurry!" I started running. "To the clock tower. We'll cut them off before the heathens make it into town!" I didn't take the time to see if they followed as I sprinted straight to Front Street, making it before the car lights drew close enough to catch me in them. I rushed inside and was surprised when both twins were right behind me, slamming the door behind them.

Panting in the dark, we grew still and listened. Moments passed, then a door closed softly but not softly enough. The click seemed to echo through the still night. Muffled voices came closer.

"What now?" I whispered, staring off into darkness, sweat trickling down my back.

Neither brother answered me, but like a slow-motion action scene, the door crashed open and only sparks caught my eye before bottle rockets zipped between us and the trespassers.

Loud yelps rang out, mingled with swear words as heavy footfalls echoed down the road.

Someone cried out. "I've been hit!"

Fred stepped outside the clock tower and cupped his hands around a megaphone I hadn't realized was strapped to his belt by a long cord. It emitted a screeching sound before he began crooning in a creepy childlike voice. *"One, two, Freddy's coming for you. Three, four, better lock your doors . . ."* Before he could continue singing the morbid song, the car took off into the night.

Hyped-up and overly proud of ourselves, we gave each other high fives.

"Bet them fools ain't comin' back!" Fred whooped.

Froid did a soulful jig and we followed suit until the victory started wearing off.

Hands on my hips as I caught my breath, I surveyed our surroundings that were shrouded in darkness. "Guys . . . we can't do this every night."

"We know." Fred nodded, hitching up his sagging camo pants. "That's why we made a tic-tac and a snap-crack."

I dropped my hands and straightened. "A what and what?"

"TikTok and Snapchat," Froid corrected. He gave his brother a glare and then turned to me. "It's quicker at getting the word out than news outlets these days. We stood over there." He pointed toward our burn pile on the other side of the clock tower. "And Bash showed us how to record a snap and then how to turn it into a tac. We told viewers we wanted to respect the family of the child who was found, and if anyone wanted to help, they should visit."

I sucked my teeth, ready to lay into them. "Why would you do that?"

"Whoa! Wait." Fred held up a palm. "We told them to visit once the town is complete in September. Then we gave out the address to the children's hospital in Charleston and the information on how to donate. We can't do nothin' for Douglas, but maybe we can help young'uns goin' through health crises."

My anger dissolved into a puddle as I wrapped my arms around the two goofs. "Aww, guys . . . that's . . . so . . . so . . ." I blubbered uncontrollably, thanking God in my inarticulate way for answering my unexplained cry for help earlier. These two men, with the help of a homeless teenager, showed me God hadn't wasted the gift of free will on us humans after all.

CHAPTER 18

LOWCOUNTRY LOST'S MOTTO was that nothing was ever too far gone. Even though we tried living by that, sometimes it didn't work out that way. I hadn't expressed this to the investors just yet, but I'd made up my mind already on the fate of the feedstore. It needed to be torn down. The idea of making a dead child's resting place a novel attraction of sorts made my stomach sour. No matter how anyone worded the proposals, they all read the same—disrespectful.

Propped in the shade of the saloon, backs pressed against the scratchy bricks and our knees drawn, Nita, Desmond, and I studied the vacant lot where the flower shop used to be while mulling over ideas about how to fix this hole in our plans.

"How about a giant pergola? Running it off the side of the saloon." Nita patted the wall to our backs and then pointed forward. "So there will be another outdoor gathering space."

Humming, I tilted my head one way and then the other. "I thought about that at first, but we already have the outdoor gazebo behind the pecan warehouse. Plus the county is putting in a park, so I think another place like that would be overkill."

"We need to build something." Desmond readjusted the towel he sat on, making sure no dirt touched his tailored trousers.

"Yeah, but we don't have time to draw up plans and have them approved." I combed my fingers down Preacher's back. He'd plopped down beside me as soon as I sat and nudged my hand to give him attention. I think he had properly trained me a whole heckuva lot quicker than I had him. "I hate to shoot both your ideas down, but . . ."

The sound of a vehicle approaching had Preacher perking up, lifting his head to check out the visitor. I hated to admit it, but I knew that purring sound belonged to a certain oversize truck. A beat later, Rowan came into view and parked in front of the dirt lot. He had been using his truck more than the bike lately, claiming he needed it for running errands, but I knew it was really so he could load up the dog for joyrides.

Preacher bounded toward him as soon as the driver's door opened.

"Traitor," I mumbled while watching my dog slobber all over my ex.

Rowan squatted down and happily showered Preacher with lots of attention. My mind wandered to the what-ifs, forming an image I couldn't turn back off. Rowan coming home from a day of work, dropping his briefcase and blueprints by the door as a pack of wild children attacked him, all vying for his attention. Each one would receive a hug, maybe a hair mussing, hair I pictured in various shades of red. He'd listen to what they had to say, present in the conversation, because the man would have been a hands-on daddy. He'd be a hero to all of us.

I pictured the children talking over each other, and Rowan would lift his head and catch me standing by the kitchen door grinning at them like a lovesick fool. Returning my smile, he'd rise to his feet and say something silly and flirty, like "Okay, kids, do let me love on your mom before she gets jealous."

They'd giggle while their daddy wrapped his arms around me and peppered my face with loud smooching kisses until finally landing a solid one on my lips . . .

"Did you hear me?"

Blinking, I looked up at Rowan standing in front of me, Preacher now back by my side, panting contently. "Sorry, what was that?"

"I'm about to be your hero." Smiling, he held up the tube in his grasp.

Face heating, I felt like the man had read my mind. "Yeah? How's that?"

"Let's go inside so I can roll out my surprise." Rowan walked to the door and held it open for us, introducing himself to Nita as we headed toward the conference table.

"It's nice to finally meet the famous Juanita Aguilar." Rowan tipped his head in her direction.

"Call me Nita. And just where did you get this 'famous' notion from?" She gave him a side-eye.

"Des says you have a decent following on TikTok. I've looked into it and he wasn't kidding. A hundred and fifty thousand followers . . . That's impressive."

My spunky friend beamed with his praise. At only twenty-four years old, this firecracker of a woman had an old *abuela* trapped inside her petite frame and she'd let that ole gal loose on TikTok. While she prepared traditional Mexican dishes, such as tamales and pozole, Nita told the cheesiest jokes. The funniest part? Her cracking up at her own self.

What do you call a three-legged dog?

Nothing. You don't call him. It'd take the poor thing too long to hobble over!

That's Nita. Joyia was her only child so far with her soldier hubby Enzo. They hoped to expand the family as soon as he wrapped up this last tour overseas. I don't know how she managed to do it all—raising Joyia pretty much on her own, working with Desmond and me, and having this lively side hustle on social media.

"Funny, ain't nobody told me who you are, Mr. Hero." Nita aimed a weighty look in my direction, the look I referred to as her guilt-tripping glare. Admittedly, I couldn't help but be impressed that Desmond hadn't gone and blabbed everything to her already.

"He's an engineer," I explained.

Nita's intense stare didn't lessen, catching on my omission. She slid her focus over to Rowan and flicked her wrist. "How about impressing us with whatever you got in this tube."

Rowan popped open the tube and unrolled a set of blueprints. Des helped him secure the corners with paperweights we kept on the table for such a thing. "My firm built this restaurant a few years ago in Spartanburg. It looks like an old-fashioned gas station."

"We don't need a gas station or another restaurant," I said, shooting his idea down too.

"I know, but wouldn't it be nice to have a country-style bodega for residents to grab groceries at instead of having to leave town each time they need something?"

"That's not a bad idea." I leaned close to the blueprints and studied the floor plan. "Will it be hard to modify this and remove the kitchen?"

"No. My buddy should be sending me the updated version minus the kitchen this afternoon. And Jonas said if the boss lady approves, we have permission to move forward."

Desmond's phone began to ring. "I need to take this." Desmond moved away from the table, the phone already to his ear.

"Does Maudie still have that antique gas pump?" Rowan asked as I began jotting down notes.

"You should know since y'all are best buds." Wincing, I answered in a nicer tone, "She has two now."

"I believe we have that giant collection of vintage signs in one of our storage units," Nita said. "Remember we found them in that warehouse we flipped over in Magnolia?"

"Yeah. Those will be perfect."

"Sounds like we have a solution. I'm going to head back to Lexington and start fishing out the signs." Nita collected her bag and a water bottle. "I have a few people who might be interested in leasing the bodega."

"Thanks, Nita. Keep an eye out for anything else we could possibly use."

"You got it, babe." She gave me a playful wink and disappeared out the door.

I slumped in a chair and noticed Rowan watching me closely.

"You look tired, boss lady."

I rolled my eyes. "Gee, thanks. Just what a girl likes to hear."

He took the chair beside mine. "You're beautiful as ever, but tired. I'm not trying to insult you, I'm concerned."

"Don't be. I just had a rough night . . . Bad dreams." I shrugged my shoulder.

"Wanna talk about it?"

A flash of the nightmare came to mind before I could stop it. Me pushing a stroller. This time instead of a dead baby it held a small skeleton. "No. I'd rather not poke at the memory of it. Leave it be and it'll fade away."

"Like the way you handle most memories. Feigned ignorance ain't bliss."

My eyes snapped up to meet his. "What's that supposed to mean?"

"Nothing. Never mind."

I snorted. "Yeah. Just like the way you handle most any confrontation. Buck up but back right down like a limp noodle."

Desmond returned before we could go another round. "How about calling it the Grocery Depot?"

I nodded. "Has a nice ring to it, for sure."

"Good. I'll order the sign." Desmond jotted some notes on his iPad. "Rowan, as soon as you have the approved blueprints, will you get them to Avalee so she can start securing permits?"

I refrained from groaning. *Great. Just great.* This new project would have me working even more closely with Rowan. Seemed I couldn't avoid this man for the life of me all of a sudden.

Rowan tipped his head and typed something into his phone. "On it."

Desmond gathered his belongings. "Lots to do, people. Now I have more shopping. Avalee, let me know what you decide on flooring so we can get the guys on the schedule to install it. ASAP."

"Yes, sir." I saluted him and he rolled his eyes.

I watched him leave and thought about doing the same, but Rowan spoke before I could.

"Bash still won't stay in the apartment?" Rowan pointed to the rolled-up sleeping bag over by Preacher's fancy dog bed. Both were in similar shades of burgundy.

"Nope. He said he'd rather stay down here so he could keep an eye on Preacher for me." I huffed a breathy laugh. "Like that dog needs anyone tending to his free-spirited self."

"Why are they still staying in here anyway?"

I winced. "I sorta played up me being a scaredy-cat after the firecracker night and asked him to hang out a few more days. This way I can feed him easier, but he was antsy this morning and took off to who-knows-where. I just hope he comes back."

"He will," Rowan said with confidence as he rolled up the blueprints and stuffed them back into the tube. "He won't leave Preacher."

"Speaking of. Guess what your dog stole this time."

He chuckled. "I like how Preacher becomes my dog when he gets up to no good. What was it this time? A measuring tape?"

"Nope. The seat cushions off both Froid's and Fred's lawn chairs."

"Good. Maybe that'll motivate them to work more and sit less." Rowan grinned, resembling the boy I fell so hard for in high school. Sweet and mischievous.

"Preacher didn't get away with it for long. We've all learned to look in the chapel when things go missing. And Fred zip-tied the cushions to the chairs, so he can't swipe them again."

Rowan's phone beeped with an incoming message. He checked it and started replying. Seemed the meeting had come to an end, so I stood and started out the door to make my getaway.

Rowan caught my wrist. "Where're you going?"

I almost told him it was none of his business, but I had no fight left in me today. "Over to the diner. Des is waiting on my opinion on flooring options."

"Want another set of eyes?"

Did I want another set of eyes? Rowan's eyes to be exact? No. Nope. Sure didn't, but I didn't have the energy to shoo him away. Every time I found myself alone with him, it made it that much harder to resist him.

"Sure." I pulled my arm free of his hold and led the way across the street. We shuffled inside and when I flipped the switch and the lights came on, it lifted my lips in a small smile. Electricity meant we were getting closer to completing this one.

"So, what vibe is Des going for?" Rowan surveyed the blank space.

Hands on my hips, I stared down at the floor samples. "He said we could go one of two ways. Either a retro diner with the black-and-white tiles in a checked pattern or a more modern farmhouse diner with this barnwood flooring."

Rowan crouched down and picked up the wide wood plank. Straightening, he traced a nail hole with his finger. "Is this reclaimed?"

"Yes." I eased closer and inspected it with him. "It'll cost a pretty penny, but I like the idea of keeping with the farming community vibe. Aesthetically, it goes better with the rest of the town." I moved to a stack of boxes, took out my knife, and sliced through the tape on top. "Let's see how the tile looks with it."

"You still using that old knife?"

I glanced at the well-used pocketknife, its red handle scratched and aged. The blade had been sharpened so many times it now looked paper-thin, but I couldn't bring myself to put it away for a newer one. "I need one and it still works just fine."

We exchanged a meaningful glance, but otherwise didn't acknowledge just how sentimental this small pocketknife really was to me. Our very first Christmas as husband and wife, Rowan had put it in my stocking.

Clearing my throat, I put away the knife and the memories it evoked. I plucked a few pieces of white tile from the box and placed them on top of the floor sample. "You can't go wrong with classic subway tile. It's a good contrast with the rustic wood."

"Seems like you've made your choice." He knocked his knuckles against the plank. "Modern farmhouse it is."

"Humph. Easiest thing I've done in forever."

Rowan bumped his shoulder against mine. "How was the rest of your day? Uneventful, I hope."

"Detective Wolf stopped by," I said through a yawn.

"Did he have any news?"

"Yes. They've closed the case. He said they found evidence in the garbage bag that linked Harvey Parker to the murder, but he died in prison, so there's nothing else they can do." I gathered the floor samples into a stack to bring back to the saloon. "He also wanted a personal tour of the town. He's pretty interested in the revitalization initiative."

Rowan snorted, reaching and taking the stack of flooring from me as we straightened.

"What?" I asked, following him out.

"That's not all he's interested in."

I opened the saloon door and held it for him. "What do you mean?"

"The man is into you." Rowan placed the flooring on the portable shelving unit we were using to house the samples.

It was the truth, but I played off his comment with a laugh. "He's just being nice."

"His niceness makes me want to punch him."

I laughed again but Rowan did not. He was practically seething. "Why?"

"'Cause you're my wife."

His declaration wiped the smile off my face. This was the second time he'd slipped and called me that recently. "I'm not your wife anymore, Rowan."

"I made a covenant between us and God. Divorce papers don't change that."

I wanted to beg to differ but wasn't sure if he was wrong. Either way, I needed to shut this mess down. "Look, Rowan, we have a job to do here. Let's focus on that."

"But—"

"No." I opened the door and dismissed him with a jerk of my head. He didn't move. "Please."

Finally, he brushed past me but paused long enough to whisper firmly, "We have things that need sorting between us, so put it off all you want, but it's happening."

CHAPTER 19

DURING THAT FIRST YEAR WITH ROWAN AS MY SIDEKICK in elementary school, I spent more time in time-out than I had the three years prior to the third grade. He'd been trouble from the get-go. One time he had the brilliant idea that we should play leapfrog, jumping from one desktop to the next. We broke a total of three. My dad and Rowan's parents had to split the cost to replace them and we had to spend a week in time-out during recess. Not a good thing for two high-energy kids needing to burn that off so our teacher wouldn't pull out all her hair. Another time, Rowdy dared me to swipe our music teacher's can of Dr Pepper. Sure, I got it without Mrs. Byrd seeing, just eased up to her desk and slipped it behind my back undetected while she scribbled music notes that none of us understood on the chalkboard, but she noticed when he popped the tab and started guzzling it. I didn't drink a drop but got put into time-out for taking it in the first place. It had gotten so bad that the principal threatened to separate us, moving Rowan to another class. That threat was enough to make us straighten up . . . a little.

With all those silly time-outs on my mind, I walked into the firehouse to get away from the sticky humid day for just a little while. Summer had crept up and tried to surprise us, but this is the South and so we were expecting it well before now. Thank goodness, the air was already up and running in here and the sweat on my body began to evaporate under the coolness seeping from the vent overhead.

I lifted my hair off my neck and sighed while scanning the vast lobby, completely cleared in anticipation of the arrival of a fire truck and a rescue vehicle. Most of the front wall had already been removed and reframed to retrofit the giant bay doors. Even with that major transformation, the building still resembled a bank.

With no one in sight, I slipped inside the bank vault. After a few moments, I sat down on the floor while gazing up at the fancy woodwork on the ceiling. The cavernous room had a luxurious ambience, with dark-green walls and warm lighting. This would be a pretty neat hangout space for the fire and rescue crew once Desmond dressed it up all nice.

A throat cleared.

I angled my head to the side and found Rowan leaning against the doorjamb. He wore what had become his daily uniform, nicely fitted T-shirts and naturally distressed jeans. Today's pair were a dark wash with a hole below his right knee. The hole had been created just last week when his pants leg got hung on an old manual washing machine he was attempting to remove from the inn.

I waited for him to speak, but when he didn't, I spoke up, "Yes, sir?"

"What are you doing on the floor?"

"You ever heard of someone taking a time-out in a bank vault?"

His lips twitched. "Can't say that I have."

"Well, now you can."

He pushed off the doorjamb and hovered near me for a few beats before dropping to the floor. Close enough for the subtle hints of his cologne to reach me. The man always smelled good enough to eat. "Remember that time we were put in time-out in the cafeteria for finger painting the floor in the art room instead of painting that ugly beige construction paper?"

I caught myself leaning closer to sniff him just before I actually did it. I pretended to stretch to cover my folly. "That paper was the worst. The paint never really popped against it." I couldn't help but laugh.

"It sure did pop against that white tiled floor though." The mischievous glint warmed his brown eyes even further and boy, did he look all Rowdy in that moment.

Grinning, I crossed my ankles. "I was just thinking about our lengthy time-out history."

"That cafeteria time-out was my favorite though. They thought leaving us in there during recess was punishment." He let out a throaty chuckle. "Didn't take into account us being wily kids, the fools."

"We probably ate our weight in brownies that day." Every time the cafeteria workers turned their backs on us, Rowan snuck brownies off the food line. "They should have known better than setting up time-out chairs by the dessert section."

Looking smug, Rowan ran his fingers through his hair. The coppery-brown waves fell carelessly back into stylish place. "Yeah. Most kids would have sat there mooning for the sweets. Not us."

I laughed until it turned into a lingering yawn.

His smile slipped. "Still not sleeping well?"

"Not really."

Rowan laid back and tapped my knee. "I think you need your teddy bear."

I rolled my eyes but didn't deny it.

I had friends who were in perfectly happy marriages, but they couldn't sleep if someone was in their space. They needed room to sprawl. Not me. Even during the silent seasons of my marriage to Rowan, we always came together at night. That had been the case right up until the night before he moved out. Sleepless hours passed while we had clung to each other like lifelines. Lifelines that could no longer bear the strain of loss.

I yawned again.

"Come here." Rowan hooked an arm around me and pulled me into his side.

"What? Why?" I tried shoving away but he wasn't having it.

"Use my chest as a pillow." He maneuvered me until my cheek pressed right over his heart.

The familiar scent of him surrounded me. It was nostalgic, that scent, and now it made perfect sense as to why he reacted so strongly to my change of perfume. "I don't think this is a good idea," I mumbled even as I snuggled closer.

Rowan placed his hand on the back of my head. "Don't make it weird, *a stór*. Just rest your eyes for a few."

My body tensed. "You just did by calling me that. I'm not your treasure anymore, Rowan."

"You'll always be my treasure." His voice softened into a velvety murmur. "Nothing will ever change that."

"Rowan—"

"Maudie is my treasure too. So are my friends and family." His reasoning for the term of endearment didn't change the fact that I'd never heard him call anyone else *a stór* but me.

I wanted to argue this point but he began combing his fingers through my hair and I'll be darned if I wasn't close to drooling. Slowly, the steady rhythm of his heartbeat lulled me, my body loosened, and my eyes drifted shut.

I woke up later in the same position and realized Rowan had also drifted off to sleep. The faint dusting of freckles across his nose and cheeks were a hint of the ginger boy he once was. Caught in the memory of a younger us, I leaned over and kissed the bridge of his nose just as I used to do.

His eyes opened and studied me. Minutes ticked by, and as if he'd come to a decision, he began leaning forward.

I placed a hand on his chest. "No."

"Why?" Rowan whispered, his voice gravelly and rough.

"Because . . ." I wiggled away from him and stood. "You make me feel things I don't want to."

He rolled into a sitting position and rested his arms on his knees. "Why not?"

"Because we ended a long time ago. It's too late for this."

Rowan considered me for a moment before pushing to his feet and eliminating the space I tried placing between us. "We're still breathing, *a stór*. It won't be too late until there's no breath left."

Unable to breathe, I moved out of the vault and into the spacious lobby. Thinking of something to put an end to this intimate land mine we found ourselves skipping over, I blurted, "I want you to condemn the feedstore."

Rowan stalled in his steps toward me, appearing rather perturbed. "Change of subject . . ." Frowning, he planted his hands on his lean hips and grumbled. "Smooth . . . Real smooth."

I wagged a finger at him, daring him to get all huffy. "Time-out is over. We need to get back to business. You know as well as I do we need to figure out what to do with the feedstore sooner rather than later with all the deadlines looming."

"That's fine, but I can't just go around condemning any and every building on a whim."

"You did with the flower shop."

His eyes narrowed, features hardening in a defensive expression. "Because it was structurally *unsound*."

"The floor joists are toast and the roof is mostly gone."

"That's fixable."

"I can't stomach the idea of anyone profiting from the location of where that little boy's body was disposed."

"So what do you expect us to do? Just level it and leave an empty lot? Isn't that what you dragged me over the coals for with the flower shop?" His voice was low but stern, indicating I had a hard sell before me.

"I did no such thing." I jabbed a finger in his direction, daring him to oppose. "You came up with a perfect solution, though, with building that country-style bodega."

"Yeah . . . But we don't have time to pull more blueprints out our backsides for another fresh build, plus the feedstore shares a wall with that boutique."

"It's all brick and most of the roof is already gone, so tearing it down with a thoughtful plan of action should minimize any damage to the building next door."

Rowan rubbed his jaw, appearing to be on the fence. "Then what?"

I walked over and gripped his elbows. "We can turn the space into a memorial garden to pay proper respect to Douglas Holt. I've thought a lot about his mother. Rowan, we could give her this."

Staring at the ceiling for several seconds, he finally dropped his gaze to meet mine. "Do you have a landscape architect in mind?"

I managed to withhold a smile of victory, knowing I had him, and nodded. "Yes. The same firm working on the parks and sidewalk beautification design has agreed to work on the garden as soon as I get the go-ahead. I've also contacted two artists from Sunset Cove who specialize in murals. It's a married couple who go by AJ Bradford."

Rowan sucked in his bottom lip, distracting me momentarily. "I like the idea of a mural."

Blinking away from his lips, I refocused on the task at hand. "I think the mural needs to be a nod to Somewhere, South Carolina. Maybe include some pecan trees and a dirt road. And an appropriate quote to go along with it. They're sketching up some ideas."

Rowan moved out of my grasp for once. "Keep working on the design and I'll call Jonas and try to get him on board with this." Rowan started walking away.

"Thank you!" I nearly shouted and he threw a hand up in acknowledgment before disappearing out the front door.

Between my nap and the passionate debate with Rowan, I felt more invigorated than I had in ages. With my newfound get-up-and-go, I got to work on finally making something right out of a terrible wrong.

CHAPTER 20

"IS THERE ANYTHING MORE WELCOMING THAN A FRONT PORCH?" I grinned at my phone screen and Jonas smiled back at me. "Once we add some rocking chairs, that'll encourage folks to stay a while. Great for business, right?"

"Most definitely. What did you call the design concept for the diner?"

"It's modern farmhouse with a Scandinavian design. Clean lines, light and airy."

"Do you mind flipping the screen and scanning the exterior again so I can record it this time to share with the other investors?"

"Sure. No problem." I stepped off the new front porch, reluctantly leaving the shade. I could seriously use another kiddie pool day after working outside today. Turning around, I tapped the camera icon to show off the gorgeous white exterior of the diner. "We updated the exterior with vertical board and batten siding. I think the black tin roofing and the light stained wood door and shutters really play into the modern farmhouse design."

"Are those gas lanterns?" Jonas asked.

I zoomed in on the black lanterns flanking the pinewood door. "Not anymore. They were originally from the inn. Desmond had them revamped." I zoomed out and showed off the covered porch. "Today, I completed the decking and tomorrow I should be able to finish wrapping the porch posts in pinewood."

"What about railings?"

"It's ground level so railings aren't required. This goes well with the light and airy concept."

"It's lovely, Avalee, just like everything else you and your crew have done so far. Somewhere is going to be one charming little town."

"That's our goal." I returned to the shade of the porch and swiped a hand across my sweaty forehead. My blue tank top and the waistband of my tan work pants were pretty much soaked through. Thankfully, I could angle the camera so Jonas didn't have to see any of that. And the blue bandana kept my sweaty hair in check.

"You're a busy woman, so I won't keep you any longer. Thanks for the update."

"You're welcome. Take care." I waved at the phone like a doofus before ending the call.

I admired my handiwork while polishing off a bottle of Gatorade. After the long night I'd had, today had called for a one-person job so I could be alone with my thoughts. I hadn't been able to sleep—nothing new there—and my mind wouldn't shut off about Douglas Holt or the other boys who had lost their lives at the hands of that serial killer. Smart thing to have done was turn on a movie, something light in subject matter and humorous, but at one in the morning I tended to not do the smart thing. Instead, I opened up my laptop and went down the Internet rabbit hole once again. Most of it I already knew about, but I kept reading anyway, wondering how on earth those poor families had moved on after such horrific tragedy. I'd finally given in and emailed Loreen Holt, letting her know I was the one who found her son and that if she ever wanted to talk, I'd be willing to meet her. I'm not sure why, but I felt like I couldn't get any closure until I at least reached out.

From the sounds of tools being slung into the back of trucks and vehicles cranking up, work crews were wrapping up for the day. I was ready to do the same, but first I needed to track Desmond down and go over a few things. I crossed the street and checked inside the saloon but it was empty. I stood there a minute and let the cool air wash over me, relishing in the way it sent goose bumps along my exposed arms. The air-conditioning was almost enough to convince me to end my quest right there, but I needed to find Desmond so I kept moving, going out back to see if his car was still parked behind the saloon, which it was.

Snickering caught my attention before I could decide where to start looking. I glanced around and spotted Fred and Froid peeping in the back windows of the boutique next door, their identical Clemson-orange bucket hats shielding them from the relentless sun. "What are y'all up to now?" I hollered, startling them both.

"Shh!" Froid hissed at me.

Shaking my head, I walked over and peered inside the building. It was small and shotgun-style so you could see all the way to the front. "What are we supposed to be looking at?" As soon as I asked, my gaze snagged on something over the front door. Squinting, I leaned closer until realizing what I was staring at. "Aren't you guys too old to be pulling pranks?"

Fred clucked his tongue and shoved his hands into the front pockets of his jean overalls. "You're never too old for some good clean fun."

"This ain't good clean fun, mister." I side-eyed him then returned my attention to the box fan suspended over the door, a small can of paint hung precariously above it on a pulley system that appeared to be attached to the front door. At least they picked a good location to pull this stunt. The drywall and flooring wouldn't be installed until the end of the week. "Who's supposed to be coming through that door?"

The brothers looked at each other and shrugged, before Froid answered with a rascally grin. "Bash. It's past time to initiate him."

I snorted. "Initiate him into what?"

"The construction family. Remember that summer when we got you?" Froid elbowed his brother and they snickered, sounding like two naughty little boys instead of the grandpas they were.

Folding my arms, I leveled a glare at them while fighting back a smile. "How could I forget? Y'all crazy-glued all of my tools to my very first tool belt. Maudie was ready to wring your necks for that one. We couldn't unstick any of them, so she had to buy me a new set of tools and belt because of your foolery."

Fred wheezed out a guffaw.

Froid shushed him. "That boy is gonna hear us if you don't pipe down."

Our heads swung toward the window when we heard the door creak open.

"Wait!" I shouted as loud as I could, but it was too late.

"Ah shoot. That ain't the boy!" Fred groaned as we helplessly watched peach-colored paint rain down on a sharply dressed Desmond.

I moved past the brothers and pushed open the back door. We halted just inside, safely out of harm's way.

Several moments ticked by in silence, only the whining sound of the fan interrupting it. Desmond stood unblinking with his hands on his hips as paint dripped down his handsome face and navy suit. The light coral color really popped against his dark skin and clothing, but I wouldn't be pointing that out.

Fred started to speak up, but Desmond raised a painted palm and shook his head. Taking off his fedora, he stepped out from underneath the fan and stared at the splattered walls and floor.

"You ain't Bash," Froid said, as if that cleared everything up.

"Nope." Mouth flattened into a thin line, Desmond continued surveying the mess.

"I was trying to stop them," I admitted, trying to clear my name of their shenanigans.

Desmond's eyes cut to mine briefly. Seemed he didn't believe me.

I nudged Fred in the side. "You better tell him I had no part in this!"

"Avalee told us to use the pink paint." Fred shrugged and Froid nodded in agreement.

Gasping, I popped him in the shoulder with the back of my hand. "You lie!"

"What's going on?" Bash walked up behind us, making all three of us jump like the guilty.

I glared at the brothers. "These two thought it would be fun to pull a prank on you. Except poor Des got here first."

Bash looked at painted-up Desmond with wide eyes. "M'kay." The teenager turned on his heels and disappeared out the back door as fast as he'd appeared.

"Des?" I took a few cautious steps toward him, worrying he'd gone into shock.

"*Pink Sea Salt*," Desmond muttered.

"What? Will that get the paint out of your clothes?" I had my doubts.

Desmond sighed heavily. "No. The suit's ruined." He sliced a sharp glance at the brothers. "The name of this paint color is *Pink Sea Salt*. They used one of my samples for . . ." He jabbed a finger up at the box fan, then tilted his head while studying the wall. "I think it's the right color for this boutique instead of the soft green hue."

"Okay . . ." I was dumbfounded that he wasn't pitching a fit over his ruined suit and the grueling task it would be to scrub off all that paint. I know I would have, but Des just stood there in work mode among a prank gone awry. "So I can go ahead and order the paint?"

"Yep." Without so much as a glance back at the pranksters, Desmond yanked open the front door and strode outside.

I followed him out and then around to the back of the saloon. "You want me to hose you down or maybe take you through a car wash?"

"Not funny." Desmond carefully shucked off his clothes down to his satin boxers, draping the ruined articles on top of a sawhorse. "I'm going upstairs to shower."

Giving him some space, I headed inside the main level to make note of the paint choice for the boutique and placed an order for it. After checking and refilling Preacher's water and food bowls, I went upstairs.

I figured it wouldn't hurt to rest my eyes while Desmond showered, so I sat on the couch, reclined my head, and let the gentle breeze from the ceiling fan wash over my body. It felt like a cool weighted blanket and everything began to drift . . . the room, my thoughts, the sound of the shower . . .

A combination of a snort and snore jolted me awake as the cushion dipped beside me. Blinking, I looked over and saw a freshly washed Desmond sitting beside me with his favorite jar of moisturizer in his hand. The citrusy scent of his bergamot bodywash perfumed the air. He kept the fancy bottle underneath the bathroom sink to keep me from using it, but that didn't stop me from sneaking a squirt of it every now and then.

"I didn't mean to wake you."

"I didn't mean to fall asleep." I rubbed my eyes and angled myself on the couch to face him. It was then that I noticed a speck of paint on his ear. "You missed a spot." I plucked a tissue from the box on the end table and cleaned it off.

"Thanks," Desmond grunted, taking the tissue and rubbing his other ear for good measure. "I'll probably be finding paint on me for the foreseeable future. I'm sure there's some stuck in my nasal cavities." He sniffed. "Your text earlier said we had some things to discuss?"

"Just a few updates I wanted to run by you." I wrestled my phone out my front pocket and pulled up the list I'd made. "The paving crew is scheduled for the last week in this month. They're paving the roads and pouring the walkways. Does that work for you?"

"I believe so." Setting the jar of cream on the cushion beside him, Desmond picked up his leather portfolio off the coffee table and retrieved his iPad. "Good thing I dropped this off up here before doing a walk-through at the coffee shop."

"No doubt." I watched him bring the screen to life and check his calendar, noticing he'd changed into a light-blue polo shirt and chinos—his idea of dressing down.

"If they come in on that Tuesday, that'll work for me."

"I'll let them know." I glanced at my list. "Do you have any updates on the windows shipment?"

"Let me see . . ." He tapped the screen with a stylus pencil. "The delivery date is showing the day after Memorial Day."

"Good. The sooner we get the windows installed, the sooner we can get started on the deli." I made note of the delivery. "I finished most of the diner's porch today and I have everything cut for the porch posts. The plan is to knock that out first thing in the morning. Oh, and Jonas Facetimed me for updates. He seemed pleased with all the progress."

Desmond tapped the screen once more and set it aside. "You've been a busy lady. Rowan said you didn't eat lunch with the crew today."

"Rowan needs to mind his business." I huffed. "And why exactly are you talking to him about me again?"

"That, my dear, is your fault." Desmond opened the jar of cocoa butter cream and scooped out a small dollop. He smoothed the cream along his forearms and elbows, making his dark skin glow. "Ever since we've started work on this town you've been tight-lipped. If you would talk, I wouldn't have to rely on your ex-husband to fill me in on things."

I repressed a cringe. Desmond had been rather salty about that tidbit ever since he overheard Rowan and I talking in the tree that day. Desmond had expressed to me several times that you share something as significant as being divorced with your closest friend.

Not when you keep them at arm's length, like I did with Desmond.

My hackles rose. "It's neither one of your business where I eat lunch or do anything else, for that matter."

"I care about you and your well-being. Stop trying to make me feel guilty about that." Desmond slapped the lid on the cream with a bit of aggression and screwed it tightly.

"You can care about me without going to Rowan about it," I snapped instead of apologizing or at least thanking him for caring. I dropped my phone in my lap and scrubbed my palms down my face.

"We've known each other for over five years. We've shared a lot in that time, haven't we?"

"Yes." I shrugged.

"Remember that car accident I was in?"

"How could I forget?" I'd been terrified of losing someone else so dear to me. It happened about a year after we'd met and was a firm reminder to keep Desmond at a distance. That way the hurt wouldn't hurt so much if I lost him somehow.

"You beat the ambulance to the hospital and didn't leave my side after I had surgery to repair my leg." He surveyed the room, as if looking for something. After a few silent beats, he returned his gaze to mine. "I attended the funeral with you for your great-aunt, I've met and fell in love with Maudie, you've met and fell in love with my parents, we started this tremendously successful business together. I could go on and on . . . Heck, you've even met my ex-fiancée. So forgive me if it makes no sense in my mind why you've never shared much about your past with me."

I crossed my arms, feeling sticky from the dried sweat and itchy from the uncomfortable conversation. "My past . . ." I took a forceful inhale to suppress the sudden stinging in my nose. "It hurts, Des. I've lost a lot more than a husband—much more—and I'd just rather keep it in the past."

Desmond placed his warm hand on my shoulder. "But it might help if you talk about it."

Shaking my head, I dabbed the corners of my watery eyes. The pressure in my chest built until I finally found enough nerve to spit out what was stuck on the tip of my tongue. "Have you lost a son or daughter, Des?"

The sudden intake of breath indicated that I'd caught him off guard. His brown eyes glassed over as he shook his head.

"I've lost both." I coughed to clear the sorrow wedged in my throat. "Talking about it doesn't help. It just picks at the scab until I'm bleeding all over again." Leaving my friend speechless, I rose from the couch and locked myself in the bathroom.

I closed the lid of the toilet and sat down, resting my face in my hands. The tidal wave of grief unleashed the tears and I gave in to it.

Some time passed by before I heard a gentle knock on the door, but I didn't move to unlock it or answer him.

"Avalee," Desmond said in a hoarse voice. "I had no idea." He sighed heavily enough that I could hear it through the door. "I'm sorry I pried."

I still didn't respond. I couldn't.

"I'm going to head out . . . I don't want to but I know that's what you want, so . . ."

I remained hunched over for a long time, watching my tears make a puddle on the tiled floor. I remained that way until I finally heard the front door shut.

Why couldn't keeping the past from coming home to roost be as easy as shutting a door? Between Rowan returning with all our ghosts in tow and Desmond determined to make me open up about it, the hinges had been well and truly blown off, eliminating the possibility of keeping the past locked out.

CHAPTER 21

JUNE

Sometimes the only thing you can do is keep moving forward . . .

At least that was the case with this darn wagon of sorts I'd made. Technically, it was a bench on wheels, but for some reason when I welded the bench to the frame, I managed to mess up the axle. So . . . going forward was the only option. There seemed to be a life lesson in that somewhere, but I had other things to focus on than trying to decipher it. Specifically, the layout for benches around town.

I pulled the bench wagon along the bumpy dirt road down Main Street, stopping every so often to test out the location. So far, I'd determined that the spot in front of the boutique was a no-go. Reason being—no shade. Moving on, I stopped between the deli and coffee shop and took a seat on the bench. Shielding my eyes, I scanned the ghost town, thinking about patrons coming out with steaming cups of java from the coffee shop or a bag full of goodness from the deli, meeting up with others to conversate a moment or two right here in this very spot. Yeah, it needed a bench.

A shadow fell over my clipboard as I made a notation to put a bench in front of the coffee shop. His shoes came into view. The fancy leather boots with one lone splatter of peach paint. Paint from where he interrupted my progress the other day in the clothes boutique. *Rowan.*

I looked up. "Yes, sir?"

"What exactly is this contraption you're sitting on?" Rowan grabbed the handle and rolled me forward a few paces.

"It's a portable bench. Roll me across the street to the town hall, please."

Rowan did as I said, then motioned for me to scoot over and I reluctantly agreed. He sat down and wiggled his butt, causing the bench to shake. "You make this?"

"Yep."

"Why?"

"I'm working on the layout for the benches around town." I handed him the clipboard with the town's map.

"How many benches do you have?" He studied the map.

"Five so far. Nita's been working on getting prominent figures from South Carolina to donate them. The governor, an author from near Myrtle Beach, two of the guys from the band Hootie and the Blowfish, and a celebrity chef from Edisto Island. Each bench will have a placard on the back with the donor's name on it."

"That's a good idea." Rowan tapped the map. "Definitely need one by Sweet Silo."

"Yeah. I think each corner needs a bench too." I placed the pen behind my ear and climbed down, hoping he'd take the hint to move on.

"Light travels faster than sound. That's why some people appear bright until you hear them speak." A rumble of laughter pushed past his smiling lips as he gestured toward the chapel sign. "That's kinda harsh."

I thought that one was pretty funny, in an honest sort of way. "Just truth speaking."

"Speaking of truth speaking . . ." He rubbed the back of his neck, hesitating.

I waited while sounds of productivity swirled around us. Power tools whining away, hammers pounding, a generator rumbling behind one of the buildings.

"I have work to do, Rowan, so spit it out already." Frowning, I motioned toward him with my clipboard. I'd felt awkward ever since our time-out in the bank vault, an itchy combination of wanting to be around him and dreading it at the same time. A little embarrassed as well. I couldn't believe I kissed his nose.

He looked away, his handsome face crumpling. "Used to, I could do or say something to annoy you into a grin. I knew it was over when you stopped giving me your smile." His eyes collided with mine and I wished I had my sunglasses to shield me from his intense gaze. The overwhelming need to cry washed over me. "If I couldn't give you that," he went on, "then I knew you needed to move on and find someone who could."

I swallowed down the tears and shook my head. "That's the problem, Rowan. I didn't want anyone to give me that. I wanted to be miserable, to just stay drowning in it *alone*."

"But alone is lonely," he whispered.

"I'm sure you've found someone else to annoy into smiling."

Rowan scrubbed a hand down his face and gave me a sidelong look. Finally he shook his head and forced a smile. "Nah. You're the only one I enjoy annoying."

"But I thought you just said being alone is lonely."

"Yeah. It's been a lonely six years."

It really wasn't that hard to understand why he'd remained single too. Grief had robbed so many aspects of my life, desire being one of them. I barely felt human most days, much less a woman. It's hard to feel attraction when grief is a constant companion.

"Welp . . ." I hopped off the mobile bench, wiped my hands across my jeans, and tried walking away like I didn't have a care in the world, but Rowan didn't let me get far. He wrapped his hand around my wrist. I opened my mouth to deter whatever was about to come out of his, but his phone rang before I could.

Rowan pulled the phone out and winced. "I need to take this, but don't go far, because you'll want to hear whatever this is about."

I stood awkwardly beside him and waited for the conversation to conclude. From the grunts and his twisted facial expression, it couldn't be good.

Sighing, Rowan ended the call. "You may want to sit back down."

My stomach revolted against his request, spasming painfully. "Why?"

Rowan placed his phone into his pocket. "Don't get mad."

"Every time you've ever prefaced something with that I've gotten mad!" I tapped the clipboard against my leg. "Just tell me."

"A friend of mine's wife is a private investigator. I had her look into Sebastian."

I took his advice and plopped down on the bench, jostling it. "Please tell me Bash isn't a criminal on the lam."

"He's not a criminal on the lam." Rowan settled beside me, arm slung on the back of the bench. His hand gently squeezed my shoulder. "But he is a runaway."

My head jerked in his direction. "What do you mean?"

Rowan glanced around just as a subcontractor emerged from the barbershop. The guy grabbed a box of supplies by the door and disappeared back inside. Others were milling around working, too, so Rowan lowered his voice. "His grandmother has custody of him. She thought he's been staying with a friend."

I held Rowan's stoic stare as that sunk in. "He's not nineteen . . ."

He shook his head. "No. He's sixteen."

I leaned forward, placing my elbows on my knees and my face into the palms of my hands. "But . . . Bash seems like he's got a good head on his shoulders, so there has to be a reason why he ran away."

"Think he'll tell us?"

I sat up and sniffed a dry laugh. "You know how stingy that kid is with his words, what do you think?"

"He's not going to have a choice." Rowan sighed. "Avalee, we can't not do something about this. He's a minor."

"Where's Maudie when you need her?" I muttered, looking skyward.

"We're adults, so I think she'd tell us to handle this ourselves."

My eyes dropped to meet his. "How?"

"Where's Bash?"

"The pharmacy, cleaning. The inspector is coming tomorrow to sign off on it."

"Good." Rowan stood, then helped me to my feet. "I say we hole him up in a corner so he can't make a run for it." He looked around animatedly. "Maybe bring some rope just in case."

I slugged him in the arm. "Now's not the time for jokes."

"Who's joking?" Rowan winked. He was right though. It was a fair probability that Bash would take off as soon as we confronted him.

We made it to the entrance of the pharmacy, but Rowan latched onto my hand and pulled me to a stop. "I think you need to lead the talk."

"Why me? You're the one *leading* the private investigation."

"You're the one who hired him without a background check," Rowan fired back, his eyebrows raising dramatically.

"Oh, the blame game. Gotcha." I nodded. "Then go away and let me handle *my* mess, alone." I shoulder-checked him on my way inside, but Rowan followed anyway.

Bash looked up while dumping a dustpan full of sawdust and wood scraps into the large garbage can. "Wassup?"

"Umm . . ." I glanced at Rowan and he gave me a subtle nod. "You like working here, Bash?"

Bash's gaze ping-ponged between us. "Yeah."

I moved closer but Rowan hovered by the door, as if guarding it. "Good, because we like you working here, and . . . Well, we need to talk about how that can keep happening."

Bash squinted suspiciously. "Did I do something wrong?"

"Not that we know of," Rowan piped up.

I shot him a look that said to keep his mouth shut and then turned back to Bash. "Look, I like you. I trust you. In the last few months, you've proved how invaluable you are to this project, but . . . I'm . . . Is there any reason why you might not be able to continue working with us?"

Bash shrugged. "No."

I moved a little closer and dropped my voice. "I'm your boss, but more than that, I'm your friend. I'd help you in any way if you needed me to."

"M'kay." He started to sweep up some more debris, but I placed my hand on the broom handle.

"Bash, we *know*."

The teenager glanced over my shoulder before meeting my eyes, his lips pinched firmly shut. No surprise there, but boy did I hate having to do all the talking.

I spoke softly, "Did someone hurt you? Is that why you ran away?"

Again, he glanced over my shoulder to where Rowan stood.

"No one knows but me and Avalee," Rowan said, coming closer at a slow pace. It reminded me of how I approached Preacher that first day in the chapel. "We're here for you, man, but you gotta tell us what you need."

Bash retreated a step, but I moved with him.

"Don't you want to stay here?"

Bash's entire face frowned, lips, eyes, brow. Even his high cheekbones seemed lower. "How?"

"You tell us why you ran away and then we work together on finding a solution. You're sixteen—"

"I turned seventeen two days ago." His jaw set firmly, making him appear much older than that. I guess surviving a hard life did that to a person.

"Okay." Now I felt guilty that his birthday had passed with no celebration. I added that to my list to remedy ASAP. Just as long as he didn't make a break for it.

"Technically, I didn't run away. My grandma gave me permission to stay with my friend. In the state of South Carolina, that makes me legit, not a runaway, so I'm good." Bash lifted a shoulder.

"Where's the problem in what you just said there, Bash?" Rowan asked, firm but with a hint of kindness. "You're not staying with that friend and your grandmother doesn't know where you're at."

"Please don't bother her. Money's tight. And Grandma's health ain't good. I didn't want to be a burden to her anymore." Bash motioned around the room. "And I've been doin' just fine on my own."

"You're squatting in the chapel," Rowan said, as if that proved Bash wasn't fine on his own. But you had to give the teenager credit. He'd managed pretty well on his own, all things considered.

I stepped in front of Rowan, ready to block Bash from anything I possibly could. "We've been fine with you staying in the chapel."

Bash seemed hurt by this. "You knew?"

"For a while," Rowan answered. "We're cool with you staying as long as you let us help you figure out how to do this legally. We can ask your grandmother—"

"Please don't! That'll just worry her. Seriously, man, her health is real bad." Bash bowed his head and studied the floor. "I'll tell her. Just give me some time. Please."

I exchanged a look with Rowan and could tell he wasn't on board with that, but when I tilted my head and gave him a slight pout, he huffed in agreement.

"Fine. You have a week to tell her and get this sorted. Avalee and I can go with you, if you need us to."

"M'kay." Bash's shoulders slumped, the weight of his world pressing down on him. And what a world it was for the young boy. But come hell or high water, we'd figure this out with him. If he'd just trust us enough, that is.

CHAPTER 22

SURPRISES WEREN'T FOR EVERYONE, me included. Surely, I'd experienced enough, but that didn't stop me from planning one. Bash needed a proper birthday celebration and how cool would it be that he could say he had one in a ghost town. I'd gotten the entire crew in on it. Fred and Froid were cooking what we'd learned was Bash's favorite meal, chili. I had his favorite cake—plain vanilla with buttercream icing—up in my apartment, along with a new pair of steel-toe work boots. His high-tops were a faded black, so I went with black boots, hoping they would be his style. Others had gifts for him too. The kid was going to be so surprised!

I chose to work alongside Bash in the pecan grove today to keep him away from the party preparations some of the guys were helping pull off. Even Nita was going to make a trip out here to help celebrate, bringing a batch of homemade tortillas to go with Froid's chili. We'd worked steadily all morning, gathering broken tree limbs and debris.

I tossed another branch into the wheelbarrow and glanced at Bash. The kid worked with gusto, as always, yanking and pulling on underbrush like it was no big deal. "Just get the big stuff. The bush hog should be able to handle the rest," I reminded him.

"M'kay."

Wiping my sweaty hair out of my face, I scanned the five rows of bountiful trees. If the tiny green balls sprouting along the branches were any indicator, we'd have a decent harvest of pecans come September. The ground was coated in rotted pecans, making me sad that these trees had given so many years with no one here to accept their offerings, but also hopeful that it would never be the case again.

Speaking of celebration. I looked in Bash's direction as he yanked a broken branch from the snares of vines. He glanced up and caught me staring. Turning away so he couldn't see me grinning like a doofus, I plucked another limb from the overgrown grass. I was struggling to contain my giddiness over the surprise and from the looks he kept tossing my way, he knew something was up. Hopefully I could make it a few more hours without totally giving it away.

Bash cleared his throat. "You all right?"

"Yep," I answered, keeping my back toward him.

A week had passed since we confronted Bash about his situation. Each day I awoke fully expecting Bash to have disappeared in the night, and was fully thankful each day he met me in the pecan warehouse for his daily assignment. Through some unspoken agreement, we were a team. A team he wouldn't be bailing on. At least, I hoped not.

"Who's that?" Bash asked, nodding his head toward a blue sedan parking in front of the saloon.

"Not sure." I shucked off my gloves and shoved them in my back pocket. "I'll go see."

"M'kay."

I spotted the blonde middle-aged woman exiting the car. I'm not sure why, intuition perhaps, but I suddenly had a pretty good idea of who she was. Perhaps Bash did too because he shoved his hat down further, shadowing his face as he backed slightly behind one of the pecan trees. Thankfully my favorite twins were setting up outside the barbershop. I moved Bash in the opposite direction of the woman and told him, "Froid is feeding us his famous chili for lunch today. He's got this big ole cooker in the alley over there. How 'bout helping him out. Traffic is busy on Main Street, so take the back way." A total lie, considering only two work trucks were parked in the middle of the rutted road.

Bash hesitated, his eyes shifting between me and the woman across the street. Thankfully, she hadn't spotted us yet. Head down, he started weaving through the trees without a word.

I hurried over to the woman dressed in slacks and a button-down blouse at the same time Rowan came out of the diner. We both met her at the same time but Rowan spoke first.

"Beth?" He reached his hand out and she accepted it.

"Yes." Beth offered him a smile, then looked in my direction.

"Avalee, this is Beth. She's Sebastian's caseworker," Rowan introduced, revealing the seriousness of this situation. "Let's go inside the saloon and have a talk." He led the way. Just a short walk, barely a few yards, but it gave me enough time to teeter on a full-blown freak-out.

I stopped Rowan after Beth stepped inside. "Can I talk to you for a moment, alone?"

Rowan glanced inside where Beth was placing her briefcase on the conference table. "Beth, we'll be right with you. There's a Keurig on the sideboard. Help yourself." He shut the door and whispered, "What?"

"We gotta go in there as a team on the same page or we may chance screwing this up," I whispered back, feeling a bit panicky.

Rowan nodded and leaned closer. So close I could smell his cologne, and that familiar scent with hints of crisp apple and sandalwood seemed to settle me a bit. "Okay, okay. What's the plan?"

"The plan is . . ." Taking a deep breath, which was my sly way of sniffing him, I thought about that for a moment. "We know nothing until we have to."

His lips pouted as those thick brows puckered together. "Come again?"

"I said what I said." Huffing, I repeated it slowly on a hushed hiss. "We know nothing until we have to."

"So basically play dumb?" He scratched the back of his neck, already playing the part rather well.

"Yep. Sure."

Appearing a bit doubtful, Rowan led me inside and we took a seat directly in front of the woman. Her hair was in such a severe bun, I could imagine it practically pulling a headache out by the roots.

Beth shifted in her chair. "Is Sebastian here?"

"Uhh . . ." Rowan looked at me.

"Not sure," I quickly added.

Beth gave us a questioning look. "But, Rowan, you said you've seen him."

"Maybe?" Rowan smiled awkwardly and shrugged. Man, he was a terrible liar.

"I want to keep him," I blurted, sounding like a weirdo.

"We'd like for him to stay in our care, if possible," Rowan corrected, placing his hand on top of mine, making us appear like a unit. I went along with it, thinking it would be best for Bash's sake.

Beth's faded blue eyes darted between us. "You two married?"

"Yes," Rowan said without hesitation as I said, "No."

An awkward pause settled around the table, so I amended, "Were . . . We were married."

Three distinct lines formed vertically between her eyebrows as she assessed us. "I'm not sure I should be telling you anything about Sebastian, but his mother died in an accident close to two years ago. I oversaw placing him with his great-grandmother and once that was complete, I closed the case. I didn't realize until now anything was wrong."

My stomach did a double-dip, as if on a roller coaster as I realized if Beth knew Bash then surely Bash knew Beth. He'd seen her, but I hoped beyond hoping he hadn't come to the wrong conclusion on why she was here. I wanted to sneak my phone out of my pocket and send Froid a text to check on him, but I refrained.

"I'm not sure anything is actually wrong. His grandmother gave him permission to stay elsewhere." I wanted to high-five Rowan for his quick thinking.

"Rose gave him permission to specifically stay with a certain friend's family. Not in a construction zone."

"You said great-grandmother?" I asked.

"Yes. No other relative came forward." Beth glanced to the right. "I shouldn't even be telling you that."

Before I could stop myself, I reached underneath the table and gripped Rowan's knee. I squeezed, a plea of some sort. I shouldn't have done it, but it was too late to take it back.

Rowan cleared his throat and placed his palm over my hand still clinging to his knee. "What if Rose gives Sebastian permission to stay with us?"

I flipped my hand and squeezed his, so proud of how fast the man thought of this on the fly. "Yes," I said too loudly and then tried to tone it down. "That sounds like a good idea . . ." I looked at Rowan and then Beth.

"Do either of you know Rose?" The three vertical lines between her eyebrows softened.

We exchanged unsettled glances.

"Vaguely," Rowan answered with a lie of sorts. "But if you give her a call and let me speak to her, I'm sure we can clear this up." He gave her a lopsided smile. "Sure would make your paperwork load a heckuva lot less. You got enough of that. Am I right, Beth?"

Beth didn't answer him right away, but I saw the pink bloom along her cheeks. Ole Rowdy had pulled out the aw-shucks flirt and it seemed to be working. She stepped out the back entrance to make a phone call.

Freaking out, I whisper-yelled, "We're going to jail!"

"Calm down, *a stór*." Rowan rubbed my shoulder. "We've done nothing wrong. Let's just see what she has to say."

The door opened moments later and Beth walked in with her phone extended in Rowan's direction.

He accepted it and said, "Hello?" Then he proceeded to *uh-hmm* and *yes ma'am* through ten solid minutes of a conversation I couldn't hear. He handed Beth the phone and then she carried on a similar conversation for a much shorter time frame.

"So . . ." Beth pocketed her phone. "Rose is giving you permission, Rowan, to take in Sebastian."

I gasped. "Seriously?"

"This is a unique situation. One I hope I won't regret." Beth packed up her belongings. "Even though I'm not technically his caseworker anymore, expect me to be checking in."

"Of course." Rowan gave her another aw-shucks smile but it didn't beam the way it did earlier. I was pretty sure what he'd just signed up for was sinking in about as lightly as a ton of bricks.

We talked a little longer before Beth left. After she drove away, I started up the street.

Rowan snagged me by my belt loops and hauled me back. "Whoa there, teammate."

"What?"

"Now we need another plan before we approach Bash with all this."

I rubbed my forehead. "You're right." I held a finger up. "Don't get bigheaded over it." I dropped my hands to my hips and spun in a circle, thinking. "Why don't we just be straight up with him. We've gone through the proper channels and have gotten permission for him to stay here."

Rowan nodded. "Yeah. Okay. Say it just like that and I think we'll be fine."

I clucked my tongue. "Fine? I can't believe you'd speak that word to me." I pretended to clutch my pearls.

He smirked—the specific smirk with one corner of his mouth curled slightly higher than the other he used to give me just before giving me a loud popping kiss—but today he didn't do that. "Let's go tell him the good news, smarty-pants."

We walked to the alley where Froid was stirring the gigantic cast-iron pot of chili. It reminded me of a witch's cauldron but with a lid.

"Hey, Froid, where's Bash?"

Froid tapped the long wooden spoon on the edge of the pot and placed the lid on, the pinging sound of iron against iron ringing out. "I ain't seen 'em."

Sharing wide-eyed glances, Rowan and I rushed to the chapel and found exactly what I had feared but expected.

The sleeping bag gone. The tattered blue backpack gone.

Sebastian gone.

CHAPTER 23

MAUDIE AND I ONCE HAD A VERY SHORT-LIVED ASPIRATION of becoming quilters. At her insistence, we joined a local quilting club at the library and set out to do the things quilters do. Make quilts. But man oh man. Those old ladies' nimble hands did something my impatient ones couldn't do and that was to sew with precision. I spent more time using a seam ripper to tear out my awful stitches than I spent with the sewing machine. I didn't want to think of all the squares of fabric I ruined. At the end of that summer, I counted the quilting challenge as a fail and never sat in front of a sewing machine again. Reflecting back on my life, I couldn't help but focus on several patches of fails woven deeply into its design. I often wondered if I could cut those threads out, but quickly realized the action would only cause it all to unravel.

My goal had always been to make a positive mark on the world, but seemed all I was good at was making disastrous smudges.

Brooding inside the saloon, Rowan and I sat shoulder to shoulder at the bar, staring straight ahead. Rows of jewel-tone bottles were lined up before us. I worried a seam in the bar top's wood grain with the tip of my finger, wishing one of those bottles actually held something stronger than the water I'd filled them with.

Sighing heavily, Rowan raked his fingers through his hair. "I can't believe we lost him."

Bash had disappeared into what seemed to be thin air. Seriously, the boy had mad Houdini skills and if I ever caught up with him, I'd make him divulge his secrets. Work had come to a screeching halt while everyone came together to comb the entire town and surrounding woods for over three hours, finding no sign of the teenager. Not even Preacher could find him. And how that dog whined with his nose to the ground, I truly believed he searched as hard as we did.

I huffed a haughty laugh. "Story of our lives."

Rowan's face swung in my direction. "What is?"

"Losing kids . . . Or maybe it's just the story of my life." Frowning, my eyes burned and suddenly I could hardly swallow.

"Avalee—"

I slashed a hand through the air. "Sorry I brought it up. Let's not go there today, okay?"

Rowan pressed his lips firmly together, reluctantly agreeing. I wanted to ease his worry with a smile but I was too darn sad to pull one off.

"We were good to him . . . I just don't get why he'd run . . ." I sniffled.

Rowan's hand met my clenched fist. "We'll find him, Avalee." He wore an irresistible cloak of confidence. It made me want to pinch him.

As I began to slump forward with all intentions of laying down my throbbing head, I heard the distinct beeping of a large piece of equipment backing up. "What's that?" I swiveled on the barstool and glanced out the front window but saw nothing.

Rowan checked something on his phone. "That would be the surprise I set up for you."

I shook my head. "I've had enough surprises for one day." Beth showing up and then Bash running off were more than enough . . .

"It's only a little after two." Rowan stood and pulled me to my feet. "There's time for one more surprise and I promise you'll approve of this one."

Grumbling, I reluctantly trailed him outside and found a yellow long reach excavator rolling past. "What's that for?" I hollered over the beastly rumble.

"I got approval to tear down the feedstore." Rowan waved a hand toward the machine. "Surprise!"

His forced cheer didn't fool me; we were both miserably disappointed and worried, but I followed him to the feedstore to do right by at least one lost boy.

We gathered an assortment of chairs and set up across the street from the feedstore, making the building demolition the afternoon's entertainment.

Froid rolled the giant pot of chili next to a foldout table and Nita helped him spread out the food, minus the birthday cake. He dabbed his brow with a handkerchief. "Food's ready. Y'all come an' get it." When I remained in my camping chair while everyone else dug in, Froid came over with a bowl and placed it in my hands. "Little Avalee, stop worrin' 'bout that boy. He'll show up."

I gave him a weak smile and nodded my head, doubting that very much. Everyone seemed to think Bash would turn up by dark, but I wasn't so sure.

Soon the chili pot was empty and the group had settled into their chairs to take in the demo show across the street.

"I need to get going, lady." Nita tucked her black hair behind her ears, leaned down, and gave me a hug, something we didn't do often but I think she knew I needed one. "I'll do a loop around the area before I head home."

"Thanks. And thank you for the tortillas." I pointed toward the table where her aluminum pan was now empty. "The crew tore them up."

"Glad everyone enjoyed them. I'll call you later." She squeezed my shoulder, straightened, and walked away.

"Food's getting cold." Rowan pointed his spoon at my bowl and took a seat in the chair beside mine.

I glanced down at the chili, thick with chunks of beef and four different beans. Normally the spicy aroma would make my mouth water, but it only made my stomach recoil today. "Here." I shoved my bowl in his hand.

Rowan stared at the bowl and then at me, as if stewing on something. Finally, he took the bowl and chowed down.

I folded my arms over my abdomen, wishing that alone could push the pain away, and watched as the excavator's claw dropped a piece of roof to the side. The splintering crash was marked by a plume of dust. A two-man crew aimed their water hoses at the dust, tamping it down before it tried choking us. Good thing, because I was already struggling to breathe with ease. *Where is that kid?* I kept asking myself over and over, scanning the area around me, as if he were hiding in a shadow nearby. Other possible answers flickered through my head while everyone chattered around me. Was he hitchhiking to parts unknown? Hiding out in the woods just past these buildings? Or did he simply vanish as easily as my own children had vanished from my life?

The group let out a collective gasp. I blinked out of my haze and glanced up as bricks rained down. The excavator's ability to destroy something with such precision was quite impressive. As the claw came down on the brick wall, it sounded like a giant monster crunching on cement potato chips.

Preacher trotted over and rested his head on my lap, looking up at me with the saddest puppy dog eyes.

I opened my mouth to repeat the same line of assurance Rowan offered me, that we would find him, but I didn't have it in me to offer something I wasn't one-hundred-percent sure about. I scratched behind his ear instead.

Once the feedstore was nothing but a pile of rubble, I slipped away and made it inside the saloon before a strong yet gentle arm slipped firmly around my chest. I knew that protective hold, even though it'd been years since I'd felt it. I wanted to pull away but was too drained to do anything but let him hold me.

Dragging me closer, Rowan's heartbeat pressed against my upper back. He brought his mouth to my ear and whispered, "I got you."

Three simple words, but that was all it took for me to splinter. I let go and fell into his embrace, crying for Bash, crying for how I'd failed the kid, crying for already missing him. I cried. Cried some more. And when Rowan whispered, "It's okay. Let it out," I cried even more.

Rowan stood holding me upright while I crumbled, but I heard his quieter sobs mingling with mine. I wasn't certain if his tears were over losing Bash or if they were over losing in general, but I did know they were just as valid as mine.

Pain. It was much like a quilt. Even if the squares formed different patterns and were stitched together using different techniques, in the end, they all still formed a quilt. Our traumas and losses might have different patterns, and different stitches of life held them together, but in the end, all of them still formed pain.

CHAPTER 24

AS DAYS TURNED INTO A WEEK AND THEN ANOTHER, my expectation of Bash showing up waned considerably. Rowan had dodged Beth and Rose so far, but it wouldn't hold right on.

Lying in bed and staring into the darkness, I mapped out everywhere we'd searched and started considering other spots to check out. Around four I'd had enough of the tossing and turning game, so I shoved the blanket aside and made my way to the living room in the dark. I moved to the window and peered out. Darker than dark with no moon or stars in sight, it was difficult to make out anything. The streetlights wouldn't be installed until the paving was complete, so I had no view to gaze at, but I settled a shoulder against the wall and stared out at nothing anyway.

I straightened and started to turn toward the kitchen, but stopped when a tiny flash of light broke the darkness and started moving from behind the diner across the street. Blinking, I leaned closer to the window to make sure my eyes weren't playing tricks on me and sure enough I saw what looked to be a small flashlight beam. We hadn't had any trespassers ever since Fred and Froid had handled it. Then I thought of someone else it could be.

Without thinking it through, I yanked on a pair of jogging pants and ran downstairs barefoot. I hauled tail, my long legs making quick work of running down the street and through the alley between the diner and the mercantile. A piercing pain shot through my foot and up my leg. I cried out, unable to help myself, and dropped to the ground.

Suddenly, a light shined my way, blinding me at first and then landing on my foot. The beam glanced off the nail sticking out my heel.

I averted my eyes and groaned. "Dang it! Dang it! Dang it!" Each word managed to slip through my gritted teeth.

"You need to pull the nail out."

I looked up, momentarily forgetting all about the nail and the pain. "You stinker! I've been worried sick about you!" I wagged my finger. "Just where have you been?"

Bash shined the light in my face, blinding me this time on purpose. "Don't you dare think about leaving me like this. It's your fault!"

"It's my fault you were walking around a construction site barefoot? Seriously, how many times have you lectured me about safety?"

Shocked again, I gasped. That had to have been the most words I'd ever heard Bash speak all at once. "Because I saw someone slinking around my town in the middle of the night. So this is your fault."

"I still don't see why you neglected to put on your shoes."

"I have to protect what's important to me." Mad as fire, I yanked the nail out and slung it. The tiny weapon pinged against the brick wall. "And if you'd stuck around instead of running off, you'd know you're important to me too." I felt a wet trickle of blood seeping from the wound.

Bash picked me up like I weighed nothing and started for the saloon. For a lanky teenager, he was freakishly strong.

"Put me down. I can walk."

He didn't respond, just kept walking. Preacher seemed to have appeared from out of nowhere just like this runaway punk. The dog barked once, adding his two cents to the conversation, and followed beside us.

Once we were inside, Bash helped me into one of the chairs at the conference table. He retrieved the first aid kit from behind the bar while I inspected the mess on my throbbing foot. We worked together, cleaning the wound with alcohol pads which set it on fire, then pressing a wad of gauze to it to stop the bleeding.

"I can hold it. Thanks." I moved his hand out the way and kept pressure on the wound.

"You need to go to the ER or something?"

"I think it'll stop bleeding on its own. How about having a seat with me." I tipped my head toward the chair beside me.

Bash obeyed but kept his sights on my foot, handing me a fresh pack of gauze. "You need to get a tetris shot or something?"

"Tetanus?" I snorted. "Anyone working construction needs to have enough sense to keep that vaccine up-to-date . . ." *Ah, shoot!* I felt like a class A failure, knowing darn well I never verified whether this kid had had an updated one. "Bash, are you current on your tetanus vaccine?"

He pressed his lips together and shrugged. I took that as a no. I also took in his appearance, and the poor kid looked a little worse for wear.

"We gotta get that updated. Being on a construction crew . . . that's a must."

"Am I still on the crew?"

"Yes, even though you ghosted us." I elbowed him, hoping to lighten the mood, but he continued to frown.

"You said I was important to you?" He seemed puzzled by that.

"You are important to me. To Rowan. Even the work crew. We've all been sick with worry."

"But you turned me in." His voice cracked.

"It wasn't like that and if you'd stuck around you would have known." I swapped the bloody gauze for a fresh wad, covered it all with a bandage, and tried ignoring the pain. "Your grandmother gave

Rowan permission for you to stay with him, as long as you promise not to pull whatever you did with your friend's family on us."

Bash's brow furrowed as his eyes narrowed. "Rowan wants me to stay with him?"

"Yeah. In the apartment beside mine. Nothing has to change except you don't have to camp out in the chapel anymore. You'd have your own bedroom and everything." I placed my hand on top of his and waited until he met my eyes. "Bash, you wouldn't have to worry about hiding."

He stared at my foot, but I doubted he saw it. His gaze appeared a million miles away, perhaps coming to terms with the choice he had to make. Did it even seem appealing to him? I had no clue.

Preacher walked up and laid his head on Bash's lap and Bash began petting him.

"That poor dog has done nothing but mope since you left us." I stretched my hand and ran it over Preacher's back. "Ain't that right, boy?"

"I'm sorry," Bash said quietly, his attention remaining on the dog.

"It's okay. I get why you did it, just don't do it again. We all missed you." I placed my hand on his shoulder briefly. He needed to know someone genuinely cared. Genuinely wanted him. "Whatever you need or want, all you gotta do is tell me."

Eventually, he lifted his gaze—now glittering with unshed tears. "Avalee?"

"Yeah, Bash?"

He let out a long, staggered exhale. "I'm really hungry."

His declaration both broke and lit my heart. "Then let's go get something to eat."

"What about your foot?"

I peeled the bandage away and checked the puncture wound. "Shoot. It's still bleeding." I pressed the bandage back into place. "How about we head upstairs so I can prop up my foot and I'll have Rowan pick us up something?"

"M'kay."

For once, I was totally happy to hear that word. And happy that he told me exactly what he needed and trusted me to deliver. Or I hoped so anyway.

After we made the long, agonizing journey up the eighteen steps to the second floor, I grabbed my phone and texted Rowan. It was past five, so chances were good that he'd be up.

In need of Waffle House. ASAP. Chocolate chip waffles. Hash browns scattered, smothered, & covered. Fiesta omelet. And get yourself something too.

Bash read over my shoulder. "You make that up?"

"No. It's all on the menu." I plopped on the couch and kept an eye out for Rowan's response. Nothing so far.

"You know the menu from memory?"

I placed my foot on the coffee table, willing it to quit hurting so bad. "The Waffle House was Rowan's and my favorite place growing up."

"You two together?"

I raised an eyebrow, surprised at his steady stream of questions. "Just friends." My phone pinged. Rowan's only reply was a thumbs-up emoji, no questions asked about why on earth I needed a breakfast feast before sunrise. He'd been my ride or die for most of my life. Always ready for whatever, as long as we were together.

"Just friends. Ya sure?"

I looked up from the phone, a bit taken aback that this young man seemed to have read my thoughts. "Why do you say that?"

Bash sat down beside me and I caught a whiff of him. "You said, 'My ride or die.'"

I rubbed my eyes and yawned. This sleep deprivation was really messing with me to the extreme if I was saying my thoughts out loud without realizing it. "It'll be a little while before Rowan gets here with the food. You're welcome to grab a shower." I motioned to the spare bedroom. "Des keeps extra clothes in the dresser in there. Help yourself."

"You with Des then?"

I laughed a little too long. "Bash . . . if you must know, I'm with Preacher. He's currently the only male in my life."

Bash gave me a strange look. Yeah, perhaps that didn't sound as humorous as I had thought it would.

I grabbed the throw pillow and put it on the coffee table. Cringing, I placed my aching foot on top of it.

Bash cringed too. "Man . . . I'm really sorry about your foot."

I waved off his concern. "I'm not worried about my foot. It'll heal."

His face puckered as he gripped the back of his neck, sending another whiff of that unclean teenager smell my way. "It hurts though, right?"

"Yeah, but not nearly as much as it hurt me when you ran off." I leaned against the couch cushion and sighed. "Bash, you mean something to me. I've been sick with worry."

"I didn't mean to make you worry."

"I know." I lolled my head in his direction and noticed his eyes reddening. Wanting to put him at ease, I teased, "You'll just have to make it up to me."

"How?"

"That dang nail went through my right foot. You know what that means?"

Bash shook his head.

"It means I won't be able to drive for a bit. Know what else?"

He shook his head again.

I held up my hands and wiggled my fingers, most of the blue polish gone from me chewing on my nails. I'd skipped out on my appointment with Starla last week, too bummed to pamper myself. "I've not had such hideous nails in a very long time. I'll need you to drive me to a manicure appointment."

His shoulders drooped. "I would but I don't have a license."

Shoot, there I was trying to lighten the mood and didn't even think he wouldn't have a license, something Maudie made sure I had as soon as I was old enough.

"I have my permit though," Bash added.

"That's all you need to drive me around. We'll get you ready for the driver's test and then I'll have Rowan take you to the DMV, if you'd like."

Bash's blue eyes sparked with some life. "Really?"

"Yep. I glanced at my phone, realizing I had never seen Bash with one. "You don't have a phone?"

He shook his head. "I had one of those pay-as-you-go, but it stopped working."

"We'll take care of that this week too."

"You don't have to—"

"Yes, I do. From here on out, I need to be able to get ahold of you." We would have a talk about having the tracker switched on at all times too. "Now how about using my bathroom to get yourself cleaned up." I dipped my chin in that direction. "The food will be here soon."

Maybe Bash was aware of his serious need of a shower, because he beat a quick path to the bathroom, detouring to grab a pair of sweatpants and a T-shirt from the spare room first.

As the shower turned on, Preacher hopped onto the couch and snuggled beside me. Running my fingers through his coarse fur, I offered up a prayer, thanking God for keeping the teenager safe and bringing him back to us. Too many situations didn't allow a child to return. My lost babies. And then little ones like Douglas Holt who had their lives stolen. I knew it in my bones that having Bash was a gift, one I prayed God would allow Rowan and me to keep.

CHAPTER 25

THERE WEREN'T MANY THINGS MORE APPEALING than a man in a plaid shirt rolled to the elbows, worn jeans, and work boots carrying two Waffle House bags. The bags declared in red ink, *GOOD FOOD FAST*. Amen to that.

"You're my hero."

"What's wrong with your foot?" Rowan kicked the door shut and was by my side in a flash. He placed the bags on the coffee table and picked up my foot.

"I stepped on a nail."

He glanced up. "You did not."

I cringed. "Yep. But it's okay. The bleeding has stopped. Almost."

Rowan peeled away the bandage to see for himself. "You gonna tell me how this came about and why you needed all that food?" He tilted his head toward the bags without looking away from my wound. His lips were puckered in concentration, making him look rather kissable. His eyes rose to meet mine. "You're not going to answer me?"

Before I could say a word, the bathroom door swung open, letting out a cloud of steam and a much fresher Bash. He'd been in there a good thirty minutes. Thank goodness, because he was definitely past due.

Rowan's jaw about hit the floor as he shot to his feet. "You found him?"

Bash froze by the bathroom door, but just briefly, because as soon as he spotted the bags of food his long legs were on the move.

I scooted off the couch and began limping into the dining room. "We'll fill you in over breakfast."

We set all of the carryout containers on the dining table and tucked into the feast with fervor. I guess with Bash showing back up, my appetite had, too, with a vengeance. Between unladylike bites of waffle and hash browns, I told Rowan about our eventful morning. Bash matched me bite for bite, but Rowan barely touched his food. He slipped Preacher pieces of bacon and biscuit, his eyes never leaving mine as I talked.

"So, whatcha think, man? You gonna stick around?" Rowan offered his plate and Bash gladly accepted it.

After swallowing down a forkful of omelet, Bash took a long swig of tea since I didn't have juice or milk to offer him. Regular grocery shopping suddenly moved high up on my to-do list. "I like it here and I like y'all, but what does this all mean exactly?"

I wiped my hands on a napkin. "It means what I told you earlier. You stay next door with Rowan. It also means you need to get back into school."

Bash's lips puckered with a rebuke but I held a palm up. "I've already done some research and you can do it all online at your own pace, if you want. Or you can attend school. There's a high school about twenty-five minutes from here."

Bash seemed to chew on that while he chewed on some more food. He finished off the hash browns. He used a wedge of toast to scoop out the rest of the grits Rowan had added to the order, then the last few bites of waffle disappeared into his bottomless pit. Finally, he placed the fork on the table and sat back, sprawling like teenage boys do.

When he didn't answer, I prompted, "Well?"

His gaze darted between me and Rowan. "M'kay."

I took a sip of tea and looked past Bash's shoulder at the mountain of gifts on the counter.

"Good. We need to celebrate. Rowan, you want to grab his gifts?"

"Gifts?" Bash looked confused as Rowan placed them in front of him on the table.

"You didn't just skip out on us that day, you skipped out on your surprise birthday party."

"For real?" He frowned. "I didn't know."

"Of course you didn't. It was a surprise." I waved toward the gifts. "Go ahead and open them. Most of the crew got you a little something."

Rowan and I leaned back in our chairs and watched Bash unwrap his gifts, grinning like a little kid on Christmas morning. He made out like a bandit. The work boots from me. Rowan got him a pair of high-dollar safety glasses and work gloves. The twin brothers got him a drink thermos. Desmond and Nita went in together and gave him an entire bag of clothes, all Carhartt, our favorite brand for work attire. I'm talking even underwear and socks.

After tossing the gift wrap, Bash grabbed up the stack of clothing and disappeared into the bathroom. He came out wearing a pair of dark-wash jeans, an Army green T-shirt, a thick pair of socks, and his new boots. A new hat sat low on his head with tufts of blond hair sticking out around it. He looked like a brand-new person. A brand-new person who was frowning.

I hobbled to him. "What's wrong?"

His bony shoulder hitched slightly. "I don't deserve all this."

"Don't even. All we did was make it easier for you to work hard with us. You're a fundamental part of this revitalization project, so our gifts are just us being selfish." I downplayed it enough that his lips tipped up on one side. I hugged him. "Happy birthday."

He returned the embrace after hesitating a second or two. "Thank you." He released me and shocked us by giving Rowan a hug while thanking him.

"I'm glad you're back." Rowan clapped him on the back and then held him at arm's length. "Now that's all settled, how 'bout explaining to us where the heck you've been." Rowan used a fatherly tone and it made my insides go all warm and gooey.

"Here," Bash replied, simply.

Rowan scoffed. "No you haven't. We've looked everywhere."

"I have, though."

Rowan and I said nothing, just looked at him expectantly.

"I've been in the basement underneath the diner."

Now I scoffed, crossing my arms. "The diner doesn't have a basement."

Bash gave me a smug look.

Five minutes later, after managing to cram on a pair of shoes, I hobbled behind Rowan as Bash led us across the street. We followed him into the kitchen's pantry. He moved aside a stack of Sheetrock, revealing a small door.

"I found this when you had me clean out the closet. Some of the wall fell off when I accidentally shoved against it." Bash opened the door and motioned for us to follow.

"And you didn't think to tell me?" I asked as we descended down creaky stairs, Rowan's and my cell phone flashlights helping to light the way.

"I planned to tell you eventually."

We reached the bottom, our feet landing on a hard dirt floor. The stale air was a bit cooler, which was perfect for this space.

"This is a root cellar." I pointed to the shelves lined with dusty jars of various produce. Green beans, okra, beets, peaches, lots of honey. Piles of what looked to be decomposed potatoes were along the back wall. The only thing out of place was the burgundy sleeping bag rolled out in the middle of the floor with a comic book on top of it.

Rowan huffed a laugh while scanning the large room with his flashlight. "This ghost town keeps on offering up secrets, doesn't it?"

I shook my head. "I can't believe the investigators didn't find it during their search."

Rowan bent down and picked up the comic book. "Where'd you get this?" He opened it and turned the pages with a careful gentleness.

"From that crate on the top shelf. It's full of them." Bash pulled the crate from the shelf and placed it on the ground so we could see for ourselves.

I suddenly had a sneaky suspicion as to why Rowan was handling the article with such care. "Rowan?"

He shook his head in bafflement while thumbing through the crate. "Bash . . . I do believe you've found a legit treasure."

Bash's nose wrinkled. "But the cover says it's only worth ten cents. It ain't even DC Comics." He curled his lip, unimpressed.

"Action Comics *is* DC Comics," Rowan mumbled, still flipping through the crate in awe.

I held my foot aloft while holding onto the shelf. "Maudie has a few appraisers on speed dial. You wanna take this crate to Beaufort?"

Rowan glanced up. "I'm allowed to see your grandma?"

"You ain't stopped seeing her, so don't even." I hobbled toward the stairs. "Bash, gather your stuff and put it in my apartment for now. Then get Preacher and yourself loaded up in Rowan's truck. If you're sticking around, we need to introduce you to the greatest human you'll ever meet."

"I take back what I said about you earlier," I grumbled under my breath. My grandmother and I had only been waiting in this exam room at the urgent care for about fifteen minutes, but that was fifteen minutes too long.

"What'd you say?" She didn't bother to look up from the game of sudoku on her phone.

"Nothing." I lay back on the table, the paper cover crinkling underneath me. As soon as she had caught wind of my injury, Maudie left the guys at her place and took me to get my foot checked out. I tried protesting but she wouldn't listen, only carrying on about how I'd be in a pickle if my foot fell off.

"Aha!" Maudie held her phone out so I could see the screen. "I beat my highest score."

"Go you," I offered, mustering up a little enthusiasm.

My grandmother had been playing that game for as long as I could remember, saying it kept her brain from going to mush. I guessed it worked, because Maudie was sharp as a tack.

"I like Sebastian."

I rolled my head in her direction. "Me too. He's a good kid."

"I like Rowan staying with you too." Her eyes twinkled.

"It's not like that and you know it."

"Well, it should be." She pointed a finger at me. "You two just work. We both know it."

"Ain't you a fine one to be talking, Miss I've-been-single-since-forever."

Maudie rolled her eyes. "Don't even go there with that, young lady. I didn't have a Rowan. I had a dirty rotten rodent!" Her words came close to a hiss.

I never met Grandpa Bryce, although I'm pretty sure the dirty rotten rodent could have helped it if he'd wanted to. Maudie said she'd had no choice but to run him off when he wouldn't stop chasing tail. Maybe that's why my father didn't understand how to be a daddy since he never had a decent role model himself in that department.

Maudie cleared her throat on a haughty cough. "We both know you and Rowan together would also work in that boy's favor. Y'all could give him a stable, loving home." She pointed at me again when my lips parted. "You got it to offer, so don't be stingy."

"Wow . . . Guilt-trip me, why dontcha." I squinted at my meddling grandmother. "This is the real reason why you rushed me to get my foot checked out, isn't it? To grill me about Bash and Rowan."

"No, I brought you to get your foot checked because you should never monkey around with your health. But also . . ." She made a face. "You were hovering over that poor boy like you fully expected something to pounce on him at any moment."

I sucked my teeth. "I was not." I totally was, but still . . .

Maudie copied me, sucking her teeth too. "Were too."

"I just want him to feel safe." I started folding the edge of the paper covering.

"Honey, you have a runaway willingly keeping close to you. There's a reason for that. It's because he feels safe with you. Trust me." Maudie tucked her phone into the front pocket of her denim overalls. She reminded me of a cross between those two older friends from *Steel Magnolias*, Ouiser and Clairee. She wore overalls rolled up mid-calf most days but got all dolled up for church on Sundays. Prissy with a side of salt. That's how my father has always described his mother. "It won't hurt him and Rowan to have some time alone. I told Rowan to take him fishing after the appraiser leaves. It'll do them good to bond some if they're going to live under the same roof."

The nurse practitioner entered the room, ending our little heart-to-heart. Swift and precise, she cleaned the wound properly and dressed it. Everything I had already done, minus the alcohol. Apparently, that was a no-no. Once I was given a paper on how to tend to my wound and a prescription for an antibiotic, we were on our way.

Maudie made me sit in her truck while making a pit stop at the grocery store. No way would she be allowing us out of Beaufort before stuffing our bellies with some of her Southern cuisine.

We arrived at the house and found Desmond's shiny silver sedan parked beside Rowan's truck. He came out of the house with Rowan and Bash.

I opened the truck door. "Des, what are you doing here?"

My friend reached in and helped me out. "Rowan called. He told me about all the mischief you'd gotten up to this morning."

Maudie rounded the hood of the truck. "Desmond!"

Desmond straightened his hat and grinned. "My lovely Maudie."

"Now I have almost all my favorite people here." She wrapped an arm around his waist, pulling him inside while chatting up a storm.

The guys were quick to help unload bags filled with ingredients for barbecued chicken legs, seven-layer salad, and corn bread casserole.

"Is your foot gonna fall off?" Bash asked, holding the door for me. He looked genuinely concerned.

"Nah. All's good." I patted his shoulder as I hobbled past him.

"We have some news," Rowan said as we reached the kitchen. He shared a grin with Bash. "It looks like Bash is a rich man."

Bash's smile fell. "Me?"

"You found it."

"But it belongs to the town."

I eased into a chair at the breakfast nook and propped my foot on the one across from me. It continued to throb like a toothache, but I ignored it the best I could. "Actually, that's sort of a gray area. Finders keepers and all that. It's yours." I turned my attention to Rowan. "How much does the appraiser think that crate is worth?" I took a sip of the water Maudie offered me.

"At least three million."

Water sprayed all over the table. "No way!" Shaking my head, I grabbed a napkin from the napkin holder in the middle of the table and cleaned up my mess.

Rowan plucked a package of iced oatmeal cookies from one of the shopping bags and leaned over and kissed Maudie on the cheek. Those were his favorites. "The appraiser has to double-check with this comic book collector, but he's pretty sure his estimation is correct and that his guy will want to buy them." He swiped at least five cookies and passed the pack to Bash, who grabbed a handful and then passed it to Desmond.

I leaned back in my chair and took in the sight before me. Maudie already in the process of seasoning the chicken. Rowan, Desmond, and Bash leaning against the counter, chowing down on cookies. It really did look like this worked. Everyone fit.

I was so scared it wouldn't last.

CHAPTER 26

GOOFING OFF TAKES MORE EFFORT THAN ONE WOULD THINK. It legit means to avoid doing any work, but you end up working on a plan to goof off, right? Take the scene I'd just stumbled upon on Main Street this morning. All of the construction equipment had been moved into the alleyways and bright orange lines had been haphazardly drawn with spray paint. Lined up on the orange line at the beginning of the street sat two old tractors revving their engines, while the group gathered along the edge of the street whooped and hollered.

Shaking my head, I moved closer to the ruckus and waited until a shirtless Rowan and a subcontractor zipped down the street on two rusty tractors. I had no idea where they got them from. The loud machines coughed and sputtered as the men turned around and raced back with Rowan taking the win.

Dust whirling around in the bright sunshine, Rowan tossed his fists in the air and did the Rocky victory shuffle right there on top of the tractor.

"What in the devil are you doing, Rowdy?" I yelled over the noise of the farm equipment and small crowd.

"Rowdy?" Bash looked around, his brow furrowed.

"That's me," Rowan declared, oh so proudly, before hopping down.

I shielded my eyes and squinted. "Maudie nicknamed him Rowdy. She also used to call him a hellion."

"Affectionately though." Rowan grinned at me over his shoulder as he fiddled with something on the tractor.

I pushed out a haughty laugh. "Whatever you need to say to make yourself feel better, buddy."

Rowan swiftly interjected, "We both know I'm Maudie's favorite." His T-shirt was hanging out of his back pocket where he'd stuffed it, and he yanked it out and slung it over his left shoulder as he turned and started walking over to me. The man was all loose-hipped swagger, full of natural confidence. The closer he got, the more his physique came into view.

I gawked. "Where'd those come from?"

He readjusted the shirt as if making sure to keep his chest covered for some reason. "Where'd what come from?"

"Those." I wiggled my fingers in the direction of the impressive peaks and valleys etched along his abdomen. "You didn't have those while we were . . ."

The amusement fell from his face. "I've had a lot of free time on my hands in the last several years." He turned his back to me and hurried into his shirt.

"No need to be modest now. You've been flashing the entire town."

His head tipped back as he chuckled. "A *ghost* town." Once his throaty laugh cut off, he leaned into my face. "How about knock it off with the scolding and let's have a little fun." His voice darkened as he said, "I'll even let you on my tractor."

I shoved him back into his place. "We should be working."

"You were the one complaining that most of the crew is already over fifty hours this week. Problem solved. Now go put that fine behind of yours in a chair and relax for a bit"—he hitched a thumb over his broad shoulder and smirked—"while I smoke Bash in this next race."

Bash snorted and muttered with confidence, "Bring it."

We hadn't had a Friday off in months, so I flicked a wrist in the air. "Go on then, Rowdy. Show us whatcha got."

Giving me a rascally wink, Rowan turned on his heel and strode away.

As I watched the guys circle around and pop can tops, razzing each other, I stood off to the side and just took it in for a beat or two. They all looked happy. I'd go as far as saying joyful. No sagging shoulders from the weight of life and responsibility. No thin-lipped frowns. Just a lightness.

For a foggy time in my life there simply wasn't any joy. Anytime a sliver of joy would peek through the clouds of despair, I was quick to turn my back to it. Finally reaching a breaking point, I had packed up my pride and went to counseling. With the help of my counselor, I'd come to understand that joy didn't disprove my pain. The wounds didn't go away, but joy simply worked as a salve for a little while.

With this in mind, I went and grabbed my mobile bench, joined the other spectators, and enjoyed the silly men's shenanigans.

"We gotta protect this noggin," Rowan said, helping Bash fasten a hard hat on his head.

His fatherly display pierced my heart. Another facet of grief—numbness. Watching others experience emotions while none touched me. It was tempting to turn on the numbness now. Instead, I took the sting, let it pierce for a good long moment, then I discreetly wiped the tear off my cheek and returned my focus to the joy. It was right there for me to accept, Rowan caring for this teenage boy, showing him true kindness.

Around one, the crowd began bellyaching about needing food, so Froid rolled out the grill while I made a trip to Publix. I picked up another plain vanilla cake for Bash, several pints of vanilla ice cream, and all the fixings for the burgers.

Under the shade of the pecan trees, we feasted.

"Bash, you did a good job getting this grove cleared out," Milo, our painter extraordinaire, commented.

Bash looked around the freshly cleared land—land he'd broken his young back to get into tip-top shape. Freshly mowed and free of debris, the grove now showed off how appealing it could be as a gathering place. "Avalee helped me," he answered, nonchalant, deflecting any credit.

I leaned my back on the tree behind me and shook my head. "This was all Bash. Now before he denies the fact, let's get to that overdue birthday cake." I shoved to my feet and retrieved the cake from the warehouse.

Once we sang a silly rendition of "Happy Birthday" to Bash and devoured most of the cake, the group began packing up and calling it a day.

With a plastic garbage bag in hand, I helped Bash clear the impromptu picnic until Rowan sidled up to me.

"Wanna see what we can see?"

Aka: Wanna get up to no good?

I scoffed. "You know that question ain't nothing but trouble."

Rowan reached up and tested the strength of a lower branch just over his head, causing the leaves to rustle and a few to float to the ground. "You used to like trouble."

My eyebrow rose dramatically. "Used to be I was quite *dumb*."

He moved closer, playing with a lock of my hair that had escaped the ponytail. "Just take a walk with me, Avalee."

I hemmed and hawed on an answer, but in the end, I allowed him to take my hand and lead the way to what could only be a bad decision.

Rowan reminisced about the dares and challenges we used to do like a bunch of heathens while we meandered through the woods. "Remember that one time you dared me to eat all that raw garlic? I'm talking an entire bulb, not just one clove but the entire bulb. Really, that was cruel."

I made a face. "Yeah. That one backfired. I couldn't stand kissing you for like a week."

Rowan chuckled. "I couldn't help it. No matter what toothpaste or mouthwash I tried, I couldn't get the taste or smell to go away." Grinning, he nudged my side. "How 'bout that time you got stuck in the train caboose."

I laughed, having recalled that very memory not too long ago. "There's no forgetting that day. Ever."

He nudged me again. "Because of that kiss, right?"

We needed to get off the kissing subject, ASAP, so I rummaged around for a dare. "Talk about cruel. You made me run down the hallway in high school, yelling I had lice!" I shoved into him a little harder than he'd nudged me.

Rowan laughed loudly. "I forgot about that one. You were called out of the next period to have your head checked."

"I was so embarrassed, but it got me out of class."

"We got up to some fun back then, didn't we?"

"I guess." I could hear the steady rhythm of water swishing along nearby, and the smell of damp earth grew more noticeable as we picked our way through the woods.

He bumped his shoulder against mine. "Let's play."

"No." I bit my lip, recalling that crazy season of mischief and the naivety of love that had made me do half the idiotic things I'd agreed to.

We reached the edge of the wide stream. Rowan seemed to be contemplating something as he stared at the glittering body of water. "We used to go skinny-dipping."

"When we were married."

He snorted, calling me out on my fib. We both knew darn well there had been times even before then.

I took a step back, standing my ground. "I'm not doing that now. We know better."

His eyes sparkled wildly. "Do we?"

"Knock it off." I shoved into his arm and retreated another step. "No dropping trou, Rowdy!"

"I can drop trou if I wanna. You ain't my boss anymore." The gleam in his golden-brown eyes and the smirk on his full lips declared a challenge, one I knew this sucker would see through to the end. "I'm swimming with or without you."

"I don't care how hot it is today, that stream is going to feel like ice." I moved past him, putting on my air of indifference as I taunted. "Ain't no way your behind is getting in there."

Rowan grabbed my arm before I could skirt his grasp. "Would I kid about something like that?"

I arched a brow. "Is water wet?"

"Why, yes. Yes it is." He gave me his rowdiest grin, releasing me and moving toward the stream. Whipping his shirt off, soon the pants followed.

My gaze shot up to the treetops just as a splash interrupted the natural sounds of the forest. A loud throaty whoop sent a scattering of birds as they abandoned their perches in the tree branches above.

"Hot dang! That's cold!" Rowan's high-pitched wails had me giggling.

I dropped my sight and found him in the middle of the stream. "That's what you get, you fool!"

Suddenly, he stood, the water only waist-deep, enough to cool him down but not enough to do the same for me. My mouth gaped as I watched his bare form wade out of the crystal clear stream.

Rowan sauntered past me, lifting a finger to touch underneath my chin to close my mouth. "You're catching flies, *a stór*."

It was then that something registered. I whirled around and caught sight of his bare backside just before he slipped on his shorts. "You have a tattoo on your chest!"

His back stiffened and his head dropped, as if checking to see if the ink remained over his heart. Without responding to me, he plucked his T-shirt off the ground, but I hurried over and yanked it out of his grasp.

"What's this about?" I studied the four lines of Roman numerals.

Rowan traced a finger over the small dark markings glistening on his damp skin. "The worst days of my life."

I studied the first row, the numerals starting to make sense, then I figured out the next two rows. Realization knocked the wind out of me. Rubbing my chest in the same spot as his ink, I felt my eyes begin to sting. "The days we lost our babies."

He exhaled a heavy breath and nodded, eyes finally looking up to meet mine.

"What about the last row?" I couldn't figure out the significance of those numerals.

"That's the day I gave in and signed the divorce papers."

An ache crept through my body, the sensation similar to coming down with the flu. Clearing my throat, I whispered, "Why would you permanently put such sadness on your skin that can never be washed off?"

Rowan looked heavenward and swallowed hard enough I could see his throat bob. "With or without the ink, that pain's never gonna wash off."

I understood, but said nothing, mostly because I could hardly breathe, much less talk. Unable to bear looking at my ex-husband or the painful reminders of our failures broadcast on his chest, I turned away and left him by the stream. Leaving Rowan had become the only thing I was good at, after all.

CHAPTER 27

FRIDAY'S FUN HAD STAYED WITH ME ALL WEEKEND, and when Rowan and I took Bash to church yesterday, I thought things were on the right track. But as soon as I opened my laptop to go through my emails before getting Monday started, the train derailed. I reread the email for the third time to make sure I understood it clearly. Surely it couldn't be, because if it were, then it meant that Rowan Murray was the new owner of the old Victorian in the woods behind the firehouse. That house was supposed to be mine, doggone it.

"I should have never told that jerk I wanted it." I slammed the lid down on my laptop, pushed it to the side, and stormed downstairs into the saloon. I beelined to the table where Rowan and another engineer were leaning over a set of blueprints. "You're just as bad as that thieving Preacher!"

The other guy's eyes rounded and his mouth gaped, but Rowan looked at me blandly before asking, "What are you going on about now?"

I slammed my fist against the table. Pens went rolling and clanking against the floor. "My house! You mind telling me why you stole it?"

Rowan sighed in a way that said I was acting absurd. "Relax, Avalee."

I clucked my tongue. "Telling a woman to relax is like lighting the dang fuse. Don't tell me to relax!"

"You're popping off like a valve on an air compressor." His eyebrows shot up. "That better?"

Crossing my arms and glaring, I refused to show the humor his comment provoked even though it was a little funny.

Rowan turned to the guy who was doing a stand-up job of studying the blueprints while pretending me *popping off like an air compressor valve* was perfectly normal. "Cal, I'll be back in a little while."

"Uhh . . ." Cal avoided eye contact. "Sure."

Rowan placed his hand on my elbow but I shook him off. Sighing that long-suffering sigh again, he waved a hand for me to lead the way outside. "Let's take the golf cart over there and I'll fill you in on a few things."

"What could you possibly need to fill me in on?"

He slid behind the wheel. "Just come on. Let's go see what we can see."

"Fine." I plopped down beside him. "But I'm not happy about it."

"Duly noted." Rowan wove around various work trucks, waving at crew members as if we were out for a joyride.

Preacher must have thought the same, because he trotted out from the alley beside the pharmacy as we passed by and hitched a ride on the back of the cart. Rowan rounded the firehouse and took the narrow lane up to the house, stopping just a few yards shy of the porch. I noticed someone had been clearing away some of the overgrown vegetation around the house. Probably him, but I didn't say anything.

We just sat on the cart for a minute or two, taking in the house. Three stories with an imposing turret. The right side of the wraparound porch sagged and several of the railing spindles were missing. From the broken windows and the peeling paint faded to the point of holding no color, this place would make for one seriously creepy haunted house, but I could see past the decaying facade. I saw the potential of it being restored to something quite grand and had been dreaming of doing such for years now.

Preacher was the first to move, hopping off the back and finding a shady spot on the porch. He looked right at home, lying down in that sprawling way of his. Rowan climbed off the cart and started up the porch without looking my way. I watched him disappear inside before I followed. Surprisingly, he flipped on some lights, illuminating the thick coating of dust on every surface and the peeling wallpaper.

As if reading my mind, he said, "It'll need to be rewired, but I went ahead and had the power turned on. The electrician said it's safe enough for now. The house has good bones. The inspection came back clear. No structural issues other than the porch, but that'll be an easy fix. The floors are in good shape throughout. They just need refinishing." He scrubbed a foot against the dusty oak boards. The varnish had darkened considerably and was gummy in spots from age.

"Why would you buy this, knowing I planned on buying it myself?" I crossed my arms.

Rowan massaged the back of his neck and sighed. "I bought it for you. Was going to start with some of the reno before I surprised you." He shook his head. "Guess that's shot now."

Shaking my head, I gazed up at the high ceilings draped with cobwebs in the corners. "This makes no sense."

"It does to me." He sat on the stairs and asked me to join him. When I didn't move, he patted the step. "Please, Avalee. Let me explain it to you."

Uncrossing my arms, I moved over and wedged myself onto the step beside him. Our thighs touched but I stoically remained there. "Go ahead. Explain this to me."

"My firm in Greenville has been partnering with Jonas for years on projects. I heard about him taking on this town and asked that I be a part of it." He rested his elbows on top of his knees and clasped his hands together. "They put me on the selection committee. I was the one to encourage Jonas and the other investors to pick your proposal."

My throat began tightening, making it difficult to swallow. "Why would you do that?"

"Because, first and foremost, it was the best one." Rowan leaned back, chin jutted stubbornly, and met my glare with a stern expression. "Plus, I knew we'd have close to a year together. I figured that was enough time to get you to fall in love with me again. That . . . or hate me even worse. Some days it's been a toss-up, but dang it, woman, I want you back."

Stunned by his admission, I stared at the front door. It was ajar, inviting me to flee, but I couldn't move. "It's been over six years."

We sat there in that tension, Preacher's tail thumping against the floor planks the only sound.

Rowan cleared his throat. "You wanted me gone back then, so I got gone." His voice softened. "I waited this long, because . . . I was hoping I'd given you enough time to want me again."

It was on the tip of my tongue to tell him I hadn't ever stopped wanting him, but I chickened out. "I was too broken to keep you, Rowan. It was for your own good."

He cupped my jaw, redirecting my attention to his sad, handsome face. "You're wrong about that. Way back in the third grade, I knew you were my people and it would always be *best* if I went wherever you went."

Our marriage vows flickered through my mind. The man seemed determined to live up to his part of the vows even though we'd legally severed them.

Rowan ran his thumb along my heated cheek. "Just think about it, okay?"

I eased away from his touch and stood. "Okay . . . I better get back to work." Shoulders slumped, I walked out of my dream home and away from my dream man. The idea of keeping both of them was slim to none. Odds never worked in my favor.

I walked the short distance back to town and wandered down Meeting Street. I paused to read my latest pun on the chapel sign. *Writing with a dull pencil is pointless.* So much felt pointless at the moment. Like things working out for me and Rowan.

The sudden need to cry came over me, so I decided to go poke around the inn until I could get myself in check enough to be around people. As I made it inside, my phone rang. I half expected it to be Rowan but was surprised to find my father's name instead. I'd put him off enough recently, and maybe talking to him would distract me from the bomb Rowan just dropped on me, so I answered.

"Hey, Dad."

"Hi, sweetheart. What's my girl up to?"

"You know me . . ." I surveyed the small reception area in its final stage of restoration. The walls were painted a muted grayish green, complementing the brick floors. We'd refinished the floors with white grout and a whitewash sealant, softening the vibrant reddish-brown brick. "Tearing something up in order to put it back together."

"Ah. The ghost town?"

"Yes, sir." I flipped open the lid of a box, finding a matte bluish-gray fish scale tile. It was for the bathroom attached to the Carolina Coast room upstairs. I wedged the box under my arm and headed that way. "How 'bout you? What are you up to?"

"I'm in California, finishing up some business. Same ole, same ole. I miss you though. Let's plan us a father-daughter trip soon."

I glanced out the window at the top of the stairs, catching sight of Bash and Preacher making their way inside the chapel. I pulled the phone away from my ear and checked the time, confirming it to be lunchtime. Bash still preferred lunch with the dog in the chapel most days.

"It'll have to be around Thanksgiving. The town is set to open in September but I'll be tied up here until at least late October." I placed the box of tiles on the floor and started gathering the supplies to get to tiling the walk-in shower.

"November works for me. Let me know where you want to go and I'll have the travel agent get it all squared away for us." Dad paused. "You're doing good, right?"

I gave him the answer I'd been giving him for too many years to keep count, even when it wasn't true. "I'm good, Dad."

"Good. We'll talk soon, hon."

"Okay." I ended the call and wondered if what we'd just done even classified as actually talking. Shaking that off, I put the phone away.

After setting up shop, I began installing the tile, mudding the cement backer board first, then setting the tile in place. My hands were busy but not my mind, so it wandered to my father and our lousy communication. We were skim-the-surface-only conversationalists. Maybe Dad had never figured out how to handle his own loss and grief, much less mine.

"Errr!" I yelled, my anger echoing off the bathroom walls. With just that one thought, a flood of other thoughts came crashing down. When I looked at my father, I saw his loss of my mom. I wondered if people saw the loss of my three babies and my husband when they looked at me.

I sat back on my haunches and stared at the tile without seeing it. Dad wasn't the only one who avoided the topic of my pregnancy losses. No one ever brought it up, as if this type of death was off-limits.

Sure, in the beginning I had no desire to talk to anyone about it, but no one really offered either. It was as if an unspoken rule existed, prohibiting anyone from bringing it up. Was that for my benefit or for theirs? Did it make them too sad? Too uncomfortable? If they acknowledged my loss, were they afraid it might rub off on them?

No matter the reason, and I'm sure it was never anyone's intention, but it left me so very isolated. Eventually the isolation became my norm. That's probably why I always seek it out when overwhelmed by something. Like my ex-husband buying me a dang house and declaring things he had no business declaring. How could he even think we could just dust off the hurts and mistakes and start down a path we already knew didn't end well?

Still unhinged by that, I hunkered down and got back to work. Alone.

CHAPTER 28

JULY

I took to avoiding Rowan like I'd done at the beginning of this project. Had it already been five months since then? At least this time he took a hint and gave me some space. Well, as much as he could, considering we were now next-door neighbors and sort of co-parenting a teenage boy.

Standing on the new sidewalk along Front Street, I regarded the town that we were slowly resuscitating. The air held the acrid odor of asphalt. I breathed it in as my eyes skipped over each building. Roof repairs had been completed, as well as new windows being installed. Next on the list would be refinishing the exteriors. Desmond was completely giddy over choosing paint colors.

I swept the back of my hand over my sweaty forehead, moving my damp bangs to the side. A rain shower had shown up earlier this morning just long enough to get everything good and wet, leaving behind steam rising from the freshly paved streets. Heat was one thing, but layer in sticky humidity, and it became unbearable around here. Work crews scurried to find indoor jobs in the buildings with electricity. The purr of AC units drew them like bees to honey.

Fred shuffled out of the bakery and joined me on the sidewalk. "It might take an extra day to get the trim work done in there." He motioned toward the bakery. He and his brother had slowed down considerably since the relentless heat had set in.

"That's fine. The appliances are going in Thursday."

Fred didn't shuffle back into his air-conditioned haven right away. Apparently, he had more to say. "You gonna let us light this place up on the Fourth?"

I snorted, shaking my head. "After your firework fiasco back in May, I don't think so."

"Nobody got hurt and nothin' got messed up. And you know as well as I do, you helped shoot off the bottle rockets that second night when another group of fools showed up."

"The fireworks definitely did the job with taking care of the trespassers." It only took about a week for things to settle down about the feedstore after the twins and Bash started guard duty and making the social media posts. "I'm just not sure we need another pyrotechnic show so soon." I crossed my arms and pretended to mull it over. I didn't mind celebrating Independence Day out here, but only with a great deal of caution. I couldn't risk us accidentally burning down the town. But before I could say yes or no, an uproar broke out over by the firehouse.

I took off running down the street, splashing in a few puddles instead of slowing enough to dodge them. I turned the corner and saw workers running inside the firehouse. I followed them and came close to passing out when I found Rowan sprawled out on the floor near the back of the lobby. A cracked wood beam lay on the floor near his head.

"Rowan!" I shoved through the group and dropped to my knees. His eyes opened and he blinked slowly. "Rowan, are you all right?"

"Stop yelling, *a stór*." He struggled, trying to sit up, but I stopped him.

"Whoa. Don't move just yet." I knew he didn't feel right when he lay back without any protest. "How the heck did this happen?"

Bash spoke up as he knelt beside me. "He thought he could handle the beam alone. It sure showed him."

Holding Rowan's hand, I reached for my phone in my pocket and called for an ambulance, trying to relay to the 911 dispatcher what had happened.

"And what's your location?" the dispatcher asked.

"We're out in the middle of Somewhere."

"Uh . . . I need more than that. Any location markers?"

"The ghost town in Colleton County. It's been renamed Somewhere, South Carolina. We're located on Meeting Street at the old Calhoun Brothers Bank."

"Ah, I know where you are now. Seen y'all on the news." The clicking of her rapid-fire typing could be heard in the background. "Help is on the way. Don't move the patient."

After agreeing and listening to some more instructions, I disconnected and looked down, meeting Rowan's eyes. I took that as a good sign that he was alert. "You hanging in there, Rowdy?"

"Yeah. Nothing hurts but my head." His words were stiff and just above a whisper. "I don't need an ambulance."

"Let's just be on the safe side, okay?" I rubbed my thumb along his wrist, hoping to soothe him.

Soon, an ambulance arrived, its red lights flashing without a siren. The paramedics secured Rowan's neck to a board before loading him up.

"I'll meet you at the hospital," I promised as they closed the back doors. I ran to my truck and pulled out behind the ambulance, my knee jumping the entire drive.

Thankfully, I was allowed in the exam room at the hospital when Rowan requested that they let me in. They were quick to send him down for scans. Once he returned to the exam room, I scooted my chair close to the gurney and held his hand.

"You hanging in there?"

"Yeah." His eyes remained closed but his voice sounded steady. "This is unnecessary. Can't we go now?"

"It won't hurt to get you checked out. Like you and Maudie insisted I do with my foot, remember?" Two worksite injuries within two weeks of each other. Not a good record to have. "I can't believe we've both managed to get hurt. Let's not make this a competition, okay?" I smirked but dropped it when I caught sight of the grimace on his face. "Where's it hurting?"

Eyes remaining shut, Rowan gently placed his hand over the crown of his head. "Right where the big knot is."

I reached and lightly touched the spot he pointed at. "Dang. You got yourself a giant goose egg there."

"They need to hurry it up. I've had about all I can take of this place." His tone was rather grouchy but I suppose he had a good reason for being in a bad mood.

A doctor came into the room, wearing teal scrubs and a white lab coat. He was younger than I expected, perhaps fresh out of med school. He smiled and tipped his head at me before addressing Rowan. "Mr. Murray, I'm Doctor Cortez. I heard you got into an altercation with a wood beam."

Rowan peeled his eyes open, red and puffy. "I put up a good fight until he got the best of me."

Dr. Cortez pulled on a pair of blue gloves and inspected Rowan's head. "I'm going to raise you up into a sitting position." The doctor helped him sit up. Then, he had Rowan follow his index finger in several directions. While examining him, the doctor asked all sorts of questions. *Are you nauseated? Does your head hurt?* Yes to both questions. *What time did you arrive at work? Who got you to the hospital?*

"Mr. Murray, good news is you'll live. The scans didn't show any bleeding in your brain. The bad news is you do have a concussion."

Rowan sighed. "Well, that stinks."

Dr. Cortez shined a small light into Rowan's eyes. "I'd like to keep you for observation."

Rowan barely shook his head. "No can do. I don't feel all that bad and I got a kid at home to take care of."

Him saying that took me by surprise. I supposed it would for a while until I got used to Bash being in our care.

The doctor glanced to me, as if looking for an ally.

Having no authority over Rowan, I shrugged.

He looked at Rowan. "I guess I could release you as long as you won't be alone for at least the next twenty-four hours. We need to ensure your symptoms aren't worsening."

Rowan met my eyes and I nodded my head.

"I'll keep an eye on him. Can we get him something for his headache?"

"Stick to Tylenol. No ibuprofen or aspirin, both could cause bleeding."

"Okay. Thanks, Doc." Rowan motioned for me to hand him his shoes. Even though he couldn't move quickly, he was in a hurry to leave.

On the way home, I swung by a Chick-fil-A since we'd both missed out on lunch. Rowan protested, but as soon as I handed him the bag of food, he hushed up and started unpacking it.

"You want your sandwich?" He held it out. He was wearing my rose-gold aviators to block the glare of the cloudy sky. He should have looked downright silly, but the man pulled them off surprisingly well.

"Nah. Just put my container of fries in the cupholder. But you can have the pickles off my sandwich."

"You sure?"

"Yep." Had I remembered quicker, I would have ordered him a side of pickles, too, but it had been almost seven years since I considered his food preferences.

"Thanks for going to the hospital with me, and for the food."

"No problem." I recalled how uncomfortable he'd acted while we were in the ER. "Since when do you get weirded out over hospitals?"

He finished his waffle fry. "Do you really need to ask that?"

"Huh?" I glanced his way before returning my attention to the highway.

"The last time I was in a hospital was the day I lost my last child and my wife."

I dropped the fry I'd just picked up back into the container and wiped my fingers on my jeans. I didn't die that day, came close, but I guess it could be argued that it was the day he lost me as his wife. We lost a lot before I was released from the hospital the following week.

Clearing my throat, which felt overly greasy, I took a long swig of tea. "Is that why you kept your eyes closed the entire time?"

Rowan slid his sandwich back into the wrapper and dropped it in the bag. He propped his elbow on the passenger door and cupped his forehead. "I see it, even with my eyes closed."

Unwanted memories pressed heavily, like someone was gripping my shoulders to make me stay put. But staying put in the past had become a terrible burden, one I wanted at least a little relief from.

We both pressed our lips firmly together and remained that way for the rest of the drive. The silence lingered as if it couldn't quite figure out when to exit. Much like the way I knew the scent of Chick-fil-A would still be lingering in the cab of this truck tomorrow. And the heaviness of our conversation too.

I got Rowan settled in his bed and scooted a wingback chair close.

"What are you doing?" Eyes closed and voice drowsy, Rowan pulled the blanket up to his neck.

"I'm on guard duty." I kicked my shoes off and dropped into the chair.

"You really don't have to. Bash can check in on me a few times. Where is he anyway?"

"Still working at the firehouse. They'll be wrapping up for the day in about an hour." I propped my feet on the edge of the bed and started thumbing through emails on my phone. "Let me know if you need anything."

"Uh-huh," Rowan muttered and the exhaustion in his voice had my own eyelids growing heavy.

With the low drone of the ceiling fan and Rowan's heavy breaths, soon the melody lulled me into a stupor. The emails grew blurry before it all went dark.

>

Another day showed up but something felt peculiar about it. Not ready to figure it out, I snuggled into the warmth and soft fabric of the blanket. My arm had grown numb, so I flexed my fingers a few times and by the time the feeling had returned I realized my fingers were squeezing someone's arm. Eyes flying open, I found myself staring at the side of Rowan's neck.

"You finally awake?" His groggy voice rumbled through me.

I tried to scoot away, but his arm tightened around my waist. "Awake? I . . ." I glanced around the room. "I don't even remember falling asleep, much less how I ended up in your bed."

"You really stink at guard duty."

I met his eyes and noticed dark circles underneath them. "How do you feel?"

"Like someone used my head for a basketball."

"You need to go back to the hospital?" I finally sat up, still fully dressed in yesterday's work attire.

"Nah. Just some Tylenol please."

"On it." I hurried out the bed and went to the kitchen. Bash was at the dining table eating a bowl of cereal.

"Wassup?"

"What's up? What's up is you letting me sleep when I should have been watching Rowan."

Bash shrugged. "You looked comfortable. And Rowan said not to wake you." He took a large bite of Special K. I wondered if he liked it or made do since that was Rowan's favorite cereal.

I filled a glass with water and grabbed the bottle of medicine. "So you checked on him through the night?"

"Yep."

"Thank you."

Bash nodded his head, chewing on another bite. From the way he was inhaling it, I guess he actually liked the cereal.

I made it to the door of Rowan's bedroom and froze as realization hit me. "I slept through the night."

Rowan sat up stiffly and propped his back against the headboard. "Yes."

It scared me to think I had just slept—thirteen? I checked out for *thirteen* freaking hours. No wonder I felt energized and ready to take on the world.

"I haven't done that since . . ." I gazed at the bottle in my hand.

"I know," Rowan said softly.

I unstuck my feet and stepped up to the bed, handing Rowan the glass and then shaking two pills into his palm.

Bash popped his head into the room. "I'm heading over to the inn to paint trim. Is there anything you need me to do?"

"Nah. The trim work will keep you until schooltime. Let the crew at the firehouse know I'll be by in a bit."

"M'kay."

"And your lunch is in the fridge next door." He already knew that, considering that had been the norm in the last few weeks. Breakfast with Rowan, I packed his and Preacher's lunch, and then we typically ate supper together downstairs in the saloon like a family. A family made up of an estranged couple, a runaway, and a thieving dog.

"Thanks, Avalee." Bash turned and walked out, leaving me alone with Rowan.

I put the lid on the bottle and placed it on the nightstand. "You hungry?"

"Not really." He pulled the covers back a bit and patted the spot beside him. "Let's just rest a little while longer."

"You can. I need to get to work." I practically bounced in place.

"I thought you were taking care of me?" He pouted.

I grew still. Rowan wanted me here with him. Hadn't he made that clear just the other day at the Victorian house? "I am . . . I won't be far."

He patted the spot beside him again. A spot that looked quite dangerous. "Stop overthinking it, *a stór.*" His accent slipped through his words. The hint of Irish brogue mingling with Southern drawl. Also dangerous.

A scalding heat bloomed on my cheeks. "Stop that."

"Stop what?"

"Your accent. Put it away, right now." I fanned my face.

His expression turned devilish. "Nah. I don't think I'm gonna."

Close to being a goner, I took several steps backwards and then did an about-face and sprinted out of the room before I did something stupid like launch myself at him. His deep chuckle chased behind me, but Rowan let me go. *For now . . . I think . . .*

CHAPTER 29

VISION BOARDS ARE LIKE COMPASSES IN THE DESIGN WORLD, leading you to the end product. But it doesn't mean those boards, aka compasses, always remain the same from start to finish. Loosely, changes are acceptable. That being said, I never cared for changing the vision along the way in my personal life. I liked making a plan and sticking to it. All at once, it seemed like every darn thing had decided to shift into something way off course, no matter how I tried keeping to the plan.

After tending to a newly formed blister on my thumb from spending the day stripping paint from several ornate doors, I stretched out on the couch and began poring over Desmond's vision boards for the bodega, making notes on selections. We needed to finalize the paint color and decor by the end of the week. The gas station theme was fun but I had to reel Des in a bit. He'd even found a vintage Cadillac, teal with a white stripe, but I wasn't sold on it.

An hour passed and I still couldn't narrow down the paint choices. So many of the buildings were in muted hues, white, gray, soft greens. The easy choice would be to grab up some leftover paint, but Desmond had his heart set on a new choice. I thought about texting Rowan for his opinion but second-guessed it. He was in Alabama on business and I hated to bother him. His work trip seemed like a good way of putting some breathing room between us as well. We'd spent most of the last two weeks together with me hovering while he recovered from his concussion. It blew my mind how easily we'd fallen into a domesticated routine reminiscent of our married years together.

I reached for my phone to text Desmond. I started to thumb off a message to just pick whatever color his designer heart desired but froze when I heard what sounded like a young child giggling. I held my breath and cocked my ear in the air. After several beats of silence with no more creepy sounds, I chalked it up to hearing things.

My body began reclining on the couch but shot upright when the child laughed again. No way did I not hear that. Casing the room, I settled on the umbrella by the door, gathering it in my hand and peeking into the hallway. No floating figures but then I heard Bash's distinctive voice from next door. For a scrawny teenager, he had a rich baritone. I bet he had a decent singing voice, but he barely spoke much less sang.

Feeling foolish, I lowered my weapon. He was probably watching something on TV. Just as I turned to go back into my apartment, a child distinctly said, "Bash!" followed by more giggling and Bash making a shushing sound.

At least it wasn't a ghost, but a real-life child was just as scary. Somewhere, South Carolina, didn't have room for either at the moment.

I charged inside unannounced and found Bash coloring with a little boy at the dining room table. Their crayons froze as they stared at me with matching pale-blue eyes.

"What on earth?" I pointed the umbrella at the child. "Please tell me you didn't kidnap a toddler!"

"I ain't no toddler!" the little boy fired back.

Still clutching the umbrella, I rested my balled-up hands on my hips. "How old are you then?" If I had to guess, I'd have put him in the ballpark of four.

"Seven and a half," he lisped, his two bottom teeth missing.

I scrutinized him, hardly believing his declaration. "You're mighty tiny . . ."

His blue eyes narrowed. "You mighty *big*." *Big* being delivered with as much attitude as the miniature package could deliver.

"Koda," Bash reprimanded.

"I ain't lyin'. She's real tall." Koda waved a hand toward me while holding the other over his head in the universal gesture of indicating a tall height. I had to bite my lip so not to laugh at the feisty kid.

"It's time to wash." Bash pointed to the bathroom.

The little boy's face soured, somehow showcasing a smattering of freckles on his upper cheeks. "But—"

"No buts." Bash began shoving the crayons into the box. "And be sure to use soap. I'll be checking."

Koda made a show of pouting and dragging his feet, but he listened.

Once the door shut and I heard the water turn on, I plopped into one of the dining chairs across from Bash and asked him slowly, "Who is that?"

"My brother. I swear he's seven." Bash stared at the closed bathroom door. "Koda was born about ten weeks early. All's good with his health now, but he's just growing slow. That's why he's so small for his age."

A weight formed on my tongue and slithered down my throat before settling with a thud in the bottom of my belly. Ten weeks early and he made it . . .

Sniffing away the stinging onslaught of tears, I stared up at the light fixture above the table. A black lantern style, new but reminiscent of the time when this building had been built. Finally, I lowered my gaze and said, "Bash, please tell me you didn't take him without permission."

"Grandma's in the hospital, so I had to go get him." Bash scrubbed his hand over his shaggy hair, the same sandy-blond shade as his brother's. "And Rowan said I could borrow the truck while he's out of town."

"Is Rose okay?"

"She had another ministroke." His blue eyes glassed over. "She's had a lot of them."

"Oh, Bash. I'm so sorry."

Blinking, he turned his face away. "She's tough."

"Okay." Making a mental note to call and check on her tomorrow, I propped my elbows on the table. "How'd I not know you had a brother?"

Bash shrugged. "I figured Grandma or Mrs. Beth told you."

"No. Beth was hesitant to tell us anything about you. She sure didn't offer anything up about Koda . . . That's an interesting name."

"Our mom was obsessed with Disney movies." He tried to chuckle, but it fell flat, revealing cracks of grief. "He's named after the cub in *Brother Bear*."

"Oh . . ." I wanted to tell him I was sorry he'd lost his mother, that I'd lost mine, too, but the timing didn't seem right to talk about it. Especially with his brother just in the next room.

The bathroom door sprung open and a buck naked Koda barreled into the living room, making a lot more noise than seemed possible for such a small kid, more like a darn elephant. Bash had to be delusional if he thought it was possible to keep his brother's visit a secret.

"Whoa, dude. Back in the bathroom!" Bash stood and moved over to Koda who was riffling around in a Walmart bag, pink-skinned and still damp from his bath.

"But I need my new stuff you got me." He freed a set of green and tan dinosaur pajamas and a pack of underwear. I wondered if the poor kid was in need of anything else. Before I could ask, Bash pulled out a new toothbrush and handed it to his brother, who acted like it was a shiny new toy. It made my heart ache.

Watching the little boy skip his naked behind into the bathroom, I asked Bash, "Y'all eat?"

"Yeah."

Dang that kid and his short answers. It was like trying to squeeze blood out of a turnip. "Y'all need anything else?"

He smoothed his hair out of his face and looked around the living room. "We're good."

I wasn't so sure about that, considering they were basically both runaways at the moment. I motioned to the front door. "I'll be back in a sec."

Bash fidgeted. "M'kay."

"I'm just grabbing my computer to get your opinion on something." I hurried to my apartment, going straight to my phone first, and put in an emergency call to Rowan but he didn't answer.

Five minutes crept by without a response, so I grabbed my laptop and returned next door. The boys were sitting on the couch, looking at something on Bash's phone.

"Have you heard from Rowan?"

"No."

Close to panicking, I scanned the room while debating my options. Call Bash's caseworker? Take the boys to my place? Clearly, I wasn't equipped to make any parental decisions. Among the chaos of my thoughts, only one thing solidified even though I hated to admit it. I needed Rowan.

As if sensing my escalating panic, Bash rose from the couch and motioned for Koda to do the same. "Time for bed."

Koda frowned. "But it's the weekend."

Instead of debating with his little brother, Bash simply ushered Koda into his bedroom and shut the door.

I took their spot on the couch and stared at my phone while willing it to flash with Rowan's name. Moments later the bedroom door creaked open and Bash joined me. "Please don't call Beth."

Placing my phone on the cushion beside me, I rubbed my forehead. I'd already ruled out calling her. Everyone was safe and sound. Really, that's what mattered. "Your grandmother has custody of Koda, correct?"

"Yes, ma'am."

I couldn't help but worry about what would happen if their grandmother didn't recover.

"I'm crashing on the couch tonight. We can sort this out tomorrow."

If Bash wanted to argue this, he hid it well. He grabbed a pillow and extra blanket off Rowan's bed and handed it to me like a proper host.

Hours later, staring at the dark, my mind got hung up on those boys losing their mom and then having a grandmother take them in. It felt so similar to my own story, even though I had a father in the picture. Either way, we'd experienced terrible losses.

My mother passed away when I was only a baby, so Maudie had stepped in to give me the woman talks. My grandmother was the one who explained the monthly deal and she was also the one to explain the gift of intimacy in a marriage.

After not allowing Rowan to touch me for nearly a year after the second pregnancy loss, I flipped a switch and sex became a chore instead of a gift. Charts, temperature checks, both of us taking ridiculous amounts of vitamins and supplements. Rowan teased me, saying he felt like he was training to join an elite task force, but I had found no humor in it. Ignoring his comments and jokes, I focused all of my attention on having a healthy baby.

Thirty-one weeks in, we were in the homestretch! The nursery had been completed and the baby shower thank-you notes mailed out. This time I had no doubt we were bringing a baby home. Instead, our baby boy was brought to the funeral home.

I remember poking my deflated belly, wondering if new mothers did the same while holding their newborns. Did they marvel at how the baby had felt so much bigger in the belly than in their arms? I had nothing but emptiness to compare it to.

Something withered inside me after that and I never recovered. Swathed in grief, I withdrew from our friends, church family, and gradually from Rowan. Instead of talking about it, we both went quiet. By the end, silence had become the only thing we shared. I desperately wanted to bridge the gap between us, but it was like my body went into lockdown. My entire being, mind and body, grew dormant after the stillbirth of our son and my emergency hysterectomy. I didn't just shut down, I shut Rowan out. They say you hurt the ones you love the most. I'd always thought that was the most absurd saying until I witnessed it during the demise of our marriage.

I didn't just lose my husband in the divorce. An entire procession followed him out of my life. Childhood friendship, first love, first kiss, dares, making love, sharing love, creating a child from that love . . . It all abandoned me.

I allowed the horrible memory a moment, just a brief moment, before hiding it back away behind a wall of faux indifference. Hopefully, it would remain there in the morning.

CHAPTER 30

A PROPER LADY. That's what Maudie said when I showed up for church in a flowery sundress this morning, but her teeth about fell out of her head when she realized this proper lady had not one but two runaways in tow. She recovered quickly, of course, and then demanded we have a *proper* Sunday dinner with her. My grandmother spent most of the afternoon cooking up a storm. I'm talking fried pork chops, rice and gravy, buttermilk biscuits, fried squash, sliced cucumbers and toma- toes lightly seasoned with salt and pepper, and blueberry dumplings.

Close to being in a food coma, I sat with Maudie underneath the shade of a mossy oak tree. We watched Bash and Koda fish from the end of her pier. It reminded me of all the times I fished from that very same spot with Rowan while my grandmother hovered nearby. Her property spanned the inlet and always seemed like the perfect playground.

"I'm glad you brought the boys to church today," Maudie spoke just as the breeze carried Koda's giggle over to us.

"Seemed like the right thing to do. Bash likes going, and Koda didn't complain about it too much." I considered taking a sip of my tea but was too full to pursue it, so I doodled designs through the condensation on the glass instead. My father traveled a lot for work, so attending church regularly had never been a top priority. Dad said you could worship God anywhere, and I agree, but Maudie always made it a priority to have me attend services with her.

Koda came running up to us, breathless, his cheeks pink. "Miz Maudie, you heard what *she* named that town?" He pointed an accusative finger at me.

"Yes. Somewhere." Maudie combed her fingers through his messy hair.

Koda took a step out of Maudie's reach and shooed her hand like it was a fly, his little upturned nose wrinkled. "But ain't that weird?"

"Unique," I interjected. "It'll stand out easier. You want to hear some weirder names than that for towns?"

Koda shrugged like he couldn't have cared less but the little stinker remained put.

I took that as a sign that he actually wanted to know, so I told him, "There's this town in Kansas named Protection. And another town named Truth or Consequences in New Mexico. And Fries, Virginia, is a weird one too."

"Fries?" Cackling like a little hyena, Koda ran off. He shouted, "Bash, there are worse ones than Somewhere!"

Maudie snickered. "That's a little spitfire."

"He sure is. It's wild how opposite he is from Bash." I watched Koda prancing around his tall older brother, talking animatedly with his hands, while Bash just stood there and listened.

"Koda reminds me of another spitfire who used to keep me and those Murray boys on their toes." Maudie hummed another laugh.

The mention of Rowan's family stung a bit. They were a rambunctious, loud, fun family and I all but ran them off when I ran Rowan off. I didn't want to be around any form of joy and the Murray family divvied that out like gifts on Christmas morning.

I checked the time on my phone and sighed. "I could be content in this spot for the rest of the day, but I need to drop the boys off at the apartment and then head to the airport."

Grinning, Maudie rose from her chair. "I'll go pack up the leftovers for y'all."

I stood too and followed her. "What's that grin about?"

Maudie laughed that tittering type she did when gloating. "You and Rowdy sure seem to be gettin' along like a house on fire."

I scoffed. "More like a dumpster fire." I helped to clean the kitchen while Maudie reminisced.

"I never had to worry if you two were being mean to each other. I just had to worry about what kinda mischief y'all were gettin' into." She clucked her tongue. "Remember that one time y'all weren't no older than ten but thought you were old enough to drive. I just never figured out how you ended up puttin' your Dad's gettin'-'round truck in the pond."

Shaking my head, I dried a plate, and recalled my dad's little S-10. He used it for hauling trash or just to putter around the countryside. "That's a great example of why we don't really get along. We both wanted to drive, so I changed the gears while Rowan did the pedals. We couldn't get into a rhythm and weren't paying attention. That pond came out of nowhere."

Maudie laughed fully and I couldn't help but join her. "I thought your daddy was gonna skin you both."

"He didn't even notice for the longest time." I think my father didn't notice a lot of things and when he did, he never made much of a fuss over it. As if he were guilty too.

"You need to call him."

"Yes, ma'am." I dried my hands on the kitchen towel and draped it over the edge of the sink. "I just talked to him last week, I think, but I'll give him another call."

"I know my son stays too busy for his own good, but I think that's the only way he knew how to deal with losing your mother. To stay busy. And he spoiled you rotten with gifts and such because that's the only way he knew how to make it up to you."

"I get it." And truly I did. I'd come to terms with it years ago. My father wasn't a bad man in any sense of the word. Just neglectful when it came to paying me any attention. Always an afterthought, never the main focus. "Time to head out. Love ya." I kissed my grandmother's soft cheek, catching hints of her comforting fragrance of jasmine. Between our conversation and her perfume, I felt surrounded by my childhood.

After dropping the boys off, I set out for the airport in Rowan's truck. Since he'd given Bash permission to drive it while he was away, I figured I could too. It was such a sweet ride. One with all the bells and whistles. It practically drove itself.

I pulled up to the curb in front of the airport just as the rotating door spit Rowan out. He was dressed in a dark suit, something I hadn't seen him wear in a few weeks. He'd looked like part of the construction crew lately in tees and worn jeans. Darned if he didn't pull off both looks remarkably well.

After tossing his suitcase into the truck bed, Rowan popped open the passenger door and slid in. "Thanks, man . . ." His eyes widened. "You're not Bash."

"Nope. He's a bit busy, so I volunteered." I winked at him and put the truck into drive. "When did you get a haircut?" He looked more distinguished with the shorter hair, making him even more handsome.

"I squeezed it in before my flight last week." His smile lit his entire face. "You missed me, didn't you. So much so you had to come pick me up?"

"I needed to talk to you. What's up with you not answering your phone all weekend?"

His smile vanished. "I dropped my phone in a retention pond and I couldn't find it."

I glanced his way as I came to a stop to pay the parking fee. He beat me to it, leaning over and handing the attendant a ten-dollar bill. Once we were squared away, I asked him, "How'd you manage chucking your phone in a pond?"

"We were walking the property with the surveyor and just dumb luck struck me." He snickered, looking more perturbed than amused. "I went to point out something and my dang phone flew out of my hand."

I laughed.

Rowan turned the radio down. "What did you need to talk about?"

"Uh, well, our lost boy situation doubled."

"Say what?"

"Rose is in the hospital so Bash had to go get Koda. I called and checked on her this morning. Sounds like she's doing okay."

"Good. Who's Koda?"

"Bash's little brother. Apparently, Beth was serious about not telling us any more about Bash than she had to." I changed lanes and took our exit.

"Wow. Another kid . . . I'm sorry you couldn't get in touch with me. Next time, I'll make sure to let you know what hotel I'll be staying at."

"It's okay. I stayed over and then took them to church this morning. Then Maudie insisted on feeding us until we were miserable."

"Wow. That's very adult of you."

"Right?" I pulled to a stop at the red light. "Speaking of being very adult . . . What happened to your motorcycle?"

Rowan worked on unknotting his tie. "It's back at my house in Greenville. The truck makes more sense while I'm hands-on with this project."

Nodding my head, I tried to envision what his home in Greenville looked like. Was it a rental? A condo or town house? The little bungalow we'd shared in Beaufort kept popping into my mind. Just over a thousand square feet, the Craftsman made up for the lack of space with charm.

"You know, I never thought to ask you where you were staying before moving into the apartment beside mine."

He tugged and the tie slid from his shirt collar, the smooth sound easily filling the cab of the truck. It brought to mind other old memories I'd shared with him. "I was staying at a hotel."

I brushed off my wayward thoughts and refocused on what he'd just said. "Oh my gosh. For the past five months you've been living in a hotel?"

"With the exception of a few nights in Greenville every now and then, yes."

"That's a pretty big sacrifice."

"I didn't mind it."

I pondered that for a beat or two, still thinking about his family from earlier. "How's your family?"

Rowan adjusted his air vents. "Good. Mom and Dad moved to Tybee Island last year."

"Tybee?"

"Yeah. That's where Brannon and his wife Darcy live. Darcy had a bad bout of postpartum depression, so my parents moved there to help out with Neve."

"Neve . . . That's pretty."

"Mom was bummed that they didn't name her Talulla after her." Rowan chuckled. "She got over it fast after meeting her though."

I smiled with effort, gripping the steering wheel a little too tightly. No matter how far we moved away from losing our children, I couldn't get away from what could have been. I wondered how it would have felt to fuss over something like name choices. Or who got to hold our baby first. Or what outfit to dress the baby in for the trip home from the hospital.

Rowan cleared his throat. "Liam and Heather . . . You remember Heather?" he asked, and I nodded. Liam and his high school sweetheart were a year behind us in school.

"So they got back together?"

"Yeah. She came back from college and asked him out on a date." Rowan shrugged. "The rest is history. They married a few years back and moved to Asheville to open a microbrewery."

"Children?"

"Not yet. They want to establish the business more first." He fiddled with the air vent. "Shaun is still single and swears he's staying that way. He travels a lot so I guess that's best for him."

"What's he do?"

"He's a producer for film documentaries."

"Sounds about right." I laughed softly. "He was always filming something with your parents' camcorder."

"Adam got married last summer. Her name is Becca. She just gave birth to a baby boy they named Connor after Dad."

I glanced his way. "Wow. That was fast."

"Yeah. I think . . . how's Maudie put it . . . they put the cart before the horse."

We both laughed, but it did nothing to soothe the sting in my chest. His family was doing well. A family I had claimed as my own for most of my life. Hearing about them and their families made me miss them bone-deep.

"I'm glad they're all doing well. I can't believe your baby brother has a baby . . ." We drove in silence for a few beats and all I could see was our baby boy.

And just like that the heaviness caught up with me again. I wished grief would release its grip on me but I'd come to realize it never would completely. Some days the grip loosened enough I could take a deep breath. Some days the hold was so tight it left claw marks.

Clearing my throat, I said, "Congrats, Uncle Rowdy." I looked over and flashed him a wink to soften the tension that had settled in the cab of the truck.

He smiled but it seemed forced. "Thanks."

I wanted a genuine smile so I blurted the first thing that came to mind. "You wanna see what we can see?"

His head shot in my direction. Probably stunned at my suggestion. His lips lifted into a crooked grin. "Don't tempt me with a good time."

Well, darn. Now I had to come up with something . . . . I flipped on the blinker and took a right.

"Where are we going?"

"You'll see." Me and him both, but then I thought of something to show him. So I made another right.

"Are we just going to drive in circles?"

"You'll see."

CHAPTER 31

OVER A HUNDRED FEET IN THE AIR, our legs dangled off the side of the giant steel structure. The evening air had cooled slightly so that the metal didn't scorch us. Thank goodness I had changed into jeans and a blouse before picking Rowan up from the airport. I closed my eyes for a moment and just listened. Crickets chirped and every so often something dinged against the metal framing. A loose chain, I assumed.

"I can't believe you'd brave doing this after the caboose incident." Rowan reached over and dug out a handful of Cracker Jack from my bag. When we were kids that would have been impossible. Back then it only came in the small boxes, which made it easier for me to protect my snack.

"Hey! You have your own snacks." I elbowed his arm out the way and motioned at his bag of pizza-flavored Combos. We'd made a pit stop by a convenience store on our way here. "And a water tower is nothing like the caboose."

Rowan leaned up and looked over the edge of the railing while he munched on the popcorn. "We had to jump that fence over there.

And the ladder could fall off and we'd be stuck way up here. So it's sorta the same."

I glanced down and made sure the ladder remained put. The rusted rungs appeared to be solid. "It's welded on. It ain't goin' anywhere."

He wiped his hand on his jeans. Jeans that he had changed into right after we arrived here. The wild man had just stripped right down to his boxers like it was no big deal to be half naked in front of God and everybody, then he rummaged in his suitcase for the pants. Sin or not, it's an image I'd have in my thoughts for a long time. "You reckon we could get arrested for being up here?"

"Not unless we get caught." I flashed him a smirk and then took a swig of my cherry-flavored ICEE. We'd somehow managed to get the slushies up here without spilling them. Well mostly. Rowan had red and blue stains running down his white T-shirt. Stains that would not be coming out. We'd tied the bag containing the cups to his belt and looped it around his neck. Not the wisest beverage choice for climbing but we committed to seeing it through. It could have been a page right out of our childhood together.

Rowan looked at me with scorching hot spice. "We were pretty good at not getting caught . . ."

I swiped a fistful of Combos, crammed them in my mouth, and chomped down. "Ouch!"

Rowan flinched beside me, fumbling around and coming close to losing his cup over the side of the tower. "What?"

Pressing my palm against the throb in the side of my face, I mumbled, "I bit the tater out of my cheek."

He *tsk*ed. "I've told you about eating too fast."

Yes, he had. Way back say six or seven years ago. Not recently, but it still catapulted me right back to the old us. I was always rushing to eat and Rowan was always telling me to slow down so I wouldn't end up eating my jaw.

We quieted for a spell, most likely remembering the same thing. I wanted to spit the Combos out, but continued chewing slowly until I could safely swallow.

Rowan cleared his throat. "Seriously though. We have a kid at home depending on us returning."

We have a kid. That still struck me each time that we were actually co-parenting a teenage boy. So far it had gone rather smoothly. "Two kids, actually. We'll make it back to Bash and Koda. No worries. This is my tower."

Rowan stopped sucking on the straw and squinted at me. His lips were stained blue from his blue raspberry slushy somehow making them look even more kissable. "You own a water tower?"

"Yeah. Well, Somewhere owns it. The city got a new one and they were planning on just tearing this one down. I talked Jonas and the illionaires into buying it for a steal. After we get it painted up with a town logo on it, I think it'll be a nice addition to the town."

"You have a town logo?"

"We're finalizing it. *Somewhere* will be in a stylish chalkboard calligraphy font in the state's indigo blue, and instead of the state's palmetto tree, our logo will have a pecan tree towering over the wording." I fluttered my hand in the air. "With some of those loopy scrolls beneath it."

Rowan angled his head and studied the tank behind us. The rusty structure had seen better days. "We don't need a water tower though. The town is hooked up to the public water and sewer system."

"I know. It'll be just for looks. We're having it moved to that field near Front Street. It'll help attract visitors. They'll be able to spot this metal giant miles away." I scanned the horizon. From our vantage point, we had a clear view of the sun beginning to set over the tops of trees. Vivid hues of orange and pink streaked the sky.

"I can't believe the investors would dish out money for something like this." He shook his head and popped a handful of Combos in his mouth.

"We basically paid what the city would get for scrapping this thing, pennies really." I worked on unlodging a popcorn kernel from my tooth and took another slurp of slushy. "I think this ghost town flip is an experiment of sorts for them. I really don't care as long as it works in my favor and we get to do fun stuff like this." I raised my cup and tapped it against his in a toast.

"Look at us, hanging out on top of a water tower. Our younger selves would be proud of us." He smiled with his entire face, my favorite smile. Staring at my lips, he leaned toward me.

I drew back and pretended to slap at a mosquito on the side of my neck. "Dang mosquitoes. I guess our fun is over." I started gathering our garbage and tossed everything in the plastic grocery bag.

Rowan scoured the sky, then his arms, searching for the varmints that hadn't arrived quite yet. "I haven't been bit."

"Well, I have. I'm sweeter," I sassed, gripping the railing and climbing to my feet. "Plus we have a busy Monday ahead. I need to get home and write out the schedule."

He didn't move. "I don't have anything going on when we get back. I'll help you."

Shaking my head, I tried beckoning him to get the lead out, but the stubborn man didn't move. "You have Bash and Koda to get home to. I can handle it."

Rowan sucked down the rest of his slushy, making me wait a little longer. He placed his cup in the bag, tied it off, and then dropped it over the edge. I barely heard it hit the ground. Finally, he stood and led the descent back to the ground.

A few rungs in I made the mistake of looking down and a wave of vertigo crashed into me. Gulping for air, I clung tighter to the rung. "Shoot. It's harder going down than up."

"I'm not minding it."

I glanced over my shoulder and caught Rowan checking out my backside. "Eyes down, Rowdy. Get me off this thing."

His dark chuckle echoed off the metal structure, sending a shiver to zip through me. We kept moving downward but I still felt the heat of his gaze on me.

Near the bottom, Rowan's hands gripped my waist and pulled me off the ladder. I only managed a squeak as his arms encircled me and held me close to his chest. His body was like marble and my body felt like Jell-O.

"Hmm . . . you smell good." Rowan's cold lips grazed my ear as he spoke, eliciting a burst of shivers to overtake me.

Gripping his forearms, I huffed. "I thought you said you didn't like my new perfume."

"No." His nose tickled my neck as he skimmed it along the delicate skin. "I said you smelled different, but I'm getting used to it now. It's a little spicy, like my *a stór*."

My fingers tightened. "Don't."

"Don't what?" As he asked, his warm lips moved down my neck.

"This." Wiggling out of his grasp, I put some space between us and wagged my finger at him. "You enchant me."

"What's so wrong with that?"

I raised my hands then dropped them, slapping my thighs, hoping to sturdy my weak knees. "You've always enchanted me and I hate you a little for it."

Red-cheeked and smoldering, Rowan said resolutely, as if it were a done deal, "Then fall in love with me again."

"That's not a good idea. Last time I screwed up the landing."

"What if I promise to catch you this time?"

"Seriously, Rowan. I'm damaged goods."

"So am I."

"Not like this." I pulled up my shirt and shoved the waist of my jeans down low enough to show off the silvery shadows of stretch marks and the imposing scar along my pelvis. Dropping my shirt, I cupped my breasts. "The stretch marks still exist here too." After Declan was born and buried, my milk came in. That had to be the lowest point of my life. I wrapped my arms around my waist and looked away, thinking about how my body showed all the signs of pregnancy yet my arms never held the fruit of my labor.

The muscle in Rowan's jaw flexed. "Avalee."

I held up a hand before he could spit out what he was chewing on. "You deserve someone better. Someone that you can celebrate life with by creating another life."

He laughed with no humor. "Oh, that ship sailed long ago."

"How so? You're young enough to find another wife and have her pop out some kids."

He shook his head and rubbed his chest. "The same month I got these tattoos I also got a vasectomy."

Stunned stupid, I reached out and gripped the ladder for support. "Rowan . . . No . . . Why would you do that?"

He scrubbed his face with his hands. "Because . . ."

A numbness crept over my body, one that almost stung. As if I'd been submerged in ice water. "But . . . I thought you hadn't been to a hospital since . . . ?"

"The procedure was done in a doctor's office. I didn't have to go to a hospital." His golden-brown eyes swam in tears.

Shaking my head, I stomped to his truck and let him drive us home. Shoulders stiff and jaw clenched, I waited for him to pick up the argument, but Rowan turned the radio up instead and didn't say another word.

Somberly, we trudged up the stairs to our apartments. Rowan stood at his door without opening it, so I stood at mine and waited.

Hand on the doorknob, he turned to look at me. "Wanna know what I can't get over? How you just let me go. After everything . . . You just let me go." Without waiting for a response, he went inside.

Later, lying in bed, wide awake, I replayed the early evening with Rowan. How could being around him both feel so good yet hurt so bad at the same time? Over the last several months— more like years really—I kept expecting my heart to just give out from the strain of it all.

I have a favorite band saw. Big ole clunky thing, but such a versatile piece of equipment. My father gave it to me for my sixteenth birthday. Yes, I was completely ecstatic over this gift. Twenty years of never letting me down, it stopped working right in the middle of a project. The crazy thing about that, only a tiny spring broke, halting the function of the entire machine. It seemed so insignificant, yet the machine depended on it to work.

When I examined my heart, missing four distinct pieces, it made no sense that it could continue working.

CHAPTER 32

MUD CAKES WERE MY SPECIALTY GROWING UP. I'd use empty SpaghettiOs cans as molds, packing the mud inside and unmolding it like one would do a sandcastle. Then I'd frost it with more mud with a plastic knife. I thought I was pretty good at it and had a short-lived dream to open a bakery one day. Not long after setting this aspiration, my grandmother introduced me to power tools and I forgot all about my bakery dreams.

"It's as easy as frosting a cake." I held out the trowel but Bash just stared at it, his hands secured in his back pockets. You'd think I was offering him a snake. "You've never frosted a cake?"

He shook his head.

"Well, I know for fact you know how to smear peanut butter on a cracker."

He shrugged. "Yeah."

"That's all German smear is. Smearing mortar onto the brick. Easy peasy. Here." I tried handing the tool to him again and this time he accepted it. After putting on a pair of work gloves to protect my new purple manicure—*Violet Visionary*—I pulled a bandana out my back pocket and secured my hair back with it while I scanned the Lowcountry Mercantile storefront. A long expanse of red brick, just like the Pet & Plant Store next door, making the two stores blend together. Today, we would remedy that.

Bash slid his hat on backwards, preparing to get to work too. "Wouldn't it be easier to paint it?"

"Yes, but paint is boring. This will give the building texture and style."

"You had the inn painted that blue color," Bash pointed out.

"Different buildings require different mediums. The inn has a clapboard exterior, this is brick."

He still seemed skeptical so I pulled out my phone and showed him pictures of another building I applied this technique to.

"Oh. I get it now."

"Good." I picked up the other trowel and loaded it with mortar. "Let's ice this baby. Bottom to top." I slapped the trowel against the bottom of the wall and spread the mortar upwards. "Just like that. Come on and give it a try."

Bash stepped forward and loaded his trowel, repeating the application as I had shown him. "This is making a mess." He shook his shoe to try to get the mortar off but he'd soon realize that was a lost cause. We'd be covered in it before the day was done.

"That's the fun part. We're allowed to make a mess today. The tarp we laid out will catch most of the fallout. So just relax and enjoy." I smeared another section. "It's like a big ole art project really." We smeared for about five minutes then returned to the first section. "Now we scrape it off and use a wire brush to clean it up a bit." I demonstrated, scraping away the top layer and then brushing some spots to expose a little more brick.

"I'm getting it all over me," Bash muttered.

"Scrape sideways. Like this." I went left to right. "You'll get less on you."

Bash did as I said and cleared the section with a pace only someone with youthful vigor could pull off. While I played the role of teacher and Bash the student, in the last four months I'd learned a good bit about him and his work ethic. Did someone instill that in him or was it a survival instinct he had learned the hard way? Either way, I'd also discovered that he was a visual learner. I only needed to show him something once, and the young guy quickly picked up on whatever task it was and set in to doing it.

"We'll get all that we can reach, then I'll get some guys to come over and help us set up some scaffolding to get the top of the walls."

"M'kay." That was another thing about Bash. He would answer questions and make the occasional comment but never stopped working. Gosh, I loved this kid. He reminded me of me in so many ways.

Soon, we got into a rhythm of smearing and wiping. The gritty sound of our tools scraping along the brick mixed with other noises. The high-pitched pop of a nail gun firing off, the whirl of a circular saw munching away through lumber, workers calling out orders. It was all music to my ears.

An hour in, Bash floored me by initiating conversation. "You know what Rowan eats for a snack at night?"

I had a pretty good guess but shrugged.

"Dill pickles." Bash used the wire brush to clean a spot of brick. The poor guy had speckles of mortar head to toe, same as me. "I'm talking right out the jar. Like he gets a fork and sits down and snacks while watching TV." He wrinkled his nose.

Laughing, I used a rag to wipe away some mortar that had gotten on the doorframe. "He's done that forever. I've never seen someone like pickles as much as that man. He once opened a jar in our truck on a road trip and I thought I'd never get the smell of vinegar out of the cab." I picked up the trowel and went back to work. I thought I could almost smell pickles now within the earthy scent of the mortar but I knew that was only my imagination. "Besides the pickles, y'all getting along as roommates?"

"Yeah. He's teaching me how to play poker." Bash cut me a sidelong glance.

I scoffed. "He better not."

"No." Bash chuckled at his own joke, making me laugh too. "But we play War and rummy."

"Well, I guess that's okay." I could picture the two of them hunkered down at the dining table, seriously focused on their card game.

"You know he gets up every morning at five to read his Bible and drink coffee?"

"He still does that?"

Bash glanced my way and I almost knew what he was thinking, that I was closer to Rowan at one time than I'd admitted to. "Yeah. He normally reads a verse or two to me over breakfast."

I kept slapping mortar on the bricks, remembering how I would settle on our couch way back when beside Rowan and while snuggling close to him, he'd read verses to me. I'd forgotten all about that until now. It made me smile even though my chest tightened.

Needing a change of subject, I asked, "How's classes going?"

"Good. I got a ninety-four on that geometry test." Bash bent down to get underneath the window.

"Excellent. You like the online program so far?"

He scooted farther along the wall, doing a great job making less mess than me. "I like that I can work half a day on the town and still get my school in after lunch."

The program allowed students to work at their own pace, even during the summer, but at the rate Bash was going he'd be caught up in no time. So far it was going surprisingly smooth. As smooth as his German smear technique.

"I talked to your great-aunt. They're moving your grandma to a rehabilitation center."

Bash paused with the trowel in the bucket. "I thought Grandma was doing better."

"She is, but she still needs therapy. The stroke left her pretty weak." I slathered on another section of mortar. "Your great-aunt says she'd take Koda but she's helping her daughter, who's fallen on hard times."

Bash sighed with the indignation of a grown man. "I've been

saving up . . . My plan is to get my own place and then get custody of Koda, but . . . I need more time. My aunt can't handle him. Grandma barely could."

Their great-aunt picked up Koda after we had him that weekend, but she'd expressed the same sentiments as Bash just had, that the young boy was too headstrong and didn't want to mind her.

"Koda seems to like it here."

"Yeah." Bash scratched his elbow, flaking off a splatter of mortar.

"I'll talk to Rowan and Rose, but I'm sure it's fine for him to stay here with us as long as you help keep an eye on him."

"I will." Bash sounded desperate and relieved at the same time. "He's excited about helping plant the flowers in the memorial garden."

"The plants should be here by Friday. We can make it a family project." I said it without thought, as if it were perfectly natural to refer to us as family.

Apparently, it caught us both off guard. We worked in an awkward silence for several minutes.

Stretching my back, I turned and surveyed the work going on across the street at the memorial garden. It was coming along quite nicely. A small team from the landscape company were hunched over, laying out the reclaimed bricks to form a walkway. It would meander from the front entrance, around a fountain, and to the back. We were hoping to find room in the budget for a fountain for the middle but that hadn't happened yet, so the fountain would probably have to wait. The outline of the mural on the deli's newly exposed brick wall was complete and the artists planned on returning each evening this week to work on filling it in.

"Are we?" Bash said quietly.

I glanced away from the garden and found him watching me carefully. "Are we what?"

He shrugged. "Family."

I shrugged too. "Maybe not in the traditional sense, but I think so." I nudged his arm with my shoulder. "I'm not a fan of tradition anyway. You?"

He twisted his lips. "Yeah. It's overrated."

We exchanged a knowing smile and went back to work until the smooth purr of fancy vehicles caught our attention. Three shiny SUVs pulled onto Main Street and slowly drove by like a high-class parade. One black Range Rover, a white Mercedes, and one silver BMW.

"Looks like the illionaires are doing a drive-by," Bash mumbled, busying himself with scraping off another section of drying mortar.

I bit my lip but smiled anyway. For some reason it tickled me every time he picked up on something we said. Good thing most of us didn't cuss on a regular basis.

A few minutes later the motorcade did another loop, then parked in front of us this time. I placed my trowel in the bucket and watched the men pile out of the SUVs. All dressed in various golf shirts and chinos. The brands PING and Callaway etched on their shirts and hats.

"Gentlemen, what a pleasant surprise."

They walked over, heads bobbing around to take in all the changes.

"We were in a charity golf tournament in Hilton Head, so we figured we'd swing by and check on things." Jonas motioned around. "The town is really coming along."

I nodded in agreement. "Several projects are down to short punch lists. And the fire truck will be delivered next week, so some very exciting things are happening." I waved toward Bash who had lowered his head and hunched his shoulders, working steadily, as if hoping not to be noticed. Poor guy needed to realize he was nearly a head taller than most so going unnoticed would never be an option for him. "Gentlemen, this is Sebastian. We call him Bash. He's the best worker on the entire crew."

Leveling me with a look that said *knock it off,* Bash's face reddened as he straightened and turned to acknowledge the group of men. He tipped his head but didn't say a word, in true Bashful Bash fashion.

"Ah, just the young man I wanted to see." Jonas held up a finger and hurried to his Range Rover. He came back with a slim leather portfolio. He opened it and withdrew an envelope. "Here's the money from the comic books auction. They went for a pretty penny." He tried to hand it to Bash.

Bash held up his mortar-caked hands and shook his head. "That's okay. I'd rather the money be put toward the town."

Jonas narrowed his eyes but looked amused. "Son, this is a fairly substantial amount of money. You discovered the abandoned comic books, so this money is rightfully yours."

Bash looked intently across the street. It seemed that garden meant something significant to us all. "I'd like to donate it to purchase the fountain for the memorial garden."

The older men glanced at one another, as if they could hardly believe it.

"Tell you what." Jonas slid the check inside the portfolio. "We'll buy the fountain and give you whatever is left."

Bash shook his head. "That's okay. Y'all can use it all for the fountain."

Jonas's lip twitched. "At most, how much will the fountain cost, Avalee?"

"If we go for the nicest and biggest that can fit into the space, we're looking at right around twenty grand."

"Have it ordered." Jonas tucked the portfolio underneath his arm. "Avalee, do you have time to give us a tour of the new renovations?"

"Sure." I turned to Bash. "You good to keep smearing without me for a bit?"

"Yes." He picked up his trowel and went back at it.

I pulled my gloves off, giving myself a second to inspect my nails. Still good to go. I led the group of about a dozen men down Main Street. "The inn is almost complete. Let's start there."

Kendrick chuckled, pointing to the small marquee in front of the church. "What's that about?"

I silently read this week's message. *Don't trust stairs. They're always up to something.* "Just me having some fun. I'll be sure to put something appropriate on it before the ribbon cutting." I opened the inn's door and stepped aside to allow the men in. "Y'all take your time looking around and let me know if you have any questions. I'm going to stay right here so I don't get mortar everywhere."

Jonas stopped beside me and waited until the men were out of earshot. "Rowan told me about Sebastian's situation. I think it's commendable what you two are doing for him."

Feeling protective, I said firmly, "He's an exceptional young man. He deserves a fighting chance and I just want to help give him one."

Jonas nodded. "I agree. If you're okay with it, I'm going to have my lawyer set up a trust with this check." He held up the portfolio.

"That's fine, but would you please take out the money for the fountain? I think it's important to Bash to contribute to the memorial garden."

"I can do that." He tapped the portfolio against his palm. "That's why I asked for the tour, to have a moment to discuss this with you. I know you're busy, so we can show ourselves around."

I smiled. Jonas had really grown on me and I knew why Rowan thought so highly of him. "Thanks, Jonas. For everything, really. You've made a dream of mine come true by backing this revitalization initiative."

"I'm honored to be a part of it." He hitched a thumb over his shoulder. "We all are."

I started stepping backwards. "You know where I'll be if you have any questions or need anything. Waters and such are in the saloon. Feel free to help yourselves."

Jonas tipped his head and disappeared inside.

Feeling lighter, I practically skipped over to the mercantile. I decided not to tell Bash, but would secretly call him an illionaire in my head from this day forward.

CHAPTER 33

AUGUST

I was banned from the local library at age nine. I had no idea there were more rules than the universal one about being quiet. No one told me I couldn't skip down the aisles. And really, what's the harm in that? It's not like you could break a book by accidentally bumping into it. But the battle-ax librarian found harm in it, apparently, and banned me from the premises for a month. She said I needed to learn some respect. Even after the month-long sentence had been served, that old bird never really welcomed me back. In all fairness, I've met plenty of perfectly nice librarians over the years, but that bad experience certainly left an impression.

Tonight, I planned on dedicating my shenanigans to Miss Hazel-Mae Goodall. Well past dark to ensure the crews were gone for the day, I let myself in the back entrance of the coffee shop and headed upstairs to the newly completed library. The smell of old paper and fresh paint wafted around me as I walked through the dim, silent space. I flipped on the light above the media center and got to work on annihilating the silence.

"I can't believe we're sneaking into the library," Nita whispered.

Snorting, I looked at my phone screen, her face grinning at me. "We?"

She huffed. "I'd be there if Mama hadn't had to cancel."

I walked deeper into the library, flipping the screen so she could look at the archway we'd created with bricks painted to look like book spines.

"Oooh! I love it!"

"Same. This has really turned out to be the quaintest library ever." I ducked inside the children's nook and rotated in a circle to show it off. "Joyia is going to love this room." Two tiny table and chair sets grounded the space and the walls were lined with low bookcases filled with colorful books. A few beanbag chairs dotted the corners, luring children to sit a while with a book.

"Aww . . . She definitely will. I can't wait to bring her out there. The county really came through with the book donations."

"Yeah. They even ordered a nice collection of new releases too. The twins did such a killer job on the shelves."

"I like the ones on the wall that have the arched tops. That's a really nice touch."

I flipped the screen back to me. "Okay, my friend. Time to get off here and get up to some shenanigans."

Nita laughed. "Please do that 'Gangnam Style' dance for me."

"Of course."

We said our goodbyes and I returned to the front of the library. I powered up my portable speaker and placed it on a nearby bookshelf. After syncing it to my phone, I cued the new playlist entitled *Library Dance Party*. The first techno beats of "Pump Up the Jam" started streaming around me. Head nodding, my body began swaying until catching the rhythm.

I pumped up my jam, then caught some good vibrations and my foot got loose. Several songs into the playlist and in the midst of twerking, the music stopped playing.

"What the . . . ?" Straightening, I whirled around and there stood

Rowan, Bash, and Koda with their arms crossed like they were the fun police here to bust up my dance party. Rowan wore a look of amusement while the boys appeared a bit dumbstruck. I certainly didn't kid myself and mistake it for *awestruck*.

"You wanna tell us why you're disturbing the peace on a Tuesday night?" Rowan made a show of checking his watch with a raised eyebrow. "It's past your bedtime, young lady."

"Because I can," I said a little breathless. I took several inhales to steady my breathing.

Rowan's lips twitched. "This on the list of things to get away with in a ghost town?"

"Something like that. Now how 'bout turning my music back on." I flicked a hand at the speaker, but no one made a move.

"Look, no judgment is allowed here. Y'all can go on to bed or have some fun with me." I waved toward the speaker again. Rowan finally reached over and turned the volume back up but not quite as loud as I had it originally. "Electric Boogie" started playing and my legs began moving me to the right and then the left. Taking it back, I went to turn it out and realized Rowan had fallen in beside me. He had as much rhythm as me—not much—but what we lacked in skill we made up for in enthusiasm.

I couldn't stop the flashes of us doing this very dance at our wedding reception. The difference between now and that day was that then, we were all over each other, earning catcalls and silly remarks during the entire reception. Another difference, we cut out early because we couldn't keep our hands off each other. We were young, naive, and absolutely in love.

"Y'all doing it all wrong," Bash yelled over the music.

"Then get your butt over here and show us the right way," Rowan yelled back just as we bumped into each other. Laughing, we stumbled around until getting back in line, sort of.

"Cha Cha Slide" came on next, and even though I was getting winded from laughing more than anything else, I clapped my hands and prepared to get *real smooth*.

Soon, Bash and Koda walked over. Standing between Rowan and me, Bash started directing our steps. The teenager was a pro at it and easily transitioned into the "Cupid Shuffle" next.

"How do you know these line dances?" I asked as we strutted the "walk it by yourself" part.

"I thought there was no judgment here?" Bash turned his hat backwards and swiveled his hips to the beat like he owned it. Koda tried mimicking him, but he looked like he was being electrocuted.

I threw my head back and laughed, bumping into Rowan once again.

Smiling with flushed faces, we shuffled and strutted and did a version of all the moves, song after song. And then the whimsical opening to the "Chicken Dance" began and Bash froze. Not me and Rowan. Nope, we immediately started flapping our wings and making beaks by tapping our fingers to our thumbs. Another silly dance we did at our wedding.

"This is so lame!" Shaking his head, Bash motioned for Koda and started walking away like he hadn't just been dancing his little too-cool-for-school heart out.

Typical Koda, the little stinker stuck his tongue out before trailing behind his big brother.

"Where are y'all going?" Rowan called out as we watched them start down the stairs.

"To bed." Bash tossed a hand up without looking back.

We continued going through the chicken motions, and I laughed until I could hardly breathe. When Whitney Houston started belting out "I Wanna Dance with Somebody" Rowan reached for my hand and spun me around. The song felt too intimate, and I knew he felt it too when he pulled me closer until I could feel the heat of his chest.

Time slowed even though the song did not. Then, Rowan began walking me backwards until we were between two bookshelves. "I know something else that would be fun to get away with in a library." A determined look settled on his face as he advanced toward me.

I tried to come up with a flippant response to defuse the mounting tension, but reasonable thinking left me as Rowan placed a hand on my hip and then slid it into my back pocket, slipping my phone out. He held it behind my shoulder, the blue light of the screen lighting his face as he concentrated on whatever he was doing. His eyes moved from the screen and locked with mine just as the first tinkling notes of "Everywhere" by Fleetwood Mac began playing. Our song.

Eyes burning, heart thumping aggressively, I shuffled to keep some space but he soon eliminated it. My back pressed against the wall, halting my retreat altogether.

Rowan caged me in by placing a hand on each side of my head, as if reading my thoughts. "What'll happen if I kiss you, *a stór*?" His Irishman slipped into his words.

I grabbed ahold of some anger before something else more dangerous took hold, like affection or lust. "Do that and I'll coldcock you."

He huffed a husky chuckle. "I don't doubt you, but I think it'll be worth it."

Sweat broke out along my hairline and I could hardly take a deep breath. "Please don't."

Rowan leaned forward and skimmed his nose along my jaw, pressing a featherlight kiss just below my ear. "Why not?"

A shiver moved through me even though my skin was close to overheating. "Because it's gonna hurt."

He edged back and met my gaze, his eyes a molten honey. "Doesn't it already hurt?"

Lips trembling, I nodded. Gosh, did it hurt so bad. I was absolutely exhausted by it.

My back stiffened as Rowan angled his head to the side, his eyes pinned to mine. I was prepared for the zap of his lips meeting mine, not for the tender caress he gave in its place. Instead of stealing that kiss, Rowan wrapped his arms around me and tucked me close. The tremble in my lips veined out until my entire body shook. My walls were collapsing, but Rowan's firm grip reassured me he'd hold me up. I knew he would, so I fell.

Soon, tears soaked his shirt where my face burrowed against his shoulder. Clinging to him, I cried as our song played on repeat several times. I'd cried alone so often over the years, but this solidarity of shared pain gave me a freedom I'd robbed myself of for way too long.

Being alone in this long season of despair had really been troubling in so many ways. One, I pushed those that I loved away, even keeping my grandmother and father at arm's length. I allowed the loneliness to rob me of my peace and rest. That verse from Ecclesiastes came to mind: *Someone who falls alone is in real trouble.*

Rowan cradled me to him and began to gently rock until I joined him. We danced to our song for the first time in almost a decade. Unrushed, we swayed side to side. It was rather settling to just be in the moment instead of running away from it.

I would never be able to walk down the nonfiction section of this library without recalling the night I let out enough of my grief to let Rowan back in.

CHAPTER 34

I STRETCHED MY ARMS OUT and spun slowly around the main room in the mercantile. A hodgepodge of tables, desks, and hutches were strategically placed and ready to be filled with merchandise. "What do you think?"

Desmond rubbed his chin. "I can't envision anything past the paint fumes and polyurethane."

I dismissed his comment with a flick of the wrist. "We just need to exorcise that with a good-smelling candle. Something floral and known from this region. A gardenia or . . . magnolia."

His face lit up. "Magnolia. That fresh lemony fragrance is what this place needs to bring it to life. Remember that quaint shop on the coast we visited a while back with all the eclectic furniture pieces? Bless This Mess?"

"Yeah."

"They have candles. I'll make a trip this afternoon and grab some."

"Great. You're a peach."

"Just call me Steel Magnolia." Desmond winked.

A chiming sound, one I'd not heard in the last several months, caught me off guard and made me jolt like I'd been shocked. Desmond looked a bit shocked too.

"Is that the clock?" he asked, wide-eyed.

We both darted to the door and found a small group gathered at the base of the clock tower.

Froid saw us and started waving. "It's fixed!"

"This place is starting to really come alive," Desmond commented as we made our way to the clock tower.

"I have goose bumps!" I showed him my arm. As we joined the crowd, our clocksmith emerged from inside the tower. "Andy, you're a magician!"

Andy wiped his hands on a rag, shrugging his shoulders. "It's not the original. This one's computer operated." He pulled a slim remote out of his coverall pocket and handed it to me. "You can work it from anywhere in town."

"I liked the sound of the chimes. It wasn't jarring."

"Not replacing the bell and all those mechanisms kept us in budget."

"Now that's music to my ears." As soon as I said that a screeching kid ran up and nearly plowed me over. "Whoa!" I grabbed Koda to steady him but he quickly wiggled out of my touch.

"Can you make it sing again?" He jabbed a finger toward the clock while jumping up and down.

I handed Andy the remote, having no clue how to do such.

He pushed a button and the clock tolled a pleasant tune twelve times. "The original clock would have set the bell to toll at noon and then at midnight, but with the digital age, we can set it to chime just at noon. You can even change up the tune if you'd like."

"No. The one you've selected is perfect. It has such a soothing melody."

"It's a popular choice. This green button that says *test* is the one to press to test it. It's fairly dummy-proof." Once again, Andy handed me the remote and told me he'd send the invoice for the final payment before leaving us with our shiny new toy.

Koda tried snatching the remote while I held it easily out of his reach.

"Knock it off, Koda," Bash reprimanded, but when his little brother began to whine, he shut that down. "If you wanna help with the garden, you'll dry it up right now."

Koda mashed his pouting lips together and started following in Bash's shadow back toward the memorial garden.

The little stinker looked so pitiful that I couldn't help myself. I pressed the test button. As soon as the first chime rang out, he wheeled around and pumped his dirt-caked fists in the air. I half expected him to shout, "Rock on!"

"Silly kid." Desmond chuckled while fishing out his phone. "I'm going to make a call about those candles."

"Okay." I pointed a thumb over my shoulder. "I'm going to go work on the memorial garden with the others. How about putting this remote somewhere for safekeeping."

Desmond took the remote. "How about the wall in the fabric store. Well . . . deli now. Seems like the safest place to store something in this town." He chuckled at his own joke, heading to the saloon. "It'll be behind the bar in the saloon."

"Okay."

At the memorial garden, all hands were on deck to get the plants and a few small ornamental trees in the ground. Well, except for Rowan. He'd had to head up to Greenville for a few days on business. I hated to admit it, but I missed him.

I caught sight of Koda talking Froid's ear off, a gerbera daisy clutched in his fist. "Hey, tot, we're supposed to be planting the flowers, not choking them to death."

A deep scowl on his face, Koda growled. "Don't call me that."

I took the flower from him. "Then don't act like one by mishandling the plants. Come on and I'll show you how to properly plant this."

Giving me a run for my money, Koda spent most of the day sassing me every chance he got while we worked on finishing up the flower beds. I believe the kid would have argued that the petunias were orange if I had told him they were purple.

Out the corner of my eye, I caught him about to pull off his shoe.

"Don't even think about taking those shoes off."

"Why can't I just go barefoot?"

"Because this is a worksite. You could hurt your foot." I wiggled a flower from the tray, waiting for him to obey before handing it over.

He crossed his little arms and glared. "But my shoes ain't workin' right."

"Ain't working right? What do you mean?" I put the flower back into the tray and dusted off my hands.

Koda shrugged. "My toes don't fit."

Squatting beside him, I prodded the tip of his shoes. "How on earth did you get these things on?"

Shrugging, he started to step away.

"Whoa." I glanced around and found Bash helping the landscape crew leader dig a hole for the Japanese maple tree in the back. "Bash!"

He looked up, "Yeah?"

I gestured with my chin. "Come here a minute." Once he reached us, I asked, "Your brother got any more shoes?"

Both brothers shrugged.

Bash looked down at Koda. "Something wrong with the ones he's wearing?"

"They're way too small," I answered.

Slumping, Bash's lips mushed firmly together. He was too young to have so much weight on his shoulders.

"No worries." I straightened. "Koda, I'm ready for a break. Let's you and me go grab a pair of shoes."

Both brothers said no at the same time.

"We'll get ice cream too. I'm hungry." That's all I had to say and the younger brother was sold. He dropped his little work gloves I bought him last weekend and started hobbling in the direction of my truck down the street.

"I can give you some money," Bash offered.

"Nah. I owe Koda for helping with the garden. We'll be back later."

"You've been letting him stay with us, feeding him, and taking us to church. I think we owe you."

"Hardly." I stood my full giant height, as Koda liked to say, and steeled my shoulders. "Now. I'm the adult and what I say goes."

Bash squinted. "M'kay."

I winked at him and walked away, feeling really parental in that moment instead of like an imposter.

After swinging in at Sonic for ice cream to butter him up for shopping, we went to the mall for new shoes. Wearing dirt-smudged clothes and worn ballcaps, I knew we looked thrown away, but I didn't care what anyone thought. My only concern was getting this kid some shoes that fit.

Sporting new light-up Skechers, Koda let me drag him to a few stores for new clothes. We spent the rest of the day shopping and goofing off. He whined about the new-wardrobe mission I went on but was all smiles when I spotted one of those jump parks and made a U-turn. We jumped until working up an appetite.

"I could go for some pizza," Koda declared, pulling his new shoes back on with ease.

"Pizza it is." I lucked out and found a Chuck E. Cheese. We definitely bonded over our love for cheese pizza and Skee-Ball.

I'd never tell the little spitfire, but it was the most fun I'd had in years.

Tuesday evening, I decided to use Rowan's kitchen to make supper while I quizzed Bash for his US History test, since he wasn't feeling the best.

Stirring the pot of grits, I scanned the sheet of paper I printed off. "What was the Cold War?"

"An ongoing political rivalry between the United States and the Soviet Union."

I looked over my shoulder to where he was sprawled on the couch, a pillow pressed to his stomach. Maudie always made me do that when my stomach hurt, so I insisted he do so too. He humored me and did as I said. "Why was it called the Cold War?"

"Because war was never declared."

Rowan stormed into the apartment, nostrils flaring and a stern frown smashing his lips together. In a navy suit, he looked like a grumpy business exec. "Where's Koda?"

"He's spending the night with Froid and his wife. They have their grandchildren tonight and they're having a big sleepover. They're crazy, if you ask me, to take on three boys under the age of ten." I made a silly face but dropped it when I noticed Rowan still seemed worked up about something.

Rowan pointed at me and then the door. "Next door. Now." He pointed to Bash, who was slowly sitting up. "You stay put."

I cut a look toward Bash and mouthed, *What'd you do?*

He shrugged and made a face.

Reluctantly, I turned off the stove burner and followed in Rowan's wake to my apartment. Barely in the door, Rowan's hand captured me as he kicked the door shut.

"What th—" Before I could finish my thought, his arms wrapped around me. My back remained straight as a board for a few beats before I melted into his embrace.

"I missed you, *a stór.*" Rowan nuzzled my neck, pressing his lips to my thrumming pulse.

A breathless giggle escaped me as I twined my fingers in the short, soft strands of his hair. "It's only been three days."

"No." A deep groan vibrated through him as his arms tightened. "It's been six years and three days."

"Rowan . . ." I heaved a sigh and leaned against the door so I could see his face. His eyes were molten honey, cheeks tinged pink, lips curled on one side.

"You missed me, too, so don't even deny it." Growing serious, Rowan tugged me flush against him and placed his lips against mine.

To be honest, I went willingly and stayed there for much longer than I should have before breaking the kiss.

"Whoa." I wiggled until he loosened his grip. Chest heaving, I righted my shirt and smoothed my lopsided ponytail. "What's gotten into you?"

His swollen lips formed a devilish grin. "Seemed you were into it too."

I shoved him off and moved around him. "Seriously, Rowdy?"

"You know I love it when you call me that." He stepped forward, his hands already reaching for me again, but I countered his action and reversed several steps.

Doing my best to erect some walls, which were flimsy at best, I said the first thing to come to mind. "Bash has diarrhea."

Well, that did it. Rowan halted. The smolder gone, replaced with a furrowed brow. "He okay?"

"Froid made his Bloody Mary sausage and rice. It's really spicy and I think that's what got ahold of Bash."

Rowan took a step in the direction of the door, looking very much like a concerned daddy. "He need medicine? Some of that Pedialyte stuff?"

Now I felt awful for making him worry. I clutched Rowan's arm to stop him. "He's okay. Don't go over there all willy-nilly and embarrass him."

Rowan stared at the wall between the apartments, as if he were considering it. "But . . ."

"I gave him some Imodium and I was in the middle of making him some grits for supper when you interrupted. He's fine." I gestured toward the dining table. "How about we sit down and you explain to me why you showed up in such a . . . mood."

His lips quirked to one side as he blocked me from the table. "I got you a surprise." He reached into his suit coat and pulled out a black velvet gift box.

My eyes rounded as I poked him in the chest. "You better not have!"

Undeterred, Rowan dropped to one knee. "Avalee Elvis, would you do me the honor of becoming my BFF again?" He snapped the lid open, revealing a shiny new pocketknife with a gorgeous wood handle.

Laughing, I popped him in the shoulder. "You're not funny!"

"That was totally funny." Chuckling, Rowan stood and offered me the gift box. "Your other knife is worn out. It was time for you to have a new one."

I removed it from the box and flicked the blade out. It performed the task smoothly. My old one had so much grit built up inside that it was a challenge to open and close it. Shutting the blade, I weighed the knife in the palm of my hand. It was small, just what I needed for small tasks. "This wood handle is exquisite."

"It's actually a piece of wood from the oak tree by the firehouse. I had it custom-made."

I glanced up. "Really? That's so . . ." My attention returned to the knife.

"That day in the tree gave me hope that we could be friends again. You showed me you still cared." Rowan took it out of my hand and flipped it over, showing off the engraving. *Wherever you go, I go.*

A sensation close to a tidal wave slammed into me and my body swayed. Unable to hold it back, I hiccuped a gasp.

Rowan's arms encircled me again and mine responded by draping over his shoulders. "From day one, way back in third grade, you demanded I follow you, and I have. You're my best friend, Avalee. I will always want to go too."

I looked over his shoulder and studied the knife in my hand, the words engraved more specifically. *Wherever you go, I go.* "Rowan, I am your friend. I'm sorry I didn't work harder to take care of our friendship." My mind rewound to the conversation Maudie and I had back in Beaufort. The one where she gave me insight on how Rowan had suffered after our life together broke apart. *For better or for worse.* I'd failed that part of our marriage by not being there for him in his suffering. Maybe now, after all this time and some healing, I could be the best friend he deserved. "I promise to do a better job at being your friend this time."

"Me too." He pressed a kiss to my forehead. "I like being your friend."

"A friend who is now sharing responsibility of two boys with you. This is a pretty serious endeavor." I wiggled free and sat at the dining table.

"Something happen?" He joined me.

"Nothing major. We just need to pay more attention to Bash and Koda's needs."

"Sounds to me like you're already handling that."

I looked up and narrowed my eyes. "How?"

"Bash called me last night and told me you took Koda shopping for new shoes and clothes."

I clucked my tongue. "The poor thing was hobbling around in shoes two sizes too small. How'd we miss that for *weeks*?"

"Boys can sprout inches overnight. I grew up in a house full of them, I should know."

"Still. I should have noticed."

"Don't beat yourself up over something you've already fixed."

"I just want to do my best for those boys . . ." I glanced off, then back to him. "I know we haven't known them long, but it feels like they're family."

"I know." Rowan grew somber and stared off to the left. Blinking slowly, he brought his gaze back to me. "I think God put Bash and Koda in our life on purpose. Like it's meant for us to take care of them."

"If God deems fit for us to take care of Bash and Koda, then why didn't he do the same for our own children?"

Rowan frowned, shaking his head. "I have no answer for that, but I do know you're a natural at taking care of Bash and Koda." He reached out and took my hand. "Didn't you come up with the quote for the mural?"

I nodded, my eyes trained on the beautiful knife sitting on the table before me.

A new start doesn't negate the past. It learns from the roots of history and blooms into a better version." He squeezed my hand. "You know the truth in that or you wouldn't have come up with it in the first place. Avalee, we have a strong root system. Sure, we also have some damaged branches, but we could heal . . . We could have our own new start."

"I know we're in this together . . . I'm just trying to figure out what a new start looks like for us."

"It can look like whatever we want it to." Rowan scooted his chair away from the table and stood. "I'm going to go check on Bash and change out of this suit."

"Okay." I grabbed Rowan's hand as he walked by. "You're a natural with those boys, too, ya know."

He stopped and smiled at me.

I didn't have a sentimental gift for him, but I could give him my words. "You're one amazing man, Rowan Murray. I'm grateful to have my best friend back . . . I've really missed him." I rose to my feet, my focus on his lips. Always able to read me as easily as I could him, he leaned down and kissed me.

Loving this man was as easy as breathing. I just needed to figure out how to stop suffocating under the weight of our grievous past.

CHAPTER 35

THE AUGUST NIGHT WAS AS HOT AS ALL THE JULY NIGHTS, but I was too busy admiring the completed memorial garden to care. With the warm glow from strings of lights zigzagging between the buildings on each side and the sounds of the hushed gurgling of the water fountain and the tinkling of wind chimes, the intimate outdoor space held a magical quality full of whimsy, exactly what I'd envisioned. A place where Douglas would have enjoyed visiting. My little ones too.

A minivan pulled up in front of the entrance to the garden, and moments later a heavyset woman dressed in purple scrubs helped an elderly lady into a wheelchair. I had reached out and invited Loreen Holt to visit the garden before the town opened so she could have privacy, but I hadn't expected her to be in such poor health. She was hunched and wafer-thin.

I rose to my feet, about to go greet Loreen and her aide, but the older lady's face crumpled as she read the bronze memorial plaque mounted to the brick column at the entrance. *Withered* came to mind as I observed her, like life had been whittling away at her, little by little. Not much remained but a husk. And in this moment the poor husk nearly folded in on herself. Deciding she deserved space to mourn, I caught the nurse's attention and mouthed, *I'll be back later.* She nodded her head.

I made the three-mile loop around town before returning. As I walked by the entrance, I saw Loreen hunched in her chair by the three-tiered water fountain. The creamy white granite glowed underneath the string lights and the underwater lights cast a green hue to her face. The murmur of water seemed to have her in a trance.

"Hello," I said gently as I joined her by the fountain, taking a seat on the bench beside her chair. I looked around and caught sight of the aide sitting on another bench, far enough away to give Loreen some privacy yet close enough if the elderly lady needed her. I gave her a smile and turned my attention to Loreen. "I'm Avalee Elvis. You must be Loreen Holt."

A moment passed before she cleared her throat on a frail cough. "Yes."

"Thank you for accepting my invitation."

She finally glanced away from the fountain and met my eyes with a pair of cloudy blue ones, but said nothing. Surely, this had to be beyond overwhelming, so I didn't push for conversation. Sometimes situations didn't require words, so we sat there for a long spell of quiet as she took in the space. Her gaze moved from the fountain to the mural of the pecan tree with my quote on a ribbon beneath it. *A new start doesn't negate the past. It learns from the roots of history and blooms into a better version.* She nodded as if she agreed with the saying. Then she looked to the left back corner, where we'd installed an interactive musical nook. It was a garden in memory of a child, after all, so we'd installed drums that looked like red-capped mushrooms with white dots, an upright xylophone shaped and painted like a butterfly, lily pad cymbals, and my favorite, three giant bamboo rainsticks.

The warm breeze gave the garden movement and I could all but imagine little fairies hiding in the flowers and shrubbery. I looked over at Loreen and watched her ease up in her chair to look over the lip of the fountain. I did the same and admired the coins glittering underneath the lit water. The day we'd finished installing it, workers kept stopping by to dump their spare change in at Koda's insistence.

I fished a coin out of my pocket and offered it to her.

"Oh . . . no, dear. I don't believe in wishing."

"Good. Neither do I." Wishing only ever let me down. "But I like to toss coins in Douglas's fountain because all the money will be collected and donated to the March of Dimes in his memory each year from here on out."

Her chin wobbled as I expected it would. "You were the one to find my son."

"Yes," I answered even though it wasn't a question.

Loreen reached for the coin and I gave it to her. She flicked it into the bottom basin, barely making a splash. With our eyes trained on the rippling water, she caught my hand in hers and held it. An unspoken thank-you, I was sure.

We sat there staring into the water until I had the overwhelming urge to tell her my story.

"I've lost three children," I whispered, my voice cracking. "Two miscarriages and one stillbirth." The two words felt all wrong leaving my tongue. Two words that shouldn't exist, right along with the two words *kidnapping* and *murder*. I couldn't believe I just said them out loud and to a stranger no less. But somehow it felt freeing.

Loreen held my hand tighter with more strength than she appeared to have. It should have felt odd holding this stranger's hand, but perhaps our similar grief made her feel familiar to me. "We're in a club no mother should ever be a part of, my dear."

I trained my bleary gaze at the illuminated water. "I want to ask God why . . ." My throat filled with pain, making it impossible to speak further.

Beside me, Loreen shifted in her chair, slowly crossing her ankles. After some time, she interrupted the silence with her own confession of hurt.

"I spent the first year with hopes that my little boy would return home. I couldn't fathom it any other way. And then years moved forward without giving me my son back. My husband planned a funeral against my wishes." She shook her head and sighed. "I refused to attend. I was so mad at Doug Senior for giving up hope. Then, after he left me, I finally gave up hope too. My grief got the better of me. I put up a wall between me and my other two children. Years later when Jacob and Jane were grown adults, I realized the mistake of pushing them away, but the damage had been done and my children kept their distance."

I wiped a tear off my cheek. "I'm so sorry, Loreen."

We grew quiet until she spoke again.

"I made a list of questions long ago, questions I would demand God answer once I got to heaven. But now, at ninety-two years old, I see how it doesn't matter. I don't want answers anymore, I just want peace." She squeezed my hand before letting go. "I suggest you do the same. Focus on peace. Not the questions we can't answer."

"I want to but . . ." I motioned at nothing in particular and shook my head.

"I lost my son at the hands of a sick man. But I lost the rest of my family at my own hands. I let grief and anger rule over me to the point that's all I had . . . It's been a lonely life."

Soft footsteps approached and the aide appeared at Loreen's side. "Ms. Holt, we need to get you back. It's close time for your meds." She offered me a sad smile, clearly having heard our conversation. "This garden is beautiful."

I returned her sad smile with one of my own. "Thank you."

"I'm Florence." She unlatched the wheels on Loreen's chair and turned her around.

"Avalee." We shared a better smile this time.

"May I give you a hug, Loreen?" I asked before they moved away.

"I could use one, yes."

I rose from the bench and stooped over and gently embraced her. It felt like hugging a frail twig, but the scent of her floral perfume softened the hug. Slowly, I released her and took a step out of the way, then followed behind them.

"Please say hello to your handsome husband for me."

I stumbled a bit but recovered. "Oh, uh, I don't have a husband."

Loreen looked over her shoulder, her brow puckered. "Rowan? He called you his wife."

Laughing softly, I veered around the wheelchair, and held the gate door open for them to pass through. "That man has a bad habit of doing that." I shifted to face her. "You know Rowan?"

"He's come to visit me just about every week the last two months. Brings me flowers." Loreen smiled warmly. "You have yourself a catch." I started to correct her but she held up her arthritic hand, several fingers bent in painful looking angles. "Don't make my mistakes. That man wants to be caught. I suggest you stop lollygagging and catch him." She tipped her head resolutely.

"Maybe I'll just let him catch me," I joked.

"That works too." Her smile lit up her pale eyes.

I helped Florence get Loreen in the van. Before closing her door, I spoke softly, "You don't know how much I needed to hear what you shared. Thank you for that and please know you are welcome to visit the garden anytime."

She patted my hand where it rested on her arm. "Thank you, dear. You have no idea how much it means to me what you've done to honor my son. Take care of yourself."

"Yes, ma'am." Smiling, I shut her door and watched the van drive away. Glancing one last time at the tranquil garden, I headed down the street toward the saloon. I grabbed the door handle but stopped before going inside when I caught sight of Rowan sitting on the tailgate of my truck.

"Whatcha doing?"

"Waiting on you." He patted the spot beside him. "C'mere."

I hesitated, but the need to talk outweighed my discomfort. I hopped up beside him and studied my dangling boots. "That was Loreen. I invited her out to see the garden in privacy."

"I know."

Glimpsing him out the corner of my eye, I *tsk*ed. "You really get around with the old ladies, Rowdy. Maudie is gonna be jealous."

Rowan chuckled. "Your grandmother already knows. She's the one who encouraged me to go visit Loreen in the first place."

"I'm still trying to figure out how you manage to sneak off and spend so much time with my grandmother." I pushed my shoulder against his.

He just smiled at my comment instead of responding to it. "My visits with Loreen . . . It's been nice to talk with someone who knows what we've been through, to an extent. It's like only parents who've lost a child can understand, ya know."

I nodded, moving my gaze back to my dangling boots. "I'm sorry I never let you talk about it."

A soft sigh left him. "We did what we had to do to survive. Don't apologize for that."

I listened to a medley of croaking frogs, wondering what they had so much to talk about while trying to find the right words to share. "You wanna know what hurts the most?"

"What's that?"

"Not getting to hold him. I didn't even get to say hello or good-bye." I had no recollection between glimpsing the blue baby to waking up two days later with a stomach full of stitches and emptiness.

Rowan wrapped an arm around my waist and tugged me closer. "I met him," he said in a scratchy whisper.

The moon hung heavily over the pecan grove, whitewashing the treetops as fireflies flashed in a twinkling effect around the trunks. Eyes focused in that direction, I braced myself and asked, "Will you tell me about him?"

Rowan didn't talk right away, opening his mouth a few times but then pressing his lips tightly. Lips that were trembling. He'd not even started talking about it yet, but we were already ripping open the poorly healed wound by finally accepting it had happened. That acknowledgment was profound in itself, but once he began sharing, every raw spot on my soul burned.

"I'd hoped the doctors were wrong and Declan could come out crying." Rowan's voice cracked. Clearing his throat, he continued, "My boy came out pouting like his mama. His little face was all scrunched up and his bottom lip poked out." With silent tears slipping down his cheeks, Rowan mimicked a pouty face.

Laughing through my own tears, I shook my head. "I don't pout."

"Oh yes you do. Just yesterday when the inspector came in and said we couldn't continue with the chapel reno until the electrician fixed the fuse box? Boy, you pouted the rest of the day." Rowan puckered his face again, lips protruding in such a way that I almost kissed them.

I drew back a bit. "So he pouted?"

"Yeah. I think he was as mad as I was that he wouldn't get to stay." Rowan wiped his face with the back of his hand and swallowed with difficulty, coughing a little. "You were in surgery and Declan . . . As soon as they placed him in my arms, his little face relaxed."

We cried a while, holding on to each other, and I wondered with deep regret why we hadn't done this very thing during those hard moments. Why hadn't we clung to each other? Where had that wall come from that prevented us from doing this then?

Eventually, Rowan pulled himself together enough to speak. "They gave me some time alone with him. At some point, I noticed he was starting to get cold, so I undid my shirt and placed him on my chest. It wasn't to keep him warm. I . . . I knew better than to try, but I did it so I could soak up his warmth." Rowan choked on a sob.

"Oh, Rowan." I hiccuped.

All these years and I never really considered my husband's grief. I was too wrapped up in my own to see anything past it. At least I was unconscious during the most horrific moment of our lives. Rowan didn't have that escape. He lived it, *alone*, and those memories of holding his dead child . . . I couldn't help him carry them any more than he could help me carry mine.

But maybe we could find a new way to carry each other.

"What did he smell like?" I asked, after regaining some composure.

Rowan didn't even bat an eye at my odd question, just gave me a sad smile. "He smelled like perfection. A faint sweetness. He smelled so pure . . ."

Each of my questions sent a jolt of pain through my chest, but I continued anyway, allowing myself to feel it all. "Did he have any hair?"

"A little." Rowan leaned close and said softly, "It was red."

I giggled through a sniffle and squeezed his forearm. "I knew it!"

"Knew what?"

"Your red hair vanished. I had a feeling our babies stole it from you."

A grin lit up his damp face. "I like that idea." Rubbing the back of his neck, he stared up at the dark indigo sky. "I would have given them my soul if God would have allowed it."

"Me too." I mopped my face with the collar of my shirt.

With my head resting on Rowan's shoulder, I marveled at how we finally braved unsealing the silence where we had kept all the hurt, all the grief.

More fireflies came out to join us as we continued talking. The talking sounded a lot like healing.

In a lull of conversation, our eyes met and held. For the first time in almost a decade, I initiated kissing him. Leaning into his space, I pressed my lips against his and held on for dear life. A roller coaster of emotions tumbled through me but I continued kissing him. Rowan wrapped his arms around me and lowered us onto the bed of the truck. Arms entwined, hands searching for purchase, we kissed like we used to before life got hard. The kind of kissing that's reckless with abandon. The kind that you'll be recalling the next day with a smile on your bruised lips.

A throat cleared and startled us apart. Jackknifing up, I found Bash at the back of the truck, peering at us with his arms crossed, Preacher and Koda by his side.

"Not together . . . I'm calling bull." Bash's eyes narrowed.

"Eww! Y'all was kissin'!" Koda shook a finger at us.

Rowan and I chose selective hearing at that moment while straightening our shirts and hair, neither one of us addressing the boys' comments.

Rowan drew up his knees and draped his arms, trying to appear casual even though his lips were swollen. "What's up?"

"We're about to make some popcorn." Bash glanced between us, fighting a smile. "I was going to see if y'all wanted some, but I see you're busy."

"We gonna watch a movie too." Koda jumped up and down, trying to get a better look at us.

"Pick one out. We'll be there in a minute." Rowan tipped his head, dismissing them.

Bash turned and started walking away with Preacher and Koda following. "For what it's worth," he said over his shoulder, "I like y'all together."

He wasn't the only one.

CHAPTER 36

SEPTEMBER

People, lots and lots of people, were starting to encroach on my town. At this point, I guessed it was time for me to stop referring to it as *mine*, but still. It would take some getting used to, not having the run of the place like we'd had the last seven months. Adjusting the backpack on my arm, I peeked out the saloon door. Delivery trucks and other vehicles lined the street and boxes littered the sidewalks. Today was move-in day for the business owners. Seeing all the activity had a spike of adrenaline rushing through me. We did it. We brought the ghost town back from the dead and managed to meet the September 24 deadline.

Blinking away the sting in my eyes, I kept my head down, crossed the street, and took the back way through the new park to the chapel. I had one last order of private business to take care of before the ribbon cutting in four days. I glanced at the marquee. It was now boring. *Welcome to Somewhere.* But I smiled at my new message. The message welcomed a new beginning.

I entered the chapel and took a deep inhale of the freshly scrubbed space. The podium had been moved off the platform up front in preparation for the floors to be refinished tomorrow. I had a crew lined up to help move out the pews later today. But first . . .

Placing the portable speaker on the front pew and syncing my phone to it, I pulled up the only song needed for this task. "Shake" by MercyMe. Once the lively beats started piping through the speaker, I put it on repeat and pulled my special shoes out of the backpack. Another unexpected gift from this old town. There had been a few pairs of tap shoes in a box in the old theater, one being my size, so of course I swiped them.

Once I had the shoes on, I moved onto the platform, already giddy from the clinking sound coming from the shoes. I tapped one foot, then the other until I matched it to the rhythm of the song. Well, it sort of matched . . . Close enough, I'd say, to have some good ole fun.

By the third time through the song, sweat had collected at my hairline and my entire body was shaking just as MercyMe told me to. Heel to toe. Tap. Toe to heel. Tap. Over and over . . . I twirled, shook, tapped till I was pure winded but I didn't slow the shaking or tapping.

A loud bark broke the dancing spell. I spun around and found Preacher standing beside Rowan, Bash, and Koda by the back pew.

I hurried over to the speaker, shoes tapping the entire way, and turned the music off. "Hey!" I took a deep breath and wiped my damp forehead with the back of my hand. "You're early."

"We surprised this one and picked him up from school a little early." Rowan's lips curled to one side as he mussed Koda's hair. His amused gaze slid to my feet. "Where'd you get those shoes?"

I popped a leg out and admired the ancient relics. "I found them months ago when I was cleaning out the old theater. I almost forgot I had them until this morning when I was going through my closet."

"Eww . . ." Koda wrinkled his nose. "Your feet are gonna get cooties."

Hands on my hips, I clucked my tongue. "There's nothing wrong with these shoes. I cleaned them and sprayed them with disinfectant."

"This another one of your bucket list items?" Rowan asked.

"Yep."

Desmond came in, dressed in a tan linen suit with a matching fedora. "What'd I miss?"

"Your friend actin' the fool," Rowan answered, amused eyes trained on me. "I didn't even know you took tap dance lessons, Avalee."

"I don't." I tapped around, shimmying in a circle with jazz hands. "I'm self-taught."

"That's why you're so bad," Koda interjected. To that I danced some more, my shoes clickety-clacketing in a satisfying way. "You're so weird."

I gave him my best weird face. "*Weird* means fun in my book, so thank you for the compliment."

Desmond grabbed one of my jazz hands and inspected it. "At least your nail polish is on point."

I looked at my sparkling nails, hot pink with flecks of black and white. "Thanks. It's called *Finish Line*. How perfect is that!" I did another happy dance.

Shaking his head, Desmond smirked. "I thought we were here to shop, not monkey around."

"There's always time for both." I shimmied to the front pew and took the tap shoes off, replacing them with my plain, boring canvas slide-on shoes. "Where's Nita?"

"She texted us in our group chat and said she couldn't make it. Joyia has a fever. I guess you were too busy monkeying around to check your phone."

I checked it then and saw the message. "Poor Joyia. I hate that Nita is going to miss our shopping date. I'd say let's postpone it but today is our only chance."

Desmond started toward the exit. "Nita understands that. We can buy her and Joyia some gifts."

"Okay. So here's our goal for the day. We are going to be the very first customers for every business in town. I already booked Maudie a room at the inn for this weekend's grand celebration and I opened a checking account at the bank." I pulled out my trusty clipboard and crossed those two places off the list. "We're starting the fun at Beauty and the Barber. I know two guys in serious need of haircuts. Diesel and Jillian are expecting us."

Koda grumbled in true Koda fashion but seemed smitten by the very pretty and very blonde Jillian when she offered to cut his hair while her dad cut Bash's. Bash only got a trim, leaving his locks long, but at least there was shape to his style now.

After the haircuts we wasted no time moving on next door to Pet & Plant, which turned out to be a big mistake.

A few minutes later, we stood on the sidewalk, trying to collect ourselves after that mayhem.

"Preacher is already banned from the pet store." Bash snorted. "I can't believe he tore down the doggy treat rack like a boss."

"Not like a boss. Like the thief that he is." I turned and eyed the dog, who seemed pleased with himself. "Two hundred dollars' worth of treats . . . you're grounded."

We paused our shopping spree while Rowan took Preacher up to his apartment for a time-out.

At the Lowcountry Mercantile I bought a few of the magnolia candles Desmond had recommended to the shop manager. I got several so I could share with Nita. The guys got T-shirts with the pecan tree mural on the back. Except for Desmond. He purchased hand-dyed handkerchiefs.

"I'm hungry," Koda groaned at the checkout counter.

I slid my credit card into the machine. "Well, you're in luck. Next on the list is Dinah's Diner."

We grabbed a booth at the diner and chowed down on fat, juicy burgers and hand-cut fries, but were careful to leave room for ice cream from Sweet Silo. After being overwhelmed by the many flavor options, I settled on butter pecan. Rowan chose peach cobbler. Desmond picked sweet potato, which was actually very tasty. Bash picked strawberry and Koda got a scoop of chocolate and a scoop of red velvet.

"We're going to have bellyaches," Rowan grumbled as we ventured into Back Home Bakery.

The smell of yeast and sugar drew me straight to the glass display case. "We're picking up cupcakes and sandwich rolls to go with sliced meats and cheeses that we'll get from the deli. All of which we're bringing to the crew at the firehouse as a welcome gift."

That was the plan, but Koda talked me into buying him a dozen cookies and Desmond bought pecan praline muffins.

Once we crossed the street to continue our shopping spree, Rowan took over footing the bill, beating me to the register each time. At the Grocery Depot we were treated to freshly squeezed orange juice that we saved for later. At the Sandlapper Boutique Desmond bought a beaded bracelet for Nita and I got Maudie a head wrap in a sunflower print. Rowan veered into the Bluebird Deli to get the meats and cheeses I'd preordered earlier in the day, while we picked up a few gallons of tea and cold brew coffee from Coffee & Chapters. The Smokehouse wouldn't be up and running until tomorrow, but I'd already placed an order for them to cater a thank-you lunch for the construction crews, with the help of the diner.

"We'll come back by the library after we drop this stuff off to the firemen." I motioned for everyone to continue down the sidewalk, lined with halved wooden barrels with flowers spilling over the edges.

"Yay!" Koda skipped ahead of us. "Can I sit in the fire truck?"

"You sat in it the other day," Bash said. "Plus they've already promised you can ride in it in the parade on Saturday."

That didn't stop the little boy from talking his way into the truck once we arrived at the station. A quick visit stretched past an hour with him exploring the truck as if it were a jungle gym. The fire chief sat in the driver's seat, answering the million questions Koda rattled off.

Finally, we made it to Founder's Pharmacy and Rowan held the door for me, our eyes snagging for a few extra seconds.

"What are we gonna get from here?" Koda asked, his lip curled skeptically.

"Flu shots!" I clapped my hands in mock excitement and both boys started backing away. "Just kidding!" I laughed. "I need to restock Band-Aids and Neosporin." I pointed to Koda's bandaged knees. "Someone keeps using all mine."

Once that small purchase was complete, we walked next door and went upstairs to the library, where we each signed up for library cards. I noticed Rowan eyeing the nonfiction section with a small smile on his face, which put a smile on mine.

We made it back to the sidewalk and paused. "Well, I guess that's every store."

"But what about that big ole building over there?" Koda pointed.

"That's the town hall. It holds the sheriff's office, the chamber of commerce, the mayor's office, and some other offices. No one's there today though."

"That's boring. Let's go to the park!" Koda skipped in place.

"We can't. They're installing the playground equipment," Rowan told him, while checking something on his phone. "But you can go to the memorial garden."

Koda about-faced and started marching down the sidewalk. "Bash, come play with me!"

"Go keep an eye on your brother. We'll be there in a little while." Rowan nodded his head toward the garden.

Bash's phone chimed in his pocket. He pulled it out and read the message. "M'kay." He followed behind Koda.

"I'm going to bring Nita and Joyia their gifts." Desmond gave me a side-hug and gazed around. "We did good, darlin'."

"We sure did. Time to find a new project, I guess."

Desmond chuckled. "I need a vacation first."

I laughed. "Same."

As he walked away, I turned my attention to Rowan. He grabbed my hand and started leading me in the opposite direction. "What are you up to?"

"One last free pass." He walked us inside the quiet town hall. "Wanna see what we can see?"

I tried to stop but he kept pulling me along with him. "You're gonna get us in trouble."

"Just a little." Rowan looked at me over his shoulder and winked. He pushed open the courtroom's door and walked straight up to the judge's bench. We'd decided to leave this room as is, thinking it could be nice for town meetings.

"We've seen all this before."

Rowan didn't stop in front of the bench, instead moving behind it. "Yeah, but have you ever been kissed on a judge's bench?" He nudged the chair out the way.

I snorted out a laugh. "Not that I can recall."

"Good." Rowan grasped my hips and, in one fluid motion, sat me on top of the bench and placed his lips against mine.

I thought about Loreen's words. *Focus on peace.* Instead of protesting, I laced my arms around Rowan's neck and leaned into this stolen moment with him. I let go of the worries racing through my thoughts and focused on his firm embrace, soft lips, and warmth. We kissed until I lost track of time and forgot where we were.

Rowan's phone vibrated in his pocket. Groaning, he broke the kiss to check it. Sighing, he tapped out a reply and shoved the phone into his pocket. "The boys need us at the garden."

"Are they okay?" I jumped down.

Rowan took my elbow to steady me. "Yes. Just need us to see something that's been added to the garden."

There went that peace . . . I smoothed my hair. "What is it?"

He seemed a little nervous, which made me nervous. "You'll see." He hooked an arm around my shoulder and led me over to Main Street.

We walked to the memorial garden, our long strides making quick work in getting there. I was anxious to check things out and make sure the garden hadn't been messed up in any way. "Was there some vandalism?"

"No." Rowan held the gate open for me and then led me to what we referred to as the bird corner, where several bird feeders were secured on poles and a birdbath sat in the shade of a Japanese maple. The boys were crouched down looking at something on the brick path.

"Oh no. Did something happen to a bird?" I asked.

"Nothing like that." Rowan sidled up beside Bash, who stood. "Come see, *a stór.*"

They parted and let me through. My eyes landed on three new bricks with something engraved on them. Squatting down, I read *In loving memory of Baby Murray. In loving memory of Helen Murray. In loving memory of Declan Murray.* Gaze blurring, I landed on my backside and just stared at the bricks.

"The town hall . . ." I sniffed. "That was a distraction?" I motioned toward the three bricks.

"Partly, but mostly I wanted to kiss you real bad." Rowan winked at me. Could a wink look somber? His sure did.

Koda made a gagging sound. "Eww!!"

"Hush," Bash reprimanded his little brother while tapping him on the upper arm.

"They were delivered while we were at the library. This was Bash's idea," Rowan said softly as he settled beside me. "He paid for the bricks with his own money."

One blink and the tears plopped heavily onto my cheeks. "How'd he know?"

"We have some pretty intense conversations while playing poker," Bash answered.

Wiping my cheeks, I rolled my damp eyes at his old joke.

"We play no such thing!" Rowan playfully popped him on the leg with the back of his hand.

I pulled Koda to my lap and was surprised when he didn't protest. Then I took Bash's arm and tugged until he sat on the brick walkway with us.

Koda's sticky hand wiped another tear off my face. "I'm sorry your babies have already gone to heaven."

"Me too." I reread the bricks. "Bash, this was so very thoughtful of you."

Bash shrugged. "You made sure Ms. Loreen had a special place to mourn her son and well . . . I thought you needed a special place too."

I swallowed past the lump in my throat. "You're an exceptional young man, you know that, Bash?"

He blushed. "You keep telling me that."

I placed my hand on his shoulder. "Because it's true and I don't want you to ever forget it."

That sticky hand of Koda's settled on my cheek and turned my attention to him. "What about me?"

"You're—"

He made a face, then burped like a grizzly bear. His ill manners shattered the serious moment, cracking us all up.

Laughing, I leaned back a bit. "You're an exceptional mess!" I tickled him mercilessly, making him squeal like a little piglet.

Youthful giggles and roaring laughter mingled perfectly with the tinkling sound of wind chimes and the rushing water from the fountain. I'm fairly certain the combination breathed a new life into this town and finished chasing off the ghosts.

CHAPTER 37

WHITE BANNERS WITH THE SOMEWHERE LOGO waved overhead and the air was perfumed in sweet and savory scents from food vendors as we all gathered around the town hall steps.

Mayor Higgins stood on the top step, a wide grin on his face, Preacher by his side. "I'd like to welcome you all to Somewhere, South Carolina."

The large crowd cheered. A rainbow of balloons bobbed up and down, as beacons throughout the group to indicate where the children stood.

"I'd like to introduce you to Mayor Preacher Elvis."

Preacher barked at the mention of his name and a wave of laughter moved through the crowd.

"His office is located at the chapel, but I've heard his office hours are unreliable." Mayor Higgins shook his head. "And if something of yours goes missing that's where to look first. You see, our mayor has sticky paws."

A roar of laughter erupted, some of us louder than others because we knew it to be true.

"Jonas got us a good mayor," Rowan said beside me.

"Yes he did."

Reginald Higgins was a Southern comedian and Jonas's good friend. He actually favored the comedian Kevin Hart but Reggie was a bit taller than five two. He would be the interim mayor until the town was more established and a proper election for the position could be held.

"I'd like to give Mayor Preacher the first key to our city." Mayor Higgins took the vintage skeleton key from his assistant and secured it to Preacher's collar.

"Is that the key I found in the coffee shop?" Desmond asked.

"Yes. I thought it was fitting since that's where I saw the mutt for the first time."

"Don't call him that," Koda sassed before slurping a mouthful of his snow cone. He had become attached to Preacher and was quite protective over the dog.

The mayor—the real one, not the dog—concluded his welcome speech, and the people began moving toward various activities set up all around town.

"There they are," Maudie called out from behind us.

We turned and I had to do a double take. "Dad!" Shocked but so grateful, I made my way through the crowd and gave him a big hug.

He laughed in surprise, not used to me being affectionate toward him. "Hey, sweetheart."

I stepped back. "I thought you were in Chicago this week."

Dad ran a hand through his salt-and-pepper hair, eyes crinkled in the corners. "I cut the trip short so I could surprise you."

"Well, you succeeded."

Dad looked over my shoulder and extended his hand. "Rowan. It's been a long time, young man."

Rowan shook his hand, stepping around me to give Dad one of those half-hugs guys do while shaking hands. "It's nice to see you, Gregory."

Dad's eyes cut to me and I could see all the questions he wanted to ask but wouldn't. I'd tell him all of it anyway, sometime soon. But first we needed to celebrate the town.

"How about we give you a grand tour, Dad?" I hooked my arm with his and started down Main Street.

"I thought there were guides doing that," Maudie spoke.

"Yes, ma'am, but I'd like to give y'all one myself."

Nita waved from another group passing by. She'd lined up tour guides to show off our town and was taking a tour herself. Joyia was on her hip but as soon as the toddler spotted me, she began reaching for me.

"Hey, hey, hey!" Joyia's chubby little fingers dancing out toward me.

Laughing, I scooped her in my arms and settled her on my hip.

Nita's eyes rounded, then narrowed slightly as a smile brightened her face. She glanced in Rowan's direction, then winked at me.

"Don't start with me," I sassed, walking away with Nita's daughter as if it were the most natural thing. Holding someone else's baby didn't hurt as bad as I thought it would. Planting a kiss on Joyia's forehead, I thanked the good Lord for healing some of my brokenness in the last year.

I led our group around, sharing stories about the renovation as we went. It had been one wild adventure and it felt bittersweet now that we'd finished it. Inside the pecan warehouse, a slideshow played on a loop. Images of the renovation projects and candid shots showcased the long journey it took to resurrect this town.

"Look!" Koda pointed out, cackling. "There's my dog and my giant!"

We turned our attention to the screen and there I sat on the floor of the chapel, a pencil behind my ear and safety glasses perched on top of my head, with Preacher beside me.

"Rowan took that the day we caught Preacher red-handed."

"He calls you his giant?" Maudie grinned, pleased as punch over the teasing endearment.

I shrugged. "I guess he could call me worse."

After making a loop around the warehouse to check out the

displays, we moved back outside to the vendors set up around the clock tower.

We sampled all the food offerings, purchased souvenirs from various vendors, and grabbed ice cream cones to enjoy during the little parade. Koda rode with the firemen who led the procession in the shiny new fire truck, and a few businesses put together small floats. Beauty and the Barber won the float contest with theirs. It was based on the fairy tale with the Beast sitting in a barber chair while Belle pretended to trim his mane. After that we made another round for food and beverages with Koda riding on my mobile bench with Maudie since they both decided they were too tired to walk another step. We took turns pulling them around until we declared *we* were too tired to walk another step.

All in all, the day went off without a hitch until a storm blew in near dusk. The only thing we had to cancel was the fireworks show, so I still considered the opening day of Somewhere, South Carolina, a success.

As the streets cleared in record speed, Rowan took the boys back to the apartment and I set out to find my wandering dog.

Of course he was exactly where I knew he would be. In the chapel. Pacing. A seemingly universal trait for preachers. Back and forth, while sharing the message. Apparently, our dog had this trait as well.

With my legs crossed at the ankles and my arms stretched out along the back of the front pew, I watched Preacher pace back and forth as the rain shower picked up into a heavy downpour just outside. The scoundrel refused to come with me over to the saloon. Being the pushover that I am, I decided to ride out the storm with him here so he wouldn't be alone.

"You're spoiled rotten, you know that, right?"

Preacher paused and gave me his best puppy dog eyes, neither confirming nor denying it. He continued his pace as lightning lit up the windows.

The door swung open. "There you are."

I craned my neck and watched a soaking wet Rowan saunter down the center aisle.

"Whatcha grinning at?" He plopped down beside me, sprinkling me with cool raindrops.

"You reminded me just now of our wedding day."

He chuckled. "Ah yeah. A flat tire in the middle of a thunderstorm on the way to the church. You married me anyway with wet hair and mud splatters on my tuxedo pants."

"What a wild day that was." A low rumble of thunder crept along just outside.

"Seemed to always be our style." He used the hem of his shirt to dry his face, giving me a peek of the dates stamped over his heart. The bad days. He dropped the hem and peered at me with a frown. "What's the matter?"

I shook my head and shrugged both shoulders, trying to brush off the hard truth. "We had a lot of fails."

Rowan studied his shoes thoughtfully. "Yeah . . . But what about the wins?"

"Wins?"

He looked up and nodded firmly. "We had plenty of wins, but the bads were just so . . . *bad*, they overshadowed all the good."

Preacher wandered over and laid his muzzle in my lap. I began petting him, soothing us both. "We used to leave groceries on the doorstep of that little old lady's house down the road from our place." I felt Rowan's gaze on me, so I clarified. "That was one of our wins."

He hummed, as if just remembering that. "We always held each other at night, even if we weren't talking. One of my favorite wins."

I smiled even though it wobbled. "That's one of my favorites too." I leaned my head on his shoulder.

The rain pitter-pattered on the tin roof, lulling us to just sit in peace and listen. Even though Rowan's shirt was damp, his warmth and the crisp scent of his cologne drew me in, so I snuggled closer.

"Taking care of Bash and Koda is another favorite win," I said softly, smiling at the memory of Bash laughing and acting like a kid for once today while Koda kept calling me his giant.

"Mine too." Rowan took a deep breath. "I visited Rose yesterday."

I sat up. "Yeah?"

"Yeah. They're moving her to a nursing home."

"Oh no. That poor woman." I shook my head. "When we went last weekend, I could tell she wasn't doing much better."

"Yeah. That's why she wants us to adopt the boys."

My entire body jolted. "Adopt them?"

"I told Rose I had to talk with you about it and get back to her, but time isn't on her side."

I stood and walked over to peer outside. Dark and gloomy, the sky appeared bruised and crying at the same time. "That's a big step."

"It is." Rowan joined me by the window and we both gazed out until suddenly the sky lightened and the rain turned off. "We need to make a run for it in case the storm decides to loop around." He took my hand and hurried out the door but not toward the saloon.

"Where are we going?"

"You'll see."

And see I did.

We cut behind the firehouse where a few men in uniforms were hanging out near the open bay. We exchanged waves but kept moving.

I knew where we were heading and my heart rate picked up considerably. For some crippling reason, I hadn't allowed myself near the Victorian since the day Rowan admitted he bought it for me. Fear of life falling apart kept me from giving the house any hope. I didn't want to get attached if I had to say goodbye.

We emerged from the thin line of trees and I all but fell to my knees.

Like a fairy tale, the house glowed an alluring warmth, welcoming anyone who happened to stumble upon it in the middle of nowhere. It no longer looked like a haunted house, but an enchanted one.

"Oh my gosh, is it pink?" The hue was a little hard to pinpoint in the dark.

"Yes. I had a historian research the house, so I could restore it as close to the original as possible. This was the original color." Rowan waved toward the house. "It's a soft coral pink though. Not garish." He winked.

"Rowan . . ." I shook my head and tried to take it all in. The gingerbread trim was now a bright white with what looked like a darker shade of pink accenting it. Three rocking chairs lined each side of the double front door.

"Let's go inside. See what we can see." He pulled me up the steps and opened the front door.

It was like stepping back in time.

"It's the same wallpaper pattern." I ran my palm over the satiny paper, a creamy background with a dusty blue damask pattern.

"I had it recreated."

I turned toward him in wonder. "I'm . . ." I shook my head.

Rowan led me around on a tour of the house. In the kitchen the gray marble had been salvaged, but the old appliances had been replaced by stainless steel. The original chandeliers, now dust-free and sparkling. The four bedrooms upstairs had resurfaced wood floors and fresh coats of paint but were empty. We stood on the balcony off the master suite and gazed down at the backyard. The rain had brought out the aroma of nature. I took a deep inhale, smelling the sweet notes of honeysuckle and lemony hints from the magnolia tree.

I braced my elbows on the railing beside Rowan. "How'd you manage this without me noticing?"

"You've been pretty distracted with the town and then the boys. I just made sure the subcontractors used the back entrance we added for the town houses. That way you wouldn't see them coming and going."

I turned and peered through the French doors. "I . . . Rowan, this is just all so exquisite." I shook my head, dumbfounded. "Wow."

His cheeks warmed in color. "I didn't furnish it. I thought maybe you'd like to pick out the furniture."

I breathed a faint laugh. "I can't take your house, Rowan. You should furnish it however you want."

He sighed. "Let's leave that for now. We need to get back to discussing what to do about Bash and Koda long-term."

The abrupt topic change had me reeling a bit. Blinking, I nodded. "Okay."

"I don't want anything to get in the way of those boys being able to stay together." Scratching his stubbly chin, Rowan tilted his head. "But there's something we need to nail down first before we get the ball rolling on a plan to make that happen."

"What's that?"

He closed the distance between us and rested his hands on my hips. "Marry me."

I sputtered a laugh, nearly choking. "Why would you possibly want to marry me again?"

His hands tightened on my hips, as if making sure I didn't make a run for it. "We could give those boys the parents they deserve. And if we marry again, it'll make it harder for you to get rid of me. 'Cause I promise you, *a stór*, I won't go down without a fight ever again."

Both stunned and panicked, a swarm of butterflies filled my chest as my ears began to ring. "You're serious?"

"Let's make this house our home with those two boys." He stood so close the puffs of his breaths tickled my lips. "Please say you want that as much as I do. That you want *me*."

"How could I not want you, Rowan? You're my treasure too." I touched my lips to his, just barely. "Yes."

"Yes?"

"I'll marry you."

With trembling fingers, he lifted my necklace, revealing my claddagh ring. After some fumbling, he managed to unclasp it and take the ring off.

"How'd you know I was wearing it?"

His lips twitched mischievously. "You've been wearing it since

Loreen's visit to the memorial garden. I sort of looked down your shirt and saw it."

"Sort of?"

He grinned.

"When?"

"Uh . . . a few times." Rowan lifted my hand and placed the ring in its rightful place, where it would remain.

As we sealed our promise with a kiss, I couldn't help but reflect on how in the midst of restoring this ghost town, I'd been restored in more ways than one.

Can a person be a ghost town? I believed so for a very long time. Similar to an abandoned town, I felt like everyone and everything had abandoned me but the trauma, the grief it produced, and the silence that followed. I could do nothing but accept the forsakenness while the passing years began to weather my soul. Rusting the hinges of my heart until the corrosion made it nearabout impossible to open to anything or anyone.

But, just like the revitalization project, I felt God doing a restoration in my heart during these last seven months. The rusty hinges of my heart had been replaced and now opened freely to the possibilities of love. I thought I was beyond lost. I'm glad I got it wrong.

EPILOGUE

I STOOD IN THE MIDDLE OF THE DIMLY LIT RUIN, dust motes and dustier memories whirling around me. It wouldn't have been my first pick for our next project, but today wasn't about me. Still, I had to ask.

"Are you sure, Bash?" I stepped cautiously over the busted tiles. "Don't most college grads want a new car?"

Dressed in his black cap and gown, Bash spun in a slow circle, assessing the dilapidated space. "It has potential."

Rowan chuckled. "Only our kid would want a trashed building instead of a car." Sure, he was teasing, but he couldn't hide the pride in his voice.

An hour ago had been the proudest moment of my life, witnessing Bash walk across that stage as they announced, "Sebastian Murray, graduating magna cum laude, bachelor's in structural engineering." It had been a long road to get to this point, helping him get through high school and then taking the tests to get into college, but he did it. Bash overcame some pretty tall obstacles to get here, so if the young man wanted an abandoned train station, that's what he'd get.

I placed my hand on Bash's arm. "Why this place, Son?"

Bash cleared his throat. "I stayed here before . . . before I found you."

Now I had to clear my throat. Bash had opened up to us over the last five years, but he hadn't shared much about what happened before he wandered into our ghost town. I surveyed the crumbling space with a different perspective, my stomach recoiling at the idea of him here alone, barely surviving.

Desmond stepped over a pile of trash with his iPad and stylus in hand. "What's your vision for this train station, Bash?"

Bash scratched the back of his neck. "This place was somewhere for me before I moved to Somewhere. I'd like to make it a somewhere for others."

"A shelter home?" Rowan asked.

Bash winced. "No. Like, maybe affordable housing for people down on their luck. I've been reading up on how sliding fee scales work. I was thinking maybe we can use something like that to figure out rent. There's the caboose, ten train cars, and this long building. We could easily flip about twenty small apartments from this."

"I like your thinking." Desmond scribbled some notes, his face bathed in blue light from the screen.

"That caboose out there might cause Avalee nightmares though," Rowan teased.

Bash turned to eye Rowan. "Why's that?"

"Because that's the very spot Rowan tricked me into falling in love with him," I piped in.

"No way." Bash grinned. "So this place is already a 'somewhere' for y'all too."

Rowan chuckled. "Yep."

"Mama! I found a kitten!" Koda came barreling in, a tiny furball tucked in his arms and Preacher hot on his heels. "Can we keep it? Please!"

My heart beat an extra beat every time Bash or Koda called me their mama. Sure, we'd made it official and adopted both of them, but I never expected to be blessed with that sacred label.

"Please!" He batted those blue eyes and I already knew that darn kitten was coming home with us.

"We'll see."

Maudie wandered in. "I told him you'd let him keep it."

I clucked my tongue. "I said we'd see."

Koda jumped up and down. The little punk had me wrapped around his pinky and he knew it. We all knew it and were perfectly fine with it. He'd been denied enough in this life. No harm in giving him the small wins, such as a stray animal.

"This is all your fault," Rowan muttered close to my ear, sending shivers along my neck as he pressed a kiss in the very spot.

"You know I have a special place in my heart for abandoned things."

"More like lost boys," Rowan teased. "We should call you Wendy."

While Koda and Maudie showed off the kitten to Bash and Desmond, I wrapped an arm around Rowan's waist.

I'd always envisioned diaper duties, first steps, first words, and potty training when I thought about having a family. What I ended up with—an ex-husband I remarried, two abandoned boys, friends from all sorts of backgrounds, and stray animals—may not have been my original dream, but this was my reality. A reality I wouldn't take anything for. Hugging my husband to my side, I thanked God for opening my eyes to what a true family consisted of, and for us, it didn't require shared DNA.

Rowan and I had endured tremendous loss, losses that no parent should ever experience. After almost a decade of barely hanging on, we managed to survive. We'd lost a lot, but look at how much we'd found within the ruins of our loss.

A Note from the Author

FOR THE PAST SEVENTEEN YEARS, I've wrestled with a mix of guilt and thankfulness regarding childbirth and pregnancy loss. My story had a happy ending, but I am all too aware that for so many, that is not the case.

Twenty weeks into my second pregnancy, we thought we'd overcome the hardest hurdle, the first trimester. Yes, I still had morning sickness, but I'd had it the entire pregnancy with my son, except for the seventh month, so I figured this second one would be no different.

A crazy thing happened during this time. I broke out in hives for the very first time in my life. I had used a different clothes detergent. Worst idea of my life. Head to toe, an angry red rash attacked me. As if my morning sickness, which went on all day, wasn't bad enough.

Well, I thought that was the worst it could get, but then late in the day I began living a nightmare. Cramping and spotting. Two other things I never experienced during my first pregnancy. Horrified, I called the emergency number for my doctor and told her what was going on. She was calm. I was not. The doctor said there was nothing we could do, so it was best to wait until morning to head to the office. She told me to take some Benadryl for the rash and to try to get some rest. Easier said than done. I thought she was out of her mind. No way would I be resting, knowing I was most likely losing my child.

After a long night of no rest, my somber husband drove me to the doctor's office. We sat in the waiting room filled with ripe women who seemed minutes away from giving birth. They were all joyous and ready to meet their child. Bernie and I sat in fear while I continued to bleed and cramp. It felt surreal.

Devastated, we shuffled into the ultrasound room, where the nurse avoided eye contact with us. After some searching with the ultrasound wand, I could hardly believe my ears when it picked up my daughter's strong heartbeat. Surely, I was imagining it. No way was she surviving with what my body was going through. But sure enough, there she was, still hanging on.

I am beyond grateful that God saw fit for me to meet my incredible daughter in this life. She is artistic, more creative than me by a long shot, and has such a pure spirit. I can't help but think of how different my life would have been, had the doctor not found her heartbeat that day. I'm devastated to even think it.

Those memories and the fear I felt have stayed with me all these years. And it gave me the tiniest glimpse into what so many parents face: the ultrasounds that show no life. The unfound heartbeats. The mourning when they should be celebrating. I don't understand why God chose to extend his grace to my family in that moment, but with this book I hope to honor those who did not get my outcome. The ones who, like Avalee and Rowan, did not get to bring their precious babies home with them. By telling this story, I'm paying my respects to those who were lost. My genuine hope is that I did just that.

Acknowledgments

A BOOK IS ONLY PAGES AND WORDS UNTIL IT IS READ. Then it becomes a story. I am forever grateful for each and every person who reads my stories. What an extraordinary gift it is to share my imagined worlds and the characters who live in them with my reading friends.

Even though writing is a solitary endeavor, so many are a part of the publishing journey. It's such an honor to work with the fabulous fiction team at Tyndale House Publishers. You give me the freedom to create and the guidance needed to make my stories shine. Jan Stob, Karen Watson, Andrea Garcia, Elizabeth Jackson, and Amanda Woods, I'm honored to work alongside you!

Kathryn Olson, your patience and encouragement throughout the process with *Lowcountry Lost* was such a gift, as always. It was a tough year for me to write, but you helped me see this story through and I am darn proud of it! I couldn't have done it without you. Thank you.

To my agent Danielle Egan-Miller and foreign rights agent Mariana Fisher, I have so much respect for what you do. I am so fortunate to have Browne & Miller Literary Associates in my corner. You ladies are simply fabulous!

I want to thank my daughter, Lydia Lowe, for creating the map of the town that appears in the front of the book. I absolutely love it. Lydia, your creativity far surpasses my own. I'm so proud of you.

Bernie Lowe, we are still trucking. I love you and am so glad to have you by my side through thick or thin, never more so than during the past year.

Nathan Lowe, my Stevens family, and Healy family, I love you and truly appreciate your support in my writing career.

Marybeth Whalen, I'm so grateful to have a partner-in-crime in this writing world. You are a voice of reason that I need so often. Creatives are also weirdos. I love being able to be freely weird with you! Those voices are always talking to us . . .

Kari Clark, Samantha DuVal, and Laura Krooswyk, thank you for sharing your poignant stories with me. I hope I respected you and so many others in the writing of this book.

The cheering squad: Trina Cooke, Teresa Moise, Jennifer Strickland, and Stephanie Wilhelm. They say when the world walks away, true friends remain. Thank you for remaining.

To our bowling partners, Dave and Vicki Baty, y'all are just good people with such big hearts and that is so rare to find. I feel like I am constantly learning something about life and/or history when we go "bowling." We've only known you a handful of years, but the love and respect I have for you feels more like a lifetime's worth. I count Bernie and myself blessed to have your friendship.

Even though I have grown weary recently, my heavenly Father has not. Thank you, Lord, for propping me up when all I wanted to do was give up. "He lifted me out of the pit of despair, out of the mud and the mire. He set my feet on solid ground and steadied me as I walked along" (Psalm 40:2).

Lowcountry Lost Recipes

Y'ALL PROBABLY KNOW BY NOW THAT I LOVE EATING as much as writing. Every chance I get to share some of my Southern roots through recipes, I like slipping them in. Froid was the cook of this story, so I decided to come up with some original recipes from Froid to share with y'all! I hope you enjoy them. Let me know if you try them out!

Froid's Bloody Mary Sausage and Rice

> 1 large yellow onion, diced
> 2 tbsp. olive oil
> 2 12-oz. packages smoked sausage, diced
> 1 tbsp. chicken base
> 1 10-oz. package Mahatma yellow rice
> 1 cup long-grain rice
> 1 14.5-oz. can fire-roasted diced tomatoes
> 1 cup spicy Bloody Mary mix
> 6 cups water
> 2 tsp. parsley
> Hot sauce to taste

In a large pot on medium heat, sauté onion in olive oil until translucent. Add sausage and chicken base. Once browned, add both types of rice and cook five minutes before adding tomatoes and Bloody Mary mix. Once it's bubbling, add water, parsley, and hot sauce. Cover and cook on low heat for twenty minutes or until rice is tender. Serve with corn bread for the best tasting experience!

Note: The chicken base and Bloody Mary mix should be enough seasoning, but if you need to, add salt and pepper to taste.

Froid's Fiery Chili

  2 lbs. ground beef
  1 large yellow onion, diced
  2 1-oz. packages Kinder's chili seasoning (or whatever brand
     you prefer)
  1 bottle of beer (nonalcoholic if preferred)
  1 40.5-oz. can light red kidney beans
  1 40.5-oz. can dark red kidney beans
  1 26.5-oz. can black beans
  1 28-oz. can fire-roasted diced tomatoes
  1 cup salsa, fresh or jarred
  Hot sauce to taste

Brown ground beef with onion. Add the rest of the stuff and cook on low as much of the day as you can pull off—at least four hours. Serve with . . . you guessed it! Corn bread. Or tortilla chips. Top with cheese and sour cream or whatever you prefer.

Lowcountry Lost Playlists

"Heart Like a Truck" by Lainey Wilson
"Memory I Don't Mess With" by Lee Brice
"Easy on Me" by Adele
"Weary Traveler" by Jordan St. Cyr
"You Ain't Here to Kiss Me" by Brett Young
"Something's the Same about You" by Old Dominion
"Not over You" by Gavin DeGraw
"Little One" by Highly Suspect
"I Try" by Macy Gray
"Happier" by Marshmello ft. Bastille
"You Should Probably Leave" by Chris Stapleton
"Way Less Sad" by AJR
"Memory Lane" by Old Dominion
"One of the Good Ones" by Gabby Barrett
"Come What May" by We Are Messengers
"Free/Into the Mystic" by Zac Brown Band
"Broken Things" by Matthew West
"Roses in the Rain" by Christina Perri

Avalee's Library Dance Party Playlist

"Walking on Sunshine" by Katrina and the Waves
"I Wanna Dance with Somebody" by Whitney Houston

"Cupid Shuffle" by Cupid

"Footloose" by Kenny Loggins

"Electric Boogie" by Marcia Griffiths

"I Ain't Worried" by OneRepublic

"Cha Cha Slide" by DJ Casper

"Let's Hear It for the Boy" by Deniece Williams

"Good Vibrations" by Marky Mark and the Funky Bunch

"Pump Up the Jam" by Technotronic

"Walk Like an Egyptian" by the Bangles

"Straight Up" by Paula Abdul

"Copperhead Road" by Steve Earle

"Jump" by Van Halen

"Rhythm of the Night" by DeBarge

"Achy Breaky Heart" by Billy Ray Cyrus

"Everywhere" by Fleetwood Mac

Discussion Questions

1. When we first meet Avalee, she is in need of healing. What are some of the steps she takes toward healing during the course of the book? Is her journey realistic? Are there parts of her story you could identify with?

2. Avalee tries to focus on "small happies" since she thinks she can't have any of the "big happies" of life. How can this approach be helpful in dealing with life's disappointments? In what ways might it fall short?

3. *Lowcountry Lost* is like an HGTV house-flipping show on steroids. Which building flip interested you the most? Is restoring an old home—or even just a piece of furniture—something you have done or would like to try?

4. Avalee had quite a unique, albeit silly, ghost town bucket list. If you had total access to a ghost town, what would be on your bucket list?

5. The crew finds all sorts of hidden "treasure" as they renovate the town. Hate mail in the post office, a burlap bank bag with no money in the fabric store, a box filled with metal crosses from the flower shop. Have you ever discovered hidden "treasure"? If so, what?

6. Second chances are a unique treasure that many are unable to discover. What are your thoughts on Avalee and Rowan discovering this treasure for their relationship?

7. Miscarriage and stillbirth are both sensitive topics explored within this story. How do you feel the author did at presenting these topics? Were they talked about enough? Too little?

8. A lot is lost in this story—items, people, relationships—and a lot is also found. What is your favorite lost and found? Do you have a lost and found story of your own?

9. Bash is a unique young man who is cautious with sharing too many words. Do you think it would be interesting if he chose to say more?

10. Do you or someone you know have what might be considered an unconventional family? What are some of the special blessings families like this can experience? What are some of their special challenges?

About the Author

 *T. I. LOWE* is an ordinary country girl who loves to tell extraordinary stories. She is the author of twenty novels, including the bestselling *Indigo Isle*; the #1 international bestseller and critically acclaimed *Under the Magnolias*; and her debut breakout, *Lulu's Café*. She lives with her husband and family in coastal South Carolina. Find her at tilowe.com or on Facebook (T.I.Lowe), Instagram (tilowe), and Twitter (@TiLowe).

CONNECT WITH T. I. LOWE ONLINE AND SIGN UP FOR HER NEWSLETTER AT

tilowe.com

OR FOLLOW HER ON

 T.I.Lowe   tilowe

 TiLowe   T_I_Lowe

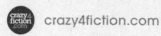
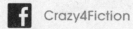

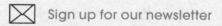